DOWN THE RIVER

RIVER CITY BOOK 2

J. SCOTT COATSWORTH

Published by
Other Worlds Ink
PO Box 19341, Sacramento, CA 95819

 Formatted with Vellum

CONTENTS

This book is dedicated, like all my work, to my amazing husband Marco, who sometimes doesn't see what a remarkable human being he is, and who read and critiqued the story as I was writing it.

It's also dedicated to Kim Fielding, who read every single chapter as I was writing it, and to Allison Behrens, my tireless editor and copywriter who had to go through the whole thing twice. You guys are amazing.

FOREWORD

I first started *The River City Chronicles* in 2015, before most of the current insanity. It was inspired by Armisted Maupin's *Tales of the City*, only instead of sharing it weekly on the local newspaper, I published it on my blog.

Even though it took two years to finish, it remains a bit of a time capsule for the "before times."

Last year, during the interregnum, I decided to go back to River City to see what had happened to my characters in the last nine years. And there were some surprises! I'll let you discover them for yourself.

Once again, I published it on my blog as a weekly serial. It's now complete, and I am thrilled to finally be able to share it with you in book form, along with a new short story volume, *The River City Companion*, which gathers a few connected short stories and novellas.

I hope you enjoy them both!

LIST OF CHARACTERS

Major Characters:

- **Ainsley Kim:** 23 – Waitress at Ragazzi
- **Ben Hammond:** 44 – Trans author and restaurant manager
- **Brad Weston:** 39 – Lives with Sam in Tucson
- **Carmelina di Rosa:** 64 – Semi-retired redhead who runs a bakery and flower shop with her partner Daniele
- **Daniele Amoroso:** 49 – Carmelina's partner in life and business
- **Dave Ramos:** 56 – Human resources consultant and Marcos's husband
- **Diego Bellei:** 56 – The chef at Ragazzi restaurant, married to Matteo
- **Giovanni (Gio) Bellei:** 26 – Diego's son who works at Ragazzi
- **Marcos Ramirez:** 48 – Web designer married to Dave
- **Marissa Sutton:** 26 – Bi woman who works for a local corporation
- **Matteo Bianco:** 56 – Co-owner and host at Ragazzi restaurant, married to Diego Bellei.
- **Sam Fuller:** 32 – Suspense novel writer, now semi-famous

Minor Repeating Characters:

- **Alyn Cranford:** Ricky's boyfriend
- **Arthur di Rosa:** deceased – Carmelina's husband
- **Dante Bellei:** Valentina's son and Gio's cousin
- **Elena Romano:** Daniele's lesbian cousin in Rome
- **Jackie Vaughn:** One of Ricky's friends
- **Jake Myers:** Jun Seo Jang's US manager
- **Jason Clark:** One of Marissa's friends at McClatchy High
- **Jim Oberkrom:** One of Brad & Sam's old neighbors
- **Jun Seo Jang:** A non-binary South Korean artist
- **Kelton O'Malley:** Owner of the Red Roof Gallery
- **Lorelei Miller:** Ben's upstairs neighbor
- **Miz Faye Min Fortune:** A drag queen matchmaker
- **Ricky Martinez:** One of the homeless kids from the LGBT center
- **Sole Biondo:** Gio's cousin and Stella's daughter
- **Stella Biondo:** Gio's aunt
- **The Stranger:** Mysterious individual stalking someone at Ragazzi
- **Valentina Bellei:** Diego's sister who lives in Italy

1

RAGAZZI

Ainsley Kim stared out of the window at the cars as they passed on Folsom Boulevard in a steady row of sparkling red and white, their lights scattering and twinkling like fairy dust across the rain-splattered glass. It was mesmerizing—so much life out there… and in here, as she was rudely reminded by the diner clearing his throat behind her.

"So sorry!" She spun around, reaching for the Toast point-of-sale device that hung from a custom-made pocket in her clean white apron that said Ragazzi in neat black letters. She turned her attention back to her customers. "Are you ready to order?"

The one who'd cleared his throat was a sharply dressed man in his mid-fifties—lawyer if she'd had to guess—his neatly trimmed black hair turning silver on the sides. He glared at the menu as if it were opposing counsel, squinting through his wire-framed glasses and scowling. "Damned print is so small on these things."

His dining partner, another man in a black suit and tie, but without a hair on his head, chuckled. "You're just getting old, Andy. Order the tagliatelle. It's what you always get." Bald Head offered her a warm smile. "So sorry for my partner's behavior. Rough day in court today."

Ainsley hid a grin. She *was* good at reading people. "Not a problem. So… the tagliatelle?"

Andy nodded. "Sure. With arrabbiata sauce. And ask the chef to make it a little *extra spicy*."

She tapped it into the POS, feeling more like a glorified data entry clerk than a waitress. "You got it. And you, sir?"

"Don't let him fool you. Kel knows what he wants. He just likes to play with his prey." Andy grimaced, then managed a weak smile. "Sorry for the foul mood. I hate losing."

Rich, white, and a lawyer to boot? *You have no idea what losing is.* "Not a problem." She flashed him her best *you're the customer so I'll pretend I like you* smile.

"I'll have the gnocchi in a ragu sauce, and an appetizer of your delightful burrata." Kel flipped the menu over. "Add a glass of Chateau Ciel. I, unlike my friend here, had a lovely day. Signed a new artist for the gallery, a talented Korean painter named Jun Seo Jang." His eyes fixed on her. "Do you know him?"

Ainsley blinked, caught between the casual racism of assuming that all Koreans knew each other—maybe he didn't mean it that way?—and the fact that she *did* actually know them. Or of them, anyhow. Jang was one of her idols.

Customer service won out. "Yes. *They* are very good. I studied them in art class."

Kel grinned. "Then you must come see his… their pieces. Sorry, old dog, new tricks. I'll be getting the first of them next week." He pulled out his wallet and extracted a card. "Kelton O'Malley, Red Roof Gallery."

She took it, staring at it. It seemed to sparkle under the restaurant's mood lighting. She blinked and the sparkle went away. She stuffed it in her pocket.

Nobody used business cards anymore. *So old school.* "Thank you. I'll try to come by. It's a bit busy, with school and work and all…" And taking care of her mother.

"Ah, what's your major?"

"Molecular biology." It came out automatically. Her father had wanted her to "make something of herself," not just be another poor immigrant like himself, working at minimum wage jobs. She'd been at it so long, doing what her parents wanted her to do, that it almost seemed like she wanted it, too.

"Impressive." He winked. "Still, it's good to hear that you have an appreciation for the arts as well."

She blushed. That comment hit a little too close to home. "I'll find some time to stop by."

"Wonderful. Jun Seo will be there next Thursday night, if you want to meet... them."

Ainsley touched the edge of the table to steady herself. "They'll be here... in town?" She was already calculating how she could rearrange things to be at the gallery.

"They personally supervise the set-up at all their new galleries." He grinned. "See, that whole pronoun thing's not so hard."

She suppressed a snort. Boomers were always making such a big deal about it. "Let me get those orders in for you." She gave them a small bow —ingrained behavior from two decades growing up in the Kim household —and slipped away.

"Need anything here?" she asked her next table, a young gay couple from the looks of it, who were busy staring rapturously into each other's eyes like a couple lovestruck teenagers.

"Just some water," the blonde said, never breaking his gaze, his hand wrapped tightly around the other man's. A single plate of pasta sat between them.

"You got it."

A two-for-one, or twofer, they called it—when two clients shared a dish, usually to save costs.

Matteo had needed to raise prices again last month to account for inflation. Luckily Ragazzi was doing well enough that they'd expanded into a new addition, taking over the old bar next door for Diego's cooking classes.

She twirled through the restaurant like a ballerina, checking on tables, her footsteps lighter than they'd been in months. Jun Seo Jang was coming to town. She had so many questions for them.

How did you find your inspiration? When did you know you wanted to be an artist? How did you let your parents down gently?

Ainsley Kim had a secret.

She wanted to be an artist more than anything else in the whole wide world. She wanted to create things, pieces of art that would make people frown and smile and nod knowingly as they stood in front of them, stroking their chins. Like her father did as a hobby.

She wanted to meet the artist, but she also wanted to *become* them.

The thought of life as a medical researcher left her cold, but her parents had invested so much in that dream, both money and hope. How could she bear to disappoint them?

Maybe it was better if she didn't go to the gallery on Thursday. Better for everyone involved.

Right?

2

PANE E TULIPANI

Carmelina di Rosa stirred the muffin batter by hand, blending in fresh-cut apples, caramel, and just a touch of cinnamon and nutmeg. The spicy blend filled the small kitchen with a heavenly aroma, reminding her of her *nonna's* kitchen when she'd been a child.

It was glorious to finally have a space of her own for her business, inspired when Matteo had asked her to take over for Diego for a short stint as a restaurant cook nine years earlier. She'd never considered herself a chef, but it had rekindled her passion for cooking and helped her to start moving past the loss of her late husband, Arthur.

The new kitchen practically sparkled with anticipation, even at the ungodly hour of 5:30 in the morning, marred only by specks of flour floating in the air. Daniele had helped her move her things the week before, from home and from the commercial training kitchen Diego had been letting her use just down the street at Ragazzi.

As if summoned by her thoughts of him, her business and romantic partner slipped into the kitchen from the adjacent flower shop. "How is the proud new co-owner of *Pane e Tulipani* doing?" Her still-handsome man—fourteen years her junior, and wasn't she a lucky girl—embraced her gently from behind, slipping warm hands around her apron, careful not to disturb her mixing. "It smells heavenly in here."

She twisted out of his grasp and pecked him on the cheek. "My co-owner needs to leave me be. I've got a ton of baking to do before seven." One of the downsides of having a bakery that supplied not only their own small venture, but also half a dozen local restaurants.

"It's only half-past-five," he protested, pulling her back for a quick kiss on the lips. "But I know you need your space. Anything I can do?"

"You must have floral deliveries to attend to." Mixing a bakery and a flower shop had seemed like a stroke of genius when they'd come up with it in the late spring of 2020, trapped at her house together in the heart of the pandemic. She'd already been taking shifts as the dessert chef at Ragazzi and baking at home in her spare time.

The name—bread and tulips, in English—had been inspired by a wonderful Italian film about a woman whose family left her behind by accident on a bus trip, and who started up a whole new life working at a floral shop. *An apt metaphor.*

"Already done, my love." He stuck his finger in the batter and stole a taste. "Mmmm. *Delicioso.* Are we still on for dinner at Ragazzi? I have some news."

"Hey, health codes." She batted him away with her wooden spoon. "And I think so." One of the perks of starting her day at four AM was that she was usually back out the door and headed back home by just after three in the afternoon. "What kind of news?"

"Let me have my fun." He winked at her and retreated, leaving her alone to her baking.

She was halfway convinced he'd just popped in to make sure she hadn't fallen asleep in the kitchen. It had happened before… once, and he'd never let her forget it.

She popped open an oven door to check the strawberry tarts—it was late in the season, but she'd found a good local supplier with a greenhouse and reasonable rates.

She hadn't been prepared for all the math that went into running a successful small business, but thankfully Daniele was adept at it.

He'd opened his heart and his family flower shop to her. They'd spent two years planning the renovation together, adding a commercial kitchen and reconfiguring the main space to allow for seating amongst the buckets and vases and cold cases filled with flowers. It reminded her a little of the

Dish Room at Mulvaney's, where they'd had their first date—a working space where the hustle and bustle of the flower business was a part of the experience. The floral dining room had opened two months before to great success, and she was finally working there full-time.

She opened the second of her four ovens—the coconut macadamia cinnamon rolls were almost done too. She sighed with pleasure.

I can do this. Sometimes it seemed overwhelming, but mostly she was just… happy. *Life is good.*

She scooped the muffin mix into an industrial-size muffin pan inside little cups wrapped with the *Pane e Tulipani* logo, and popped the pan into the oven. She set the timer for 12 minutes and spun off to the next thing.

It was like a magical dance, even if her knee throbbed a bit as she turned. *Have to be careful about that.*

Getting older annoyed her. *Not dead yet.* Whistling, she waltzed into the next thing on her list.

~

It was 3:30 in the afternoon when she pulled into her driveway at home. The weather was gorgeous after the previous night's rain—warm, with unexpected gusts kicking up the edge of her flour-covered shirt, but the sky was still clear and blue.

They'd repainted the duplex a lovely tan a couple years earlier, just as the world was starting to move past the pandemic. She'd needed a fresh start.

Daniele had promised to meet her at the restaurant at five—he had some "floral accounting" to do. *Enough time for a shower and a little relaxation before running off again.*

The house was warm. It was early May, and the days were getting hotter every week. Inside, all traces of her former life with Arthur had been replaced, one by one, over the past decade, as she and Daniele had built a new life together. All but one.

Arthur's smiling face greeted her from its place on the fireplace mantle. Daniele never said a word about it. *One of the reasons I love him.*

She blew Arthur a kiss and popped out of the front door to grab the mail—a few assorted bills, a money mailer, and, curiously, a handwritten envelope postmarked from Strangolagalli, Italy. It seemed to sparkle in her hands.

Her brow furrowed. Hadn't that wonderful Italian mystery series she'd been reading been set there? The one with the woman with the perfect memory and bumbling style that always seemed to nab the bad guy? *Teresa Papavero.* Strangolagalli was a small town just south of Rome, if she remembered right.

Curious about who would be writing her from Italy, she retreated to her living room and worked open the envelope with a long fingernail. A handwritten letter slipped out into her palm.

It was in Italian, but she'd gotten pretty good at reading the language these last few years with Daniele:

Ciao, Carmelina, my name is Angelo Farelli. I don't know if your mother ever mentioned me, but I'm your uncle, and I would love to meet you. I have so many things to tell you. Things that you ought to know…

She stared at it. *Wait, I have an uncle in Italy?* Her mother had most certainly never mentioned it.

Carmelina was naturally distrustful of strangers, especially those who tried to play upon her good nature and sense of family.

She sank back in her armchair and squinted at the letter, her curiosity piqued.

What do you really want from me, Mister Farelli?

3

CARDBOARD BOX

"You're doing it wrong."

Marcos Ramirez grinned. "You wanna come do it?"

"I offered." Dave's voice carried from the kitchen. A tantalizing aroma of chicken curry casserole emanated from the oven with it, making Marcos's stomach growl.

"Besides, how can you tell?" He glared at the old VCR, bought off an online auction site the week before. *Damned thing doesn't even have HDMI.*

"There's a coax to HDMI converter in the wires box, in the laundry room cabinet."

"It's like you read my mind." He shook his head in wonder. Nine years in, and Dave could still surprise him. "Dinner smells heavenly."

Dave snorted. "Yeah, if you don't mind the curry stench lingering for a day or two."

Marcos pecked him on the cheek on the way by. "Hope this is all worth it. The VCR, not the curry."

It had started with one of Dave's infamous "clear out the house" projects, something he'd been doing increasingly with his free time, as their business had begun to tank the year before. No one seemed to need web designers or graphic artists anymore in the age of algorithms and artificial intelligence. *Intelligence my ass.*

Dave had come across a box of old VHS tapes with the labels mostly missing. Before they paid to have them converted to DVDs, he wanted to see what was on them. Which of course meant getting a VCR, which cost money, something that was in increasingly short supply as their business plummeted. But it would make Dave happy, so Marcos had acquiesced and found a cheap one on eBay.

He pulled the old Amazon box down from its perch above the washer and rummaged through it. Sure enough, there was the adapter.

Something glittered, catching his eye. A worn envelope sat at the back of the box, held in place by an assorted clump of cords—lightning, USB, USB2, USB-c. *Why are there so many kinds of USB cords?*

Curious, he plucked it out.

Inside, he found a variety of papers… tickets from the Sacramento Zoo, from that time they fed the giraffes. A playbill for Tribes, the first play they'd ever seen together at Cap Stage, and a coffee-stained napkin from the Everyday Grind just down the street. Mementoes from their early days. *He saved them, all these years.*

And at the back…

Marcos's breath caught.

It was a photo of Dave and his ex-partner, John, who'd passed away some fourteen years before. The same photo that had sent Dave into shock one fateful night, not long after they met.

"Find it?" Dave's voice floated in from the kitchen. "Dinner's almost ready."

"Yup. Got it!" He hurriedly stuffed the keepsakes back into the envelope and put it where he'd found it. He eased the box back up into its cabinet and closed the door almost reverently.

He'd always known Dave loved him. But seeing how he'd saved all those little pieces of their courtship? It was the first time he understood that his husband loved him as much as he'd loved John.

The slow decline of their business had taken its toll on both of them. They fought more often, and had less of a buffer—Dave's word—for the idiocy and ignorance of the world. But in a strange way, it had also brought them closer. Two warriors fighting a common enemy.

He slipped back into the kitchen and put his arms around Dave from behind, pulling his warm body close. "I love you, you know."

Dave paused chopping cucumbers for the salad. "What's that for?"

Marcos shrugged. "Just realized I don't tell you often enough." He kissed the back of Dave's neck, then headed for his nemesis again, across the living room. "Give me two minutes and I'll have this hooked up." Hopefully the old beast still worked.

"Perfect. Then we can test it out after dinner."

Dave grinned as Marcos sat back and patted his ample tummy. He'd grown more comfortable with himself over the years, seemingly no longer afraid that Dave would leave him if he didn't keep himself always trim and in shape.

Not that he wasn't still a handsome man. The extra weight suited him, and Dave loved to grab a hold of it when they made love, kneading it like putty. Or bread dough. "Good?"

"Fantastic." Marcos grinned. "Where'd you get that recipe again?"

"Friend of my mother's. Mom passed it along. You sure you don't mind them coming for Thanksgiving?"

"Not even a little. Especially if your mom will make us a batch of her famous *calabacitas*." The tomato, cheese, and zucchini dish was one of his favorites.

"I think she could be convinced." His parents were getting older. Dad had a pacemaker, and Mom couldn't play the piano anymore with her arthritis. He was looking forward to seeing them both. "Let's clean up, and then we'll see what's on those tapes?"

Fifteen minutes later the moment of truth arrived. "Which one?" Hopefully none of them had anything too embarrassing.

Marcos picked up a black VHS tape at random. "This one?"

"Sure. Pop it in." It was strange to see one of those again, after years of DVDs and now streaming for almost everything.

The tape started, and music blared through the speaker's TV.

"Oh my god. I can't believe you recorded Three's Company." Marcos stared at him, eyes dancing with merriment.

"It was the closest thing to something gay I could find at the time." He'd mooned over John Ritter as a kid.

"Uh huh. Keep?" Marcos sounded doubtful.

"Nah. Toss. Next?" He didn't need an old seventies actor now. He had Marcos.

His husband cued up another. Grunts and moans filled their little apartment. "Closest thing to gay, huh?" Marcos grinned.

Dave grabbed the remote and put it on mute, his face on fire. "In *mainstream* television, yes." He'd forgotten about that one.

"Wait… how many arms does that guy have?" Marcos cocked his head. "Oh, I see. It's a three-way. Kinky."

Dave snorted. "Like you didn't do anything like that when you were younger… or worse." Marcos had shared some of his tales of sexual conquest, and submission.

"Touché. Keep?"

Dave nodded sagely. "For old time's sake."

Marcos wrinkled his nose. "Of course." He set it in a second pile, and tried the next one. "I think this one is one of mine."

Static filled the screen, and when it cleared, a ten-year-old boy in a purple princess costume, complete with conical hat and matching lilac nails, stared solemnly at the camera. "I swear to protect the kingdom of Narnia, to rid the world of the One Ring, and to make all the boys kiss."

Dave blinked. Here was a side of Marcos he'd never seen before. "Wow. Just… wow."

It was Marcos's turn to blush. "We can, um, dump that one…"

"Are you kidding? This is priceless. I want to take screenshots and share it will all of our friends."

Marcos stuck his tongue out at him.

Dave watched it a moment more, mesmerized, then leaned forward and popped out the tape, setting it as far away from Marcos as he could without leaving the couch. "Wait, did they have VHS cameras back then?"

"My mom shot that on reel-to-reel tape. She had it converted to VHS later." He sighed. "When my Dad saw that, he almost threw me out of the house."

And he had done so later, when Marcos was older. Dave was glad they'd patched things up before his father had passed away. He gave Marcos a kiss on the cheek. "Next."

The tape popped into the player with that familiar mechanical loading sound, and as soon as it started to play, Dave knew what it was.

So did Marcos. "Maybe I should go to the next one…"

"No. Let it play." It was John's thirtieth birthday. Dave had surprised him with breakfast in bed, filming the whole thing, which had been… awkward. Those old cameras were bulky, and holding a plate full of breakfast, syrup, and the camera had put his ballerina abilities to the test.

"Wake up, sleepy head."

John lay on his back, eyes closed, his hands behind his head, his beautiful chest half-hidden under the sheets. Those blue eyes fluttered open. "What's this?"

"It's your birthday. I made you eggs and pancakes." The camera jiggled as he set down the tray.

"Oooh, those smell amazing, D." He reached up and his hand pulled down the camera for a kiss for the chef.

"Sweet for my sweet—"

Dave hit the pause button, and closed his eyes.

"You okay?" Marcos sounded worried.

With good reason. Reminders of John had sent him spiraling before.

He took a deep breath. "Yeah. I'm… okay." John was his past. Sometimes painful, sometimes uplifting. More of the latter lately. He squeezed Marcos' hand. Whatever they were going through, however difficult it became, they would get through it. *I'd live in a cardboard box with you, if it came to that, and still be happy.* "He would have liked you, I think."

"Keep it?" Marcos raised an eyebrow.

Dave nodded. "Keep it. It was a good time in my life. But so is this, with you. Even better, actually."

And as soon as he said it, he knew it was true.

4

PAPÀ AND BABBO

Diego Bellei laid out his ingredients with care on the wide white marble countertop. Italian flour from Corti Brothers in a large white ceramic canister covered in lemons—always better than that bleached powder Americans used. A blue ceramic chalice of water. A pinch-bowl full of salt. A bottle of Kirkland olive oil, which even the Italians here in Sacramento rated the best locally available. A canister of sugar. And a metal container of beer yeast.

The marble was cold to the touch, and the whole place felt… empty, despite Gio banging around, prepping the other workstations around the wide room for the class he'd be teaching in half an hour.

The Raven Tavern next door to Ragazzi had gone out of business during the pandemic, and Matteo had worked out a deal with the bank to buy it on a short sale. It had taken almost eighteen months to gut the place and set it up as a proper training kitchen, but he could now teach ten pairs of students at once, each with their own countertop, sink, and oven.

Gio dropped a stainless-steel bowl on one of the counters, creating a racket.

"You're a menacer."

"It's *menace, Papà,* and if you can find someone else to help you out for free, be my guest." He flashed his trademark Bellei grin, white teeth almost glowing.

"*Porco cane*, I hate when you call me that." He grinned in spite of himself. In nine years, his English had improved greatly, but Gio now spoke it like he'd been born to it. It wasn't fair. And truth be told, he loved being the young man's father. Just not having to *be reminded* about it. It made him feel old.

Gio finished setting up the last station. They'd have a full house tonight.

So why do I feel so empty?

He knew why. *Carmelina.* She'd taken the last of her things to her new kitchen at *Pane e Tulipani*, and the clutter was gone. He should be grateful. How many times had he complained about her leaving his kitchen a mess after her early-morning endeavors? There was always flour scattered about and a couple dirty dishes left forgotten in the sink. But she'd been a part of his life here for so long. If felt… strange now that she was gone. *Like a lost limb.*

"Have you given any more thought to my proposal?" Gio pulled up a chair and propped his head on his hands, his dirty-blond hair a messy mop on his head.

Diego frowned. "It's… a lot to considering." In truth, he'd been too preoccupied with other things, including *the other thing*, and he hadn't had much time to give thought to his son's idea.

"C'mon, *Papà*. This place is great. Everyone loves it. What you and *Babbo* have done to bring Italian food, culture, and the language to this city is nothing short of miraculous. Why not share it? If you franchised, you could help do the same in a bunch of other places." He fidgeted, as if stuffed so full of the promise of the thing that it was itching to get out of him.

Ah, the energy of the young. Even a pandemic hadn't dulled Gio's lust for life, for something new. "I'll talk it over with *Babbo*." *And why does Matteo get to be babbo?*

"Thanks, *Papone*." Gio grinned and looked around the room. "Full class tonight?"

"*Alla grande.*" He leaned back against the stainless-steel counter that ran along the back wall and looked at Giovani, really looked at him. His unexpected son had grown into a strong, confident, intelligent man, full of plans for his own life. And theirs, apparently. "*Sono molto orgolioso di te, Giovanni.*"

His son blushed. "Proud of you too, pop. Gotta run. *Babbo* needs me in the restaurant."

"Go. Thanks for the help." Diego busied himself with the handouts, making sure each station was ready to go for his new class.

"*Figurati!*"

So there was little Italian in him yet. Diego grinned. *Not such a bad life we've built here.* He hoped it would stay that way.

Matteo was checking inventory in the kitchen, enjoying the pause between the lunch and dinner crowd. Ragazzi was closed between three and five to give them time to prepare for the next meal.

It had been an unusually busy day so far, with four large groups coming in, coworkers from local businesses. It was good to have them, but sometimes these big parties strained their small waitstaff.

It had become increasingly difficult to find good workers as inflation had taken a toll on their bottom line. They had raised their pay several times over the last few years as the new minimum wage laws took effect, and thankfully their operation was doing well enough to afford it. But he shuddered to think of the damage those market forces were inflicting on some of his friendly competitors.

The door between the restaurant and the new training kitchen next door swung open, and Gio practically bounded into the room.

"*Papà's* got it all in hand over there. What do we need to do here?"

Matteo hid a grin. Gio had grown into a fine young man, following in his father's footsteps. "The front of house is prepped. Everything ready in the kitchen?"

Gio took a minute before answering, biting his lip, clearly considering the question. "I think so. We had some extra mussels from last weekend that were about to go bad, so I'm doing a special ravioli. Natasha's coming in a little early to help me prep them. Oh, and we have some extra apples, so I made some *torta sbriciolata.*"

Matteo's mouth watered. The crumbly apple cake was one of his favorites, and Gio knew it. The young man had taken to being a chef as if he were born to it. And maybe he was—Gio was Diego's son, after all. "That sounds perfectly."

"*Perfect, Babbo*. Perfectly is an adverb." Gio winked at him. His stepson had long since surpassed his own near-mastery of the English language. Gio's children, if he had any, would be American to the core.

The thought both thrilled and saddened him. "Sounds like you have it well in hand. I'm going to count down the drawer. You got everything out here?" He was proud of his mastery of that most American of words, *got*.

"Yep. I'll call you if I need you." He started pulling out the ingredients for the ravioli.

Matteo removed the cash drawer and retreated to his office.

Thirty minutes later, he was staring at the pile of cash, perplexed.

Most people paid by credit card these days—swipe, insert, tap, or Apple Pay and the like—but Ragazzi still took in a fair amount of those old green bills. And for the third time in a week, the count was off.

Once was a mistake. Twice a coincidence. But three times?

We have ourselves a thief.

5

LORELEI

en Hammond pecked at the keyboard, willing the words to come like they used to. Eventually they did, but they refused to do so in any coherent sort of order:

Bleak. Cries. Winter. Plague. Throes. Denial. Pineapple.

Pineapple? That was out of left field.

He sat back in his chair, interlacing his fingers behind his shoulder-length hair. One of these days he'd have to get a haircut. Probably. If he could get himself out of the house long enough between work shifts.

Pineapple, pineapple... ah. That day in late spring, in the before time. When Ella had insisted on finding a ripe pineapple to cut up, to take with them on a picnic in McKinley Park. It had been ripe and delicious, and had reminded them of Hawaii...

He closed his eyes, the familiar pain squeezing his chest. Two long years she'd been gone, and it had all been his fault. *If only I'd been more careful... and why does it still seem like it was just yesterday?*

He glanced at the clock. *Four-thirty already?* He had the night shift at Zocalo—he'd swapped managerial shifts with Daria, because she had some kind of family thing.

With a heavy sigh, he closed his laptop and got out of the chair to stretch. *Isn't this grief thing supposed to get easier?*

After her memorial, once all their friends and family had left, endless days had stretched into sluggish weeks, devoid of light and color. Life became an exercise in simply remembering to put one foot in front of the other. Three months off work—his boss had been more than fair about it.

And then the *pretending*.

Pretending to be human. Pretending to give a crap about work. Pretending he still remembered what having a life was.

Pretending she wasn't gone.

At least he was showering every day now. That had taken him the better part of the year to accomplish. *Ella would be proud.*

He hopped in for a cursory rinse, trying not to look at the yellow shampoo bottle in the corner. The one he still didn't have the heart to throw away. Every now and then, he would use a little bit of the lemon-scented shampoo that she used to favor—something she'd picked up on their trip to Italy.

The Amalfi Coast had been stunning that spring.

He knew he was being pathetic. It was time to move on. *Past time.* Ella wouldn't want to see him like this.

"Get off your ass," she'd say. "There's someone else out there for you, you silly fool."

He grinned for just a moment, remembering the sweetness of her kiss and hearing her voice, before his face settled back into its normal, neutral, impassive glare.

He knew she was right. But *knowing* and *doing* were two very different things. So for now, he contented himself with simply getting out of bed and putting that one foot in front of the other each day. Hoping for *one good thing*.

He got out and toweled himself off, avoiding looking at himself in the mirror. At his scars.

Clomp, clomp, clomp.

Ben rolled his eyes. The elephant was back.

He'd never met his upstairs neighbor, but whoever they were, they must weigh three hundred pounds. When they stomped around their apartment, he swore dust dropped from his ceiling, like in those old Westerns. It didn't happen all that often, but it was enough to break through his self-imposed shell of numbness.

Bam!

This time the whole room shook, and the shampoo bottle slipped off its perch to spill some of its precious contents across the shower floor.

"God dammit." He scooped it up and pushed as much of the precious golden liquid as he could back inside. He set it on the bathroom counter, where he hoped it would be safe. "Enough is enough."

Ben marched out of his front door, towel tied around his waist, and up the narrow stairs to the third floor of the old partitioned Victorian house in Mansion Flats that he called home. He pounded on the door, determined to finally put an end to the elephant's sonic torture.

The door opened… and there was no one there.

"Hello… down here."

His gaze dropped to the woman in the wheelchair who held the door open. "Um… hello." His face flushed with heat.

"Can I help you?" Her brow was knitted, her blonde hair pushed back and tied behind her head.

His anger drained out of him. *I can't yell at a woman in a wheelchair.* "Um… yeah." He scratched his head, wondering how to proceed, and suddenly realized he was wearing only a towel. "I'm sorry. I… I live downstairs, and…"

Her hand flew to cover her mouth. "Oh, I'm the one who should be sorry. My kids are here for the weekend, and sometimes they get a little crazy."

As if in response, another loud crash thundered through the house.

She looked back over her shoulder. "If I have to come in there one more time…" Her voice trailed off, and so did the noise. She turned back to him. "I'm so sorry. I'm Lorelei."

She held out her hand, and he got a good look at her for the first time. She was close to his own age, pretty in a harried way. Blond, brown-eyed, with a warm smile.

He shook her hand. "Ben. I live downstairs."

Her warm laugh charmed him. "You mentioned that."

"Yeah, guess I did." He cast about for something else to say. "You have kids?"

She snorted. "Yes, two little demons. Max and Mia. Love them to death, of course, but they'll be the end of me. My ex leaves them with me on the weekends, while he's out of town."

"Of course." Work was calling. He needed to finish getting ready if he wasn't going to be late. "Sorry to bother you." He started to turn away. "Say, how do you…" He was going to ask how she navigated the stairs in her wheelchair. But that didn't seem polite. "Sorry. Have to get to work. But it was nice to meet you."

She bit her lip and grinned. "Nice to meet you too, Ben."

She closed the door, leaving him standing there alone, gaping at the door.

One good thing. Something good had happened. He'd met someone new.
Yes, Ella would be proud.

6

THAT WAS THEN

Marissa blinked, staring at the endless line of red taillights in front of her. After a pause for the pandemic, traffic in Sacramento was worse than ever, and the long line of cars inched down Folsom Boulevard a few feet at a time.

At least the rain had let up for a bit, returning the weather to springtime warmth, the air new and clear. She rolled down her window and was struck by the unexpected aroma of fresh-baked bread and rosemary.

She glanced over to find the welcoming windows of Ragazzi facing her. A smile crept across her face. *So many memories there.*

Tris and the Adolescent Army. Finding her grandmother, Carmelina. Her time with Gio.

She frowned. *It was good between us for a little while, right?* Until she'd screwed it all up with that other girl in her Econ Masters classes. *What was her name? Ally?*

She'd never told Gio, but the affair had signaled the end of them. *Not my proudest moment.*

She'd decided she was probably better off alone. She had a good, albeit somewhat boring job with a local law firm, and was slowly figuring out the rest of her life.

An open parking spot beckoned, and she pulled over impulsively. That bread had smelled so good. She'd treat herself to a quick meal and see a couple old friends. *I deserve it.*

It had been ages since she'd been to Ragazzi, and surely by now things would be smoothed over with Gio. *Time heals all wounds, right? Even self-inflicted ones.*

She fed the meter—she hoped the Kings appreciated her unwilling donation to the cause—and returned the two blocks down the street to the Italian restaurant. When had she last been there? *Let's see. It's March of 2024. Last time was… no, it can't be.*

Pre-pandemic. Probably 2018 or 2019, when she was still in school. *Holy crap.*

She crossed the street to stand in front of the place that held all those memories, like the Prodigal Daughter returned home.

It was early yet—the place was only half full. Thankfully Gio was nowhere to be seen.

She took a deep breath, steeled herself, and pushed open the door.

"Welcome in. We're a little short-handed at the moment—grab yourself a table wherever." The speaker was a beautiful Asian woman—Korean, if she had to guess—dressed in a crisp white shirt and short red and green tie, her black hair tied up neatly behind her head. "I'll be with you in just a moment."

"Thanks!" Marissa watched her disappear into the kitchen, a smile crossing her face. *Cute.*

She chose a table by the window and was just about to take a seat when a booming voice sounded behind her. "Marissa! I thought that was you. So lovely to have you back."

She spun around to find one of the owners, Matteo Bianco, standing before her. "Uncle Matty!" She threw her arms around him, hugging him tightly. "It's good to see you."

"You too. I didn't see you on the list of reservations."

She giggled. His mostly right English never failed to bring a smile to her face. "An impulsive thing. I was driving by and smelled rosemary…" She looked around hopefully.

"Ah. Diego is baking up a batch of Romagnola bread next door. I'll see if I can sneak for you a little."

Oooh. "I'd like that."

The server appeared at his side, handing her a menu. "I see you know the boss." She flashed Marissa a bright smile.

"We go way back." She glanced over the menu. Still the same old comforting dishes, although she spied a few new things, too. *I need to come by here more often.*

"I'm Ainsley and I'll be your server tonight. Can I get you started with something to drink?"

"Just water, please." She still had a lot of student loans to pay off, and the new job didn't pay *that* well.

"I'll send Gio out to say hi when he has some moments." Matteo bowed and slipped away before she could protest.

"Water coming right up." Ainsley glanced over her shoulder at the kitchen door. "So you know the boss's son too?"

Marissa nodded, hoping she wasn't blushing *too* obviously. "We… have a history."

"Ah." That little word spoke volumes. "He *is* handsome. I'll be back with that water, and to get your order." She left an aroma behind, something halfway between watermelon and citrus.

Marissa closed her eyes. *Slow down, girl. You're finally on your own now, remember?* This was not the time to start up another romance.

Her gaze slid down the menu and settled on an old favorite, the chicken piadina.

She closed her eyes, remembering her hands buried in flour, Tris's arms around hers, kneading the dough together in this very room…

"Ready to order? Matteo sent this over." Ainsley placed a basket of fresh bread on the table. The tantalizing aroma made her mouth water.

"Oh my god, that smells amazing." She broke off a piece and popped it in her mouth. "Pure heaven. Here." She held out a piece, grinning like an idiot. "You *have* to try this."

Ainsley looked around. "I really shouldn't."

"Oh come on. It's your job to know what you're serving, right? You wouldn't want to disappoint a customer." Okay, maybe she was laying it on a little thick.

Ainsley laughed, a delightful sound that sent a thrill up Marissa's spine. "I suppose when you put it that way. Just one bite." She took the proffered piece and slipped it in her mouth, and her lips widened in pleasure. "Oooh, that *is* good. We should serve it all the time."

"I know, right?" Ainsley was getting under her skin, and she wasn't even trying. Marissa imagined those fingertips on her face, those lips brushing her neck…

"So are you ready to order?" Ainsley seemed blissfully unaware of her interest. Or maybe she was just that good of a server.

"Yes. The chicken piadina? And a side salad?" She should at least make a stab at eating something healthy. Besides, she didn't want Ainsley thinking she only ate carbs.

"Coming right up." The server winked at her, and Marissa's heart fluttered.

Down, girl. She sat back in the smooth wicker chair and just *breathed,* letting herself slow down for the first time since daybreak. She should treat herself a little more often. Life was more than just work.

A squeak announced the opening of the kitchen door. Gio appeared there and stared at her for a moment. He looked the same—young, Italian, and adorable—though somehow he seemed a little more… *seasoned* than before.

She waved at him tentatively.

He frowned and disappeared back inside the kitchen.

So that's how it's going to be? The welcome sense of warmth fled, replaced by a familiar but still searing sense of guilt, a cold ball in her stomach. *He didn't know about Ally, did he?*

She'd never told him about her affair, but he had to have guessed that something significant had happened. He was a good man. Just not *the* good man—or person—for her.

Still, she wasn't dead. Just in zombie mode. She'd castigated herself for it long enough, putting her personal life on hold.

Maybe it was time to come back to life.

When Ainsley returned with her meal, setting down the beautiful and aromatic open-faced Italian sandwich on the table before her, so did the warmth in Marissa's heart. "It's perfect, thank you."

Her heart fluttered again as she watched Ainsley walk away.

Life had a way of surprising you, just when you'd all but given up.

7

ITALIAN SURPRISE

Carmelina swept into Ragazzi like she owned the place, which was not far from the truth. She'd been dining there with Diego and Matteo for nine years, not to mention serving as a substitute chef *and* cooking her own baked treats in the training kitchen next door for years. She'd first met her granddaughter there—before she'd known that she and Marissa were related—and had celebrated not one but two weddings with some of her dearest friends under its roof.

Daniele was waiting for her at their usual table, in the corner by the window, next to the shelves filled with boxes and cans of Italian goods.

"My, don't you look handsome." His sharp white Italian blazer was set off by an emerald green tie, his intense brown eyes fixed on hers.

"You're early!" By which he meant she was only fifteen minutes late—a minor miracle by her standards.

She kissed him, running a hand through his silvering hair. "Sorry, got caught up in something at home. I'll tell you later." She'd done some googling after that strange letter from her purported uncle, and the results had left her no less mystified.

She sank down into the beautiful rosewood chair, grateful to finally be off her feet. Now that she was officially running the bakery, her days were longer than ever, and after dinner she'd be ready for a bath and a foot rubbing, if Daniele was so inclined.

How was it possible that she was almost eligible for Medicare and retirement? Not that she planned to go gently into that dark night any time soon. She still had a lot she wanted to accomplish. "What are the specials?"

"Yours is already on order. Diego's sending over an Italian sandwich— something he whipped up in class today called *La Spianata Romagnola*. Oh and they have *torta sbriciolata* tonight, too." He grinned. He knew the crumbly apple treat was one of her favorites.

"*Perfetto.*" She set down her menu and gave him her full attention. "So, you have news?" She'd been wondering what it was all day. Between inflation and the upcoming election and Gaza and Ukraine and all the other horrible things going on in the world, it had been nice to fixate on something positive, for once. "*Dimmi.*" While she was still far from fluent in Daniele's native tongue, she could manage well enough.

He grinned. "Not until I get a little wine into you first." He lifted a bottle, Chateau Varnelli, if she didn't miss the mark. The lustrous, silky liquid flowed into her glass like red velvet.

"That bad, huh?" She sniffed it. It had a delightfully fruity scent, like raspberries, with just a hint of licorice.

"That *good*, actually. Drink up."

She stuck her tongue out at him, and then took a sip. It was divine, washing away her troubles. "How much *was* this?" *Like I really want to know.*

"Less than it would be at another restaurant." He winked at her, and she knew he was up to something.

"Okay, spill it. What's your news?" The older she got, the less patience she had for little games. Even with Daniele.

He sighed dramatically. "You're no fun at all." With a sip from his own glass, he continued. "Remember my cousin Elena?"

Carmelina frowned. He had about a hundred cousins. "Is she the one who lives on a sailboat in Sicily?"

"No, that's Filipa."

"The one who lives in the Dolomites and gives tours of the Alps?"

"No, that's Elia."

"The one—"

Daniele laughed. "Before you go down what I admit is an embarrassingly extensive list, she's the lawyer in Rome, with the girlfriend who runs that boutique on Via dei Condotti."

With the spiky blond hair. "Ah, of course."

"You think I have a hundred cousins, don't you?" He took another sip, staring at her over the glass.

Busted. "Don't you?"

"No. Just thirty."

She chuckled. "You know that's a lot, right?" She had seven cousins, and that had always seemed like more than enough.

"Not for an Italian family, *tesoro.*" He set down his wine glass. "So… Elena's getting married."

"That's wonderful! Wait, are lesbian weddings—"

"Still not legal in Italy, but they can have a civil union." He shook his head. "The things Italians get hung up on."

"Not just there." America had its own special brand of idiocy and intolerance.

He shook his head, and then wiped away the gravity of the moment with a dazzling smile. "She invited us to come to the wedding."

"Really?" *A Roman vacation.* She'd always wanted to go to Italy, but somehow she and Arthur had never gotten around to it, and then, with his declining health… "I'd love to see the Eternal City."

"I was hoping you'd say that." He put his hands on hers. "Imagine it. You and me wandering the streets of Rome together. All that history and beauty…."

"When is it?" She was hoping for October. Fewer crowds, and the weather was still good. They'd visit the Coliseum, explore the halls of the Vatican, wander through the Spanish Steps…

"Next weekend."

"What?" Her heart started to race. *Next weekend?* She couldn't possibly. She had the new café to run.

A thousand thoughts ran through her head. *Why so soon? Why didn't you tell me earlier? Is something wrong? Who will bake the muffins?* But all that came out was, "Why?"

Daniele, as always, knew her as well as he knew the contours of a

Madame Butterfly snapdragon. "I just found out. Apparently she had a cancellation—Elia can't make it. Otherwise everything's fine. And we can have Bethany substitute for you at the shop. She's already agreed. Sweet Nothings will be okay for a few days without you."

Bethany had interned with her a couple years earlier, before going on to open her own bakery on the Sac State Campus.

Rome's close to Strangolagalli. "I don't know."

"Just say yes." He took her hand and kissed it in that charming and irresistible way of his. "It will be *molto romantico, mia principessa.*"

She shivered the way she always did when he called her *princess.* She was helpless before his Italian charms.

"Amici!" Diego appeared at their tableside, dragging a surprised Marissa with him. "What comes you to Ragazzi?"

"Diego!" Carmelina jumped up and hugged him, unconcerned about the flour on his apron. "Date night. Daniele had a little surprise for me." She still wasn't sure about what he proposed—it was such a short notice. "And I see you brought my dearest granddaughter." She brushed the white powder off her red blouse and embraced Marissa. "It's been a while since I've seen you here."

Marissa shrugged. "It was time. Plus I missed Diego's cooking!"

Carmelina looked her granddaughter over. She'd grown into a beautiful, capable young woman.

Daniele shook Diego's hand. "*Piacere.*"

"Mine's the pleasure." Diego grinned. At fifty-six, he was still handsome, if a little… rounder than before.

Hazards of being a chef. "Daniele was just inviting me to go to Rome. *Next weekend.*" That last part came out a little sharper than she intended.

"*Che fantastico.*" Diego squeezed his hands together. "Roma is beautiful in the spring."

"I haven't said yes…"

"*Nonna*, you have to go. When a beautiful man asks you to come to Rome with him…" Marissa's eyes sparkled. "I can even help out a little with the shop, if you need me."

Gio popped out of the kitchen at the back of the restaurant, took one look at Marissa, and disappeared again.

What was that about? We'll talk about that later. Carmelina sighed. It *would* be romantic. And didn't *romantic* have the word Rome in it? Almost? Her eyes met Daniele's. "Looks like we're going to Rome."

"*Evviva!*" Daniele leaned over and kissed her cheek. "You won't be sorry."

Their dinners arrived. The *spianata romagnola* smelled heavenly, essentially a foccacia sandwich filled with prosciutto and fresh mozzarella, a festival of rosemary and olive oil and yeasty goodness.

"*Buon appetito.*" Diego kissed her cheeks and let them be.

Marissa waved her goodbyes. "I'll see you soon, *Nonna.*"

"Come by the house Saturday? We can talk about the café." *And about that other thing with Gio.*

"Sure. Late afternoon okay?"

"Perfect. We'll make dinner out of it."

Marissa slipped out the door. There was more going on than the girl—young woman—was letting on.

She set her concerns aside, and picked up half of the Italian sandwich to take a bite. It was delicious, as always, filled with notes of rosemary and garlic and olive oil.

"So what did you want to tell *me*?" Daniele asked between bites of ravioli in an arrabbiata sauce.

"What?"

"You said you had news for me, too."

Her supposed uncle. Now that she was faced with the possibility of actually meeting him, the whole thing seemed a bit… preposterous. She needed time to think it over first. To contact this man and find out more. "Nothing. Just that I'm thrilled with how well things went at the café today."

"*Anch'io.* Me too. This thing just might work." He seemed happy. And that made her want to feel happy.

We're going to Rome. It would be the trip of a lifetime.

So why was her stomach tied in knots?

8

SMOKE AND MOONLIGHT

Gio slung the garbage bag over his shoulder and headed out the back door of the restaurant, passing Justin, who was vigorously rinsing dishes to be loaded into the industrial washer. "Busy night?"

Gio rolled his eyes. "Not bad. It's my third trash run." *Babbo* had taught him to take part in all the restaurant tasks. Not only because they were a small family-owned business, but also because it *holds you humble.* Matteo's words. Gio grinned.

It was late out, but still light enough to see without the back porch light. He gave the back lot a quick scan before stepping outside—you could never be too careful. Sometimes unhoused folk hung out back there, going through the garbage for scraps of food. They were usually harmless, but they also occasionally left needles and broken glass, or worse, by the dumpster.

His heart went out to them. Without Diego, he might have ended up just like them.

The moon was just rising in the East, over the butcher shop across the street. It was almost full, its silver light lining everything with an argent glow.

Luna. It had been a long time since he'd thought about his mother. How she used to take him outside on full-moon nights. They would order

Chinese take-out and sit on the steps in front of their *palazzo* to watch her rise, as his mother recited some of her favorite poetry and shared a glass of *limonata* with him.

Her face was slowly fading from his mind as the years passed. Sometimes, now, when he thought of her, he saw the face of the moon instead.

He still missed her—that would never change. He had a good life here. He loved his *Papà* and *Babbo*, and Sacramento had become, improbably, a second home. But his heart would always be in Italy.

He lifted the dumpster lid, his nose wrinkling at the smell of old soda and decaying food scraps, and dumped the bag in. The metal lid slammed shut with a satisfying *crash*.

"Hey."

Gio spun around to find someone staring at him.

Not just anyone. *Her.*

"Hey, 'Riss." He'd managed to avoid her inside the restaurant, though he'd never admit it. It was stupid, really. They'd been *over* for years, after all, even if he'd never understood why. One day, she'd just packed up her things and fled, leaving him with an empty flat and a cat named Oscar. He'd moved back home the next day.

So it was reflex, mostly, avoiding the prickly awkwardness between them. "What are you doing back here?" Then he saw the little stick between her fingers.

"I was… I wanted to think." She held up the cigarette as if it were an explanation.

He huffed. "Those things will kill you, you know."

Her lips pursed in what might have been annoyance or amusement. "I'm aware."

He laughed. He'd always liked her dry sense of humor. "When we were… the last time I saw you, you were still vaping."

"I guess I graduated to these." She stared at the cigarette. "I don't even know why I started doing it. Studying for my Master's… it was hard. Some of my friends got me into them. They made it a little easier."

She was still beautiful to him, his mother's moon casting her face in an ethereal glow that made her look more like an Italian statue of Venus than his ex who'd stomped on his heart and then walked away. "You were avoiding me in there, weren't you?" Her eyes narrowed as she took his measure, one eyebrow raising.

"Of course not... I was busy in the kitchen and...." He laughed, his face flushing. "Yeah. I totally was."

They laughed together at his attempted denial, and for a moment, everything felt normal between them.

A car passed on 48th Street, its headlights brightening the parking light for just a minute, dispelling the magical moonlight.

"Truth be told, I've been avoiding Ragazzi, and you, for years." She lit the cigarette and brought it to her lips for a long drag. "It's a shame too. Diego's bread is to die for."

Gio grinned. "It's one of my *cibo preferito,* too."

She shivered a little, whether it was from the cool night air or his Italian accent, he couldn't tell. She'd always had a soft spot for his native tongue. That thought brought back other sorts of memories, and he blushed again.

She exhaled, smoke floating up into the sky between them. "I'd better go…"

"Why did you leave?" It slipped out before he knew he'd said it. *The* question. The one that had been burning him up inside for years. "I mean, we were good together, *certo?*"

"Oh Gio." She took another drag on the cigarette, her face displaying a disturbing flurry of emotions. Surprise, sadness, guilt?

And maybe pity. "I'm sorry. It was stupid of me to ask. After all this time." He turned to go, wishing he'd waited to take out the trash.

"No… listen, it wasn't your fault. It was me. All me." She stubbed out the cigarette under her black sneaker, and leaned forward to kiss him on the cheek. "Good night, Gio." Then she fled.

He stared after her, as mystified as ever. He had loved her, once. Still did, if he was honest with himself. There was something she wouldn't tell him yet, even after all this time. *What did you do?*

The parking lot darkened.

Gio looked up. A cloud passed over the moon, hiding her face from view.

He shook himself like a wet dog to shake off the spell Marissa had cast upon him. It was time to let her go. There were dishes to be washed, guests to be attended to, and his family, all waiting inside that door for him.

He had a full life. A good life.

So why do I still miss her so?

It wasn't clear, even in his own head, whether he meant Marissa or Luna.

~

Marissa reached the safety of her little red Mini, collapsing into the seat and slamming the door behind her as if it could keep out the memories. She closed her eyes, sinking into the familiar black leather seat, and her breathing slowed, the sweat on her face cooling.

Why did I need a smoke just then? Better if she'd just gone home. Instead, she'd run into poor Gio again, and ripped off his fragile scab.

She'd always thought of herself as a good person, but what she'd done to him… it was unconscionable.

She shoved her hand into her pocket, pulling out the napkin with Ainsley's number. She stared at it for a long moment, then rolled down her window and threw it out into the breeze.

I don't deserve to be with someone. I'm toxic. She'd hurt Gio badly—the one person in her life at the time who had seen the real her, all of her hopes and dreams. She'd thought once that she might become a chef, just like Diego…

She had a good job. A steady paycheck. Her own place.

Life is good. Isn't it? With a heavy sigh, she started the car, determined to put the bad end to a wonderful evening behind her.

The cigarettes mocked her from above the sun visor, one of them hanging out as if inviting her to smoke it. With a growl, she ripped the whole pack out from its snug hiding place and threw them outside after the napkin. *I can at least do one good thing tonight.*

She peeled out of the parking spot, heading for her safe space, four walls to block out the world.

Unnoticed on the floor behind her seat, the napkin that the wind had blown back into the car sparkled green for just a moment, before fading into darkness.

9

____

HER FIRST FAN

Ainsley lay on her back, staring up at the poster of one of Jaemin Lee's pieces of art called *Lazy Day*. Five dark-haired women in white tops lay on a red tabletop, their bodies extended like putty under the artist's insightful gaze. The women slept while a gaggle of blackbirds helped themselves to the leftovers of the meal, while verdant jungle leaves jostled all around them.

I know how you feel. She was supposed to be studying for her Foundations of Clinical Research class, but it was a warm Saturday afternoon, and words like "biostatistics," "cohort studies," and "statistical analysis" had lulled her into a state of near paralysis. She hadn't slept well, her mind fixated on the pretty blonde who'd come into the restaurant a few nights before. Marissa... something. On impulse, Ainsley had written her name and number on a napkin and had left it with the bill. When she'd retrieved the check holder, it had been gone.

That has to be a good sign, right? She wasn't supposed to be dating, not until she got out of school and had "a job to make your mom and pop proud." She'd had a few flings on campus, but mostly she'd stuck to the plan—her parents' plan—that they'd laid down for her when she was six.

"You'll study really hard and get your high school degree, and be the valedictorian of your school."

Check.

"Then you'll go to a good school. Not a fancy one, but one that will teach you what you need to know to be a great doctor."

Check.

Well, almost. She'd discovered that she couldn't deal with the sight of blood—at least not when it was gushing out of someone—and diverted into a medical research track. Which her parents had been fine with, if you defined *fine* as grumbling about it every time she saw them.

"You could have been a *real* doctor," her mom would say, rolling her eyes.

"Mom, it's a good job. I'll be able to help lots of people."

"Of course you will." Ma had patted her hand. "Your cousin Jung is a real doctor, you know. There's still time for you to change your mind."

Ainsley sighed. She rolled over and spied the card the gallery owner had given her that same night she'd met the beguiling Marissa. Frowning, she picked it up to stare at its raised black lettering. *Red Roof Gallery.*

Maybe she needed a little art to clear her head. Or better yet, maybe she needed to make a little.

She slipped off the bed and pulled on her best torn jeans and a K-Pop t-shirt, along with her bright pink heart-lens sunglasses. She checked herself in the mirror. She looked acceptable enough. Grabbing her backpack, she headed out of the dorm room.

She'd spied an art store on J Street, just this side of Midtown, last time she was in town. She checked out a lime-green scooter from the rack outside the dorm and hopped on, letting it carry her through the campus.

The semester was almost over. Soon she'd be cramming for finals, but for today she was content to let her studies rest for an afternoon.

She'd come to love East Sacramento during her time at school. Huge trees lined the boulevards, the homes had beautiful, tidy yards, and the Fabulous Forties was like something out of a romance movie—huge houses, even bigger trees, and streets as wide as the *Champs-Élysées*, at least the way she imagined it in her head.

As she got closer to the freeway, the city around her changed, first replacing single family homes with old but well-kept-up apartment complexes, and then tiny shopping centers filled with restaurants and bars and coffee shops.

Cars crammed Business 80, slowed to almost a standstill as the freeway approached the river crossing a few blocks north. It was always slow there, one of the reasons she liked riding a scooter instead of driving.

She slipped past the homeless man who had pitched a bright blue tent under the freeway underpass, praying he would leave her alone. He was lost in his own world and didn't seem to notice her.

On the other side, Midtown began in earnest. Two-story buildings lined J Street—mostly more restaurants and coffee shops, though she passed a Birkenstock store and a salon or two on the way. Just a block beyond the park, University Art awaited her.

It was a good-sized store, mismatched white and gray tile giving it anti-establishment cred. She browsed through cans of spray-paint, watercolors, posterboard in the colors of the rainbow, frames, stands overflowing with hand-dyed paper, and horse-hair brushes, finally settling on colored pencils. One set had 240 shades.

Oooh. She picked it up, staring covetously at all the pretty colors. Then she saw its price tag. $50 was a bit over her budget.

"If that's too much, there's a great set right here that has over a hundred colors and is a fourth the price."

Ainsley turned to find a young man about her age staring back at her. His face was pockmarked, probably from a bad case of acne as a teenager, but he had a broad, friendly smile and a twinkle in his eyes. "Thanks. Let me take a look."

He handed over the set, and she saw the flash of a store badge.

"Thanks, Alyn. You work here?" The pencils looked high quality, the shades different enough that she could blend them to get the colors she wanted.

"Since last year." From his voice and demeanor, it was clear he was part of the queer community. "I love art, though I've never been very good at it."

"You shouldn't denigrate yourself. I bet you're much better than you think."

"Nah, I can only draw stick figures." His frown slipped up at the edges. "What do you draw?"

"I'm not sure yet." She bit her lip. "I haven't done art since high school. I just needed a little… something."

He nodded. "I get that. Here, let me show you the best deal we have on a drawing pad…."

They spent a good fifteen minutes touring the store, and by the end, she had everything she needed.

They chatted about Sacramento, about her school, and about his own recent past.

"I came here from Wisconsin to study, but when I came out, my parents cut me off."

"Oh that sucks. I'm so sorry!" Her own parents had taken the news surprisingly well. Considering. *Oh, it's all right. So sad that you will never marry a man and give us grandbabies. But it's all right.*

"I landed on my feet. I'm working here now and saving up." He rang her up. "That'll be $22.15."

She stared at him. "That can't be right."

"I gave you my employee discount." He winked at her. "Gotta take care of family, right?"

"That's so sweet of you. Are you sure? I don't want to get you into trouble."

"It's fine. Like I said, I'm not an artist, so I never use it."

Sweet and gallant. For just a moment, she wished she was a gay man. "Okay, thank you." She paid in cash, using some of her food money so it wouldn't show up on her student ATM card when her mom opened the bill.

Alyn put everything in a bag and held it out to her. "Make something beautiful…"

"Ainsley. Ainsley Kim."

"Ainsley Kim. And come show it to me when you're done. You have a gift for art. I can tell."

She blushed. "Thanks. I will. Have a great day!" She headed out the door, feeling something light and happy inside.

Just starting out, and I already have my first fan.

10

SECRETS, LIPSTICK &
MATCHING KHAKIS

Carmelina stared at the blank screen, willing herself to type… something.

Her uncle, if he really was related to her—she'd never heard the name *Angelo Farelli* from her mother's lips—had sent an email address with his letter. Which was good, as she'd be in Italy in just a week, and she had to decide if she wanted to respond to his unexpected request.

Well, she *was* responding. *Aren't I?*

She should tell Daniele about the whole affair, but it seemed so out of the blue. So unlikely. She wanted to be sure there was actually something to tell him before she broached the strange affair with her partner.

Never my husband. The strength of the thought surprised her.

That had been her Arthur. She was convinced that she still caught glimpses of him from time to time, lounging in his favorite recliner or puttering around the backyard.

She wasn't sure she was ever going to want to cross that threshold again… not even for Daniele.

Taking a deep breath, she began to type:

• • •

Dear Mr. Farelli,

I received your letter. You say you're my uncle, but I'm sure I've never heard of you...

Too confrontational? After all, she didn't want to scare him away. *What if he's for real?*

Dear Mr. Farelli,

I received your letter. How are you related to me? My mother never mentioned a brother. Are you on my father's side? I look forward to hearing from you.

—Carmelina

She stared at it for a moment, undecided. Maybe she should just let it all go. What secret could he possibly have to tell her?

"You about ready in there?" Daniele's warm voice from the living room startled her out of her reverie.

"Yes. Be right there." She hit send before she could change her mind and pushed away from her computer desk.

Your move, Mr. Farelli.

~

A couple cities east, in a new infill apartment building along the bustling Sunrise Boulevard in Fair Oaks, Marissa lifted her head to confront the woman in the mirror. She stared back at herself, tired yet defiant, like an unfinished sketch that some painter had crumpled up and thrown into the trash. She felt *worn.*

It was a perfectly serviceable apartment. Six-hundred square feet, with a nice if somewhat boring marble-and-tile kitchen, a narrow living room, an ample bedroom that looked out over a back alley with a dumpster and a series of mismatched fences, and a bathroom with a walk-in tub—apparently intended for someone with disabilities. It had been the only available unit in the complex when she'd been ready to move out on her own after college.

Marcos and Carmelina had offered to help with the rent, but things were tight for both of them.

Marcos and Dave were having troubles with their business—the internet wasn't what it used to be, apparently, though it had always seemed like a bit of a hellhole to her. She still liked popping on TikTok to see what was new, but she mostly stuck to texting.

And Carmelina was opening her bakery and needed everything she had to pay for the renovation, the supplies, the advertising, and everything else that came with a new business.

Besides, I have a good job now. I can afford it. Still, $1800 for the little white box she now inhabited—*lived in* seemed a little too personal— seemed like a lot. Small wonder she'd never be able to buy a house.

And it was a *good job*. McKinley-Davis-Rocklin paid well, everyone in the office was nice to her, and she could work from home—from *apartment*, anyhow—two days a week.

So why did it all feel so empty?

She looked out of her bedroom window at the alley. A stray dog was sniffing the fence across the way, and lifted his leg over a lonely dandelion as she watched.

She snickered. *That's the life.* Free to go where you want, chew on what you want, and pee on whatever you want... though maybe the last part didn't sound too appealing. *Maybe I should just take a nap.*

Still, it was First Saturday, and that meant Family Dinner.

She decided to go without makeup, save for a touch of lipstick. There was no one to impress tonight, just Marcos, Carmelina, and their husbands. *Well, partner, in Daniele's case.*

Her *nonna* had something against getting re-married. *Ghosts on the brain.*

She brushed her blond hair back. It had been good to see Gio the other day, even if it had been hard. He'd seemed much the same as she remembered him. Maybe a little older, a little wiser, but still his old sweet self. She'd screwed that one up badly. She'd almost told him, but then had chickened out at the last moment. *Maybe one day...*

In any case, it was time to move on.

She slipped out of the white box she called a home and locked the door behind her. Down a flight of concrete stairs, and her Mini was waiting for her in the early evening light.

The driver's seat had slipped back a bit—she should have them look at that next time she took it to the dealer. Reaching behind the seat to push it forward, her hand brushed against a piece of paper. Curious, she picked it up and turned it over.

It was a white paper napkin, scribbled with someone's name and number. *Ainsley, the waitress.* She'd thrown out of the window a couple nights earlier. *Must have blown back in.*

She knew a sign when she saw it.

She stuffed it into her jeans pocket, and resolved to message the beguiling waitress later. *After dinner.*

Her family was waiting.

~

"Are you wearing a tie?" Dave sounded hungry.

"For a family dinner? I don't think so." Marcos snorted. "A polo and khakis should be fine."

"Gotcha." Dave popped out of the bedroom wearing the mirror image of what he had on. "Dammit." He turned to change.

Marcos laughed. "No, leave it. I like it."

"You don't think it's too… *matchy matchy?*" Dave frowned.

"No. We look like a couple."

"Yeah, one of *those* couples…" Dave's voice trailed off. "You've lost weight."

Marcos grinned. "Been trying. Not that tonight's dinner will help." It was much easier when he could count his calories and know exactly what he was eating. Though with Dave's wonderful cooking, that too was a challenge… "You like it?"

"I do. But I like you *however* you are. Thick or thin. Bear or otter." Dave's thumbs slipped through the belt loops on either side of Marcos's khakis to pull his husband closer. "Sure we can't squeeze out a few more moments before we go?"

Marcos checked his watch. "Why? What did you have in mind?"
"First, getting this belt off of you…"
Marcos didn't need any more convincing.

11

DINNER PARTY MASH-UP

Dave and Marcos dropped their car off at a parking garage and walked down Liestal Alley, past the bike repair shop and the Old Soul Coffee Shop. Marcos bit his lip. "Remember, not a word to Marissa about our troubles." Though he was pretty sure she already knew.

Dave zipped his lips. "Mum's the word."

Sacramento was big on the idea of "activating" its midtown and downtown alleys, and had given each one a name corresponding to the nearest "letter" street to the north. Thus Liestal for L street, Jazz for J, Matsui for M (which was really Capitol down here, but Marcos had always thought of it as one of the letter streets).

He was a bit confused about *Liestal.* Sacramento was known for its Jazz festival, and Matsui was a local politician's last name, so those made sense, but when he'd looked up Liestal, all he'd found was a city in Switzerland. "Why Liestal?"

Dave chuckled. "You always forget. It's one of Sacramento's sister cities."

"'*One* of'? How many do we have?"

"Last I checked? Maybe a dozen. Hey, watch it!" He pulled Marcos back from the street as a red Mini roared by and swung into the last free spot in front of Zocalo.

"Crap." Marcos stared at the car, sweat breaking out across his forehead. "Was that…?"

"Yeah, I think so. You okay? She nearly took your kneecaps off."

"Not to mention my nose." He'd been worried about his adopted daughter, but apparently she wasn't so concerned about him. He stormed across the street. "Marissa!"

She was just getting out of the car, having snagged a spot right in front of Zocalo. "Oh, hey there." The smile that blossomed across her face at seeing him softened his anger.

Marcos crossed his arms, trying to express the appropriate level of parental indignation. "Didn't you see us? You almost ran me over!"

She flushed scarlet. "I'm so sorry. I dropped my phone and I—"

"You were using your phone while you were driving?" His ire rose once again.

"Not exactly. Just the GPS." Marissa looked miserable.

"Hey, go easy on the kid. No harm done." Dave clapped him on the shoulder.

In other words, I made my point. Given that her mother had been killed in exactly the same way… "Just… be more careful next time."

She threw her arms around his neck. "Thanks, Papa."

His heart melted. She'd seemed a bit distant of late, and he was looking forward to finding out why. "Well, let's get inside. It's hot out here." He took her hand, and they squeezed past the other car—a white Tesla, of course, as they were everywhere these days—and went inside.

"Wonder if Carmelina and Daniele are here yet." Dave looked around the restaurant. It was warm and inviting—an old converted car dealership that had kept the open, bright feel of the roll-up doors, but with windows instead of steel. Raised rows of plants and pottery ran down the two wings in front of a lively bar, and a huge stone basin held hundreds of cut flowers floating on water. A cheer went up from the counter, where a soccer game was in progress on four flatscreen TVs.

Marissa checked her phone. "Not yet. They just passed Sutter Park."

"*Arrivo!*" he and Dave said together. An old joke—the Italians had a habit of promising they were arriving *any minute now*, even when they were a half-hour away.

"Do you have a reservation?" The handsome young host—Iggy, by his nametag—looked like he was ten.

Hazard of growing older, I suppose. "Yes. Ramirez, party of five. Can you let Ben know we're here?"

"Of course. He has you in the banquet room. This way please." Iggy led them down the aisle toward the back end of the restaurant, through a red velvet curtain and into the area often used for private parties. It was mostly closed off, with just a table for the five of them.

Dave raised his eyebrow.

Marcos winked at his husband. "It's all in who you know."

"You guys must be important." Iggy's eyes darted from one to another, as if he might be able to figure out who they were, if he just looked hard enough.

"We go way back with Ben." Marcos sat down next to Dave, and Marissa took one of the end chairs.

Iggy nodded. "Of course. Your server will be right with you." Iggy took one last look at them and vanished, and they had the big room all to themselves.

"Oooh, I want the Enchiladas Guanajuato." Marissa was already scanning the menu, almost drooling.

"Good choice." He tried not to stare at her. Since she'd left for college, she didn't come around all that often. "So… how's the new job?"

She looked up at him, and then quickly back down at the menu. "Ssaallite."

"What?" Marcos frowned.

"I said 'it's all right'." She frowned and went back to the menu.

I'm the one who should be annoyed. "Are they treating you well?"

She sighed. "Yes, Papa." This time she met his gaze, a mischievous smile playing across her lips. "How's your business doing?"

He looked down at his menu and muttered, "Ssaallite."

Dave intervened. "How about them River Cats?"

Marcos laughed. Dave always knew how to smooth the waters. "Do you even know what a River Cat is?"

Dave blinked owlishly. "I imagine it's something like an otter…"

Marissa laughed, and the tension was broken. "No, it's a baseball team. But you already knew that."

"Did not." But his eyes twinkled. "So, are you seeing anyone?" Dave asked the question that every young single person dreaded hearing from their family.

She surprised them. "Not right now. Though I did meet a girl the other day."

"Oooh, do tell." Dave, being the husband of the guy who was technically Marissa's father now, could get away with more than he could, apparently.

"She's pretty. Whip-smart. A waitress, but working her way through school…" She looked down, her fingers curling around the edges of the menu. "She might be too good for me."

Marcos frowned. "No one is too good for you. Why would you say that?" Marissa was amazing. She had pulled herself out of homelessness and excelled in college. Now she had a place of her own and a good job.

"It's nothing. Just—"

"You made it!" Ben popped into the room. He had a smile on his face, but there was a smoky sadness beneath it that tinged his skin gray. It ran deep into his soul.

It had been two years since Ella's death. Hence the family dinner at Zocalo, instead of at Ragazzi. Marissa had wanted to check in on him.

She must have noticed his ashen color too. She leapt up and threw her arms around him. "It's good to see you." She squeezed him so hard his eyes bulged out.

"Hey, easy! I need those ribs. And good to see you too," Ben managed when she let go. "Where's Carmelina?"

Marcos grinned. The brassy Italian American was conspicuous in her absence. "She's on her way. Have time to sit with us for a couple minutes?"

Ben shook his head. "I wish I did. I'll stop by again in a bit, though. *Buen provecho!*" He slipped away behind the curtain.

"I'm worried about him." Marissa took her seat, staring after their friend.

"He's had a rough coupla years." Marcos shuddered, thinking of what it would be like to lose Dave. He couldn't imagine it. Things were difficult, sure, but they'd find their way through.

"*Arrivo!*" Carmelina appeared, with Daniele in tow.

"*Arrivo!*" the others repeated, their laughter breaking up the somber mood.

She took the other end seat as if it were a throne. "So, what did I miss?"

12

OH CRAP

Marissa watched Ben throughout the meal, taking his emotional pulse whenever he popped in to check on them.

Her grandmother Carmelina ruled the table like a queen, enlivening the dinner with grand tales of what Sacramento had been like when she was a girl.

"Those apartments where you live now? That was all orange groves… or maybe oak trees? Anyhow, there was nothing out there when I was a kid. *Nonna* used to take us up into the hills—she knew where all the best berry patches were—and she'd wade into them and scratch the hell out of her arms, happy as a clam collecting sweet raspberries and tart blackberries to make her famous jam…"

Marissa had noted the lines on Ben's face, the gray patches under his eyes on his dark skin.

All of the Ragazzi Club had loved Ella, but she'd been Ben's missing half, the love he'd thought he would never find. Marissa struck up an unexpected friendship with him after her break-up with Gio and they'd been thick as thieves for a while, but somehow they'd drifted apart after Ella. *Time to rectify that now.*

She pushed back her chair with a loud scrape. "Excuse me. I'm going to use the restroom."

Carmelina smiled. "Of course, dear." Her grandmother squeezed her arm as she walked by. "So this one time, *Nonna* brought back two full buckets of oranges…"

Her voice trailed off as Marissa entered the bustling main room of the restaurant. She looked around for Ben. He was nowhere to be seen.

Iggy, the cute gay host who had seated them, was greeting a large party at the front door.

Marissa slipped up behind him and waited for him to finish. She loved the open, modern vibe of the place, the buzz of the crowd, the sizzle of steak and chicken and the heavenly aroma as they were brought to the tables. What was hybrid work, half her time at a tiny gray desk and the other half in a tiny gray apartment, compared to this?

"Can I help you?" Iggy turned his attention to her, his pearly whites almost blinding.

She blinked, almost forgetting what she'd come to ask. "I… I was looking for Ben?"

"Ah yes, from the VIP party." This time his smile seemed a little more genuine. "He stepped out for a break, but he should be back in…" He glanced at his Apple Watch. "…fifteen minutes."

"Thanks. By the way, I love the bowtie, and your turquoise nails are divine." She loved this new trend of men painting their nails—even some of her straight friends were doing it.

His smile widened. "Thanks. And I love your… whatever this is." He indicated her gray shirt and black pants.

She laughed. "Laundry day." With a wave, she ducked out of the front door, looking around for her friend. *If I were Ben, where would I be?*

Her gaze fell on the alley, halfway down the block, and she *knew*.

She crossed the street, on the lookout for any drivers as careless as she'd been, and ducked into the narrow lane. Halfway down to 17th street, the sign on the side of the old white one-story building beckoned her. *Old Soul Coffee.* She and Ben had spent many a Saturday afternoon at the little Midtown coffee shop, sharing details about their lives. Her break-up, her dreams of becoming a chef. His search for new treatments for Ella. The sales of his first book. What life was like as a black trans man in Sacramento.

The gorgeous mural of a woman's face floating in water amongst a bunch of lotus flowers that covered the long side of the building greeted her as she approached. The woman seeming to wink at her as a flash of reflected light illuminated the fresco. Street art was one of the things Marissa loved most about Sactown.

Sure enough, Ben was slumped in a metal chair in front of the café's industrial windows, sipping on a cappuccino. His back was to her, and he didn't hear her approach.

Is this what my life is, these days? Running into old acquaintances in alley-ways? "Room for one more?"

He turned, the pain in his expression transforming to something closer to joy at the sight of her. "Hey, 'Riss. Sure. Grab a seat." He gestured her toward the other chair. "Shouldn't you be with your family?"

She shrugged. "Carmelina will keep them occupied." No doubt she was still holding court. They wouldn't miss her for at least fifteen or twenty minutes.

He laughed. "True enough."

"Besides, I chose Zocalo for family dinner tonight so I could come see you." She wasn't sure exactly what had made her do it. She'd realized the week before how long it had been since they had hung out together.

"You could have just texted." He took a sip out of the huge white ceramic mug and frowned.

"Where's the fun in that?" She sized him up. The sadness was like a tattered cloud over his once-sunny personality. "So how are you, really? No bullshit."

He grimaced. "It's… I'm fine."

She rolled her eyes. "Seriously? Come on, Ben. When my life was in the toilet, I told you everything."

He met her gaze, and the cloud melted away. "All right. Not… fine, exactly." He bit his lip. "Truth is, everything hurts. Since I lost her, there's a hole inside me that nothing seems to fill. But I get up every morning. I try to write. I go to work." He took a measured sip, staring off into space. "That's what life is, right? A series of things you do between getting up and going to bed?"

"That's one definition." Though he'd just described her own existence, to a 't'.

He blinked, and sat back, staring at her. "So how's your life? You have a new job, right?" Ben had always been an expert at deflection.

"I… it's fine." She tapped on the metal tabletop. *First Marcos, then Ben…*

He laughed triumphantly. "*Now* who's bullshitting?"

She wished she had a coffee cup to hold onto. Instead she shoved her restless hands into her lap. "Is it that obvious?"

Ben shook his head. "Probably not to everyone else. But I *know* you. You never wanted to work in an office."

"It pays the bills." It came out harsher than she intended.

Ben nodded. "Yes. I suppose it does."

They sat there in silence for a moment, each lost in their own thoughts. A white Tesla prowled quietly down the alley, turning onto 18th street and disappearing.

"I met someone…" They both said at once.

Marissa laughed.

Ben lifted his cup with a half-smile. "You first."

In her pocket, her phone buzzed. She ignored it. Being present with Ben was more important than someone else's text. "It's weird. I ran into Gio the other night at Ragazzi. When we broke up…" Her voice caught in her throat. Other than being on the streets as a teen, it had been the darkest time of her life.

"I remember." Ben put a hand on hers. "How was it?"

Ben was the only one she'd ever told about her secret shame. "It was… all right. Too normal, maybe? Like when you're both trying so hard not to say the wrong thing… Anyhow, it was the first time we've talked… really talked… since the break-up." She closed her eyes, the old familiar shame washing over her. "I almost told him. It was right there on the tip of my tongue. Then I chickened out and bolted."

His eyes held no judgment. "You'll know when the time is right." He took a deep breath, and exhaled in that long way people do when pain squeezes their heart and there's nothing to be done for it. "You mentioned someone new?"

Her pocket buzzed again, and she ignored it again. "Yeah. That same night, there was a woman in the restaurant. A server. Funny and bright and… you know when you get that tongue-tied feeling, when you want to just bask in someone's presence, and you can't seem to remember words?"

An unreadable expression crossed Ben's face. "I do."

"It was… everything." She closed her eyes, remembering Ainsley's beautiful smile, her bright laugh. *You've got it bad, girl.* "But what about you? You mentioned someone new, too?"

Her pocket buzzed again, more insistently this time.

Ben set down his cup. "My neighbor was pounding around upstairs. It sounded like a herd of elephants charging… what do they call a group of rhinos? A crash of rhinoceroses. I went to yell at them, and when she opened the door—"

"Just a sec." Somebody was trying awfully hard to get a hold of her.

She pulled out her phone and glanced at the screen. "Holy crap."

"What?" Ben leaned forward, his brows creasing with concern.

She held her phone out to see the message from Marcos:

Where are you? Something's happened to Brad.

13

MEANWHILE, IN TUCSON...

Sam sat next to the empty hospital bed, squeezing the faux-wooden armrests of his chair so hard his knuckles were white.

A couple orderlies had come by a half hour earlier to cart off Brad's body, as if it were a thing of no consequence whatsoever. They'd been serious and respectful as they lifted the lifeless form onto a stretcher, but as soon as they'd left the room, he'd heard them talking about Sam while they pushed the transport gurney down the hall, taking it to the morgue. Taking *him* to the morgue.

"Was that Sam Fuller?"

"I think so. My mom reads his books." A pause. "Then who's this?"

"Must be his husband."

"Holy shit…" The voices faded.

Sam stared hard at the empty space where Brad had last been. It was hard to think of that pale, crumpled body, hands clasped over the blue hospital gown, as the Brad he'd been married to for nine years. The guy he'd shared his bed, his life, even his dreams with.

The white sheets were pulled back and crumpled, as if Sam's husband had just gotten up to go to the bathroom and might come padding back in his hospital socks at any moment.

Sam sat back, templing his fingers and breathing into his hands while looking around the brightly painted golden hospital room. A sunset scene of A-Mountain, half in shadow, dominated the far wall. The heart monitor was silent now, the drip line dangling sad and alone from its holder.

The Arizona sun through the window was warm on his shoulder. If he turned to look outside, he was sure he would see people scurrying along on the sidewalk below, going about their daily business, as if nothing had changed. The world felt calm. Normal.

Why isn't everything falling to pieces? Why aren't I? Because he knew that if he let himself cry right now, he might never stop.

His phone buzzed in his pocket. Sam pulled it out and stared at it blankly.

You all right? A text from his friend Alex.

He stared at it for a couple minutes before responding. *Not sure.* Words deserted him.

**hugs* Gio will be there soon.* Alex, Gio, and his other friends had been tag-teaming him since Brad had landed in the hospital, three days earlier. One of them was almost always there with him.

Thanks. He should feel grateful. Angry. Wounded. Betrayed. *Something.* Anything but this bland, flat numbness that threatened to smother him.

He put the phone down on the small table next to a potted pincushion cactus and leaned forward to brush his fingers over the sheets. Still warm, but the heat was fading fast. "Fuck."

A blood clot. Small as the head of a pin. That's all it had taken to rip away the one person he loved most in this world.

The paralysis suffocating his heart cracked open just a little, and he gasped for air as the room spun around him.

"Sam?"

Blinking back tears, he looked up to find Gio, one of his oldest friends in Tucson, poking his head into the room. They'd met when Sam was a student at the University, before he'd gone to Sacramento.

Tucson Gio. Not the Sacramento one. Funny the places the mind went when you didn't want to think about the one thing you couldn't stop thinking about.

Gio's gaze went to the empty bed, and then back to Sam. "*Oddio.*" He crossed the room in two bounds and threw his arms around his friend.

"I'm so, so sorry." His embrace was warm, should have been comforting, but it just reminded him of the *bed-that-was-no-longer-warm* and the events of the last few days and Brad and everything—

"*Fuuuuuuuck!*" He wrapped his arms around his friend and the numbness dissolved, replaced by a primal pain so intense it made him curl his toes in his shoes. "I'm not ready. Bring him back. Goddammit, I'm not ready to lose him." His vision blurred as hot tears coursed down his face, and he squeezed his friend even harder. "Bring him back."

"He loved you so much, *amico*." Gio was as lost as he was.

"Goddammit." Sobs wracked Sam's body, the tempest he'd kept at bay since that last beep of the heart monitor taking over him completely.

Memories flashed through his mind—Brad in the Senator's office in Sacramento. Their wedding day at Ragazzi. The happy home they'd made together here in Tucson, filled with light and color and love.

Brad, lying motionless on the hospital bed, his face pale as the grave, mouth slack and eyes closed.

A fresh round of sobbing threatened to tear him in half.

Gio held him tightly, riding it out with him.

Every time he thought about Brad, that last image resurfaced, so cold and diminished, and he'd start off again, until he was certain no more tears could come.

He gasped for breath, taking in a huge gulp of air, and his breathing grew slower and slower.

He was suddenly aware what a mess he must be. Eyes red, nose dripping, cheeks puffy. "I'm sorry, Gio. You shouldn't have to deal with my—"

"Shhhh." His friend held him tighter. "It's okay to cry your eyes out. I did the same for my *nonna* when she passed, late last year."

Sam squeezed his friend tightly and then let Gio go. He felt nauseous. "I think I need to get out of this room." He swayed, unsteady on his feet, trying to avoid looking at the empty bed.

"I understand. Come on." Gio took his hand and led him out into the sterile white hallway, down to the waiting room. "Maybe we should go outside for some fresh air—"

"Sammy?"

Sam's head snapped up. "Mom. But how...?" She wasn't driving anymore.

She flashed him a sad smile. "Alex came to pick me up." She approached him cautiously, as if afraid he might break if she moved too fast. Her hand came up to touch his cheek, cupping it gently. "Oh baby, I'm so sorry."

Sam threw his arms around her. "Oh Momma, what am I going to do?"

For a response, she hugged him tight.

They stayed like that for a long time, her warmth seeping into him as she rocked him back and forth, pushing back the pain. He soaked it up like sunshine. Like when he was a child, and he'd lost his first hamster. Or his first boyfriend. Or when he'd finally gotten up the courage to leave his abusive older boyfriend, Jameson.

Finally, she loosened her grip, and he let her go.

"When was the last time you ate something?" She looked up at him, her eyes narrowing. "You always forget to eat."

"Um… I had a sandwich last night…"

"Well, come on then. Food will do you good. I spent a lot of time here when your father was ill, and the cafeteria's not half-bad."

Sam started to protest that he wasn't really hungry, but she wouldn't take no for an answer.

"You going to keep me standing here?" His mother leaned on her cane, playing up the whole *I'm an old person* thing.

"No, mother." He hung his head, still seven years old whenever she was around.

She took his hand and dragged him toward the elevator. "And bring your friends. They look too skinny."

That got a laugh from Alex, who put a hand over his mouth as if he'd committed a grave sin. "Sorry. And she's right. I ate here when Gio was… sleeping."

Gio grinned. "You can say 'in a coma.' It won't hurt my feelings."

Alex took his hand.

Sam allowed himself a brief smile. "Life goes on. I guess. It's okay." He gave Alex a hug. "Thanks for bringing her."

"Of course. I'm so sorry this happened. He was way too young." Alex kissed his cheek.

Sam closed his eyes, trying not to think of Brad. Of the empty space in his heart. He took a deep breath, finding a precarious balance once more. As long as he didn't move too fast, or think too much, maybe he could keep himself on an even keel. He let his mother lead the way.

Some things never changed.

And some things would never be the same again.

THE RAGAZZI CLUB

Matteo's phone buzzed.

He ignored it, concentrating on the books. The restaurant was finally regularly turning a profit, but it was always a delicate dance between revenue and all the rest—the costs for rent, wages, meat and produce, the inevitable repairs and upkeep, and sundry expenses that every restaurant had to contend with. *Grazie al dio* that inflation had finally moderated a little. Eggs and chicken prices were both down from a couple months earlier, and long-term price contacts had helped insulate Ragazzi from some of the other price spikes. It had been a roller coaster of a year.

His phone buzzed again insistently.

"*Cavolo!*" He picked it up, and then stared at the screen, dumbfounded.

It was a text from Marcos. *Brad is dead. Heart attack. TRC?*

Matteo shuddered. How could Brad be dead? They'd just spoken on Zoom the week before…

He replied. *Cazzo. Tonight? After service?*

The response was immediate. *I think that would be best.*

Matteo nodded. Brad had helped save Ragazzi when they'd needed it most, creating an intern program for LGBTQ+ youth and inspiring the lunch pick-up plan that had provided much needed income until the restaurant was able to establish itself as an East Sacramento culinary destination. He'd also helped them secure two emergency government loans during the pandemic. *Povero Sam. What he must be feeling…*

He switched to the WhatsApp group chat.

TRC emergency meeting tonight, 11 PM. Brad is gone.

He set the phone down and sat back in his chair, massaging his temples, as the chat room exploded with questions.

Ben knocked on the back door of Ragazzi. He slipped his hands into his jacket pockets. It was chilly out, an icy breeze surprising for late May blowing through the parking lot, clearing away the stench of the dumpster next to the door. The night was cloudless, her uncaring stars sparkling in the firmament above. *Maybe one of them is Brad, looking down on us.*

He checked his Apple Watch… it was already a quarter past eleven. Everyone else was probably already inside.

He'd gone back and forth about attending. He hadn't known Brad all that well—only from the time spent at their cooking class together. And death was still triggering for him. But the look on Marissa's face when she'd received that text… he'd decided that he had to come.

The door popped open, and Gio beckoned him inside. "Hey."

"Am I the last one here?"

Gio nodded. "Marissa beat you by about two minutes." A painful pause. "I'm so sorry, Ben. About Ella. And now this—"

"I hardly knew him." He said it like a shield.

"Me neither. Still…" Gio hugged him.

Ben melted into the embrace, stifling a sob. "Thank you." *I miss you, Ella.*

When Gio let him go, he wiped moisture from the corners of his eyes. "Where are the others?"

"In the training kitchen. Come on."

The door closed behind Ben with a hollow *thud.* He followed Gio through the prep kitchen and into the main dining room. Shades were pulled down over the front windows, and the place looked dark and deserted, lit only by light from the main kitchen behind him and from under the door, where the others awaited him.

He'd stopped coming to the classes after Ella had… gone. This would be his first time seeing the new training kitchen.

Gio pushed open the door, and Ben was back with all of his friends for the first time since—

His heart started to race, and a cold sweat broke out on his arms. "Sorry. I can't…"

Marissa was at his side in an instant. Her face was puffy, her eyes red as she grabbed onto him and squeezed him tight. "I know. I know."

He took a deep breath, and let it out slowly. *Ella is gone.* It hurt every time he thought about her, like someone had ripped his heart out of his chest with jagged black nails. And yet… *I'm still here. People need me. Marissa needs me.*

She let him go and held him out at arm's length. "Please stay? I need you."

Like she read my mind. He nodded. He could do this. Brad had taken care of discarded queer kids like her at the LGBT Center—made sure they had food, a place to stay, a path to something better. He could imagine how she was feeling right now.

He looked around the room. Someone had lit a candle at each of the ten cooking stations. The overhead lights were turned down low, and all of his friends sat in a circle, looking at him expectantly. Waiting for their last member.

Marissa led him to the last empty seat.

The place felt new, clean, fresh… and yet somehow *old world*. Steel and brick. Comfortable.

They sat next to one another, and he took her hand, giving it a squeeze.

I can do this.

～

Marcos looked around the room, the pain in his heart battling with the warmth he felt at seeing his closest friends gathered together again, here where it all had started. Even Ben.

He'd been sure Ben wouldn't come. Ella had been gone for two years now, and her loss had hollowed the man out. Marcos flashed a reassuring smile across the circle at him. Then he stood and squeezed his hands together. "It's late, past some of your bedtimes, I'm sure. So let's get started."

There was scattered laughter, which died out quickly.

"As all of you have heard by now, one of our Ragazzi Club members, Brad Weston, passed away earlier today. I talked to Sam about an hour ago, and he filled me in with the details." Marcos squeezed his eyes shut.

Brad had saved his business, the last time it had been in jeopardy, hiring him to run the Center's website account, which Marcos still managed to this day. And he'd helped Marcos adopt Marissa, a debt he'd now never be able to repay.

"Is Sam all right?" Carmelina was staring at him, as if willing the information out of him, her usually neat red hair a mess. They'd all cried over the news.

"He's coping. I think he's still in shock." *As are we all.* "Sam told me that they were out at dinner on Thursday night, celebrating Sam's Netflix deal for *Read Between the Lines*, when Brad grabbed his chest and keeled over at the table. The paramedics arrived within minutes and managed to resuscitate him. They rushed him to the hospital and into surgery." Sam had sounded numb. Lost. *Like I feel right now.* Friends weren't supposed to die. Not at Brad's age.

"Was he in pain?" Marissa squeezed Ben's hand tightly.

"Probably when he first had the heart attack. But Sam said they had him on painkillers right afterwards. I'm sure he wasn't feeling a thing."

Diego shook his head. "*Non capisco.* If he had the surgery… why is he not okay?"

Marcos sighed. "He threw a blood clot—complications from the heart attack or the surgery—and this time they couldn't save him." How could someone be there one day, and just be gone the next?

He longed to pick up the phone and call Brad, to just *talk to him*. He'd been remiss in their friendship since Brad and Sam had moved to Tucson to be closer to Sam's mother.

Now that regret was a burning knife in his heart.

Marissa closed her eyes, sinking back into the padded chair and trying to think.

Brad's gone. He'd been there for her when no one else had. He'd come with Marcos to get her out of jail, that time her adoptive parents had her arrested for breaking into her own house.

He'd gotten her started with the internship at Ragazzi, working with Diego and learning how to be a chef.

Why did I ever stop? It had happened after Gio. When she'd been too embarrassed to come back to Ragazzi. She'd been busy with her classes, and the weight of the guilt kept her away…

If she were honest with herself, she'd admit that she hated her new job. The pay was decent and the people were nice enough. But the work… sometimes she wanted to pull out her hair.

How she'd enjoyed pushing her hands deep into bread dough. Rolling out pasta. Seasoning a hearty ragu with a pinch of rosemary and a splash of garlic salt. It was honest work, work you did with your hands. Work that created something of worth.

"You always did love to cook."

I know that voice. Her eyes flew open. "Brad!" In a second, she had her arms wrapped around him, hugging him so tightly he gasped.

"Easy there. Even a dead guy's gotta breathe every now and then." He patted her on the back.

She let him go. "But how… why… you can't be here!"

He grinned. "You're at Ragazzi." He touched her cheek, reminding her, strangely, of her grandmother Carmelina. "Anything is possible here."

She looked around. The whole Ragazzi Club—the OG students she'd initially scorned and then had come to love—were talking and crying and laughing, remembering their fallen friend. "Anything?"

Brad nodded. "Anything. Remember who you wanted to be." Then he was gone, leaving a green shimmer in his wake.

"Marissa, you okay?"

She blinked. Brad had vanished, and now Marcos stood before her. "I know what we need to do."

"What's that, dear?" Carmelina was wiping at the corners of her eyes with a Kleenex.

She inhaled, smelling the wonderful scent of fresh-cooked Italian pasta. "We need to cook for him."

15

———

BZZ BZZ

B*zz bzz.*

Ainsley cracked open one eye, blearily surveying her surroundings. Early morning sunlight filtered through her single dorm window, tinged green by the needles of the redwood tree that grew close enough to the dorm that she could almost touch it.

She fixed on the digital clock, a gift from her father. Its rainbow letters were a tacit acceptance of her status as a… and her father never could quite say it without a stutter… *les-bee-an.*

Closing her eyes, she settled back into the goose down pillow and pulled her silk sheets up over her shoulders. It was only 7:30 AM, she had no classes until the next day, and she wasn't on-shift until the evening. She could indulge herself and sleep in a bit.

Bzz bzz.

"*Sshi bal.*" She thrust the covers away from her and swung her feet over the edge of the bed. Who was disturbing her on a perfectly lazy Sunday morning? And before most decent folk had even had their first cup of coffee?

Her phone was on her desk, in the midst of a snowbank of crumpled off-white drawing paper, the results of her not-so-fruitful return to art the evening before. Nothing she'd sketched had felt right. Nothing captured her attention. *Except for one thing.* One person.

Bzz bzz.

"All right already." She pushed herself up and managed three wobbly steps to her desk chair. Slumping down into it with the lack of grace she normally reserved for falling into bed after a long study session, she snatched the phone and stared at it intently.

Hello. Is this Ainsley?

The message tag said "Unknown."

Maybe. Who's asking?

She didn't normally respond to unknown texters, but she was already suitably annoyed at being dragged out of bed early, and she wanted to direct her anger at someone. A perfect stranger would be perfect.

Marissa. We met at Ragazzi *the other night.*

Ainsley's heart stopped. Well, maybe not like *Heartstopper* stopped. But it definitely did this weird thumpy thing in her chest, and her annoyance evaporated.

Hey Marissa… great to hear from you—

Delete. Too cheerful, especially for early on a Sunday morning.

I was just thinking about you—

Delete. Too thirsty. Maybe?

'sup.

She hit send before she could second guess herself a third time. Then immediately regretted it. "'Sup? What am I? Ten?"

She stared anxiously at the screen for some sign that she hadn't just screwed things up with the beautiful, funny girl she'd met the other night, and fallen quickly *in like* with. Enough to scribble her number down on a napkin.

…

"Come on." She thrummed her fingers on the desk.

…

"Seriously?" What, was she typing out a novel?

While she waited, she swept the crumpled attempts at art into her wastebasket, which was already half-full of soda cans, pencil shavings, and crumpled up Kleenex.

Bzz bzz.

She snatched up the phone again.

I know that it's late notice. Are you free this afternoon? I could really use a friend rn.

Ainsley frowned. *A friend? Crap.* Still, it was a start. And she did happen to be free, at least until six o'clock.

-*Sure. Where and when?*-

-*Ragazzi. 1 PM. I'll explain when you get here.*-

Ainsley bit her lip. Stranger and stranger. She liked a little mystery. But why Ragazzi?

-*It's a date. See you then.*-

Again, the insta-regret. *Why'd I have to say it was a date? What if she doesn't like me like that?*

A smiley face popped up.

What does that mean? Is she happy I said date? Or does she think I'm being silly? Ainsley sighed. Well, done was done.

She set down her phone. The one piece of art she'd been satisfied with, out of all the previous night's endeavors, lay before her on the now-empty desk, next to the neat set of colored pencils.

Marissa's bright eyes and smile stared back at her.

A smiley? Seriously? What was I thinking? But done was done. Ainsley probably thought she was a nutcase.

Marissa collapsed against the hard seat-back of her dining nook chair. She'd gotten the set at that huge Scandinavian furniture store in West Sac, and it had looked perfect in the store, all light wood and sharp, modern, no-nonsense Swedish angles. A *kichentablesven*, or something similar. But in her little apartment, it took up the whole nook, like one of those fish that grew to fill its aquarium, making her squeeze around it to get into the tiny galley kitchen. The wood was cold and unyielding against her back.

She stared at the crumpled Ragazzi napkin. *Why did I text her?*

She hadn't meant to. But she'd been depressed about Ben, and when she'd pulled the note with Ainsley's number out of her pocket, something warm and comforting had filled her. She'd picked up her phone and sent the message without really thinking it through.

Done is done, alright. And truth be told, it would be nice to have her new… friend?… there as a buffer. She loved her *nonna* dearly, but Carmelina, like the table, tended to suck up all the air in the room.

Gio would be there too, presumably. Things might get awkward.

Well, life was an imperfect game, and sometimes she felt like she didn't even have all the pieces.

Or all my marbles. She laughed ruefully.

Marissa tucked the note back into her jacket pocket, and went to take herself a long, hot shower.

16

TORTELLI ALLA LASTRA

He sat in his non-descript Honda Fit, parked half a block down from Ragazzi. It was a rainy Sunday afternoon—unusual for May, but this one had been wetter than usual—and his windshield wipers were set to intermittent, periodically scraping across the windshield with a harsh dragging squeak.

He glanced at his phone once again, scanning the photo to memorize their features—you had to be so careful about pronouns these days, so he'd found it easier to just use *they and them*, always.

He had to be cautious—his employer wanted information, but had impressed upon him the importance of being discreet about it.

He snorted. *Discreet* was his middle name.

The rainfall increased, pummeling the little car so hard it sounded like hail. With an annoyed grunt, he bumped up the wiper speed. They *groaned* across the dirty windshield, sending brown water droplets flying through the air.

There. Someone with a yellow umbrella ducked into the restaurant. He lifted his binoculars, squinting at their face. *Nope. Not them.*

He pulled out another Jimboys taco—it was cold now, but still smelled tantalizing— and bit off a crunchy chunk, then sucked in the loose bits of lettuce with a satisfying *slurp* and wiped the drippings off on his tan overcoat.

He had time. He was patient.

He would find them soon enough.

Gio stocked each of the stations in the training kitchen with flour, water, salt, pepper, and olive oil. In the individual fridges beneath, he put covered bowls of potatoes, sausage, and some parmigiano… the real *italiano autentico* stuff, never to be confused with that American travesty called *parmesan.*

Marissa would be there, he assumed. The thought didn't trouble him the way it had even just a week before. They seemed to have reached some sort of détente, where they could manage to be in the same room again without running away from one another. *That's a good thing. Maybe, just maybe…*

"What are we making today?"

The man's voice startled Gio. He stood up too fast and banged his head on the hard edge of the dark marble countertop. "Ouch." He focused on the newcomer—a middle-aged man with short brown hair, dressed in a crisp white shirt and blue tie and gray slacks who looked strangely familiar. He was standing by the front door, though Gio was sure he'd locked it, and the bell hadn't rung. He was also completely dry, though it was pouring outside the large plate-glass windows. "Are you here for the memorial?"

The man smiled disarmingly. "In a manner of speaking." He looked around and sighed. "It's been a long time since I've been here. You guys have made a lot of changes. This used to be a bar, I think…"

Gio nodded. "They closed during the pandemic. *Papà* and *Babbo* bought it and converted it. This way we can run the restaurant *and* the classes at the same time." If only they would listen to his ideas. They had such a great thing going here, but it could become so much more if they would just franchise it.

The stranger ran his hand down his tie. "I have fond memories of this place."

Gio couldn't get rid of that nagging feeling of familiarity—

"Gio, everything is sets in there?" *Papà* poked his head into the room from the restaurant side.

"*Set.* And yes, *Papà.* I was just talking to this guy." He thumbed the front door.

"What guy?" Diego looked around the kitchen, furrowing his brow.

Gio turned to address the stranger. "What's your name again?"

The man was gone.

Weird. He shook his head to clear it. *Too many late nights, I guess.* "Never mind. Yes, we're all set." *I must be seeing ghosts.*

Diego prepped his workstation, going over the recipe for *Tortelli alla Lastra* one last time to make sure he had everything he needed.

Carmelina and Daniele were the first to arrive. Technically, Carmelina's Italian boyfriend wasn't one of the original Club Ragazzi members, but he'd been around the place so regularly while Carmelina was using their kitchen that he had become a part of *la famiglia.* They left their umbrellas in the holder by the door.

"Hey Diego." She kissed his cheeks. Despite her effusive greeting, her face looked drawn.

No wonder. They'd all liked Sam and Brad. It was hard to believe he was gone.

"Ciao." Daniele squeezed his hand. Despite showing some silver at the temples, the Italian florist was still quite handsome. *Lucky girl.*

Carmelina took up her favorite station and began getting out pots and pans and bowls.

Marcos and Dave arrived next, shaking off the rain under the red, green, and white striped awning before stepping inside.

Diego had a soft spot in his heart for them. As the other ongoing gay couple in the club—and the ones who had brought Marissa to him—he considered them among his closest friends.

"Ciao bello…" Marcos hugged him, kissing his cheek. Italian came easily to him with his Spanish language background. "It's coming down *a dirotto* out there."

Dave was Hispanic too, but somehow had never picked up the language. "Hi gorgeous."

"Glad you two make it." He could see from the twinkle in Marcos's eyes that his words weren't quite right. "*Made?*"

A wide grin rewarded his efforts. "Perfect."

"I'll never speak English as well as you." Diego sighed.

"Maybe not, but you're far more charming than the average American." Marcos squeezed his hand in reassurance, and then led Dave to their station.

Ben popped his head in, looking around the room, the sadness of his loss etched on his face. Of all of them, he was the one who most clearly understood what poor Sam was going through. He stared at his usual station, seeming trapped at the doorway. Outside, the rain was still coming down, as his American friends said, *like cats and dogs.*

Diego slapped his forehead. How could he have been so stupid? The last time Ben had been here to cook, it had been with Ella. He waved at his friend. "Ben, over here. You're cook with me today."

Relief blossomed on Ben's face, and he let the door slip closed behind him to cross the room. "Thanks. It's just…"

"I know." He squeezed Ben tightly in his arms. "*Lo so.*" He remembered how losing Luna, Gio's mother, had ripped his soul open, and they'd been long estranged. Luckily he'd gotten Gio out of the deal. How proud he was of his beautiful, sweet, intelligent son.

Last but not least, Marissa appeared, towing along a surprise guest, both of them soaked. "Forgot my umbrella. We had to run here from the car."

"*Che piacere!* What a pleasure." He welcomed them both with a hug.

Gio came out of the walk-in with an armful of flour for the restaurant and stopped dead in his tracks. He flashed Marissa a weak smile before crossing over to the restaurant side of the building.

Diego shook his head. Best to leave them to figure it out themselves. He'd never understood why they had broken up. Gio wouldn't talk about it, and Marissa had just stopped coming around. She was so talented as a chef—it had pained Diego to lose her.

"I hope you don't mind. I asked her along today." Marissa indicated Ainsley, who blushed.

"It's strange coming in here when I'm not working."

Diego shook his head. "Of course not. We all here to celebrate the life of a good friend." Ainsley had never met Brad, as far as he knew.

Watching Marissa with Ainsley—*when did that happen?*—he smiled. She seemed happy. Or like she *could* be happy. Maybe it was for the best that she'd given up on cooking. Being a chef was a hard business, always maintaining your standards, dealing with changing tastes and styles, and keeping the menu fresh.

When everyone was settled, he cleared his throat, waiting for the murmuring to die down. "We are here because a good friend has left us." He closed his eyes, remembering Brad's welcoming smile, his easy presence. The grant he'd found to help street kids learn the skills to work in the restaurant business had saved Ragazzi. He and Matteo owed Brad everything. "So before we are started, let us raise a toast to Brad Weston." He picked up the glass of sparkling prosecco that Gio had left for him. "*Cin cin!*"

"*Cin cin!*" Glasses clinked all around the room. Outside, the rain thundered as if in approval.

Once everyone had taken a sip, he set down the glass, said a quick prayer for Brad's soul, and picked up a potato. "Today, in his honor, we're making *Tortelli alla lastra*—basically a giant fried ravioli, filled with… Gio, how do you say *salciccia, di nuovo?*"

"Sausage." The youth's voice emanated from the walk-in.

"*Perfetto*. Sausage, potatoes, and cheese. I think Brad would have liked these." He smiled at the thought. "*Lastra* means 'slab' in Italian. This dish was originally cooked on a tile 'slab," but today we'll use a hotplate seasoned with a touch of olive oil. We start by boiled the potatoes…"

Marissa sank her hands into the bowl filled with flour, salt, and pepper, kneading it as Ainsley slowly added the water. The mixture gave off such a heavenly aroma, casting her back to those evenings she'd spent there as a teenager, first in the class she'd never wanted to take, and then working as an intern in the old Ragazzi kitchen. *Glory days.* She wondered idly where Tristain was now.

"You lost in space?"

Ainsley's question brought her right back down to Earth. "Sorry. A lot of memories here." She blinked. "I'm being a terrible host, aren't I?"

Her erstwhile date laughed. "Just a little, but it's okay. It must be hard losing someone you love." She lifted the measuring cup full of water away from the bowl. "Is that enough?"

"What?" Marissa looked down at her flour-covered hands. "Oh. Yeah, I think so." The dough was kneading up nicely.

"Good." Ainsley retrieved the rolling pin from the drawer below the granite countertop. "So why did you invite me, if you just planned to sit there silently all afternoon?"

She shrugged. "I don't really know." It had just felt right.

Ainsley snorted. "Way to make a girl feel special." She dusted the counter with flour. "You want to roll, or should I?"

Marissa frowned. "I meant, I *wanted* to text you. I really did. But I don't know why I did it just then. It's been a rough week. I think I needed someone to talk to, someone to hang out with who doesn't know all the same people I do." She looked across the room at Carmelina and Daniele. They looked happy together. *Content. That was the word.* "I'm not a good person." She didn't deserve that kind of happiness.

Ainsley snorted again, louder this time. "What did you do, kill a dog?"

She shook her head. "Nothing like that." She liked Ainsley. The woman was beautiful, witty, and really smart. But Marissa had liked Gio too, and look what she'd done to him.

"Tell you what. Let's set the whole *you're an awful person* thing aside for the afternoon, have some fun making this giant ravioli thing together, and honor your friend."

Marissa reached over and squeezed her hand, leaving a sticky white handprint there. "I'd like that."

"Deal. But we're coming back to this later. And watch it with the flour!" She rolled her eyes as she rinsed off her hand in the station's sink.

Marissa let go of the guilt sitting in the pit of her stomach, laughing it out of her gut. "Fair enough. Now are you going to roll this dough out before it dries up?"

Ainsley brushed back a strand of loose black hair back behind her ear.

She's adorable. Marissa bit her lip, crushing her libido. *Awful person, remember?*

"Sure. Tell me about Brad." Her new… friend?… spread some flour on the countertop and picked up the rolling pin. She started in on the mound of dough, flattening it like a pro.

Marissa closed her eyes. She could still see him seated behind his desk at the old LGBT Center, two buildings ago. "He was kind. Mostly that. He made a place for me in the world when I was thrown out on the street…"

17

A LITTLE DEATHY

Marcos stared at the tortelli, sizzling on the cast-iron grill. They looked like raviolis, and they smelled delicious, tickling his senses with the combined aromas of spicy sausage, olive oil, and the finely chopped rosemary they'd decided to add to their own dish.

The kitchen went dark.

"That smells heavenly."

Marcos blinked, looking around. He was surrounded by bright light, and next to him… He rubbed his eyes and blinked again. "Brad?"

His old friend laughed, his brown eyes twinkling. "Couldn't take the last train outta town without saying goodbye."

Marcos embraced him. "Oh my god, it's so good to see you. You're not…?"

"Dead?" Brad chuckled. "That's a complicated question. I'm not… in my old body anymore, I suppose."

"That's pretty much the standard meaning of the word dead."

"Fair point." He rubbed his chin. "I might even be just a figment of your imagination."

Marcos looked around. *Where did everyone else go?* "Am I having a stroke?"

"No, you're fine. But this *is* kind of weird, right?" He winced. "Not too thrilled to have reached the end of my time here either. I was expecting to have another thirty or forty years with Sam."

Ghost then. Probably. Totally normal. Move along, nothing to see here. "I know." He assumed he and Dave still had decades together too, but who really knew?

"Remember when we first met?" Brad's warm brown eyes searched his.

"Yeah. In front of that old pizza place in the MARRS building. What was it called?"

"Urban Pizza?"

"Pizzeria Urbano!" It had been one of his favorite Midtown hangouts. "It closed a few years back."

"Sorry to hear that. I always liked that place." Brad rubbed his chin, seemingly lost in thought.

Marcos stared at his friend. "Shouldn't you be imparting the secrets of life to me, or something?" *I really am losing my mind If I'm expecting a ghost to offer me pearls of wisdom.*

Brad shrugged. "I don't know. No one gave me a manual for this." He stared at Marcos. "Are you all right, my friend? You seem a little haggard."

Marcos considered his answer. "I don't know. I did a stupid thing, and don't quite know how to tell Dave." Things were going to get bad, and fast, and yet he felt paralyzed.

He reached out to squeeze Marcos's shoulder, and he swore he could feel those warm hands. "Just tell him. He loves you. He'll understand." He started to waver, fuzzing a bit at the edges.

"You made a difference in so many lives." Like the time he'd given Marcos the LGBT Center's website job, when his landlord was *this close* to throwing him out for not paying his rent. "I just wanted you to know."

Brad truly did look like a ghost now, transparent and wavy. Nevertheless, Marcos could make out the faint outlines of a smile. "Thank you."

Then he was gone.

"...should probably take them off now. I don't want them to burn."

Marcos blinked.

Dave was standing in front of him, staring at him as if waiting for an answer.

"What?"

"The tortellis… tortellinis. Whatever they're called. They're going to burn." Dave pointed at the grill. "You have the spatula."

Marcos looked down at the utensil in his hand. "Oh, right. Sure. Thank you." He gave Dave a quick peck on the cheek and turned back to the grill and pried the fried pasta squares off one by one, pyramiding them on a blue and yellow plate that was festooned with lemons.

"Are you okay?" Dave's unconscious echoing of Brad's question wasn't lost on him.

"I… yeah. Sorry. Just thinking about Brad." Had that really been him? *Or just my overactive imagination?*

Dave hugged him from behind, nestling his chin against Marcos's neck. "I know."

"It's just weird. Like, I should be able to pick up the phone and call him. How is he not there?" He'd lost people in his life before, but mostly they'd been older—sick and infirm. It had been expected. Nothing about this felt *expected.*

"So let's celebrate him today. That's why we're here, right?" Dave pecked him on the cheek and then let him go.

"Right." He looked around the room. The others were all wrapping up their own dishes, with varying degrees of success. Carmelina's, surprisingly, looked almost burnt.

He closed his eyes, and for just a moment caught a whiff of Brad's Cool Water cologne. It made him smile.

Just tell him.

Brad was right—he'd do that. But not right now. Not today.

Today was for Brad.

Carmelina's eyes were bigger than her mouth.

At least, that's the excuse she gave herself for her towering platter of *Tortelli alla Lastra* that she and Daniele had prepared together. She wasn't sure how it had happened… she must have unconsciously doubled the recipe, something she was in the habit of doing for her muffins, cookies, and croissants at *Pane e Tulipini.*

And worse than that, half of them were burned at the edges.

"No one will notice." Daniele was arranging them carefully on the platter Gio had provided, artfully placing the worst specimens at the bottom of the pile.

Carmelina blushed. *I'm a great cook.* Everyone told her so. How had she let this dish get away from her? "You sure?" *What's wrong with me today?*

The obvious answer was Brad, but that wasn't the only thing.

"*Certo, cara mia.*" Daniele's Italian accent melted her heart, just like always.

"*Grazie, bello.*" Carmelina gave him a quick kiss. She had been thinking about the strange letter and emails from Italy all morning. She'd agreed to go with Daniele to his cousin's wedding—they'd be leaving in just five more days—and she'd have the chance to sus out the mystery in person. But she also felt awful about it, because it meant she might miss Brad's memorial ceremony. "Should we join the others?"

"I'll carry the *tortelli.*" Everyone was gathering around the large round wooden table in the middle of the room—imported from Italy—to enjoy the spoils of their lesson. There were twelve chairs, enough for a couple from each cooking station. Two of those seats would be empty... one for Sam and one for Brad.

Daniele set their platter next to the others, amidst a smorgasbord of fresh-baked bread, a simple green salad with *aglio e olio* dressing, and a couple bowls of Diego's city-famous marinara sauce for dipping.

In Italy, bread and salad would never be served with the first course. *When in Sacramento...* She chuckled to herself, remembering how scandalized Diego had been when she had sprinkled shredded mozzarella on her pasta.

Everyone was silent as food was shuffled from platters onto plates. The aroma reminded her of *Nonna's* kitchen, when Carmelina had been a child. The heady smell of fresh-baked bread, the deeper scents of boiled tomatoes and pancetta, the light sparkles of rosemary and basil.

When plates were full, everyone just sat there, staring at one another. No one seemed to want to take the first bite.

"What is this, a wake?" Carmelina picked up her fork and dug in.

Laughter spread around the table, lightening the mood, and the *tortelli* were absolutely delicious. Even the slightly burnt ones.

"I remember," she said around a mouthful of the little pasta dipped in marinara, "the first time I met Brad. It was the day Sam dragged him to class. We were making…" She scratched her temple. "Ravioli? Lasagna?"

"*Zuppa*." Diego's eyes twinkled.

"That's right. Soup. It had raviolis in it?"

Diego shook his head. "Minestrone, with vegetables."

"Well, fine. It was goddamned vegetable soup." She glared at the table, daring anyone to gainsay her.

They all laughed instead.

Daniele touched her shoulder. "And Brad?"

She blinked. "Oh yes. I was going to say, it was for one of the classes he set up for kids from the Center. Like you, Marissa."

Marissa nodded, eyes wet. "I remember."

"Anyhow, about halfway through the lesson, he was stirring some marinara sauce just like this, and the pot belched up bright red tomato sauce all over his red shirt. I'd never before heard him curse, but that day he let out a blue streak like you wouldn't believe. Including some choice words I hadn't heard before, or since."

Marcos nodded. "He was kind of buttoned-up, until something startled him or pissed him off. Then he could curse like an injured sailor."

"What words?" Ben had a half-smile on his face. It made her heart soar to see it.

"I'll tell you afterward. I wouldn't want to soil any delicate ears." Her pointed glance at Marissa and Ainsley made the table laugh again. "So here he was, shirt ruined, and it turns out he had a very important fundraising meeting with some guy from a big local real estate company—something about funding the Center's HIV prevention programs for ten years. It was in half an hour, and Brad was in a panic."

Diego nodded. "I remember. He tried to clean off the shirt at his station's sink."

"Which just made it worse. Then in walks this guy." She pinched Daniele on the upper arm. "He's dressed as sharp as the Pope—"

"You know the pope wears white robes, right?" Daniele's tone said he didn't mind the comparison.

"And Brad says, 'take your shirt off.' Like a command. And Daniele says—"

"At least buy me dinner first."

The room exploded in laughter. That made Carmelina happy. Funerals and wakes were often depressing, life-draining affairs. Far better that they should be life-affirming, remembering the best parts of those you lost.

"And did he buy you dinner?" Dave winked at her.

Carmelina snorted. "If he did, I don't want to know about it."

Marissa wiped the moisture from her eyes. *You are such a blubbering idiot.*

The others around the table were swapping stories about Brad. Funny things he had done. The way he'd helped everyone, even to his own detriment. His kind laugh.

All she could think about was how he had come to the hospital that one night, after Justin had been beaten up, and had stayed there with them all night long. He'd always been there for his "kids," whenever they needed him. *I can't believe he's gone.*

Ainsley reached over to squeeze her hand. She smelled of citrus and mint. "You okay?"

"Not really." Brad had been a father figure to her, before Marcos had come into her life. When she'd run away from home and had been all alone, with no one else to turn to. "It's not fair." It came out as a hoarse whisper.

Ainsley squeezed her hand tighter.

What was I thinking, bringing her here? Ainsley didn't know him. Marissa freed her hand to grab her napkin and wipe another tear from her cheek. *What a fucked-up date this is. She's never going to want to see me again.*

Marcos was telling some story about Brad at the Center, something about a mixed-up lunchtime meeting and an exploding can of soda.

It made her think of the old LGBT Center building—the rickety, ancient purple Victorian house right on the railroad tracks that had been the home to the Center for so many years, before they moved to their current digs on 20th Street. The old place was gone now too, turned back into a private home.

It was as if a whole part of her life had just been wiped out in one fell swoop. Not since the pandemic, when she'd been locked up in her room at home for almost two years, had she felt so alone. Her stomach shuddered, and she tasted bile in her throat.

"I have to go." Marissa scooted her chair back, the loud *scrape* making everyone look at her direction. She ran out the door, ignoring the surprised gasps of her friends. Brad's friends.

She burst out into the rainy afternoon, slamming into a man wearing a trench coat and an old brown hat with a leather band. "Sorry!"

He grunted something in reply and hurried away down the street.

She closed her eyes and breathed in the fresh air, trying to calm her frayed nerves and rebellious stomach.

The door behind her swung open again. She halfway expected Marcos to come out after her again, just like he had done all those years ago, when she first came to Ragazzi.

"Hey."

Marissa turned to find Ainsley standing there, staring at her under the building's awning. "Hey."

They looked at each other for a moment as the rain resumed, pouring straight down out of the sky and closing off the rest of the world.

Marissa was the first to look away. "I'm sorry I brought you here. Lousy first date, huh?"

"So this *was* a date." She flashed Marissa a half-smile. "I've been on worse."

Marissa laughed in spite of herself. "Worse than being taken to a wake for someone you didn't know, and then your date bolting on you?"

Ainsley grinned, her teeth white in the semi-darkness of the storm. "Oh yeah. One time, this woman I had a crush on was an hour late, and then she got pissed off at me and dropped me off in the middle of nowhere, about an hour outside of town."

"Ouch. How did you get home?" She would never have kicked the beautiful waitress out of her car. *Or bed.*

Ainsley pulled out her phone. "Uber. Though it took them forever to get out there. I was lucky I had cell service."

Marissa managed a slight smile. Already her stomach was feeling better. "Okay then, here's to your second worst date."

"Cheers." She met Marissa's gaze again, her dark brown eyes searching. "You must've really loved him."

Marissa nodded. She leaned back against the wall, protected from the rain by the wide awning. It seemed fitting that it was overcast today, as if even Mother Nature was mourning Brad's death. "He took care of me when no one else would."

Ainsley eased back against the side of the building next to her, her hand sliding over to touch Marissa's. "Tell me about him."

She thought about it. "He was kind. He used to be a Republican. I didn't know that until recently... When he came to the center, everything changed for him. He saw his kids and... well, he never had any of his own, but he took in one of my friends when he needed it." Come to think of it, she hadn't heard from Justin in ages. She'd have to look him up.

"He sounds amazing." Ainsley's pinky finger slipped around her own, both their hands pressed against the dark wood siding.

Despite the myriad of emotions already running through her, a thrill ran up her spine. "Did you... want it to be a date?"

"I was kind of hoping." Ainsley blushed.

"You don't want to date me." Her guilt came flooding back. "I'm a mess. I ruin everything I touch."

"I don't think that's true." Ainsley's hand grasped hers, her palm warm and soft.

Marissa thought about Gio, just on the other side of the wall. What she'd done to him. "You should run as far and fast as you can."

"I'd rather do this." Ainsley took her face in both of those warm, wonderful hands, and pulled her in for a kiss.

Marissa stiffened, then surrendered to it, heat flooding her, washing away all of her pain and regret. She kissed Ainsley back, wrapping her own hands around her back and pulling her close as the rain thundered down just inches away.

"You guys all right out here—oh!" Marcos popped his head out, took one look at them, and ducked back inside.

They laughed, and then kissed again. And Marissa felt like she was flying.

When it was over, Ainsley leaned forward to touch her cold nose to Marissa's. "So... second date? Maybe something a little less..."

"Deathy?"

"Yes, exactly that. A little less *deathy* next time."

"Deal." She still had her reservations. But Ainsley was like a drug she couldn't resist.

"Come on. Let's get back inside. That pasta's not gonna finish itself, and I don't know about you, but I'm still a starving student." She took Marissa's hand and dragged her along.

Marissa followed her back into the restaurant, mouthing a silent *thank you* to Brad for looking out for her one last time. *Wherever you are.*

18

BEN AND THE DRAG
QUEEN MATCHMAKER

Ben didn't believe in the supernatural. At least, not in the way some people did.

Had he sometimes felt Ella close to him in bed, late at night, her presence a comforting warmth? *Maybe.*

But surely that was his own brain playing tricks on him in the drowsy early hours of the morning, forgetting that she was gone and how completely her loss had riven him in two. That thing when you woke up and, just for a moment, you were somewhere else, entirely convinced that it was real.

He stood on the cooling sidewalk, staring at the two-story slate-blue Victorian with bright white trim. Mansion Flats, he assumed, though he was kind of fuzzy on all the neighborhood boundaries in midtown and downtown Sac. He was trying to work out why he was there.

A seemingly random series of events, surely all coincidence, had brought him to that exact place at that exact moment. Casual harmonies of the universal harp, plucking his little existence like an inconsequential string.

The first had happened earlier in the day, during the dinner in Brad's honor. He'd been chewing his way through one of Carmelina's slightly charcoaled *tortelli*, thinking about something—work, Ella, his new upstairs neighbor?—maybe all three.

The room had gone strangely dark, as if he were losing consciousness. And then Brad was there.

Ben stared at the apparition who had appeared so unexpectedly—rather rudely, he thought, given that he was in the middle of an early dinner with friends—in the seat next to him. "You're not real."

"No, I'm not." The edge of Brad's lips quirked upward. "Are you so sure that *you* are?"

Ben chuckled. It was vintage Brad, turning the question around on the questioner. "Carmelina must have put a little something extra in that pasta." He'd never suspected her of being a pothead. His respect for her went up a notch. He blinked, willing Brad's ghost to vanish like the hallucination it undoubtedly was.

"Did it work?" Brad's warm brown eyes twinkled with amusement.

"Apparently not." Ben pinched himself, then slapped his own cheek.

Brad laughed. "Still no?"

Ben sighed. "All right, if you aren't just some figment of my imagination, and I'm not currently passed out under the table after drinking a little too much house wine, what do you want to tell me?" He was still pretty sure that he was unconscious, that this *vision* was just random firings of his neurons bringing Brad back to life in his mind. It was the most likely explanation.

Brad frowned, raising an eyebrow. "Isn't it enough that I came to see you, one last time? The angels are calling me, after all."

"Oh is that where you're headed?"

Brad winced. "I hope so. Wouldn't want the evangelicals to be right about that one."

Ben had never been particularly religious, but he'd always thought queer folks were bound for Heaven, if such a place really existed. *After all they've put us through on Earth, it's the least we deserve.*

"You're going to be all right." He put a ghostly hand on Ben's shoulder, and damned if Ben didn't feel a tingling there. "*Misfortune knows*, you've got a bright path ahead of you." Then he was gone, and Carmelina was laughing alongside him.

Ben blinked, his eyes slowly adjusting to the bright light in the teaching kitchen.

"Misfortune knows."

What in the hell does that mean?

He'd all but put it out of his mind the next day, when he'd opened the latest edition of Outword Magazine. An article caught his eye, headed by a brassy, red-headed drag queen. "Miz Fortune's Lonely Hearts Club." It was a new advice column, full of pithy love life advice and answers to readers' questions.

Miz Fortune? Surely another coincidence. If the Universe wanted him to take it seriously, it would have to do better than that. If fate wanted to tell him something, he wished it would just come out and say it.

Which led to now. He'd taken an Uber to do some shopping on Sunday evening, after the storm had passed. Somewhere about Midtown, the car had unexpectedly started lurching and belching out smoke. The driver made it to the curb and helped Ben out, offering his abject apologies.

The man wrung his hands. "I just had it serviced last week. I don't know what's wrong with it. Wait here, and I'll get you another ride as soon as I call AAA." Then he'd walked off, leaving Ben standing on a residential block full of two-story Victorians.

And there it was, right in front of him. A small, neatly-lettered sign in the middle of a healthy green lawn:

Welcome to Miz Fortune's. Entrance on the left and down the stairs.

"Holy shit." Ben stared at the sign. Surely it was another coincidence...

His phone buzzed in his pocket. It was a text from an unknown number labeled "likely spam." He glared at it, then knitted his brow in confusion. It was just one line.

What do you have to lose? B.

B. Brad? "Fuck me. Ghosts are sending me text messages now?"

The driver glanced at him, one eyebrow raised, and put a hand over his phone's speaker. "You all right?"

"Yeah." In truth, he was far from okay. The world worked in a certain way. There was no hidden plane, no gateway to a supernatural dimension just outside the human one. Ghosts didn't use cellphones. *And yet...* "Don't worry about me. I'll get another ride. I have some business here to attend to."

The driver frowned. "You sure?"

"Yes. Don't worry. I'll give you five stars. Shit happens." *Story of my life.*

The driver smiled in apparent relief. "Thanks, man."

Decided, Ben waved his thanks and followed the concrete path that led along the left side of the house. He followed it down a flight of stairs and found himself in front of a bright red door. In the little window on the right, a neon sign advertised *Miz Fortune's Lonely Hearts Salon.*

He rang the bell and was immediately encompassed by an instrumental version of *The Point of No Return* from Phantom of the Opera. *Not ominous. Not ominous at all.*

"Come in." The voice sounded friendly enough.

Swallowing his nervousness, he pushed open the door and entered Miz Fortune's den.

The color scheme of the little room was red on red on red, with a little gold thrown in for good measure. Maroon walls, carmine curtains, a bright-crimson tablecloth embroidered with gold, and even the red hair of the proprietress herself.

Her drag was flawless, her makeup feminizing her face and her red wig falling in a luscious nest of curls to her shoulders. She looked a little older than her photo, but she was still beautiful.

As a trans man, Ben had complicated feelings about drag queens. He'd enjoyed them on many occasions, but sometimes they made him uncomfortable—men playing at being women. It hit a little too close to home. Not that there weren't also a few trans women who were drag queens too.

Miz Fortune—he recognized her from her photo in Outword—offered him a broad smile. "Welcome to the salon. Did you have an appointment?" Her hand rested on a crystal ball, complete with swirling mist special effects.

"I... no, not really." How to explain that he'd been sent to her by a dead man, and had only ended up there after his Uber driver had made an emergency stop on her block?

She nodded. "Ah. You're one of my specials." She waved her hands around the crystal ball, and the smoke sparkled and sputtered inside. "Please have a seat."

"Specials?" Ben did as he was told, all the while staring at the glass, mesmerized. How did she get it to do that? There must be a switch or lever out of sight behind the table.

She reached out and placed a hand—half-covered in golden rings topped with red rubies, and tipped with flawless red nails—on his own, golden bracelets jangling together on his wrist. "Special appointments. Sometimes people find their way to me because they're supposed to. My own husband was one of those. Does that make sense?" She waved at a framed photo on the wall that showed a handsome dark-haired man in a black button-down shirt.

"I guess so."

"So darling, tell me why you're here." She was the voice of reason. Well, she *was* a fortune teller—or matchmaker?—after all. She would understand.

He got a whiff of something—patchouli oil? "I lost my partner during the pandemic. It was devastating, and I've... been stuck ever since. I don't know what to do. A friend of mine..." Well, Brad had been his friend... "told me that 'misfortune' would know. Then I saw you in Outword Magazine. Miz Fortune, I mean. And then... well, I ended up here."

It sounded stupid, even to him. *What am I doing here?* He got up to go.

She squeezed his hand, holding him back. "You made it all the way down here." Her eyes twinkled, like Brad's had, catching him off-guard. "Don't you at least want to hear what I have to say?"

He sank back down in his chair, heat rushing to his cheeks. "Forgive me. None of this is your fault. I'm behaving abominably." His mother had taught him better manners than that. "Yes, please, tell me." He steeled himself for a crock of psychic bullshit.

"That's better." She let go of his hand.

"What do I need to do?"

"Just close your eyes and think about what you want to ask me." Her voice was warm and calming.

Ben did so, feeling more than a little self-conscious.

Will I always feel like this? Is this all there is for me? Or is there something better still to come?

Just thinking those thoughts felt like a betrayal of Ella and her tragic death. How could he move on when she never would? Yet surely she didn't want him to be miserable for the rest of his life.

Something filled his heart—a certainty that he was right about that, at least. It *felt* like her—strong, funny, self-assured, full of love despite all the crap that life had thrown at her. *Ben, I want you to be happy.*

He opened his eyes.

Miz Fortune was staring at him, her own eyes wet. "She loved you so very much."

He nodded, then shook his head, torn between agreement and anger at whatever sort of trick the charlatan was playing on him. "You didn't know her."

Miz Fortune bit her perfectly rouged lower lip. "No, I didn't, but I can *feel* her here. She was sick for so long…" She reached out a hand to him again, gently touching his. "It wasn't your fault. She wants you to know that."

"How… how did you know…?" She was wrong, though. *It was. It was my fault.* Anger, frustration, and maddening grief filled him up like boiling water in a kettle. "It *was* all my fault. If I hadn't gone to work that day… if I had worn a better mask… oh God, Ella, I am so sorry."

He lost control of himself and began to sob. His body heaved as waves of suppressed pain forced themselves out of his heart. "Ella. I'm sorry. I'm so, so sorry…"

Miz Fortune was suddenly right beside him. She knelt next to him and put her arms around him, her golden lace shawl draped over his shoulders. "I know, sweetie. I know. Let it out." She pulled him tight to her.

He was six years old again, bawling his eyes out, his mother's arms warm around his little body. "She died because of me." That was the fact that had broken him, that had twisted up his insides and left him a shattered husk.

Miz Fortune let him cry it out.

His chest heaved, and tears streamed down his face to soak into her red dress. He shuddered, letting it all out. His anger, his fear, his regret. *If only I'd stayed home. If only I'd protected her. If only she'd gotten better...*

Once again he felt Ella's presence. This time he *knew* it was her. He could feel it in his bones.

He looked up, and she was the one holding him. "Ella?"

She wiped his tears away. "Hush, my little angel. It wasn't your fault. It was my time to go."

She was so beautiful, just as he remembered her on those afternoon picnics in the park, her bright red lips pursed, sunlight streaming through her blond hair. She kissed him, those lips sweet as honey and strawberries from the lip gloss she loved to wear. "It will be all right."

Then she was gone.

Ben blinked.

"Are you all right?"

He pushed himself away from Miz Fortune's embrace. "I'm sorry. I shouldn't—"

"You are one of my special appointments. Like I said before, you're here because you are supposed to be." She pushed herself up off the ground, using the chair and table to stabilize herself. "Getting older is a bitch."

Ben laughed in spite of himself. "I'm starting to understand that."

She snorted as she took her seat again. "You're still an infant, child." She leaned forward and waved her hand above his head, and smiled.

"What?"

She peered into the crystal ball. "The answer to your question. The fates have much more in store for you. Look."

The mists cleared. Ben leaned forward and gasped. Lorelei, his upstairs neighbor, smiled back at him.

"You know her?"

He nodded. "How...?"

Miz Fortune chuckled. "If I knew, I'd manufacture a thousand of these and be rich beyond my wildest dreams." Her smile slipped away. "Still, it won't be an easy path for you. But happiness awaits you, if you're brave enough to try."

He felt the last bits of Ella slip away. For the first time in a long while —years, probably—he smiled. A genuine, ear-to-ear smile. "I can try."

She squeezed his hand again. "I know you will."

He took a deep breath, steadying himself on the arms of the chair. "Thank you, Miz Fortune…"

The matchmaker shook her head. "Call me Chester. All my friends do."

"Thank you, Chester." The weight that had held him down for years was gone. He shook her hand. "You've… just thank you." He pulled out is wallet. "What do I owe you?"

She shook her head. "This one's on the house, sweetie."

"Thanks." *And thank you, Brad.* He slipped out into the gloaming, feeling the cool air of the Delta Breeze on his cheeks. It was time to try.

19

TRAVEL PLANS

Daniele pecked Carmelina on the cheek. "I've got to dash down to Bergman to grab a few travel supplies for Friday. Need anything?"

Carmelina stared at her open suitcase on the bed. "A bigger suitcase?" It was Samsonite, and easily three feet on the long side.

He snorted. "Bigger than that? It's already almost as big as you are. We'll only be in Rome for the weekend."

"I know, but do you realize how many possible wardrobe combinations that is? Two changes a day—that's pants, shirt or blouse, underwear, socks, shoes, and bra—" Her face scrunched up as she tried to do the math. "That's like 217 pieces of clothing."

Daniele chuckled. "*Tesoro*, math was never your strong suit. And why two per day? Just wear the same thing a couple times."

"And have your family laughing at me for wearing jeans to a fancy Italian dinner?" Daniele was a sharp dresser. She'd bet his mother would give her the evil eye if she showed up for dinner in… god forbid… *casual clothes.*

He laughed again, good-naturedly, and squeezed her shoulder. "You may be right. Just try to keep it manageable. I could get you some of those vacuum bags."

She grinned. "Yes, that would be perfect. I'll need about thirty—"

"Let me do the calculations. Just work on getting everything selected by the time I get back, and I'll help." He winked and slipped out of the room.

Although a day never passed when she didn't miss her first husband, Arthur, she knew he'd approve of her new man.

A minute later, the garage door closed, and Daniele was on his way.

Carmelina set about choosing her clothing for the trip. Daniele was right, in a way, though she'd never give him the satisfaction of knowing it. She *could* wear some things more than once, and mix and match them so she didn't end up wearing "the same thing" twice.

She was just debating which of seven scarves she needed most when her phone buzzed.

Sam Fuller.

She picked it up immediately, sinking down on her bed to take the call. Her massive pile of clothes tilted toward her, threatening to bury her under a cotton and polyester avalanche. "Hey."

"Carmelina?" He sounded small and far away.

Poor guy. "Yeah, Sam, it's me. I saw your name on the caller ID." She pushed the tower of clothing away to collapse across the suitcase. "How are you?"

There was a long pause. "Not so good. Things… there are so many things to do here."

She nodded, then realized he couldn't see her. "I know. Do you want to Facetime?" In reality, she was a bit of a mess. She had Mondays off when her bakery was closed, and she'd slept in. Her hair went in a number of different directions, and she hadn't yet made up her face. *Not suitable for public consumption.*

But Sam was Sam.

"Not right now. I'm running on about two hours of sleep, and I'm a bit of a mess."

If you could just see me… She laughed, then covered her mouth. "Sorry. It's… I never know what to say at times like this."

"Just hearing your voice helps." There was a sound that might have been a muffled sob. "It all happened so fast. One day he was here, and we were planning a trip to Puerto Vallarta in the fall. Next thing I know…"

"Yeah." It had been like that with Arthur, too. "It's always too fast." Her heart ached for him.

He took a deep breath and pressed ahead. "So… anyhow. I called for a reason. Give me a sec."

She missed the old landline phones, where you could twirl the spiral cord around your finger to kill time and give your hands something to do. Especially in moments like these. "Take your time."

He and Brad had been good together. There was an age gap, sure, like between her and Daniele. But they'd always been "the boys" to her. She'd let too much time pass since she'd gotten in touch with them. *And now Brad's gone.*

"Okay, so, Brad wanted to have his ashes scattered in the Effie Yeaw Nature Center." He said the words slowly and deliberately, as if he was trying to get them all out clearly, without faltering. "He's being… Sorry."

"It's okay." She wished she were there to hug him.

"Cremated. Today."

Arthur had been buried, so she hadn't had to deal with that particular issue. But a loss was a loss. "He'll like it there. By the river."

"Yes. By the river." He grabbed onto her statement like a lifeline. "He always loved Sacramento's rivers."

"That's perfect." She cringed as soon as it came out of her mouth. *Nothing about this is perfect.*

He didn't seem to notice. "I'm flying in on Wednesday. I was hoping I could stay with you. I was going to get a hotel but there's some kind of convention in town and everything is super expensive. My friend Oscar will be coming with me."

"Of course." She wasn't leaving until Friday morning. "When were you planning to spread the ashes?" She glanced at the suitcase.

"I hadn't decided. I'll be there for a week or two—"

She bit her lip. "I only ask because Daniele and I are leaving for Italy on Friday. His lesbian cousin is getting married." She cringed again. *Why did I mention marriage? And lesbians?*

Another pause. "We can do it on Wednesday."

She shook her head. "No, don't decide on my account. I can—"

"Don't be silly." He sounded a little more like his old self. "Brad would want you there. I'll email you the flight info."

"Thank you." She closed her eyes, remembering Brad as he'd been when she knew him. "He loved you, Sam. Hold onto that." She squeezed the red scarf in her hand.

"I know he did. He loved you too."

Brad was… had been a man with a big heart. He'd taken care of Marissa before Carmelina had even known she was her granddaughter. "You can stay as long as you like. I'll give you the keys and the alarm code when we go."

"I really appreciate that." Silence fell between them again. Then, "I have to run. Oscar's calling. See you in a few days."

"Bye." She stared at the blank phone screen after he hung up. It would be good to see him. *And so strange that it will be without Brad.*

With a sigh, she set her phone aside.

It was time to tackle the rumpled mountain of clothing that had taken over her bed.

20

WITH EYES TO SEE

Dave sat alone in his car just around the corner from Carmelina's place, staring at the bungalow across the street—his old place in River Park, the little yellow wood-slat rental he'd lived in for more years than he cared to remember after his life had fallen apart. He took a sip of his Everyday Grind mocha—now cold—and set it back in the cup holder.

He could think about John now without regret, without falling into the throes of a panic attack. His heart still raced a bit when he remembered John's bright smile, his laugh when Dave said something stupid that amused him. His warm touch. But in a good way.

Then those long months after John was diagnosed, as HIV ravaged his body. The meds had slowed it down, but the end had been swift when it came, overwhelming them both like a floodtide.

That last evening, he had held John's hand all night long as he succumbed to fate. Dave could still feel John's cold fingers in his palm.

Yes, he could think about it all now without his heart threatening to burst out of his chest, without gasping for breath and feeling like he was going to die. All because of Marcos.

He'd never thought he'd get a second chance at life. At love. *A fucking cliché. But it's true.*

Marcos had given him a reason to live again. Marcos and his beautiful, complicated adopted daughter Marissa. Carmelina's granddaughter.

Staring at the red front door of the bungalow through streaked car windows—it had been forest green when he'd lived there—he remembered the day she'd welcomed him in, hugging him tightly and smelling of patchouli. *Stay as long as you need.*

And he had.

Then the world had thrown them a swarm of curve balls—the oft-cited curse of living in *interesting times.*

From the moment *He* had ridden down his golden escalator with his dark visions of "American carnage," everything had changed.

Dave refused to even think the man's name, let alone speak it.

The Obama years had been washed away by a red wave, a deluge of *fake news*—for a brief, shining moment, that phrase had meant something, before *He* co-opted it to mean anything he didn't agree with.

Suddenly everything Dave's community had worked for—legality, sanity, security, peace, equality, and marriage—felt threatened.

Corruption, rage, and an avalanche of lies followed… so many lies. It felt like nothing would ever be right again.

They had held on, the three of them. Dave had moved out of the bungalow and into the condo with Marcos, and Marissa had graduated high school and had gone off to college.

Then the plague had shut down the world.

It was hard for him to remember how dark that time had been, how scary to live in fear of a virus, to be trapped indoors for months and months like a prisoner. He'd been afraid to set foot outside, for fear of catching it on the breeze from some passerby. The gift of working from home turned into a jail sentence, with friends seen only in little boxes on flat computer screens. Toilet paper and sanitizer were as valuable as gold.

And all the unhinged madness from the White House. *End times indeed.*

Dave sat back and closed his eyes. He and most of the rest of the country had blocked out those black days, and now they were paying the price.

Finally, there'd been a breath of fresh air. The inauguration, and the sight of loving, caring adult human beings with their children and grandchildren in the White House, with people in their cars honking and flashing their lights in approval—the strangest inauguration day ever.

A vaccine, and a slow, halting return to something that resembled the "normal" he used to know.

And now? He opened his eyes, looking up at the clear blue sky that belied all of the fears and worries of mere mortals. *He* was back, stronger than ever, and if *He* got back into the White House… *We're done.*

Dave shuddered. He lived in a baseline state of dull fear these days, watching his party sleepwalking with a diminished candidate toward an almost certain defeat. *I can't imagine living through another four years.*

But that wasn't why he was here, in front of this house on this sunny Monday afternoon. He'd told Marcos he had a meeting. That much had been true, but the doctor had let him go hours before.

Now he was on a tour of his former life, like a man who was already dead but hadn't quite figured it out yet.

He picked up his phone and stared at his notes again. *Wet Advanced Macular Degeneration. Irreversible. Likely near-total vision loss within six months, even with treatment.*

I'm going blind. He'd first noticed it a few weeks earlier, before he'd had to learn the difference between *Dry AMD* and *Wet AMD*. The wet kind proceeded much faster.

When he'd first moved in with Marcos, he'd taken up an old hobby. He had always loved watercolors, how the bright pigments blended and flowed together on the paper, the cheery, vivid colors.

Soon, he wouldn't be able to see them at all. Those vibrant hues would be gone, replaced with—at best—a blurry, monochrome world.

Hence the tour of the important places in his life.

How was he supposed to tell Marcos? It wasn't fair for him to have to take care of a blind spouse. Marcos was eight years younger than he was, and still had so much of his life to live, places to go. Things to *see.*

Maybe it would be better if I checked out before the worst arrives.

The thought shocked him. He'd never been one for self-pity, let alone to think of taking his own life. And yet, there was a certain appeal to going out on top.

After all, the world was coming to an end. The liar in chief would be president again. The economy would crash, and queers like him and

Marcos would be ripped apart and forced into the closet again, or worse. And the destructiveness of climate change would only get worse, year after year.

Dave wouldn't *see* any of it.

He squeezed the steering wheel and clamped his eyes shut, trying to hold back the tears that threatened to overwhelm him. Not panic, this time. Just a deep, gutting sense of impending loss.

He held himself absolutely still, waiting for it to pass.

A single tear slipped down his cheek.

Slowly, the pressure in his chest eased, and his heartbeat slowed.

Little by little, he loosened his grip on the steering wheel.

He began to breathe again, deep, slow intakes of air that calmed his soul.

This isn't the end. He would go home and talk it out with Marcos, when he was ready. *Soon.*

Together they would figure it out.

Sometimes miracles happen. He wasn't sure if he was talking about his own situation, or the plight of the world.

Marissa and her generation would have to live with the mess that Dave's generation and his own ancestors had left them. What would they do with it? Would they be drowned by the mistakes of those who came before? Or would they find a way to make things better?

Maybe, just maybe, it was worthwhile to stick around to find out.

His phone buzzed.

Pizzasaurus Rex for dinner? It was Marcos' favorite new pizza discovery in Midtown.

Dave chuckled.

Sure. See you at home in twenty.

With a sigh, he started the engine. He gave the old yellow bungalow across the street one last look, then turned the car around on the narrow, tree-lined suburban road and headed for home.

THE THIEF AND THE ARTIST

Matteo stared at the list.

It was neatly lettered in his own hand, lining out all the employees at Ragazzi who had access to the cash drawer. He had narrowed it down to four who had been working on each of the nights the cash drawer had been short:

- Ainsley Kim
- Alex Masters
- Justin Sims
- Giovanni Mazzocco-Bellei

He'd discarded Gio right away. He couldn't believe that his adopted son would steal from them—he had everything he needed, and a decent salary besides.

That left two servers and an expediter.

Alex and Justin had worked at Ragazzi for years. Alex was shallow and a bit vain—and apparently an ex of Brad's—but Matteo had never thought of him as a thief.

Justin was their longest-employed expediter—nine years now—and didn't have a dishonest bone in his body.

Which left Ainsley. She was suspect, if only because she was newest of the three. But she seemed like such a good kid, and Marissa clearly liked her. *Hard to believe she would do this.*

Matteo sighed. There was no sure way to know who'd taken money from the till. They didn't use surveillance cameras in the restaurant—maybe he'd have to revisit that decision after this debacle, but he hated the idea.

Still, he had a plan. He'd scheduled each of the three employees on separate shifts, and would wait and see if the cash drawer came up short again during any of them. Then he'd have to confront whomever seemed to be at fault.

He rubbed his temples, glaring at the list. He hated this sort of thing. He just wanted to run a good restaurant with people who were like family to him.

Theft was a betrayal, and he was not looking forward to finding the thief.

~

Ainsley rushed from table to table, doing her best to keep everyone happy. They were short-staffed—usually Alex and Justin were on shift with her, but tonight she was paired with Margaret, a sweet but not particularly fleet-of-foot woman who often forgot customer orders, but still insisted she was able to keep it "all in my head."

Connor was a perfectly fine expediter, but he'd called in sick with Covid. It was easy to forget, sometimes, that it was going around. Life had returned to some semblance of normal, and it was rare to see folks masking any longer.

The lovely Sophia was at the bar, but she didn't serve food. That left Ainsley basically alone on the floor.

She sidled up to her latest table, and pulled out her portable payment system, the one named after a crunchy breakfast food. "My name is Ainsley, and I'll be your server tonight. Can I start you off with something to drink?"

The dark-haired person looked up at her and smiled. "Yes please. I'd like a Negroni, no ice."

Her mouth fell open. "It's… you're… I mean…" She shook her head, trying to clear it, to force sensible words to come out. "Jun Seo Jang."

Their grin got even wider. "Yes, I am. Though I'm a little surprised to be recognized on this side of the ocean."

She bit her lip. "I'm sorry. That was so unprofessional of me. I'll get your drink right out for you." She turned around and practically ran to the bar, not daring to look back. She leaned as far across the dark wooden surface as she could without falling over the other side. "Is the dark-haired Korean person by the window looking at me?" she whispered to Sophia.

The bartender looked over Ainsley's shoulder. "Oooh, handsome. Nope, he's looking at his menu… wait. Yup. Totally staring at you."

"They're."

"Ah, gotcha." She grinned. "They are looking at their menu."

Her face flushed. "They are… Can I get a Negroni, neat?"

"Of course." The bartender poured the drink. "Who is that?"

"They're just an artist whose work I love. They're in town for a gallery opening later this week." She closed her eyes. "I can't believe they're sitting in my section."

Sophia grinned. "And you're too shy to talk to them." She walked the drink around the counter and took Ainsley by the hand. "Come on."

"What are you doing?" It came out as a squeak as Sophia dragged her back across the room.

"What you won't." She plonked the drink down on Jun Seo's table. "Are you the famous artist?"

Ainsley felt a full-body blush coming on, starting from her feet.

They laughed pleasantly. "In some circles."

Sophia nodded. "I'm not much for art, but my friend here really is, and she says you're the shit."

She sputtered, "I didn't say that—"

She patted Ainsley on the shoulder. "She did. And her own work is really good. You should have her help with your show."

Ainsley's mind went in three directions at once. *Why is she doing this? What will they think of me? When did she see my work? Oh yes, when she came over that one time…*

It had been a brief fling while Sophia and her boyfriend Caleb had been broken up, and they'd decided—mutually—that it should become nothing more. *But back to the matter at hand.* "I'm so sorry for Sophia, Mx. Jang…"

Jun Seo was grinning. Damn, they were handsome. Almost handsome enough that she'd have said yes, if they asked. *Almost.* "I think it's a fantastic idea. I love to meet fresh new artists. Do you know the Red Roof Gallery?"

She nodded, trying to get words out. In proper order. "It's… He… The owner was in here a few nights ago." She hoped she didn't seem to be too much of a blathering idiot. "Yes, I know it."

"Perfect. Come by tomorrow morning around nine."

"I'd love that." She had a chemistry class in the morning, but she could skip one class…

They nodded and took a sip of the Negroni. "This is excellent. Thank you. When you're ready, I'd like to order."

Ainsley shot daggers at Sophia, who just smiled back innocently as she backed away.

Ainsley took a deep breath, pushed an errant strand of hair behind her left ear, and fell back on her waiter training. "Of course, Mx. Seo. What can I get you?"

22

WHERE ALL ROADS LEAD

Gio threw his phone onto his nightstand and pulled his knees up against his chest, hugging his sweats-covered legs and banging his head against the headboard in a slow, deliberate rhythm. His bare feet crinkled the sheets between his toes. *It's time for a change.*

He'd lived in this little bedroom above Ragazzi, in *Papà's* house, for nine years now, not counting the brief stint with Marissa. Sure, the commute was great, and he loved the job, working as the host and manager—and back-up chef—for the restaurant. But Diego never listened to his ideas. Now he was twenty-six, with no college degree, no place of his own, and no real direction.

He slipped out of bed, his bare feet touching the cold hardwood floor, and began to pace back and forth from one end of the small room to the other.

Step step step.

Clearly Diego had been open to change once. He'd crossed an ocean with Matteo, taken a *buco di merda* of a failing restaurant and turned it into something great. He'd even launched a cooking class that had set Ragazzi a step above the rest.

Why is he so afraid of it now?

Step step step.

In a way, he understood it. These were perilous times. Immigrants were being demonized, rights taken away, and who knew what might happen in the November election? It reminded him of the fascist takeover of Italy he'd studied in his history classes, and how they still left sheafs of wheat at the tomb of Mussolini in Predappio.

Step step step.

Papà and *Babbo* were both gay *and* from another country. Plus they were getting older—in their fifties now—and it must be a very scary time for them to consider taking risks.

He stopped in his tracks.

I'm not old. Though sometimes he felt like he was. He lived an *adult* life, spending nearly all of his time at work. He rarely did anything for himself, and he hadn't had a steady girlfriend since Marissa. He still didn't understand what had gone wrong there.

If he were honest with himself, he'd admit it. *I'm scared too.* Prices were so high. Everyone was hot under the collar about politics. The idea of ever owning his own home seemed way out of reach. And who knew if there would even be a world to worry about in another decade or two?

Tap tap. The gentle sound brought his head up to stare at the door. *Must have been making too much noise on the squeaky floorboards.* "Come in." He sank back down on his bed, expecting *Papà* to poke his head in and tell him to get back to sleep. He put his head down and his hands in his lap.

"Sorry to bother you. I seed that the light was still on." It was *Babbo*—his stepfather Matteo.

Gio didn't bother correcting him, but his spirit brightened. "Sorry for waking you." He adored Matteo, his second dad. Though sometimes he still missed his mother. He closed his eyes and tried to remember what she looked like.

"You didn't. I was going to the kitchen for some water." Matteo closed the door behind him. "I couldn't sleep."

Gio looked up. Matteo's black hair was a ridiculous bed-sculpted mess. "You too?"

Matteo nodded. "Some worries about the work."

Gio grinned. *Babbo* Matteo was fluent in English, but little things like prepositions, articles, and past tenses still eluded him every now and then.

The bed shifted as Matteo sat down beside him. "What is it keeping you awake?"

Gio shrugged. "The usual. Worried about work. The future. *Papà*."

Matteo raised an eyebrow.

He plowed ahead. "He never lets me change anything. I have all these great ideas, and he just turns them down, like I'm still seventeen and fresh off the plane. Like he doesn't trust me to know what I'm talking about." That was the root of it. He was stuck, and his father didn't even see it.

"You have many good ideas." Matteo patted his knee. "Diego is… stubborn. Like someone else I know."

He blushed, examining his hands. "Maybe. But does he have to shoot down every single idea I bring him? *Non 'giusto!*" It *wasn't* fair, not really. He needed more than the same job, the same day, every day.

"You need a change."

Gio looked up at him in wonder. It was like *Babbo* could read his mind. "Yeah. Maybe I do."

Matteo stared back at him for a long time before answering. "Look," he said at last, "I don't want to lose you. It's special, what we have here as a family, and I know that Gio wants you to have this place, someday."

Gio's eyes widened. "He does? He never says it…" All he ever felt from his father was disapproval.

"Diego is a proud man. A good one, but a proud one. He doesn't see you like I do." Matteo put a warm hand on his shoulder. "You are a grown man. Good, like your father, but proud too."

Gio's face flushed. "Thank you, *Babbo*."

"I have an idea." He grinned, drawing out the moment, clearly enjoying his role as the peacemaker.

"Are you going to tell me, or what?" Maybe Matteo wanted to give him more responsibility. Maybe he would even help convince Diego about the franchise idea.

"I think you should go back to Italy."

"What?" Gio stared at him blankly. They were sending him away? He was far too old for boarding school. "*Babbo*, that's… look, I like it here. I don't want to go back to live there." His mind was scrambling. *What did I do wrong?*

Matteo returned the blank look, then the wrinkles around the sides of his eyes creased, his face broadened into a smile, and he laughed heartily. He covered his mouth, apparently realizing the late hour, then shook his head. "No, no, no. That's not what I meant at all."

"Then what?" Gio's eyes narrowed.

"Oh, if you could see the look on your face." He laughed again, more softly this time. "Carmelina and Daniele are going to Rome for a wedding this next weekend. Why don't you tag along, and use the time to explore Rome's culinary scene, or visit your Aunt Valentina? We have enough miles for a coach seat. Stay for a week or two, and when you come back, you and I will talk to Diego together about making some changes around here."

Gio blinked twice, not believing his ears. "Are you serious?" It was just what he needed, a break from Ragazzi, and *Papà*. And the chance to dine at a bunch of restaurants in Rome. "Are you sure she won't mind me tagging along?"

"Not at all. I run it by her earlier today."

"Ran… oh, it doesn't matter. Thank you, *Babbo*." He threw his arms around Matteo. A Roman holiday. And when he got back, they would tackle *Mount Diego* together. A stray thought crossed his mind. "You sure you can handle the restaurant without me?"

Babbo laughed. "We'll manage, somehow. So, yes?"

"Yes!" He couldn't believe that by the weekend, he'd be in Rome. He'd visited there once with his mother, when he was nine years old, but never as an adult. He'd always dreamed of going, but there'd never been time.

"Then it's settled. I'll let your *Papà* know." Matteo got up to go.

Gio grabbed his hand and pulled him back. "What about the work thing? The one you said was keeping you up?"

"Oh, it was nothing. Just a little cash register matter."

Gio knew his *babbo* well enough to see that he was hiding something. But he also knew that it would do no good to try to pry it out of him before he was ready. Instead, he hugged Matteo tightly. "Thank you, *Babbo*."

Matteo kissed him lightly on the forehead. "I am so proud of you, *mio cucciolo*." With that, he left Gio alone once again. Alone, but no longer feeling so stuck.

He didn't even mind being called *my little puppy*.

He would pack in the morning, but for now he needed to sleep.

As if he could. *I'm going to Rome!*

23

TULIPS

"I don't know why you needed me today. I've got a lot to do for… well, just a lot to do."

Even though Gio was two steps behind him, Diego could almost hear his son's eyes rolling. "I asked you to come because I wanted your help. I intend to buy a lot for the restaurant today, and your *Papà's* back isn't getting any younger."

Gio snorted. "Neither is the rest of him."

"What?" Diego glared at his one and only child over his shoulder.

"Nothing, *Papà*." Gio hung his head.

Diego waved at the Salsa Sazona guys—he and Matteo secretly called the adorable gay couple the *Salsa Gays*—and tucked the tub of mango salsa in his backpack. That was for him and Matteo later.

Then he stopped at one of his favorite produce booths at the Downtown Farmers Market. "Better. Now help me find two dozen good onions." He turned away, hiding a smile from his son. In truth, he was very proud of the boy—well, he was a man, now. Giovanni was well into his third decade, after all. He'd taken on so much responsibility at Ragazzi, and Diego was worried he'd lose himself in the work and forget that everyone needed to have a personal life. *Porco cane, I feel that way myself sometimes.*

He lifted an onion and gave it a good sniff. It was firm and plump and had a heavenly aroma. Into the bag it went.

Gio joined him, sorting through the pile of white onions.

The late spring sun was warm on their backs, and the golden scaffolding of the Tower Bridge was sparkling in the mid-morning in the distance.

Diego loved coming to the farmers markets to buy the freshest of the season. Sacramento was a "foodie" town—one of those fun English words to say—in the heart of California's breadbasket. He almost always found the essentials there, and sometimes a little something extra and surprising. Like the dragon fruit he'd turned into an exquisite *semifreddo* the previous week.

Gio cleared his throat. "Did… *Babbo* talk with you?"

Diego kept his son waiting for a minute before responding. It was good for kids these days to learn patience.

He picked up another onion and turned it over. It had a soft spot on the underside where the fruit was bruised. He checked three more, and found another one he was satisfied with. *Into the bag with you.*

"*Papà…*"

"I heard you the first time." He winked at Gio to take the sting out of the words. "Yes, your *babbo* talked with me." Matteo had an easier relationship with Gio than he did. Diego supposed it was always harder when you were blood. So it had been with his own father.

"And?" Gio was practically bouncing with anticipation.

"And… I think it's a great idea. You have a good eye for things. You'll pick up a lot in Rome." He handed the bag to the vendor for weighing and moved on to look over the heirloom tomatoes. They were a riot of colors…. yellow ones, exotically striped green ones, orange ones… so many choices.

In Italy, they didn't like you touching the produce. Here, they encouraged it. Americans were wacky in so many ways, but in this one thing, he liked their way better.

"Seriously? That's all?" Gio bit his lip.

Diego glanced at his son. Something was eating at him, and he had a good idea what it was. "Say it." He selected a few close-to-ripe tomatoes that would make for a wonderful *caprese* salad.

Gio squeezed his hands together, looking down. "You never tell me when my ideas are good. You just bat them away like flies."

Diego sighed. *You're not wrong.*

He paid for the tomatoes and onions with cash. "Thank you. These will make some wonderful meals."

Artie Johnson grinned. The Central Valley farmer—all six-foot-four of him—was a regular at Ragazzi on Saturday nights when he was in town. "Such a pleasure to know that my work goes into your divine artistry." He handed Diego his change.

"Hope to see you tonight!" Diego took care of his vendors, giving them a steep discount when they dined at the restaurant.

Artie winked. "You can count on it. You two have a great day." Then he turned to help the next customer.

All the vendors on Capitol Mall gave him *un bel sconto*. He was a regular, an accomplished local chef, and he returned the favor when they wanted to stop by the East Sacramento restaurant that was well on its way to becoming a local institution.

He gestured to his son. "Come on. Follow me." Without looking to see if Gio was behind him, he set off toward a shady patch of asphalt next to the curb. Settling down—a little slower than he once would have, if he was honest—he patted the curb next to him.

Gio sat on his hands, long, lanky legs extended out, looking over at him uncertainly.

Diego switched over to Italian, the language they were both most comfortable with. "*Mio padre* was a good man to others. He worked for the city as a garbageman, picking up waste all over Bologna, helping to keep the city clean."

Gio stared at him. "You never talk about him."

Diego closed his eyes. "My father was also a bad man. He provided for his family, but he had a fierce streak of pride, and when he felt that someone had crossed him, he became angry. *Molto arrabbiato.*" He shivered, remembering hearing his father's voice raised against his mother, the horrible sound when he slapped her in the kitchen or threw her up against the wall, as Diego and his sisters cowered in their room together. Valentina would hold her hands over his ears and whisper over and over, "It's going to be all right."

Gio reached out and took his father's hand. "*Cazzo*. I had no idea."

Diego bit his lip and closed his eyes. "I don't like to think about that time. *Papà* died in a car accident when I was thirteen. Mamma moved us all to another town, south of Bologna, called Forlì, and took a job in a local restaurant there. She never took another husband, and she never spoke about *Papà*. It was like he never even existed."

His heart ached, remembering her. His three older sisters had closed around her like palace guards, never letting anyone get close enough to hurt her again. "I know you only met her once, at the wedding. But she was a beautiful woman. Radiant, when she stepped out of his shadow." Some of his favorite memories of his mamma were of her in the restaurant kitchen, rolling out pasta dough.

Diego nodded. "I liked her. I wish…"

"I know. She lived so far away." He should have gone back to see her more often. *I meant to.* But things were always so busy at Ragazzi and he'd found excuses not to go. And then, two years later, it had been too late.

Gio edged closer and put his arm around Diego. "She knew, *Papà*. She knew you loved her."

"I know she did." As you got older, regrets piled up for all the things you didn't do when you had the chance.

They sat there together for a bit like that, each lost in their own thoughts.

At last, Gio let him go. "But why tell me now?" His deep brown eyes —almost black—sought his father's.

You beautiful boy. "I didn't want you to grow up like I did. I mean, I didn't even know you existed until you were seventeen, so you were already cooked—"

Gio snickered.

Diego shook his head, smiling. "You know what I mean. I wanted to protect you. I thought of you as my little boy—"

"Not so little anymore." The edges of Gio's lips quirked upward.

"No. You're not. But I still see you like that gangly, lost seventeen-year-old you were when I met you. *Non sei così piccolo*." He squeezed Gio's shoulder. "I need to start seeing you as an adult. I need to start listening to you more."

Gio's eyes were wet. He wiped them with the back of his hand. "That… that would be good."

Diego laughed. "Yes. I think it would."

Gio's eyebrow arched. "So the franchise idea…?"

"Don't push it." Diego let go of his shoulder. "Go to Italy. Learn new things. Have some adventures. And when you get back, we'll talk about making some changes around here."

Gio's eyes lit up. "Really?"

"Really."

This time, Gio threw his arms around Diego and squeezed him so hard that his eyes almost popped out. "*Grazie mille, Papà. Ti voglio bene.*"

Diego hugged him back. "I love you too, *tesoro.*" *And I'm so proud of you.*

He got up, picking up the bags full of vegetables. "Come on. I want to pick out some fresh flowers for Ragazzi!"

"How about tulips this time?"

Diego started to tell him that he didn't like Tulips, that they were too plain. Then he stopped himself in his tracks. *I have to do better.* "Yes. Some tulips would be perfect."

24

AT THE GALLERY

Marissa dried her head with a fluffy white towel. Her hair was naturally a little curly—when she'd been in high school, she'd straightened it, but now she let it kink up a little. She'd also given up the bleached-blond look ages before, though sometimes she added a little purple, which complemented her brown hair nicely. *Adulting* had its perks.

Still, sometimes she missed those high school days. Not the *sleeping on the streets* part, or the small room she lived in at the back of Twink. The tattoo shop had closed a few years earlier when the landlord had decided to build some of those new toy-sized apartments that were so popular in Midtown. She hadn't seen the shop owner, Rex, in ages.

She still carried his work on her arms, though—a gorgeous rose-encrusted skull on her left bicep, and a stylish black cat on her right—and she and Tris had gotten matching tats together. *Another name from my past.*

No, what she missed was the sense of *something new* every day. Of possibility. The proximity to everything Sacramento had to offer. It was no San Francisco, but the River City had its own *big small town* charm. Living out in the suburbs, the world was often boring and gray.

She checked the time—just 8:15 AM. *Not bad.*

Ainsley's text had come out of the blue the night before, asking if she wanted to tag along to help set up for some kind of gallery opening.

Which was only fair—she'd sprung the Ragazzi cooking thing on Ainsley at the last minute too.

Marissa closed her eyes. She could still feel the heat of Ainsley's lips on hers. She rubbed her finger across them lightly, making them tingle.

She hadn't used any of her sick days yet at her new job, so she'd called into work and let them know she wasn't feeling well—*No, it isn't Covid. Yes, I tested*—and took the day off.

Slipping into a bright blue t-shirt and faded jeans and her gray Sketchers—this was a working date, after all—she was off to see her maybe, possibly, could-be new girlfriend.

~

The Red Roof Gallery was tucked away on one of Sacramento's back alleys —in an old converted home with a bright-red terracotta roof.

Marissa found a spot on 19th street, chucked in a handful of quarters— parking in Midtown and Downtown was so expensive now, and she wasn't sure if the new arena was worth it, not when she could park for free back home. *Living in the suburbs does have some advantages.*

A rented box truck took up half the alley, its lift-door up and metal ramp out. A small crew was carrying narrow crates down the ramp and through the door of the open gallery.

The front of the building was painted a bright, almost blinding white, surely meant to convey *edgy-fresh-new.* Marissa shielded her eyes and ducked inside, between workers carrying crates.

The place smelled new, too. The inside walls were as black as the outside was white, making the windows look like bright portals in a sea of darkness. The whole downstairs was one large room, except for a sectioned-off part at the back—she could see a refrigerator and part of a sink through the open door- way. A white staircase rose ghost-like out of the gloom toward the second floor.

"Marissa!" Ainsley came into view as Marissa's eyes adjusted to the darkness. "I'm so glad you came." She hugged Marissa and kissed her on the cheek, making her heart beat a little faster. "This is Alyn…" She pointed to a college-age guy with dirty blond hair who grinned as he was introduced.

"I know you!" He held out his hand and shook hers eagerly.

Marissa grinned. "Of course. You're Ricky's boyfriend!" She'd met him when she and Ricky had gone Christmas tree hunting the previous December.

"Sacramento really is a small town." Ainsley laughed. "Well, *I* met Alyn at University Art last week. He's an art major. I thought this would be good experience for him."

Marissa hid a frown. She hadn't counted on this being a group hang. "Who's the artist?"

Ainsley's face lit up like she'd been plugged into one of the painted-black wall sockets that were trying so hard not to be noticed near the floorboards. "Jun Seo Jang. They're amazing. That's them, next to Kelton, the gallery owner."

Marissa nodded automatically, as if she knew who this Jun Seo person really was. *The name does sound familiar…*

"All right everyone. How many of you have hung a show before?" Kelton stepped into the center of the gallery, under the bright light, like a carnival barker. He had a booming, take-charge voice that filled the small space.

Alyn raised his hand. So did Ainsley.

"I thought you were a biology major," Marissa whispered.

"I do some art too." She sounded a little defensive.

"Sorry." *I'm here just three minutes, and am already stepping in it.*

Kelton nodded. "Great. You there…" He checked his clipboard. "Ainsley Kim?"

She nodded and stepped forward, like in the military or something. "Yes sir." Mock salute and all.

"You'll be working directly with Mx. Jang. I'll leave it up to you to direct the others."

The artist smiled at them warmly. "Thank you for coming out to help. This is my first California show, and I really want it to go well." Their English was perfect. Like *school perfect.*

Why not choose San Francisco? Marissa figured they had their reasons. "You're welcome."

"Do you know my art?" They flashed a charming smile at her.

"Not that I'm aware of… maybe when I see it…?" *I should have looked them up this morning.*

"That I can help with." They turned to Ainsley. "Want to help me crack open these crates?"

The two of them picked up hammers and used them to gently pry open the first of the painting containers. They were more like pallets than crates, assembled around each piece to protect it from the vagaries of shipping. Soon the two of them had the first one freed from its confinement. They turned it around.

Marissa whistled. It was gorgeous.

The frame was ivory, or looked like it—she hoped it was fake. It would be stunning against the black walls.

The work itself seemed to glow. It was a streetscape at night, one with a distinctly Asian feel. Golden lanterns seemed to glow with a light of their own under red awnings and sloped roofs decked out in gray, green, and blue ceramic tiles.

"It's breathtaking." She *had* seen paintings like it before, somewhere… "Did you have a show in Chicago last year, by any chance?"

The artist smiled. "Yes, at the Korean Cultural Center. Were you there?"

She laughed. *What are the odds?* "Yes. I went there on a trip with my *nonna*—my grandma—and we were walking by after dinner and popped in to see the show. This one is exquisite."

"It's called *Jeonju at Night*." They seemed pleased.

Ainsley touched her arm, sending a shiver up her spine. "Aren't they amazing?"

"Yes." Did Ainsley have a little crush on the artist?

She squeezed Marissa's arm. "Alyn, you want to show 'Riss how we hang these? The spots are all marked."

She blinked. No one had called her "Riss" since her high school boyfriend Tris. She wasn't altogether sure how she felt about it. *I think I like it?* It showed that Ainsley was comfortable around her, at least.

"Sure. Come on." Alyn took her hand and whisked her along.

Ainsley was right. Each painting's location had a tacked sticky note with the title on it. Alyn grabbed the toolbox from one corner and proceeded to show her how to hang the first one.

The work was simple enough—measure, pound the nails, hang the piece, level it off—but the paintings were heavy and awkward, and by lunchtime Marissa was sweating and her back ached a little. Plus, the day was turning out to be far less *fun date* and far more *forced manual labor* than she had anticipated. Ainsley was busy with "The Artist," and she was stuck with sweet but young-seeming Alyn and his art chatter. She was considering backing out and heading home for the afternoon when Ainsley grabbed her hand.

"Come on!" She led Marissa toward the stairs.

"Where are we going?" She was ready for a break.

"Upstairs!"

She stuck out her tongue. "What's upstairs? I don't want to go upstairs. Why doesn't Alyn have to go upstairs?"

Ainsley ignored her pitch-perfect *Gilmore Girls* impersonation. "You'll see."

"Be careful… I'm a little creaky at the moment." Her leg muscles protested as she was dragged up the white stairs to the second floor.

"Just a little farther. I promise. Kel said we could use it." Her grin was infectious.

The second-floor walls were painted a bright red, with a black spiral staircase in the center.

"More stairs?" Marissa groaned.

Ainsley kissed her cheek. "Come *on*! It will be totally worth it."

Practically dragged up the narrow metal stairs, she bit her lip to keep from groaning.

There was a short landing up top, ending in a white door. Ainsley flung it open to reveal a wide terrace, bathed in dappled sunlight. In the middle was a bistro table, covered with a checkered tablecloth and topped with a vase, filled with bright golden sunflowers. "Ta-da!"

"What is this?" Marissa blinked in the bright light.

"It's the Red Roof terrace—they use it for the wine and cheese reception during the gallery shows, when the weather is good." She grinned. "Kel… Mr. O'Malley said we could have a private lunch up here." She knelt at a small cooler next to the door. "It's not much, but I brought sandwiches, potato chips, and sodas."

Marissa perked up. "So it's *not* a group hang?"

Ainsley looked over her shoulder. "What?"

"Never mind." She pulled Ainsley into her arms and planted a kiss on those delectable lips. "It's perfect." *Maybe I'm not such a terrible person after all.*

As if on cue, her phone buzzed in her pocket. She'd told work they could reach her on her cell, if necessary. She disentangled herself. "Let me just check this."

Ainsley grinned. "I'll get lunch set up."

It was a text. From Gio, of course. She rolled her eyes. *Why right now?* She was just starting to feel better about things. Reluctantly, she opened the app.

I'm going to Rome. Be happy for me.

Sha stared at it for a moment, and then a smile spread across her face. She *was* happy for him. She really was.

And she was happy for herself that he was happy.

Good luck! She texted back.

"Anything important?" Ainsley arched an eyebrow.

She shook her head. "Just an old friend with some good news." She snuggled up behind Ainsley, putting her arms around her waist, content. "Let's have lunch."

25

"I'M A VEGAN."

Ben climbed the old wooden steps of the Victorian house, and they groaned in protest under his feet. He hardly ever went upstairs as the flat he'd shared with Ella was on the ground floor. It was easier on her that way.

He carried the feast he'd brought home with him from Zocalo in his arms in a large paper bag—a huge steak burrito, an order of chicken enchiladas Guanajuato, and sides of beans, rice and chips and salsa. It was all cold now, but would warm up fast enough in the microwave.

He wasn't sure exactly what it was about Lorelei that had caught his attention, but it had latched onto him immediately. His memories of Ella, though far from banished, had receded into the background, leaving him thinking almost constantly of the beautiful blonde in the wheelchair who lived above him.

There was something *real* about her, something authentic. She wasn't some fantasy girl. She was here, nearby, and she had seemed open and friendly with him. *At least, the one time we met.*

This is stupid. She's not expecting you. What was he thinking, showing up unexpected like this? She might be in the middle of a bath, or cooking dinner or… with other company. He paused in the dim light of the stairway. In truth, he almost turned around and headed back down the stairs.

She'd mentioned that her kids were with her on weekends, which suggested a divorced ex. What if he'd come over with a bottle of wine, ready to rekindle their old romance?

If you don't go up and knock, you'll never know. Besides, Chester—Miz Fortune—had told him Lorelei was the right one for him. But how much stock should he put into a psychic drag queen's word?

It won't be an easy path. But happiness awaits you, if you're brave enough to try.

The opportunity had seemed almost too perfect. He'd been off early that evening, and someone had neglected to pick up their phone-in order, and Miz Fortune had all but told him to go for it...

You always do this. Ella's voice whispered in his ear. If she'd told him once, she'd told him a thousand times. He needed to believe in himself.

Ben closed his eyes. *Do I always do this? Question things to death?* He banged the back of his head against the wall. *The worst she can say is no.*

Lorelei was in a wheelchair. Did it matter? He was transgender. Ella had Fahr's Disease. Everyone had a *thing*.

"Ella's right, you know. You do *always* do this."

Ben blinked.

A man with short brown hair, wearing a white button-down shirt, blue tie, and gray slacks was looking down at him from the landing above, silhouetted by the yellow light of the single lightbulb screwed into the ceiling behind him..

He knew that voice. "Brad?" *Not again.* He was starting to doubt his sanity.

The man grinned. "In the… well, not exactly flesh. Let's just call it 'making my final rounds.'"

"I thought you already had?" Ben rubbed his eyes with his free hand. *I must be more tired than I thought.*

Still, Brad had led him to Miz Fortune, hadn't he?

Ben glared at him, but Brad refused to disappear. "Why do you keep bothering me?"

"Because you're alone. Lonely. You want to be whole again. Like Sam and I were." A shadow passed over his face.

"Fine. What do you want?" If Brad was going to haunt him, the man —ghost?—could at least get to the point.

"Are you going to let your nerves get the better of you? Or are you going to go knock on this nice woman's door and woo her with slightly cold Mexican food?" Brad indicated Lorelei's door on the landing at the top of the stairs.

"It's… You're not… I must be…" Ben felt faint. He grasped at the old, scarred wooden railing and took a ragged breath. When he looked up again, Brad was gone. *I'm losing my everlasting mind.*

Still, the voices in his head were right. He needed to try something different. *It's time.*

Steeling himself, he pushed ahead to the top of the stairs, crossed the short intervening space to her door, and knocked.

"Who is it?" The voice was a little muffled by the thick wooden door.

His heart thudded a little faster. *It's her.* "Me. Um, Ben, from downstairs?"

A short pause. "Just a second."

He swore he heard that old *elephant thumping* sound. Was someone else walking around in her apartment? Maybe hiding in the closet, before she let him in? It was a ridiculous idea, but there it was. Once he thought it, he couldn't *unthink* it.

The door creaked open at last. "Hi Ben. What can I do for you?" She looked much more put together than she had the week before. Less frazzled—her hair brushed and tied in a ponytail, her brow unlined.

"I got off work at Zocalo a bit early tonight. I brought over a few things… I thought you might be hungry?" He looked over her head at the apartment for any signs that someone else was there.

She laughed. "Oh, that's lovely. I didn't know you worked there. What did you bring?"

His heart, which had slowed to almost normal-human levels, accelerated again at the brightness of her smile. "Um, a steak burrito, chicken enchiladas… some chips and stuff…"

Her smile disappeared. "Ben, I'm a vegan."

Crap. He hadn't even considered the possibility. *Stupid stupid stupid.* "Well… there's still the beans. And rice. Though I'd have to check and see if the beans have any—"

Her impish grin stopped him in his tracks. "I'm just pulling your leg. Oh, the look on your face…" She chuckled. "I love steak. *And* chicken."

She wheeled back a bit. "Come on in. You can put it on the kitchen table."

He stepped inside. "I've never been in this unit before. It's nice." The walls were painted a soothing avocado green, The furniture, although a bit mismatched, was all in good shape, and there were paintings on every wall, all in a similar style.

"Make a right into the kitchen." She rolled after him. "And thanks. I moved in two years ago, after the divorce. How long have you been here?"

"About eight years. My fiancée and I moved in together." He passed through the galley kitchen into a dining nook and put the bag down on the square wooden table that was scooted up against the far wall, under a painting of a bright red vase filled with sunflowers.

"What's her name?" There was just enough room for her to scoot into the nook beside him. He stepped aside to give her a little space.

"Ella. It was. She passed away a couple years ago." *All my fault.* He couldn't seem to think of her without mentally appending those three words.

Lorelei frowned. "I'm so sorry. Losing someone… it's hard. Even when it's just a divorce."

He gestured toward the painting. "That's lovely. Where did you get it?"

"I painted it. Art keeps me busy now that I…" She trailed off, gesturing to the chair.

He had questions—how had she gotten injured? How long had she been in the chair? Was that why her husband had divorced her? None of them were appropriate for asking someone you'd only met twice. "Ah. I see."

She leaned toward the paper bag and took a deep breath. "That smells heavenly. Thank you so much for bringing me dinner—I was getting hungry. I'll have to save some of it for the kids this weekend. They love Mexican."

Ben blinked. "Oh. Yes. I thought… Of course. Happy to help." He'd planned to have that dinner with her, but he couldn't come out and say that. Especially after she had basically just shown him the door with her words. "Just throw it in the microwave for a minute. Make sure you take the burrito out of the foil…" His gaze strayed to the kitchen. The appliance in question was one of those hood-mounted ones.

"I will. Thanks again. Let me know if I can return the favor somehow."

"Do you need any help?" He glanced at her chair, and back up at the microwave. Perhaps he could salvage the evening with a little assistance, which might lead to an offer to stay...

She must have seen his confusion. "Oh no, I've figured out all the tricks. Thank you for offering, though!" She edged the chair forward a couple inches.

Ben took the hint. "Perfect. Have a great night, then." *I'm such an idiot.*

"Oh and Ben?"

He hovered at the doorway, hopeful she'd changed her mind. "Yes?"

"You have a great night too."

"You too." *Stupid. You already said that.* He fled as quickly as he was able to without looking like a fool, trying to retain a little dignity. Down the stairs, back to the safe confines of his own apartment.

Stupid, stupid, stupid. Ella, Miz Fortune, and the ghost of Brad had been wrong, after all. *I'm better off here in my safe place, by myself.*

He threw a frozen Thai green curry meal from Trader Joe's into his own microwave—strange that she didn't need help with that. In fact, very little seemed to be set at wheelchair height in her apartment, now that he thought about it.

He turned on the TV, looking for some comfort streaming. *Heartstopper*, or maybe *Emily in Paris*?

He pulled a quarter out of his pocket and flipped it.

Paris it is.

He frowned when he thought he heard footsteps upstairs, through the ceiling. He paused the show, ear cocked. *Nothing.*

Then the microwave went off, beeping insistently for his attention, and he forgot all about it.

26

WET ADHD

Marcos stared at the screen, scrolling through line after line after line of job postings. His eyes actually *hurt* from staring at the screen for so long.

All these big job sites were the same—thousands upon thousands of job listings, and exactly none of them right for him. On top of that, there was no way to filter them properly. No matter what he tried to do, they kept showing him jobs for *doctors* and *lawyers* and *architects*, even though he was a web designer and sometime-programmer.

It was frustrating—doubly so since he'd kept from Dave just how bad things had gotten with their own business. Clients were dropping like flies, as Big Search Engine and Generative AI finished eating what was once the world wide web and spat out its dead, rotting carcass.

Marcos chuckled, shaking his head. *That's grim, even for you.*

Still, it was true. Web traffic was down for almost everyone, as search engines switched over to AI summaries that provided all the information (and a fair share of virtual hallucinations) without ever sending the user to the website where the information came from.

Who did they think was going to maintain all those directories and info sites, once they drove everyone else out of business?

Dave's head popped into the room. "About ready for dinner? Marissa should be here in about five minutes."

Marcos hurriedly switched screens, hoping his husband hadn't seen what was on his monitor. Dave had a habit of popping into the office unannounced. *Why wouldn't he?*

They owned the place together, after all.

"Just wrapping up. Be there in a minute." He blew his husband a kiss.

"Make sure it's a real minute, and not one of those half-hour ones you like to take." Dave leaned over and kissed his forehead.

A heavenly smell wafted in through the open door behind him.

Marcos sighed. Even if he couldn't find other work right away, they'd be okay for a while. They had some money in the bank, and he could probably pick up some odds and ends to generate a little income. But if he didn't find a real job soon, one with benefits... especially since the cost of the whole healthcare thing had almost killed them, even with Obama Care.

And if the election went the wrong way... he shuddered.

Pushing down his fear, he switched back to the jobs page and closed it, and then deleted his search history. Then he went to find his husband and the source of that delicious aroma.

Marissa knocked at her parents' front door. Pop and Dad—aka Marcos and Dave—had taken her in when she'd had no one else, and ever since, she'd been like a daughter to them.

It was a work night, and she'd just as soon have stayed home to veg in front of her laptop, watching a movie virtually with a couple old friends. But something in Dave's voice had made her say *yes*.

The door swung open, and Marcos swept her up into his arms. "Welcome home!"

She laughed. "What's... whatever this is... for?"

"Can't I greet my prodigal daughter when she returns home from the hinterlands?" He let her go and gestured for her to come inside.

She scrunched up her nose in delight, and kissed his cheek. "Of course you can. You're just not usually so enthusiastic. Where's Dad?"

"Your favorite gay father is in the kitchen. Where else?" He winked at her.

"Is that *calabacitas*?" Her mouth began to water as she followed him—and the scent—into the kitchen. As long as she'd known him, he'd lived in the same condo.

"Of course it is." Dave set down his wooden spoon just long enough to hug her. He was dressed in his David apron, complete with stone micro penis. "Thank you for coming on such short notice. Grab a seat there next to Marcos. This is just about ready."

She did as she was told, sinking down into one of the comfortable chairs, their royal blue cushions only slightly faded with age.

Marcos sat beside her, putting a hand on her forearm. "So thrilled you are here."

How many hours had she spent at this very table, doing homework, both at McClatchy High and later as she'd attended American River College before going to Sac State? And then during the pandemic.

Her index finger traced the lightning-shaped scratch in the dark finish that had been her long-time companion during those endless nights.

"Here we are." Dave ladled some of the hearty soup into their bowls. With the pot safely stashed back on the stove, he plopped down a basket filled to almost overflowing with warm flour tortillas. "Simple, I know, but I hope you like it."

She grabbed a tortilla and dipped it into the soup. One bite, and savory warmth spread through her. "This is delicious. Can I get you to come out to my place every night to cook?"

Dave snorted. "You couldn't afford me."

"Now we know what it takes to get our daughter to come visit us." Marcos laughed and elbowed Dave, who smiled, but slowly.

Something's up. The invitation, the dinner, the strange looks…

She filled the rest of the tortilla with zucchini, onions, bell peppers, and cheese, holding it carefully over the bowl so any extra broth would drain back into it. All the while, she watched her Dad.

He was eating, but slowly, almost reluctantly. Every now and then, something tugged at the right side of his lip. He seemed lost in thought.

Dave had always been a bit introspective, but this felt… different.

Marcos's eyes met hers. He'd noticed it too. "Spill it."

Dave blinked. "What?"

Marcos's eyes narrowed. "You asked Marissa to come over. You made a special dinner. Now you're barely eating it. It's like we're walking on eggshells with you today. Something's on your mind. So spill it."

Dave put down his spoon with a sigh. "I was hoping to have a nice dinner with you before I told you—"

"Are you dying?" Marissa didn't mean to blurt it out, but her friend Tessa's mother had told her family she had inoperable cancer, at a family dinner just like this one.

"What? No, of course not." Dave reached out to squeeze her hand with his free one.

"Then what?" She stared at him.

Dave sat back, resting his hands on his belly, and sighed. "The doctors told me that I have wet AMD."

~

"I have wet AMD." There. He'd finally said it. It felt good to let it out into the open.

"Wet ADHD?" Marissa asked, at the same time that Marcos said, "Wet Andy?" They both looked at him quizzically.

He laughed in spite of himself. "'Wet age-related macular degeneration.' It basically means my eyesight is getting worse fast." His secret had been eating at him for months, along with worries about the upcoming election and what it might mean for his family. At least this was one issue he could do something about.

"Are you... okay?" Marcos took his hand. "How long have you known?"

Am I? How did you deal with a diagnosis of eventual blindness? "Officially? Just a couple days—since Monday. I'm sorry I didn't say anything. I didn't want you to worry." He squeezed Marcos's hand in reassurance. "Unofficially? I noticed my vision started getting blurrier a couple months back. Even my glasses didn't seem to help all that much. At first, I thought it was just lack of sleep."

Marissa was staring at him intently. "Are you going blind?"

He forced a smile. It was the typically blunt kind of question she often asked.

"Yes. But there are treatments. The blood vessels at the back of my eyes have gotten a little leaky, that's all. They're giving me a monthly shot to help slow down my vision loss."

"So how do we fix it?" That was so Marcos, jumping straight to the solution.

Dave shook his head. "We don't. It's not reversible. All they can do is slow it down." As he said it, it truly hit him for the first time. *I'm going blind.*

Never to see the sunlight sparkling over the American River. No more brightly colored flowers, puffy-white-cloud skies, drops of dew on a spider's web. No more Marcos or Marissa. He squeezed his husband's hand tightly.

They sat together in silence for a moment. Then Marissa got up and threw her arms around him. "I'm sorry, Daddy." She nestled her face in his neck.

He closed his eyes, feeling the warmth of her arms and spirit. *I can get through this.* "I'm a lucky guy. I have you two."

Marcos leaned forward and kissed him. "Thank you for telling us. I noticed that you seemed worried these last few weeks. I just thought… I'm sorry I didn't say something."

Marissa let him go and settled back into her chair.

He had one more secret to tell. "It's all right. You've had your hands busy with your job search." He'd been saving that one for weeks.

Marcos's jaw almost hit the table. "What… You knew?"

Dave nodded. "You're not exactly a world-class spy, you know. You left your browser window open last week. Besides, it's not much of a secret that we can't keep doing this website thing forever." He took Marcos's hands in his again and held them tight. "We'll figure it all out, together."

Marissa snorted. "You two are such a mess. I don't know why I ever thought that gay couples had it more together than the rest of us…"

Dave laughed. It felt good to let it all out. "No, we most decidedly do not." He looked down at their cold meals. "Let me run those through the microwave. That is, if y'all are still hungry?" He needed a little *normal,* while he could still have it.

He was greeted with two enthusiastic *yesses*.

27

BACK IN SAC

The last of the rice fields disappeared behind them as the plane descended toward the tarmac. Sam held his breath, remembering the first time he'd made this trip from Tucson to Sacramento a decade before, to work in Brad's office—for a Republican Senator, no less. Such a thing would be all but unthinkable now.

He'd landed in the River City, amazed at all the greenery—from the plane, the place looked like a forest, with not one but two great winding rivers meeting in a flux of churning waters not far from downtown.

"You okay?" In the next seat, Oscar's dark eyes reflected concern.

"Yes. No. I don't know." How could anyone be okay, after they'd lost their heart mate? He'd been struggling at times just to remember to breathe.

"I'll bet a lot has changed since you lived here." Oscar scratched the dark hair of his neatly trimmed beard thoughtfully.

Distraction. Good. "Yeah, probably. Brad and I left—" He closed his eyes at a stab of pain. "We left Sactown about eight years ago. I'm sure a lot of it is different now." His mother had needed help, and Brad had seemed happy for a change of scene. Since then, there'd been *that man* in the White House, a pandemic, and now another election coming.

There was a slight bump, then another, and they were gliding smoothly along the runway toward the distant terminal.

"Thank you for flying Southwest. You may now turn on your personal electronic devices." The gay flight attendant sounded inordinately cheerful. Sam smothered his urge to get up and smack him.

He pulled his iPhone out and powered it up, waiting impatiently for the home screen to appear. Ten seconds later, Carmelina's message popped up.

Waiting in the remote lot. Let me know when you touch down, darlin'. :)

He smiled despite himself. The one thing he was looking forward to was seeing his Ragazzi Club friends again.

When the plane rolled to a stop at the gate, he jumped up and opened the overhead compartment, pulling down the duffel bag that held the urn with Brad's ashes. *We're here, handsome.*

He wished this homecoming was happier.

～

Forty-five minutes later, they were waiting by the curb when Carmelina pulled up in her silver Honda Pilot. The take-no-prisoners red-head popped out of the car and practically ran to embrace him. "Well, look what we have here. It's about damned time." She hugged him. "I'm so sorry about Brad."

"Thank you." Sam hugged her back and then let her go. "Carmelina, this is my friend Oscar, the one I told you about on the phone."

Oscar bobbed his head. "Nice to meet you." His big hand dwarfed Carmelina's, and she was not a small woman.

"Come here." She pulled him in for a hug too. "Any friend of Sam's is a friend of mine."

Poor Oscar's eyes almost bulged out of their sockets as she squeezed him tightly. "Helllp meee."

Sam chuckled, and immediately felt bad for letting a cheerful emotion ruin his grieving. *How long until it's all right to feel happiness again?* "You get used to it. *Cara mia*, can I throw our bags in the trunk?"

"Of course. Just push around the crap back there." She opened the back door and gestured for Oscar to climb inside.

Sam lifted the hatch and stared at the revealed chaos in dismay. There were half a dozen empty Trader Joe's bags shoved up against the back seat. Three umbrellas in various shades of pink—one of them busted up pretty badly—held the middle ground, nestled between two unopened Amazon boxes. And at the front was a haphazardly-folded Sac State Hornets sweatshirt, a pair of paint-stained jeans, two pairs of muddy sneakers, and—randomly—a well-thumbed copy of *Eat, Pray, Love.*

Sam moved as much of it as he could to the sides and back of the gray-carpeted space, and managed to wedge their two suitcases in between in a fragile détente.

He kept the duffel in his hands and closed the hatch, and climbed into the back seat with Oscar.

Carmelina pinched him. "Come on, sit up front with me. We'll have half an hour to do a little catch up before we get home. Oscar, do you mind?"

His friend shook his head. "I've got emails to check for work."

With a shrug, Sam changed seats.

Carmelina shot him an inquisitive look.

"Oscar's trying to open a new LGBTQ+ center in Tucson. Wingspan closed in 2015, and the Thornhill-Lopez Center closed during the pandemic." He'd first met Oscar through Brad, who had been helping out with his experience from running the Sacramento LGBT Center. Thinking about Brad brought back Sam's crushing grief. He bit his lip and stared out the passenger window, trying to keep a lid on it.

"Ah." She started the car, and soon they were zooming their way through the airport's confusing collection of winding roads. Carmelina took them as a personal challenge, whizzing in and around other cars like a racecar driver. "Is that… him?" She glanced at the duffel bag in his lap.

Sam rested a hand on the cool curve on the steel urn inside. "Yes. It's so strange. I wasn't… He shouldn't have…" Tears welled up in his eyes and he wiped them away angrily. *I've cried enough.*

She reached over and squeezed his shoulder.

"Watch out!" An RV had just pulled in front of him, going half their speed.

"I've got it." She jerked the car to the left, missing the behemoth's bumper by five inches.

Sam closed his eyes and breathed in and out slowly to calm his racing heart.

Soon they were flying around the cloverleaf onramp and merging into southbound traffic on Highway 5. The skyscrapers of Sacramento's downtown appeared on the horizon like giant tombstones.

"So Sam and I were talking about what might have changed since he lived here." Oscar's cheerful voice broke the silence.

Sam was grateful for the interruption.

"Well, let's see." Carmelina crossed a couple lanes without a signal, heading for the Highway 50 interchange. "Fifty's a mess. They've been widening it for what seems like decades, and they split each direction into two parts for a couple miles just east of downtown." She shot over another lane, and someone behind them honked. "Oh go fuck yourself."

Despite himself, despite his grief, Sam laughed out loud, all the while hanging on tightly to the handle above the door.

Oscar was glancing nervously out the back window. "Aren't you worried they might have a gun?"

"Not here in Sacramento." She waved away the concern. "Oh, and the A's are coming here."

"For a game?" Sam was proud of the fact that he knew the A's were a baseball team. *Aren't they?*

"No, for a few years. They're moving up to Vegas, but they didn't start on their stadium yet, so they'll be playing at Raley Field… I mean, Sutter Health Park."

Sam groaned. "Do corporations have to plaster their names over everything?"

"Yup. The convention center's now the SAFE Credit Union Convention Center, and the Music Circus Theater is now the UC Davis Health Pavillion. Hell, I'd let them call my house the Bank of America Certificate of Deposit Estate if they paid me a couple million dollars."

Oscar chortled.

Sam looked down as she passed a semi and cut in front of it hard. "I was hoping to go to Lucca one night while we're here. They have the best gnocchi. The manager's gay, and the dining patio is amazing—"

"Closed during the pandemic." She scurried around the long curving connector to Highway 50, slamming on the brakes when another car cut her off. "Nice driving!"

"Okay, then, Café Vinoteca. They have great Italian food—"

"Closed by a fire." They shot back onto the highway, and Carmelina cut across four lanes to the fast lane, driving like she was Mario Andretti.

Sam held on for dear life, praying to whomever might be listening that they would make it safely to her house. When he caught his breath, he tried again. "How about Roxy? Their stuffed bell peppers—"

"Nope. Shut down a couple years ago."

"Biba's? The chef is this wonderful Italian woman, and she stops by your table—"

"She passed away before the pandemic. Alzheimer's, I think. The restaurant didn't last long after her death." They crossed three lanes again and swerved onto the connector with Northbound Business 80.

Sam closed his eyes and tried to convince his stomach to stay in his gut. He texted Oscar. *We'll take an Uber back to the airport when we leave.*

His friend snorted.

"So what is still open?" There had to be something he remembered.

"Let's see. Zocalo—there are four of them now, including one near the house. Ben still works at the one downtown. There's Café Bernardo and Paragary's... though Randy Paragary passed away about three years back. Mayahuel, Trattoria Bohemia, Zinfandel Grill... There are a few of the old faves still in business."

Sam fell silent. So much had changed. So many of his favorite places were gone.

They finally slipped off the freeway, and were soon gliding down H Street under the shade of its many lovely trees—redwoods, elms, oaks, box elders, pines—planted like guardians on both sides of the street. This part of town hadn't changed. The essential character of Sacramento remained.

"How about Ragazzi?" He had fond memories of his time with Brad there, and their friends.

Carmelina smiled. "It's doing better than ever. Gio wants to franchise it, but Diego keeps putting him off." Now that they were off the freeway, she seemed to have reverted to *normal driver mode*.

"Gio?" Oscar's eyebrow arched.

"Different one." To Carmelina, he explained, "We have a friend named Gio back in Tucson, too."

"Ah. He's a good kid. He's coming to Rome with us tomorrow. I think Diego just wants to get him out of his hair for a bit."

"Kid? He's gotta be…" He frowned.

"Twenty-six. And yes, that's still a kid to me. Even though I'm still just twenty-nine." She batted her eyes.

"For the thirtieth time?"

She snorted. "Hey, watch it. You're into your thirties now, aren't you?"

"Maybe." He bit his lip.

At last, they entered River Park. As they drove up Carlson, he noticed a few changes—a new mini-apartment building. A garden mural on one of the school's walls. But mostly things looked the same here too. "Is that red-headed crossing guard still here?"

"Shelley?" Carmelina frowned. "No, we lost her to cancer during the pandemic. She was a beautiful soul."

So much loss. So many changes.

Still, it felt good to be back in his adopted hometown.

He squeezed the duffel bag tightly. *Brad, we're coming home.*

28

RED-TAILED HAWK

As the car turned the corner onto Carmelina's street, something unexpected happened—a cheer went up from people lining the street on both sides.

Sam stared out the window, unsure what he was seeing. "What's this?"

Carmelina inched the car down the road, giving him a good look at the gathered crowd.

He recognized a few of the faces… kids from the LGBT Center, now grown. People from the Ragazzi Club. Even Jim Oberkrom, their old neighbor. "Carmelina, what did you do?"

"You know these folks?" Oscar's voice was subdued.

"Yes, I think I know every one of them." He glanced over his shoulder —the people behind them were crowding onto the street, following the car.

They pulled into her driveway, and Carmelina put on the brake and turned off the engine. "I just told a few folks that Brad was gone. They did the rest." Her gaze met his. "I hope you don't mind…"

You did this for me? "Mind? Oh my god, this is amazing. Brad… he would have been crying by now." He wiped the corners of his eyes, hoping she hadn't noticed that he was.

"I don't know if you had plans for a memorial?" For maybe the first time since he'd met her, she sounded hesitant.

"No. I just wanted to scatter his ashes by the river." He closed his eyes. *This is it.* He'd done what he promised and had brought Brad home. In a short time, it would be done, and Brad would be gone forever… *Just hold it together, Sam.*

She leaned over to hug him. "Good. We'd like to join you, if that's all right. Brad had a lot of people here who loved him." She smelled of lavender.

He nodded wordlessly. With a deep breath to steady his nerves, he opened the door, laying the duffel carefully on the seat behind him, and stood to meet the crowd.

It was a beautiful May day in Sacramento. The air was fresh, a slight breeze that caressed his skin, raising goosebumps on his forearms, and thin white clouds streaked the cerulean sky. The giant redwood trees in her front yard provided shade from the bright sun, and the noise from the people around him subsided to a dull murmur as they waited for him to take the lead.

Carmelina and Oscar got out of the car behind him.

Sam looked around at the crowd and spied the one person he hoped would be there the most. "Ricky!"

The boy he and Brad had fostered edged forward nervously, his face alternating between a frown and a grin. "Hey Sam." He was taller, handsome, his pink hair neatly trimmed.

Sam swept him up in his arms. *Not a boy anymore.* He was, what, twenty-five now? They'd kept in touch sporadically through the years. "I'm so glad you're here."

"Yeah?" Ricky let go. "I'm so sorry about Brad—"

"Don't be. He loved you. You were like a son to him." The falling out when Ricky decided not to go to college… that had been hard on both of them.

"He was so angry…" Ricky looked down at his feet.

Sam shook his head vehemently. "He only wanted you to have the most out of life. He loved you, *mijo*. You look so big… so handsome." How had they let so much time pass without seeing each other? "What are you doing now?"

"I have a job at the Center, helping kids like me."

Sam's chest swelled with pride. "That's perfect. I'm so happy for you."

Ricky beamed. "Thanks." He looked over his shoulder and gestured at someone.

Another young man stepped out of the crowd. He was a little taller than Ricky. Poor kid must have had a bad case of acne as a teenager, but he had a bright, if sheepish, smile. "This is my boyfriend, Alyn."

"Boyfriend, huh?" Sam raised an eyebrow.

Alyn held out his hand.

Sam shook it, looking back and forth between the two. "I'm proud of you, Ricky." *I have to do better keeping in touch from now on.*

His former foster son blushed. "Thanks. Maybe we can get together later?"

"Of course. I'll text you." He hugged Ricky once more, and then looked around at all the other expectant faces. "Thank you all for coming. Brad… he would have loved this."

It was as if a dam burst, and they all surged forward at once. Sam found himself in the midst of a sea of friendly faces, greeting people he knew, and some he just kind of remembered, every one of them bringing him love, a warm hug, and a few kind words about Brad.

There were so many of them. He took time to greet each one, and received about a million hugs in return.

"Okay, everyone." Carmelina's voice rang out over the crowd once everyone had had a chance to say hello. "We'll have a barbeque back here afterwards. But right now we need to get on the road. We'll go first, then y'all follow. See you at the Effie Yeaw Center." With that she ushered Sam and Oscar back to the car.

This time, Sam took the back seat with Oscar, holding the duffel bag in his arms. Oscar took his hand and squeezed it. Sam flashed him a half-smile.

Daniele joined them, climbing into the front seat next to Carmelina. "So sorry, Sam. Brad was a great guy. He was really loved."

"Thanks." He'd never been close to Carmelina's partner, but Daniele seemed like a good enough guy.

Watching the crowd—there had to be a couple hundred folks—stream back to their cars, Sam could feel how much love there was here for his husband.

He bit his lip, holding back the torrent of emotion building in his chest, as Carmelina's car pulled back out onto the street and set off toward the sanctuary, followed by a long line of others.

Yes, Brad would have loved this.

The somber motorcade pulled out onto Carlson Drive, a parade of cars of various kinds—including a couple Priuses, a red Tesla, three minivans, a lime-green Fiat, a red Smart Car, a red and black mini, a Vespa scooter, and many more than Sam could see to count.

Neighbors came out to see the procession as it wound its way through River Park, pointing at the unusual sight. Carmelina had to stop for a couple minutes as a flock of wild turkeys—thirty of them, including ten chicks—crossed the street in front of them.

"They're amazing." The sight reminded him of Brad's love of nature in all its forms.

"They shit everywhere." Carmelina grinned in the rearview mirror.

"Touché."

They made their way down past Fremont Church and the Scottish Rite Center, where there was always a rock and gem show going on, and by the Sac State entrance.

"I can't believe so many people came out." Sam hugged the duffel bag tightly.

Oscar put a hand on his shoulder. "Brad touched so many people. It was the same way back home."

Sam nodded. They'd held a candlelight vigil the night before at Tohono Chul park, one of Brad's favorite places in Tucson, and over a hundred folks had come to see them off.

The caravan proceeded across the H Street Bridge—now renamed the Tara O'Sullivan Bridge. *When did that happen?*

They passed high above the American River. The watercourse was less than half its usual flow, the water tumbling down from Folsom Dam up near the foothills to rush past on its way to merge with the Sacramento River. Sam stared at the churning waters, a suitable companion for the churning in his soul.

They made good time heading up Fair Oaks Boulevard, passing the new shops at The Boulevard and University Village, the expensive looking brick buildings of the Pavillions, and Loehmann's Plaza.

In another ten minutes, they were turning off the busy regional connector onto Oak Avenue, into the quiet neighborhood that snuggled up against the north side of the American River.

A sudden thought struck Sam, sending him into a panic. "Hey, don't we need a permit—"

Daniele shook his head. "All taken care of."

He sat back and closed his eyes, relieved, but at the same time still feeling antsy. Soon it would be done. Brad's ashes would be scattered, and Sam would be… free? Resigned?

Forced to figure out what to do next with his life. Despite the fact that Brad was seven years older, he'd never considered what he would do once his husband was gone. Brad hadn't even been forty, for god's sake. *How could you leave me?*

The doctors had said something about a previously undiscovered heart defect. It made no sense to him. Brad was one of the healthiest people Sam knew. He always took care of himself, working out, eating healthy… Once he'd caught Sam sneaking a bag of Oreos into his writing cave, and he hadn't heard the end of it for a week. *What will I do now?*

Carmelina had Daniele. Ricky had Alyn. It seemed like everyone else had someone to love them. To be there at night when the trials of the day were just too much to bear. To call them on their shit.

Oscar squeezed his hand. "You okay in there?"

Sam opened his eyes. "Not even a little."

The car pulled into the parking lot, shaded by massive oak trees. Carmelina turned around in her seat, putting her hand on his knee. "You ready, darling?"

Sam took a deep breath and nodded. "Ready as I'll ever be." He got out of the car, taking the duffel bag with him. All around them, others were arriving, parking their vehicles and emerging from them silently. No one said a word. It was as if this were sacred ground, and everyone knew that to speak would break the spell.

With a heavy sigh, Sam turned toward the path that led up to the Nature Center, and his friends fell in behind him. He felt like Moses leading his people out of Egypt to the Promised Land. *I doubt the waters will part for me, though.*

The path wound through the trees, their dappled light creating a patchwork of brown earth and golden yellow grass. Things were a bit dry already with the advent of summer, but the air still held that unmistakable scent of *forest*, even if the trees were separated here and there by open meadows. It was remarkable that such a place existed, so close to the hustle and bustle of Sacramento. He and Brad used to go there for long walks on Sunday mornings, marveling at the deer, hawks, and other wildlife that populated the little slice of land alongside the American River.

They passed the two buildings that comprised the center itself, and a sign that said:

"This is a protected nature study area. Take only memories. Leave only footprints."

Sam glanced at the duffel sack he carried with his right hand. He'd be leaving something more than footprints today.

The people behind him had started to speak softly among themselves, a low murmur like the babble of a brook. Sam didn't mind. It made the whole thing feel a little less weird.

At last, they reached his favorite spot near the northeastern part of the nature refuge, where some of the trees grew right on the riverbank, dangling their roots in the water. It was usually quiet and peaceful, but that afternoon someone was mowing their lawn in the neighborhood that bordered the preserve to the north. As the crowd filed around him in a half-circle, the sound faded away, leaving them with just the cawing of crows in the trees and the tumbling of the water behind him.

Sam looked around. His closest friends were all there. Carmelina and Daniele. Marissa and her new friend. Ricky and Alyn. Dave and Marcos. Diego and Matteo. And Ben. He'd lost Ella last year—he would understand how Sam was feeling, more than most.

Sam set down the duffel on a wide rock, took a deep breath, and found the words he wanted to say. "Thank you for being here. Brad loved Sacramento. He loved all of you. If he were here today…" His voice cracked, betraying him, and he closed his eyes. A deep breath and Oscar's hand on his shoulder steadied him. He opened his eyes again, and saw his own tears mirrored in the faces of his friends… his *logical family*. "This place was special to him. When it was sunny out, and not too goddamned *Sacramento hot…*"

The audience chuckled, many of them wiping their eyes.

"…we would pack a picnic lunch and come down here to watch the water tumble by. I remember once that he told me how it fascinated him to think of where it came from. Where it was going. 'It's like our lives—starting as rain from the ocean, falling somewhere upstream, and carrying us past so many new places and people, only to end up back in the depths, where the water runs deep with knowledge of the past.'"

He closed his eyes, remembering the moment. Brad had touched his cheek as he said that, pulling him in close for a kiss. "You are my ocean."

Sam didn't share that last part—it belonged to him and him alone. Instead, he knelt next to the duffel bag, zipping it open.

Someone sniffled in the crowd.

He pulled out the urn—a beautiful black ceramic vase wrapped with a swirling rainbow band—and stood, cradling it carefully in his arms. He approached the nearest tree—a young oak—removed the lid, and knelt to scrape out a hollow space in the loamy soil all the way around the base of the trunk with his free hand. "I hope you'll like it here, love." He hugged it for a moment, and then sprinkled the ashes as evenly as he could around the circle as his friends crowded around him.

When the urn was empty, he stared at the little ashen moat that was all that was left of Brad, and started to cry. The tears came slow at first, rolling down his cheek. Then it was as if a dam burst. They flooded out of him, his whole body heaving with the tumult, shuddering like a house in a tornado.

Grief pulled at him, hurricane-force winds threatening to tear him apart.

Brad had been his house, his *home,* the place where he was safe from the rest of the world.

Gentle hands touched him from all sides, encompassing him in their warmth. The winds of grief pulled back, circling him warily, but for a moment he was safe again. *Safe like I was with Brad.*

He wiped his eyes with his dirty hand, smearing mud across his cheek. Sniffing, he leaned forward to smooth the rich brown earth over the ashes.

A hundred other hands joined his, enfolding Brad in the life-giving ground from whence he'd come.

When it was done, Sam put his hand on the trunk of the tree. It was still young, with so much of its life ahead of it. "Grow toward the sky and take him with you." He closed his eyes again, keeping the pain at bay, He held himself, feeling the bark under his palm, the sun on his back, smelling the wet river air. He never wanted to forget this moment.

"Look!" Marissa's voice.

Sam looked up, following her gaze.

A red-tailed hawk had alighted on a branch above him, fanning out its wings and tail, so that the sun shined through the rouge feathers.

"I always liked this place."

Sam blinked and looked around. He was all alone, except… He stood and turned.

A man was standing by the edge of the river, staring at the passing water.

"Brad?"

His husband turned, that slow grin on his face. "You didn't think I'd leave without saying goodbye, did you?"

"Brad!" He leapt up and ran to his husband's side, throwing his arms around him. "Please, don't leave me."

Brad's comforting arms slipped around his waist. "I don't want to. God knows I never want to let you go. But it's time."

Sam shook his head, burying his face in Brad's neck. "Not if I don't let go."

Brad chuckled. "You always wanted to take care of me." He loosened his grip and held Sam out at arm's length. "You have to be strong, my love. You have great things ahead of you. I know—I've seen it."

Sam choked back a sob. "I don't want to do this without you." Already he could feel Brad slipping away. The touch of his hands on Sam's arms was becoming lighter, colder.

"You don't have to. I will always be here." Brad leaned forward and brushed Sam's cheek with his lips, and whispered in his ear. "Whenever you see a red-tailed hawk, that's me watching over you."

"Only the red-tailed ones?" Sam managed a quirk of a smile.

"It's just a metaphor, asshole." Brad was almost transparent now.

Sam laughed in spite of himself.

"I love you, Sam." His kind eyes were the last thing to vanish.

"I love you more."

Then he was gone. Sam wrapped his arms around himself, pretending they were Brad's.

"Sam, you all right?"

Sam blinked. Oscar was standing right in front of him.

His feet were wet. He looked down to see that he'd waded into the shallows of the river.

"I… don't know." He looked around. Brad was gone, but his friends were all waiting for him on the riverbank.

"Come on then. Let's get you back to the car. Carmelina planned a bit of a celebration of life at her place for Brad." He put an arm around Sam's shoulder and led him back up to solid ground.

That sounds nice.

Something drew his gaze upward. The red-tailed hawk was circling far above, watching over him.

29

AT THE KITCHEN SINK

Carmelina pulled out her stack of assorted platters—some glass, some plastic, one an antique her great grandmother had once owned. She also grabbed a Tupperware container full of *hors d'oeuvres* she'd made for the party out of the fridge. *Well, not a party, so much. But not really a wake, either. A celebration of life.*

Brad had been a good man. A kind man. She'd seen how he cared about the kids at the Center, including Marissa, the young girl—young woman now—who had turned out to be her granddaughter. She was forever in his debt.

She stared out the window at her driveway and the front yard. The band of turkeys that had stopped them on the way to Effie Yeaw nature center earlier in the day had made its way around to her street, and they were slowly crossing the concrete, heads bobbing and shifting back and forth, on the lookout for trouble.

One of them jumped up onto the crossbeam of the rustic split rail fence that separated her driveway from the grassy circle at the corner. It hopped down to join the others, pecking for whatever it was that the skinny wild turkeys ate for lunch. "Damned pests." They tended to shit all over her driveway, and often made a mess of her flowerbeds too, clawing out the bark in their search for food.

And yet, there was something magnificent about seeing actual wildlife in her own front yard.

"Mind if I help?" Marissa appeared at her side as if summoned by her thoughts.

"Sure. Wanna pick out three platters?" She indicated the stack.

"Of course." Marissa leaned her head on Carmelina's shoulder, her arm squeezing her *nonna's* waist. Then she sorted through them, choosing an oval green glass one that had been Carmelina's sister's, a wooden one she'd gotten at the Crocker Holiday Market just down the street at the Scottish Rites Center, and finally a ceramic one covered with bright yellow lemons and bright green leaves.

Carmelina smiled at the memory. "Arthur and I bought that one on the Amalfi Coast in 2005."

Marissa ran her hand over the shiny surface. "It's beautiful."

"It really is. And they make the best limoncello there."

Behind them, Sam, Oscar, Marcos, Ricky and his new boyfriend— *Alyn, was it?*—were gathered around her kitchen table, deep into a conversation about RuPaul's Drag Race and who was the greatest contestant of all time.

My money's on Vangie. Carmelina opened the large Tupperware container.

"Oooh, what are those?" Marissa leaned in to take a sniff.

"They're called *fagottini di bresaola ai funghi*—what a name, right? They're basically dried salted beef and mushrooms on a cracker with some fresh goat cheese. Do me a favor and grab me the bunch of leaf lettuce in the crisper." She'd washed and dried it earlier and stored it between paper towels.

"Sure thing, *Nonna*." Marissa was a good kid. Bright, hard-working, and kind to everyone.

She returned with the leaf lettuce.

"Arrange them like this…" Carmelina showed her how to make a nice bed of lettuce to showcase the appetizers.

"Got it." Her hands moved with assurance, creating a beautiful, verdant backdrop for the appetizers.

They worked side by side, and soon had the platters full. Carmelina gave them a once-over. "Perfect."

Daniele was out back, firing up the barbeque. They'd spend the evening with friends, and then finish getting ready for their trip.

She was packed for the morning flight, and had made all the necessary arrangements for her absence. They had decided, in the end, to shut down *Pane e Tulipani* for the week, and Sam had agreed to look after the house while he was there.

Marissa sighed, leaning against the kitchen counter, staring out the window at the turkeys.

"They make me crazy, but there's something magnificent about them, isn't there?" Carmelina washed her hands, then dried them on a red-and-white checkered hand towel.

"What?" Marissa blinked. "Oh, the turkeys. Sorry. My mind was somewhere else." She blushed.

"You okay, *micina?*" *My little kitten.*

Marissa cocked her head, staring sideways at Carmelina. "*Nonna*, am I a bad person?"

It was Carmelina's turn to blink in surprise. "Of course you're not. Whatever would make you say such a thing?"

Marissa looked away, her gaze falling to the sudsy water in the sink. "When I was with Gio… I… cheated on him." She gripped the edge of the sink tightly.

"Oh *tesoro*." Carmelina put her arms around Marissa and pulled her close. *How long have you been carrying this around in your heart?* "That doesn't make you a bad person. We all make mistakes."

"Really?" Marissa sniffled into her blouse, shaking a little.

"Really. Did I ever tell you about Oliver Greenhorn?" *God, I haven't thought about Ollie in years.*

Marissa let her go and looked up into her eyes. "I don't think so." She wiped her nose with the back of her hand, sniffling.

"I was in high school. I was dating this guy named Johnny Walker—really! He was on the football team. He was handsome, and that was all that mattered." *Blue eyes, dark hair slicked back, and those muscles!* "Sometimes he forgot to call me—this was way before cell phones. Sometimes he acted like an asshole after his team lost a game. But he was mine, and all my friends were jealous."

Marissa giggled. "It's hard to picture you in high school, *Nonna*."

She stuck her tongue out. "Hey! Just because I'm about to start collecting Social Security… but don't distract me. I have a hard enough time keeping my stories on track." She closed her eyes, picturing Ollie. "Oliver was everything Johnny was not. Sweet, kind, an Academic Decathlon team member. He was artistic—"

Marissa snorted. "He sounds gay."

She thought about it. "He probably was. But at the time, all I saw was that he was funny and cute… and he had a crush on me. So one night, I asked him over to… study."

Her granddaughter's eyes went wide. "What happened?"

"We fumbled about a bit, and eventually… well, you know. Neither of us was very good at it. Now that I think about it, you're probably right about the gay thing!" It explained a lot. "When it was over, he made some excuse and left. I felt like a jezebel…"

"What's that?"

"An old bible word for cheater or whore." She winked. "I told my own grandmother, eventually, and you know what she said?"

"That you were a slut?" Marissa grinned.

"No. She said that everyone screws up, and the important thing is what you learn from your mistakes. I thought about it for a long time and realized that I didn't love Johnny. He didn't deserve someone as good as me. And sure, it would have been better if I had broken up with him before putting poor Ollie through that. But it taught me what I did deserve." Arthur had known how to make her feel loved and valued. She owed that understanding of herself to that night with Ollie.

Marissa looked down at her hands. "So… I'm not a horrible person?"

"You did something you probably shouldn't have, in a perfect world. But we all know this Earth isn't that." She brushed back Marissa's hair from her face. "So what *did* you learn?"

Marissa frowned. "That it just wasn't right. Gio was sweet and kind and funny… like Ollie—"

"Are you saying *he's* gay?"

She laughed. "No. Definitely not. But there was just… something missing."

Carmelina took Marissa's hands in hers. "Does this new girl have… whatever it is?"

Marissa bit her lip. "Not sure yet. Maybe?"

"Well, at least you'll have fun finding out." She leaned over and kissed Marissa's cheek. "Don't keep the poor girl waiting. She hardly knows anyone else here." She gestured at the platters. "Be a dear and take those out to each of the tables. Then spend a little time with your date." She kissed Marissa on the forehead.

"Thanks, *Nonna*." Marissa hugged her. "I love you." Then she was off delivering appetizers.

Carmelina put away the rest of the platters, her arms a little shakier than they'd once been.

She was lucky to have a relationship with Marissa. It would never make up for the loss of her own daughter. How could it? But she was a bright spot in Carmelina's life.

"Nicely done."

She froze. She knew that voice, but that was… impossible.

She turned to find Brad there, leaning against the wall, arms crossed. "You… you're not here." She must have taken too much of her blood pressure medication, or… something.

He chuckled. "I'm getting that a lot."

"Where did everyone else go?" She squeezed past him and ran to the door that led to the living room and dining area. The house was empty.

Someone tapped her on the shoulder, and she almost jumped out of her skin.

"They can't see me. I'm here for you."

She turned on him. "What the fuck, Brad? Why did you have to go and die on poor Sam like that?" Since her hallucination refused to disappear, she figured it was better to deal with it—him—head-on.

"Not my choice." He splayed his hands, palms up, in front of him, and if a ghost could show emotion, she would have sworn he was sad. "But that's not why I'm here. What are you going to do?"

"About what?" She frowned. She knew exactly what he meant, but she wasn't going to give him the satisfaction of letting him know that.

He raised an eyebrow. "Will you go?"

Tucked away in her suitcase was the letter she'd received from the stranger in Strangolagalli, the little village outside of Rome. "I don't know. We'll be awfully busy with Daniele's family, and…"

"You should go." He nodded as if he'd just decided it for her.

"Maybe so…" But he was gone.

"You all right?" Daniele put a hand on her shoulder.

Carmelina blinked. She was standing at the kitchen sink, staring out the window. The turkeys were gone. "I think so." She turned around, pulling his arms around her.

If she was going to do this, he had a right to know. "There's something I need to tell you…"

30

THE STRANGER

Warning: deadnaming.

The man in gray looked up and down the street of the residential neighborhood where his target had parked his car. River Park was an upstanding place, not far from the Sac State campus, full of huge trees, broad green lawns, and a multitude of folks out on walks with dogs of all shapes and sizes—dachshunds, corgis, golden retrievers, and even a rather prissy trio of Afghans that walked with that flouncy certainty that they owned the place.

He eyed the big trees warily. *Must be fun times in those atmospheric rivers we seem to be getting these days.* A couple years earlier, on New Year's Day, a giant elm tree had crashed into his neighbor's two-story Victorian in Midtown. Lucky for them, they'd been on vacation when it happened, but the damage had been appalling.

He sidled up to the target's car, an old Honda Civic. Easy to get into, without all that electronic lock mumbo-jumbo that was so common these days.

With one last look around to be sure no one was watching, he jimmied the door with an expert touch and slipped inside.

If he had to, he'd break into his target's apartment. A couple decades spent on the outer edges of the law had taught him the requisite skills needed to entrap a cheating husband, to break into a supposedly secure safe, or trace someone's finances through the arcane pathways of the internet and financial system, all while following his client's wishes. But he preferred to start small—far less likely to draw attention that way.

Before nosing around in the car, he glanced in the rearview mirror.

A tall, bald man was approaching, led by a giant German shepherd. Likely the dogwalker was just passing through and didn't live on the street, but it didn't pay to take unnecessary chances.

He lowered the seat and lay down nearly flat, staring up at the stained gray fabric ceiling. He counted out a good thirty seconds before popping his head up to see if they had passed.

Damn my luck. The man was standing right next to the car while his dog did his business on the lawn. At least his back was turned toward the Civic.

Hope he cleans up after it. Nothing annoyed him more than people who failed to take their civic responsibilities seriously, or worse, deposited their dog's waste in someone else's trash can.

A moment later, the man was gone.

He got right to work. First off, he rummaged through the center console. There were a few candy wrappers, a small black plastic container full of quarters, a garage door opener, three twist ties, and a mostly empty bottle of hand sanitizer. He frowned. *Nothing useful there.*

Next, he tried the glove compartment. There he found proof of insurance—in the name of Ben Hammond—which had some other information that might prove useful in his online sleuthing. He took a photo of the card.

There was also a car manual—never opened, by the look of it—a couple of probably unpaid parking tickets, and one of those little plastic-wrapped cleaning wipes from Quick Quack Car Wash. He took photos of the tickets too.

One last place to check.

He reached around the back and felt in the pocket behind the driver's seat. Sometimes people put things there and forgot about them.

Bingo. His fingers closed on a piece of paper. He pulled it out—it was an envelope.

Inside was a copy of the title for the car, dated fifteen years earlier. *This guy really needs to upgrade his life.* Same job for nine years. Same car for a decade and a half. Surprising for someone who had to be making bank as a manager at one of the city's most successful restaurants.

Paydirt. The title had Ben's deadname—Alice Hamil.

The person he was being paid to find.

He pulled out his iPhone again and dialed his client.

She answered after the first ring. "Yes?" She sounded tense.

"I found him."

"You mean her?"

He sighed. "Look. This isn't going to work if you don't respect him. That starts with using his proper pronouns." He might be a sketchy private eye, willing to work on the edges of the law. But that didn't mean he had to be an asshole.

There was a pregnant pause. "I'm sorry," she said at last. Maybe she even meant it. "She… I knew him as *her* for so long."

He closed his eyes. He'd lost his daughter when she was ten, and trying to find her was what got him into this business in the first place. "That must have been very painful."

"We… said a lot of things we shouldn't have said. It doesn't matter now." There was a bleakness to her tone that he'd only heard in someone's voice before where someone had died. In his ex-wife's voice. "I'm… thank you, Mr. Kuo. Can I… what happens now?"

He bit his lip, not willing to give into the tidal wave of emotion he held so carefully in check. "Now I make contact. Give me a few days. I'll be in touch."

He hung up before she could reply.

Someone rapped on the passenger window.

He looked up. A man stood there, his face smeared with dirt, his hiker's backpack on his shoulders soiled with grease. At his side was a mangy mixed breed dog.

He rolled down the manual window. "Can I help you?" He needed to move the man along before he drew attention to them both.

"Spare some change?"

There were homeless folks everywhere in California these days. Even in the fancy neighborhoods. "Sure." He pulled out a crisp twenty and handed it over. "Get yourself something hot to eat."

The guy blushed. "Thanks, man. God bless you."

"You too." He'd been on the streets before himself, had lived like that man for a year. Besides, he could afford the help, with his current case about to pay out.

After the man left with his dog, he rolled up the window and made sure everything was the way he'd found it when he arrived. *As soon as you get sloppy, you get caught.*

Then he got out of the car and sauntered down the road toward his own ride. *Time to enact the next part of my plan.*

31

———

THE PARTY'S OVER

"I'll probably be blind by the end of the year." Dave blinked. It felt good to finally *say it*.

The room around him went silent.

His hand flew to his mouth. He'd meant to just tell Matteo and Diego, but he must have said it loud enough for the whole living room to hear.

Carmelina poked her head through the doorway that lead to the kitchen. "What the hell did you just say?"

Correction. The whole house. He sighed. *Cat's out of the bag.* "I have macular degeneration. They can slow it down, but I'll be functionally blind, sooner rather than later." He felt calm as he said it. Carmelina's warmly appointed living room—avocado green walls, cozy leather furniture, bright accent pillows, and cheery art on the walls—had lulled him into a state of complacency.

Not that he wasn't still upset about the prospect. *Who wants to go blind?* But he'd had time to settle in with it. And he had Marcos, and Marissa.

"Holy crap." Sam had followed Carmelina into the living room. He crossed the room to throw his arms around Dave. "I'm so sorry, Dave."

"Thanks." Dave blinked owlishly. He wasn't used to such attention.

Really, he just wanted everyone to treat him like normal. It felt strange for Sam, who just lost his husband, to be showing pity on him.

Mercifully, Sam let him go and stepped back. But then everyone else closed in, each person giving him a hug, squeezing his shoulder, whispering "I'm sorry" in his ear. Dave grew more and more uncomfortable with the attention, until at last he exploded, sending Justin's new boyfriend scampering backward, windmilling his arms comically like Wile E. Coyote. "Hey, it's all right, folks. I'm not dying!"

There was shocked silence, and then the party slowly returned to normal. Dave didn't miss the worried looks sent his way.

Ben knelt next to him, putting a hand on his knee. "It's so unnerving, how they treat you differently. Sam knows."

Dave snorted. "It's like they think I'm about to meet my maker."

Ben laughed. "Exactly. But seriously, I know some great doctors. When Ella was sick…" A pained look crossed his face. "We talked to a lot of folks, including some doing cutting edge work. I can ask around…"

"Thanks. I might take you up on that." His own doctors had been clear, though. The only course of action was delay. There was no cure.

"Of course. I'll send you some names." Ben's phone buzzed. "I'm so sorry. I've got to run." He stood, looked at Dave uncertainly, and then bent over to kiss his cheek. "We'll all help you figure this out." Then he was heading out the door.

Marcos squeezed his shoulder. "That must have been hard."

Dave shook his head. "It really wasn't. I didn't mean to do it. An Ellen DeGeneres moment." He might as well have leaned over a microphone when he said it. "At least it's out there now. Everyone knows."

Matteo nodded. "*Mio padre…* my father had that. Still, he could see light and color. He used to say to me that it was like an impressionist painting. The whole world full of fuzzy, bright colors."

Dave nodded. "That's a nice way to think about it." He loved painting. Maybe he could paint what he saw once his sight diminished, even if it was just an impressionist blur. "Poor Marcos here is going to be stuck with the care and feeding of an old blind man."

Marcos frowned. "It's not going to be like that, and you know it." His face went blurry for a second, then sharpened up. "You'll be all right, *old man.* Like Ben said, we'll figure this out."

Dave managed a weak grin at the jibe. He closed his eyes. The truth was, although he felt a certain calm settle over him, it was more numbness than tranquility. He wasn't ready to never see Marcos again, or Marissa or his art or their home… any of it.

To be honest, he was totally freaking out inside, even as he struggled to hold it together for the ones who loved him. He forced a grin. "Yeah, I'll be all right."

"That's the spirit." Marcos kissed him and ruffled his hair, then turned back to Diego to discuss business at Ragazzi.

Dave nodded and kept the smile on his face, even as he felt like the worst kind of liar.

❧

Ben hurried back to his car through the gorgeous late spring afternoon, his brow creased. The text had been explicit.

Ben, it's Lorelei. Help!

He'd texted back.

Where are you?

Home.

Be right there.

He slipped behind the wheel of his old Honda and stuck the key in the ignition. The engine protested, but on the third try, it finally turned over with an annoyed growl.

Something was amiss. He felt it. *Something's wrong, and she called me!*

He looked out the windshield, down at the dashboard, and over at the passenger seat. The glove compartment was hanging open.

That's weird. It was an old car, and sometimes the thing slipped open on its own, but he swore he'd closed it. *I should really think about trading the ancient gal in.*

Except…

This was the car he'd taken Ella to dinner in more times than he could count. The one they'd road tripped in when they went down to the Bay Area to see Kinky Boots at the Curran. The car that had carried so many picnic lunches to sundry parks and hiking trails. The one that reminded him of *her.* Looking at the passenger seat, he could still see her there, her laughing smile teasing him…

Nothing lasts forever.

He put the car in gear and let off the brake, and it lurched down the street. Home was fifteen minutes away, but he'd made it in ten before.

His luck held—he made it through East Sac and into Midtown at record speed, hitting all green lights—well, there might have been a yellow or two in there, but he'd squeaked through without a cop in sight. There was even a spot waiting for him in front of the building they shared. The gods were smiling on him.

He bounded up the stairs of the old Victorian and unlocked the front door. In five more seconds he was up the interior stairwell and pounding on her door.

It swung open, and there she was, standing in the entryway, soaked through and through. "Thank God you're here." She took his arm and dragged him inside.

Standing in the entryway. He froze, staring at her. "You're… on your feet." His mind refused to accept what he was seeing, despite all the clues. The stomping around upstairs. The kitchen equipment up on top shelves, too high to reach in a wheelchair. The *walking* noise the last time he visited her.

"Yes, I am. It's a miracle. Now come on. I need your help." She pulled him through the living room and back to the master bedroom, where her wheelchair was folded up in one corner.

This was not how I hoped I'd get here. He barely had time for the thought before she dragged him into the bathroom, stepping over a couple wet towels that were serving as a makeshift dam.

None of this was what he'd planned.

The toilet was gurgling angrily, overflowing its bowl.

Lorelei took a towel and started sopping up water, wringing the damp towel into the tub. "I can't get it to stop!"

Luckily the water was clean. Or clean enough. "Let me try." He slipped past her and reached behind the toilet for the shutoff valve to give it a good twist.

No go. It was stuck.

"Did you think I didn't try that first?"

He couldn't tell if she sounded annoyed or amused. Maybe both. "Sorry. Had to check. Do you have a wrench?"

She shook her head, intent on her task. "No. My ex took all the tools." Sop. Lift. Squeeze.

"Give me a sec." He ran out of the room, slipping off his shoes in the living room so he wouldn't track water all over the floor, and headed down the stairs to his place. He kept his toolbox in the bedroom closet, and he had an old wrench there that had belonged to his father… one of the few things he had left from the man.

He found it buried at the bottom of the toolbox. He popped his head into his own bathroom, which was directly below hers.

Water was dripping down from the ceiling into his tub.

Ben sighed. They'd have to get the property manager involved, and he was a pain in the ass. The owner was a bit of a skinflint, never wanting to spend money on the place.

He ran back up the stairs and through Lorelei's apartment, holding the wrench up triumphantly. "Found it." He knelt by the still-erupting toilet and stuck his head behind the porcelain throne. Managing to get the wrench in place, he tightened it on the valve and pushed on it hard. He had very little leverage in the awkward position, but soon enough he got the valve to move—a little. A quarter turn—release, re-clamp—and then another, until it loosened up enough to turn by hand.

At last the flow stopped.

"Got it." He stepped back and set the wrench down on the bathroom counter, and picked up a towel to pitch in. "It's dripping a bit downstairs in my bathroom. We'll have to give Dale a call."

"Dammit." She squeezed out her towel again, and then sank down on the edge of the tub. "Last time I called him, he said he was about to throw me out. 'Too much trouble,' he said. 'There are a hundred other tenants who would love to have a place like this.'"

Ben laughed. "Yeah, Dale's an asshole." He squeezed out his own towel, and then wiped up more of the water.

She laughed. "He really is." A heavy sigh. "If he kicks me out—"

"He won't. This isn't your fault. I'll talk to him." He found a couple more towels under the sink. "Okay if I use these?"

She nodded. "I'm so glad you came. I didn't know who else to call. I hope I didn't pull you away from anything."

"Just a wake." He finished drying the floor and the side of the toilet, and hung the towels over the edge of the tub next to her to dry, next to her leopard print shower curtain.

Lorelei's eyes went wide. "Are you serious? I am so sorry—"

Ben laughed. "It's all right. It was over. Really. They were just about to kick all of us out anyhow." He put down the toilet lid and sat on it, fixing her with his best Will Trent stare. "So… the standing and walking around *thing?*"

She sighed. "You don't think you could just forget that you saw that?"

"'Fraid not." She'd been lying to him, after all. He didn't know quite how to feel about that.

She was silent for a moment, looking down at the still damp white linoleum tiles. At last, she nodded to herself, and looked up at him again. "I really was injured—I was driving the kids to soccer practice, and a guy broadsided me over on Broadway. Thank god the boys weren't injured." She rubbed her temples. "I couldn't walk for half a year. When Garrett left me… it was hard. But the whole disabled thing helped with the judge. She was sympathetic, and granted me partial custody. So when I moved in here… I just kept it up so Garrett wouldn't have any reason to try to change the agreement. I've been doing physical therapy, and now I can get around pretty well without the chair."

"Do your kids know?" *Did she even really have kids?* He was pretty sure he'd heard them in the background, that first time he'd come knocking on her door.

"Yeah. They won't tell their father. They don't like him much, either." She laughed, but it was a bitter sound. "I'm sorry I lied to you, Ben." She put her hand on his arm, and a shock went through him.

It didn't seem so bad, now that she'd explained it to him. "It's… all right." After all, he had his own secret. Or several. "I have a confession of my own to make."

Her warm brown eyes met his, sparkling with anticipation. "Tell me."

"When I brought you dinner the other day… I was hoping we would eat it together."

"I know." She looked away again, wringing her hands.

"You… knew? Then why did you send me away?" He'd been so sure she would say yes, that they'd hit it off, and then…

It won't be an easy path. Was this what Miz Fortune had meant?

"Things for me are… *complicated.* I have two kids. I barely make ends meet. And there's the whole *handicap deception.* You don't want to get involved with me. Believe me."

He reached out and put his hand under her chin, gently turning her face toward his. "Another confession, then. That first time I saw you, when I pounded on your door and you opened it, sitting there in your chair, looking up at me, I was enchanted. Something inside me knew I wanted to get to know you better. That you could be someone who *mattered.* It's the first time I've felt that way since… since Ella." Oof. *That hurt to say.* Ella would have liked her.

She searched his eyes and shook her head. "You *don't* want me—"

Ben grinned. "Don't tell me what I want."

"I'll bring you down."

"Let me decide that."

"I'm a liar. You really don't want to be with me."

He squeezed her hands. "Just give me one date. Then if you want to be rid of me, I'll go and leave you alone forever."

She bit her lip. "One date?"

"One date. What do you say?" He waited, holding his breath, his entire body thrumming with anticipation.

She took a deep breath, then let it all out at once. "One date, then. Saturday night. Garrett has the kids this weekend." She pulled an offending strand of blond hair back behind her ear. "Pick me up at six?"

"Six o'clock it is." He leaned forward and kissed her cheek.

"You're a rare kind of man, Ben." Her eyes followed him as he retrieved his wrench.

You have no idea. Soon, he'd have to tell her his other secret. But not on the first date. "See you Saturday." He headed out the door, feeling her eyes on his back.

He whistled all the way down the stairs to his own flat.

32

UNDER THE RED ROOF

The Red Roof Gallery was buzzing.

Ainsley stood halfway up the staircase at the back of the open ground floor, a good ten feet above the heads of the crowd, watching everyone circulate and admire Jun Seo's paintings. She was proud of the work she'd done to help them and Mr. O'Malley get everything set up, and now they all got to reap the rewards.

Her phone vibrated—text from Marissa. *Fifteen minutes.*

See you soon.

The place was already packed. Some folks were elegantly decked out in tuxedoes or fancy dresses that sparkled with gold and silver threads that practically breathed *luxe.* Others were casual in jeans and hoodies and everything in between, as if both uptown and downtown had decided to crash the midtown art house at the same time.

Attractive cater waiters in tight white tees wove throughout the assembly carrying white platters topped with champagne and little *banchan,* Korean appetizers repurposed as *hors d'oeuvres.* And more people kept pouring in. Jun's show was a triumph.

Sure, most of the art was *giclée,* and even *those* prints were going for multiple thousands of dollars, especially with the artist on-hand to sign them. From her vantage point, she could see that at least half of them were already sold.

Then there was Seo's latest piece. Most of the others showcased beautiful scenes in their home country, Korea. But this one was different… they'd chosen a vantage point along the Sacramento River that captured downtown, the Tower Bridge, and the ziggurat, the curious pyramid-shaped building on the western shore. Done in Jun Seo's signature style, the painting practically vibrated with energy and light. It was electric.

The artist stood in the middle of the chaos like a lightning bolt in the midst of a hurricane, their face alight, engaging with the crowd enthusiastically.

"They're amazing, aren't they?" A man with cropped blond hair in a sleek gray suit and silver tie ascended the stairs to meet her.

"The artist or their art?"

"Both, I would say." He stopped a step below her to survey the scene. "Though I would say the newest one blows away all the rest. I told him he needed a change of scenery." He gestured toward the Sacramento piece. "Being here this last month, it really shook him up."

"Them."

"What's that?" The man looked up at her, one eyebrow raised.

"Really shook *them* up. Jun Seo is non-binary."

He nodded. "Oh, of course. I always screw that up." He laughed.

"Then you should keep practicing." She went to slip by him to rejoin the crowd. She didn't know who he was, and didn't really care to find out.

"You're Ainsley, right?"

She stopped and spun around to look up at him. "Yes… and who are you, exactly?"

He pulled out a card—what was with older white men and business cards?—and handed it to her. "Jake Myers, at your service. I'm Jun's American agent. He… *they* told me about you."

"What did they say?" Now she was intrigued, despite her annoyance. *Jun Seo is talking about me?*

"That they'd like you to work with *them* at their studio while they're here in residency." He waited while that sentence penetrated Ainsley's head, a grin on his face.

"They *what?*" She must have shouted it, because the whole room went quiet for a second. "Sorry, it's just… something good. Keep talking." She waved at the crowd and turned away, her face burning hot. "It… that sounds amazing."

Jake grinned. "Perfect. Do you have a second? We can go over some of the details."

Her brain froze. *It's not possible.* How was she going to have time to study molecular biology and be a full-time student? Her throat went dry. She glanced at the front door—Marissa wasn't there yet. She'd text when she arrived if she didn't see Ainsley. "Um, sure."

"Then come on up. I'm using Kelton's office this evening." He turned and led the way up the stairs.

She scanned the crowd and caught Jun Seo's eye. They grinned and nodded. Mollified, she turned to follow Jake up the stairs.

"Jun Seo's going to be in residence here?" A second floor hallway led to a tiny office, where every available wall space was covered in art, many of them prints. There were classics—Van Gogh, Vermeer, da Vinci, prints of course—and more modern artists. She spotted a Doolittle, a Baumgartner, and of course, a Jun Seo. There was also a chair with a tattered cushion, a beat-up wooden desk covered in coffee-ring stains, and a wide, soft purple velvet couch. *No accounting for tastes.*

"Well, not *here*." Jake looked around the room, his lip curled. "Close the door behind you. It's a bit noisy out there."

She blinked, but did it anyhow. *I'm safe enough here, right?* There were at least a hundred people gathered in the gallery below.

Jake leaned back on the edge of the desk. "Have a seat." He gestured at the purple couch.

It did look comfortable, and she had been on her feet all afternoon. It felt heavenly to sink down into its lavender embrace. "Thank you." She closed her eyes, enjoying the sensation of doing nothing for just a moment.

They flew open when she felt his weight descend on the cushion next to her. She stared at Jake, and then scooted away as far as she was able, maintaining some personal space. "So tell me about this residency. I hadn't heard anything about it."

Jake smiled again. Was it just her imagination, or was it more of a leer? "He's… sorry, *they've* painted just about *everything* in South Korea. They were feeling uninspired, and while they were here scouting for a Sacramento gallery, they said they were sparked by all the art in the city, from the giant red rabbit at the airport to the murals all over downtown and midtown. Jun rented a ranch up in the foothills for six months, and the painting you saw downstairs was the first in a new series. They're calling it *goldeunhilseu deuliming*."

Jake's Korean pronunciation was excellent. "Golden Hills Dreaming. I like that." And if the new work below was any example, this next phase of their career was going to be stunning. "And what would I be doing?"

He edged closer to her, setting off alarm bells in her head. "You'd be working in his studio, helping him with whatever he needed. You and I would work… closely, as well."

She stood up, banging into the back wall of the office and almost knocking an Escher print to the ground. "I'm… I don't think I'm comfortable with this."

He stood too, looking far more menacing than a five-foot-six man in a business suit should be able to. "You're new, so I'll cut you a little slack. In this business, you get ahead by paying your dues." He spread his hands, as if to indicate none of this was his fault. "It's a sweet deal. You help me out, you get to work for Jun Seo, and he helps you with his connections in the art world." He reached out and brushed a hand through her black hair. "I'm doing you a favor, Ainsley. Don't be a fool."

His overly minty breath assaulted her nose, and her name sounded dirty in his mouth.

"Get the fuck off me!" She slammed her knee hard into his groin.

He screamed like a little boy and fell over sideways on the couch.

She pushed past him, feeling ill. "I don't need your kind of *favors*." Shaking, she rushed out of the office and stumbled down the stairs into the crowd, her legs threatening to betray her.

"Ainsley!" Marissa appeared before her and hugged her. "This place looks amazing! I can't wait to—"

"Let's get out of here." Her face was hot. She just wanted to be anywhere but *here*.

Marissa blinked. "What? But I just got here! Are you okay?"

Ainsley glanced over her shoulder, up the stairs, expecting *that man* to appear at any second. "Not even a little bit. Please, can we just go?"

Marissa's eyes narrowed. "Of course. Come on." She took Ainsley by the hand and plowed her way through the crowd toward the front door.

"Ms. Kim… where are you going?" Jun Seo stared after her, mouth agape. "I was hoping to talk with you…"

"Sorry, I… have to go. Emergency." She hated lying to them, but then again, did they know how their manager treated women like her? *God, I hope not.*

They cleared the front door, and the Delta Breeze brought her a welcome lungful of cool air.

Marissa squeezed her hand. "How did you get here? You don't have a car, right?"

Ainsley blinked. "Light rail."

"Come on, then. I brought my car." Marissa led her down the alley to 18th street, and then another block south.

Cars passed by on the street, but Ainsley was all but oblivious to them. She felt numb.

"This is me." Marissa opened the door to a red Mini, and beckoned her inside, then got into the driver's side, shutting the rest of the world outside. She started the car to get the air flowing. "Okay now, *talk.*"

Ainsley shook her head. "It's… nothing. Let's just go." She just wanted to forget about what had just happened. The offer, the assault… was it even an assault? *He didn't touch me…*

"Ainsley." The way Marissa said it made her look into Marissa's eyes. "*Tell me.*"

She bit her lip. "It's… he… he wanted me to have sex with him."

Marissa growled. "Who? Jun Seo?" She started to get up. "I should go back in there and give them a piece of—"

"No. Not them. Their… he said he was Jun's US agent. Jake… something." His card was still in her pocket. She pulled it out. "Him. He… he said he wanted me to work with Jun while they were in residence here. Then we went up to this office, and he kept getting closer and closer…"

"Did he hurt you?" Marissa's voice hovered between concern and thunderous anger.

"No. He touched my hair. Then I kneed him in the nuts and ran out."

Marissa stared at her. Then she laughed out loud. "Oh my God, you didn't."

"It was the only way to get past him." Despite herself, Ainsley laughed too. Not because it was funny. Not really. But because it released all the tension in her gut. And because the big scary man did look so humorously pathetic groaning on the couch.

They laughed together for a full minute—Ainsley even snorted unattractively once—and then trailed off into silence. She closed her eyes again, wishing she could just rewind the whole night and not go upstairs with him.

"You *have* to tell someone," Marissa said at last.

"Maybe." How many times had he done this before? "Not tonight, though. I'm feeling all twisted up. I just want to go home."

Marissa nodded. "How about… my place? Not for… I just don't think you should be alone right now."

Ainsley looked up into Marissa's eyes again. All she saw there was compassion. "I'd like that. I'd like someone I trust to hold me tonight."

Marissa leaned over and kissed her cheek. "I can do that. Then we'll deal with this mess tomorrow."

Ainsley nodded. "Tomorrow." She closed her eyes as Marissa started up the car. How had everything fallen apart so quickly? She'd been living her dream for a night, and then this… And why did she let a man make her feel like crap?

She'd skipped her Chemistry test for this—her parents would be furious if they knew.

Maybe she wasn't meant to be an artist.

She reached out and squeezed Marissa's thigh while her… friend? Girlfriend?… started up the car.

So many questions.

She closed her eyes and let Marissa take the reins, her mind a blur of conflicting emotions.

Tomorrow. I'll deal with it all tomorrow.

33

AN UNEXPECTED GOODBYE

"I'll be gone about an hour. You sure you're okay?"

Ainsley stared up at the blurry brown-and-white blotch in front of her. It *sounded* like Marissa, but her eyes refused to confirm the fact. Maybe something to do with the three Nitty's hard ciders she'd consumed the night before. "What time is it?"

"Four-thirty. Sorry. I need to tell Gio something before he leaves for Italy." The blob resolved itself into her friend—and maybe more—who had held her all night, after...

Ainsley blinked. She didn't want to think about it. Not yet. Thinking about it meant *doing* something about it, and she wasn't ready to deal with that just yet. Especially if she had to face her parents, and explain what she'd been doing at an art gallery, and why she'd missed an important test... "Yeah. I'm just going to sleep a bit longer."

Marissa knelt and kissed her cheek. "That sounds good. We'll talk over breakfast, when I get back."

Then she was gone.

Ainsley closed her eyes, expecting to be tormented by memories of the night before.

Instead, she fell almost immediately back into a deep, numbing sleep.

~

The city streets were all but empty so early on a Friday morning. Marissa wasn't used to being up before the crack of dawn—though a few years before, she would have still been awake after a crazy night filled with studying, eating pizza, and chugging Red Bull or Monster to help keep her eyes open.

This morning, it was mostly rage at Jun Seo's manager and a gnawing ache in her own soul at what she'd done to Gio that kept her going. That and a can of Pepsi hastily grabbed from the fridge on her way out.

She had a small window to do what she could to make things right on the latter, even if it meant leaving Ainsley alone for an hour or two.

She sailed through the lights at Watt and Howe, usually good for a five-to-ten-minute wait apiece at commute time. *What, How... why isn't there a Who Street somewhere nearby?* It was an old joke.

The businesses along the way were dark save for the occasional lit-up neon sign, and the grand houses between Morse and Monroe, some of them fancy enough that they wouldn't have been out of place in Beverly Hills, stood like silent monoliths, regarding her little red Mini as it sped by.

In no time, she found herself standing outside Ragazzi, staring up at the upper windows where Gio and his dads lived.

One was lit up—Gio's room—and she could see his shadow passing back and forth behind of the curtains. She checked her phone—Carmelina would be picking him up in another half-hour or so. Just enough time.

She sent him a text.

Gio, it's me.

The shadow stopped. Then it started moving again.

Marissa stared at her phone. Nothing. *Dammit.*

Gio, pick up!

This time he didn't even stop to look at his phone.

Marissa sighed. She looked around, spying a short branch in the gutter nearby.

A lone silver Cybertruck passed by, the inside dark, its headlights temporarily blinding her. Hard to tell if they saw her or not. She scowled at it anyhow, just for good measure.

Then, with a sigh, she knelt and picked up the branch, getting a handful of sap on her palm for her trouble. With a flick of her wrist, she managed to toss it up toward Gio's window, but the sticky stuff on her hand sent it awry.

"Dammit." There had to be a better way to get his attention.

Then she saw the linen delivery truck pull around the back of the restaurant.

Of course. You're an idiot. Diego would be up receiving the day's deliveries at the back door.

She rubbed the sap off on the side of her jeans, as best she could, and followed the truck around to the small parking lot in the back, next to the dumpsters—the last place she'd spoken with Gio. As she'd hoped, the back door was open, golden light shining out to illuminate the time-worn, cracked gray pavement.

She slipped in through the door, past a surprised man in a *Linens for Less* t-shirt, and through the test kitchen, where Diego was preparing for the day. "*Buon giorno,*" she said with a cheery wave, ignoring his shocked look.

"*Dove vai?*"

Where are you going? She remembered that one from her time with Gio. "Upstairs to see the traveler." Then she was past him and on her way up to the second floor.

Part of her was nervous, scared to finally do this, after all this time. But another part was exhilarated, ready to finally get it off her chest. Ready to move on.

The door to the master bedroom was closed—Matteo was probably still asleep. But the light under Gio's door shone bright.

She pushed her way inside, afraid to slow down lest she change her mind—and collided with a shirtless Gio, knocking them both down onto his bed. His half-full suitcase tumbled onto the floor, spilling its contents.

"*Che cazzo…?*" He looked up at her, and started laughing.

She hit him hard in the left bicep. "Why are you laughing?"

He flashed her his famous Italian grin. "If you wanted to see me this badly, you could have just called."

She stared at him. She'd been prepared for anger. For sullenness. For just about any negative reaction, actually—she'd imagined them all. But not this.

Then again, she hadn't told him her secret yet. "I texted." It sounded lame, even to her.

His glance strayed to his phone on the tiny Ikea nightstand. "From where? In front of the restaurant?"

Her face betrayed her. "Maaaybe."

He sat up, disentangling himself from her arms. "Seriously?" He looked at his phone. "I guess you'd have had to, to make it up here in such record time." He got up and lifted his suitcase back up onto the bed, refilling it with the scattered clothing. "You know I'm leaving this morning, right? In, like, half an hour?"

"Of course. I didn't want to wait." She sat up, carefully removing a sappy-sticky palm from his bedcover. *Hopefully he won't notice.* "I... I wanted to talk to you. Before you left."

He moved his suitcase aside and sat down next to her. "Okay. Talk." His eyes met hers, and for just a second she felt the resistance piling up again inside.

"It's nothing. It can wait." She started to get up.

He pulled her back down, gently, his hand warm against the skin of her forearm. "You came all this way. It's not nothing." His eyes narrowed. "Is this about the affair?"

Marissa frowned. "You... knew?" She'd gone to such lengths to keep it from him. *I never wanted to hurt you.*

He looked away. "Not for a long time. But that night you came to see me, out back, under the moon? I figured it out."

Heat rushed to her cheeks. "Oh Gio, I'm sorry—"

"Don't." He held up a hand. "No excuses. It happened, it's over."

She sighed. "I never meant to hurt you."

"Well, you did." He got up, his back to her. "We were good, you and me. Or at least I thought we were—"

"We were. I... I've been giving it a lot of thought. We got comfortable. Together, I mean And maybe I didn't want *comfortable,* just then."

He bit his lip. "What was her name?"

"You don't know her."

"*Her name.* I deserve that much." The request was more of a demand, this time.

You're right, You do. "Abby. And how'd you know it was a her?" Everyone knew she was bi, but that didn't mean she'd been with a woman.

He leaned back against the wall, starting at his bookshelf, which was full of books about food and cars and red and yellow sports car models. "I saw her once, I think. Getting into the car with you, downstairs. Red hair?"

She nodded. "Yeah. I met her in school."

"I didn't think anything of it, at the time. Only later." He stared out the window into the darkness. "Why didn't you just tell me?"

She wished she knew. "It's… I don't know. I didn't want you to think it was your fault—"

Gio sighed. "Mission *not* accomplished. I thought I had screwed something up, badly."

"And it only lasted a month. She was exciting, fresh, beautiful—"

"Ouch."

She cringed. *I'm still hurting him.* "But also a little… aimless. She had no goals. Just wanted life to be one big party. You… you were nothing like that."

He ran his hands through his hair and down the back of his neck, settling his elbows on his chest. "You know I loved you, right?" He was still beautiful to her.

Past tense. "I know. I… I think I loved you too. Just not at the right time."

He shook his head, exhaling like a bull.

Her heart hurt. "I'm sorry, Gio. I truly am. You didn't deserve it."

He was silent for a long time, so long she grew uncomfortable, her fingers flexing on her knees, as if looking for something to do. But she owed him the space to process it. Owed him so much more, in fact.

"Are you happy?" His words caught her by surprise, as did the sharp gaze that pinned her where she sat.

Am I? It wasn't a question she normally allowed herself to consider. "No. Not right now." Work felt like a dead-end. Her education a waste. And the guilt… But then there was Ainsley. "I think I could be, though."

He nodded. "Me too." Then he wrapped his arms around her, pulling her into an unexpected embrace. "I want to forgive you. I *will* forgive you. But right now…"

She nodded. "I know."

They let go, and their eyes met. "Thank you for being honest. Finally."

She bit her lip at the last word. But she nodded. "I'm sorry it took me so long. You deserved better."

He whistled. "Maybe so. But we don't always get what we want. Sometimes you just have to wait for the right time to come around." He looked around the room. "I do actually have to get packed before Carmelina gets here."

"Of course." She got up and headed for the door, relieved, but feeling afresh the pain she had caused him.

"Marissa."

She half turned, unsure what he would say next, bracing for the worst.

"Talk more when I get back?" He managed a wistful smile, a *remember how things were* smile, and her heart melted.

She nodded. "I'd like that." Two steps back to give him a peck on the cheek. "*Buon viaggio.*"

"*Ci vediamo presto.*" *We'll see each other soon.*

It was enough. *For now.*

34

____

OLD HAUNTS

I t had been an early morning.

Carmelina and Daniele left at the crack of dawn to pick up Gio and head to the airport for the long trip to Italy.

Sam had gotten up with them, sharing a cup of coffee and some memories with Carmelina in her kitchen, while Oscar dozed on, oblivious, in the guest room.

It had been strange sleeping with someone else, even if it was only *sleep*. For the past nine years, it had been Brad at Sam's side at night, having his warm back to snuggle with, his light snores a reassuring beacon in the middle of the night.

Once Oscar had woken up—at the reasonably decent hour of 7 AM—he and Oscar planned the day together. It had been a veritable *Where's Where* of Sacramento landmarks, starting with breakfast at Orphan. The cash-only East Sac institution had added on a beautiful patio since he'd moved away, marred only slightly by the Sacramento curse of being unable to create any outdoor space that wasn't two steps from a noisy, busy street. He vowed to come back at least once more before he returned to Tucson.

After breakfast, they hit Capitol Park, leaving the rental car and taking advantage of the beautiful day for a walk through the rose garden and some of the memorials on the grounds.

They'd touched the bear in the Capitol Building, and laughed at all the folksy county displays down one of the main halls. They'd even peeked into his old office, where he and Brad had worked for the Senator when they'd first met. She was long gone, replaced by a Democrat, which made Sam happy. Brad would have loved it too.

They detoured over to the new DoCo—Downtown Commons. Brad had snickered at the pretentious name for a stadium and a fancy food court, constructed where the old Downtown Plaza mall used to sit. Somehow, the planned gentrification around it had never really taken hold, and it was still surrounded with unsavory blocks of run-down mid rises, trash in the streets, and homeless tents.

The ballpark looked fancy, though, bright and new and shiny. They even checked out a few of the restaurants, but they were all super expensive.

He'd planned to have lunch at Lucca, and had been devastated to find out that it was closed. They passed by the once-vibrant restaurant with its gorgeous side patio, and Sam almost cried when he saw the boarded-up windows and the graffiti that marred the outside. He had so many fond memories of the place, and now it was lost to time.

Instead, they ended up at Mayahuel. He was happy to see that the Mexican restaurant not only had survived the pandemic, but seemed to be thriving. The cream of poblano soup was as divine as he remembered it, and he felt a little piece of home return to his heart.

The afternoon was spent at the Crocker. He'd always loved Sacramento's own local art museum. There were so many things to see, but the one that caught his eye like no other was a life-size sculpture of a young girl in a drab floral-print dress.

She was a little stocky. Her shoulder-length red hair was faded, lying flat against the back of her head, and the wallpaper behind her mimicked the dress, so much so that she seemed to fade into it. But it was the donut in her hand and the look on her face—a little guilty, a little sad—that rivetted him in place.

He saw so much of himself in the piece, a young kid, trying to fade into the background. And *his* donut was the thing he'd desired most, but was also most deeply ashamed of.

Oscar had squeezed his hand, knowing without saying what he was feeling.

Now they stood together in front of the last place on the day's itinerary, before dinner. "This is where the magic happened, huh?"

Sam nodded. He stared at the two-story Victorian he and Brad had bought together, almost a decade before. The place looked much the same, and yet different. The new owners had refreshed the paint, going from gray and purple to a more understated white with gray trim. Sam wasn't sure how he felt about that.

"Sam? Is that you?" An older man shuffled down the steps of the blue Victorian next door, noticeably shabbier than Sam and Brad's old home. Like its owner, the place had seen better days.

"Jim?" A thrill ran up his spine, and he approached the man and gave him a big hug. "I didn't know you still lived here."

Jim huffed. "Been in this house thirty-nine years. Ain't going until the last breath leaves my body or they carry me out on a stretcher." He looked at Oscar. "Hello. I'm Jim Oberkrom."

Oscar flashed him a bright smile. "Oscar Rivas. Friend of Sam's." They shook hands.

"Nice to meet you, Oscar." Jim looked around. "Where's Brad?"

Sam closed his eyes, the question tugging on the pain he'd stuffed down deep inside. "He… he passed away, last week. We came home to spread his ashes at Effie Yeaw."

Jim's face sank. It was the face of a man who had seen too many friends die. "I'm awfully sorry about that." He pulled Sam in for a hug, squeezing him tightly in trembling arms. He looked so much older than the silver fox Sam had known when they'd lived here before.

"Thanks." There was still a grim unreality to it all. Like, at any moment Brad would call or text him. Sam would forget that Brad was gone for five or ten minutes at a time, but then it all came crashing back.

"Would you like to see the inside?" Jim gestured at their old house.

Sam blinked. "Oh, I'm sure the owners wouldn't want to be interrupted."

"Pish. They're on a Caribbean cruise, and left the keys with me to water their plants. I was just headed over there. Come on. It won't do no harm." He started to climb the steps, much slower than Sam remembered.

He glanced at Oscar, who shrugged. *Your call.*

Resigned, he followed his old neighbor up the stairs and into the house.

The first thing that struck him was the smell—sandalwood, a crisp, bright aroma, but not the old homey smell the place used to have, the product of flowers and waffles and laughter.

The warm hardwood floors had been replaced with a sleek gray laminate. The walls were a stark white, decorated in perfectly placed intervals with black and white photos of buildings.

The furniture, too, was monochrome—a black sofa, white ottomans, and gray bookshelves filled with gray books.

The only pops of color were from a large ficus in the middle of the living room, and a bright green fern on the dining room table.

Even the kitchen had been gutted, turned into an open-plan space, with gray cabinets and a white quartz countertop.

Jim must have picked up on his unease. "Yeah, I know. These new folks come in and rip out the heart and soul of a house, replacing with *hospital chic*."

Sam snorted at that one. "It's… different." Everything that had made it a home—his home—was gone. Sweat beaded his brow. He wiped it away with his sleeve.

"Wife's an architect and husband's a lawyer of something or other. No kids." He shrugged, as if he had a hard time understanding that. "Want to see upstairs?"

His heart was racing. "No, I don't." He turned and bolted out the door, out into the fresh evening air. He made it down to the sidewalk and bent over, resting his hands on his knees, panting heavily.

Footsteps sounded behind him, and then Oscar's warm hand caressed his lower back. "You okay?"

"I feel like I'm having a heart attack." His chest hurt. His brain hurt. All of him just hurt.

Oscar pulled him up, into his warm embrace. "Breathe, Sam. Take a deep breath with me. In. Hold."

Sam did as he was told, taking a ragged breath.

"Now exhale slowly, and in again."

Together, they found a rhythm—*in, hold, slowly out.*

The panic began to recede, and his heart slowed in his chest. He lost track of how long they stood there together, but it was long enough for Jim to feel the need to clear his throat.

Sam took one last deep breath. "Thanks." He hugged Oscar tight, then let him go.

Oscar just nodded.

"Sorry, Jim. I couldn't—"

Jim waved it away. "Say no more. When I lost Sadie, I used to wake up in the middle of the night in a cold sweat, heart racing. Thought I was gonna die." He looked up toward the sky wistfully. "Some nights, I wish I had. Then one night, she was there at the end of the bed. All bright and glowing-like. Now don't get me wrong. I don't believe in ghosts and all that paranormal shit. But I figure she came down to check on me and let me know she was all right. She leaned over—pretty as the day we first met —and kissed me on the cheek. Then she was gone." He shook his head, a bemused expression on his face. "I haven't had a panic attack since."

Sam nodded. He'd seen *things* too. Brad had come to him at the ash scattering… or had it just been a hallucination?

Either way, his husband was gone, and he was never coming back. *I have to face that.*

"Want to come upstairs to my place for a drink?" Jim put a hand on Sam's shoulder. "I can water the plants later."

"Thanks, but I think I need to get away from here." He glanced up at the old house that was now someone else's, and remembered something Brad had said to him when they had first moved in.

"We don't really own this place, you know. We're just borrowing it for a bit. Once we move on, it will become someone else's dream."

And now it was. There was a certain comfort in that continuity.

Jim nodded. "I understand. Well, stop by for a bit while you're in town, if you have time. You and your friend here are always welcome."

This time Sam gave him a hug. "Thanks, Jim. I'll give you a call." Knowing full-well he wouldn't.

As he and Oscar said their goodbyes and walked away, Sam knew it was the last time he would ever see the old house.

It was someone else's dream now.

35

THE AFTERMATH

"Are you sure about this?" Marissa held Ainsley's hand outside the police station on Richards Boulevard as the traffic whizzed past behind them.

"You're the one who said I should do this." Ainsley shivered, even though it wasn't cold out. The late morning sun beat down on her back, sending rivulets of sweat running down her spine. Part of her wanted to run back to the car, crawl inside and stay there for a week. Or a month. *Why did I go upstairs with him?*

"And I stand by that." Marissa's warm brown eyes met hers, her lips tightening. "If you don't report him, he'll do this again, with someone else. You know that. He's done it before, I'm certain." She sighed and looked up at the bright blue sky. "But I don't want you to do it if you're not sure."

Ainsley closed her eyes. Marissa was right. *Of course, she's right.* How many times had she seen something like this on TV and not understood why the woman didn't just run to the police to tell her story? But now, it was real. It was happening to *her.* "He didn't really hurt me…"

"But he might have, if you hadn't protected yourself." Marissa's brow furrowed and her eyes narrowed. "Besides, that's *bullshit.*"

Ainsley stared at her.

"He *did* hurt you. You're in emotional turmoil, about your art, about

Jun Seo, even about your parents and what they would think. Injuries don't always show on the surface."

"Got any change to spare?" An old woman, maybe forty, maybe sixty —her skin was so sun-dried and wrinkled it was hard to tell—stared at her expectantly, her dirty, gnarled hands wrapped tightly around a red shopping cart's handle. The cart was filled with plastic bags, stuffed full with bits of soiled cloth in a hundred colors sticking out at odd angles. A single gold ring adorned the woman's ring finger on her left hand, and she wore a sari and matching headdress, both a bright turquoise with gold stitching, though its jaunty effect was diminished by smudges of dirt here and there. It was apparent she hadn't bathed in weeks.

Still, she held herself with a certain dignity.

Marissa reached for her wallet and pulled out a twenty. "Here you go."

The woman took the bill and stuffed it into a hidden pocket, then reached for Marissa's hand with both of hers, her clay-colored skin, smudged with dirt, contrasting with Marissa's white hands. "Bless, you, child." Then she turned away and pushed her cart away down the street, whistling softly.

"Aren't you afraid she'll buy drugs with that?" She covered her mouth with her hand, shocked she had said it aloud.

Marissa's eyes narrowed again. "I didn't when *I* was on the streets."

Ainsley's face went cold. "You... I didn't... you never told me." How much did she really know about Marissa? "When was this?"

"When I was in high school. My parents kicked me out for kissing a girl." She tucked a lock of dark hair back behind one ear and sighed. "I don't talk about it much. It was a rough time. Matteo and Dave basically adopted me, and I've been a part of their extended family ever since."

"So Carmelina isn't really your grandmother?"

Marissa laughed, and some of the warmth returned to her eyes. "Oh no, she really is. But that's a story for another day." She glanced at the police station doors. "Are you ready?"

Ainsley bit her lip. "Yeah. Sure. Let's go." Yes, her parents might be disappointed, and she was probably going to lose the internship with Jun Seo. But if Marissa could be strong enough to do what *she'd* done, living alone on the street, Ainsley could manage this. She'd tell the cops her story, and let things fall out wherever they might.

Time to fuck around and find out.

Ainsley trudged up the steps to her dorm building—one of the new ones along the river that sought to "reconnect the campus with its riparian environment." Whatever that meant. The river was running low—probably saving water up in Folsom Lake for the fall. California was always one bad winter away from extreme drought.

The interrogation had been grueling— she felt like she was the perp, not Jake. And the way that cop—A. Smith—had looked at her the whole time… she shuddered.

The dorm hall was dead. It was Friday afternoon, and most of the other students were probably in class or already headed off campus for the weekend. For all its new student housing, Sac State was still a commuter campus at heart.

Marissa had to go back to work—well, work at home—but she'd graciously allowed Ainsley to stay for as long as she wanted. But she could only handle so many *Squid Games* in a row. Eventually she'd given Marissa a peck on the cheek, checked the bus schedule, and had taken the 23 line down to Fulton to the 26—an hour and a half to go just over seven miles.

She reached her own hallway and stopped in her tracks. Someone was slouched down in front of her doorway, staring at a cell phone screen. A *very recognizable* someone. She stared at them for a moment, not believing her own eyes. "Jun Seo?"

They looked up, their eyes sad and red, looking ten years older without their usual makeup. "Hello, Ainsley." They got up awkwardly, stretching their long limbs. They were wearing a long black trench coat, now rumpled and wrinkled. They must be hot.

"What… what are you doing here?" She looked around, shivering at the thought that Jun Seo's manager might be with them.

Their brow furrowed. "I fired him." They didn't need to say who.

"But… why?" She couldn't quite process what they were saying. The whole situation felt surreal. *Jun Seo is in my dorm.*

Their eyes were downcast, shoulders slumped. "You know why. I… came to apologize." They held out their hands in entreaty.

Her mind ran over the night before. How could they know? There wasn't anyone else in the room when it happened. "We were alone…"

They looked back up at her, their normally dark-brown eyes shockingly purple, their hair spiky, as if they hadn't showered since last night. They looked almost exactly like a disheveled anime character. "When I saw you run out, I asked him what had happened. He told me he'd offered you the internship, but you had… 'flaked out.' But something didn't feel right. It's not like you. I've known since the moment I met you that you were intense, focused, driven. You wouldn't just *flake out*."

She felt the heat rising from her cheeks. *This can't be happening.* The world had turned upside down. She grabbed the wall to steady herself against the universe's sudden shift. "But… we were alone…" *You said that already, you idiot.*

Their eyebrow raised, a ghost of a smile crossing their lips. "Ah, but Mr. O'Malley has a web cam in his office."

"Oh shit." She covered her mouth, her eyes going wide. This close to them, she could smell the wool of their coat, heavy and thick.

Jun Seo laughed, though there was little mirth in it. "Yes. *Oh shit.* I asked Kelton to tell me more about Jake. I'd heard… whispers. But nothing definite. And he was supposed to be the best. Then I mentioned that he'd been meeting with you in Kelton's office and… he leaves it on all the time. Just in case."

"And you *saw.*" Now her face was on fire. "I'm sorry. I shouldn't have reacted like that."

Their expression turned grim, their lips flattening into a thin line. "You did exactly the right thing. No man should treat a woman… or anyone… like that."

She blinked. All her life, her mother had taught her to be yielding, to go with the flow. A lesson learned from a hard life in Korea, before coming to the States. A lesson Ainsley had never mastered.

She'd always done what her parents asked of her. What anyone in authority had asked. But now… "I'd like to work with you. If the offer is still open." It came out in a rush, and for the second time that day, she covered her mouth.

What are you doing? It would mean leaving school, at least for a while.

Her parents would be furious. And yet... she wanted this like nothing she'd ever desired before.

"Oh, you do?" That raised eyebrow again.

"You'd be lucky to have me." Her natural brashness asserted itself.

Jun Seo Jang stared at her for a moment. Then they laughed, heartily, crossing their arms as if trying to hold it in.

"What?" The blush returned, and with it, her anger. "Why are you laughing at me?"

Their laughter subsided, but their smile this time was genuine. "You are a refreshing change. Most people I meet treat me like a celebrity—"

She snorted. "Well, you are."

"But not you. I like you, Ainsley Kim."

She stared at them, not quite believing what she was hearing.

"And yes, I agree." They nodded sharply. "I *would* be lucky to have you. Could you start next week?"

Now it was her turn to stare at them. "I..." She'd have to tell her mother and father. It would mean jumping into the unknown. Abandoning her parents' dreams for her. There would be shouting and tears and — "Yes." This time she didn't cover her mouth.

They reached out a hand. "Welcome aboard, Ainsley Kim."

She shook it, while her insides turned to blades of ice.

What in the hell did I just do?

36

A ROMA

Carmelina stared out of the train window at the passing buildings, wondering what had changed since she had visited a couple decades before. Rome—the Eternal City—always looked a bit shabby on the approach from the airport in Fiumicino. Lots of old—but not *classically* old—apartments lined the tracks, many with brightly colored flags consisting of the day's laundry drying on lines hung out on balconies and across alleyways.

Graffiti tagged the sides of many of the structures, dressing them up in bold greens and yellows and pinks—at least it was in Italian, though she didn't recognize any of the words.

It could have been almost any city in the US—the L train line in Chicago came to mind, where it wound through some of the city's poorer neighborhoods.

"What are you thinking?" Daniele's hand brushed hers, his dark eyes twinkling. Even after almost a decade, he could still take her breath away with his handsome Italian looks.

She blinked and looked around. The train was only half full this early in the morning. *God, I hate red eye flights.*

Gio was in one of the opposite seats, with their luggage piled on and around the other, forming a veritable wall, and most of it was hers. Diego's son had white earbuds in and was glued to his iPad, oblivious to the outside world.

Why didn't we fly in a day early? She stifled a yawn. Attending the ceremony that very afternoon while jetlagged from a fourteen-hour flight—two flights, if she was being exact, routed through Frankfurt—was going to be brutal. "Just tired. I was wondering why they don't clean things up along the rail line."

Her handsome boyfriend shrugged. "Why would they? It's cheap to live next to the train. If they cleaned it up, it would cost more."

She laughed. Was it only Americans who were so concerned about gentrifying everything? "Where is the wedding being held again?"

"Ostia. By the sea." He moved his hands in little wavelike motions. Italians loved to talk with their hands. A slight quirk of his lips told her he knew what she was thinking. "It's a beautiful little town."

She shifted, trying to find a more comfortable position on the hard seat, and her purse flew onto the ground and dumped out half of its contents. "*Cazzo!*" she exclaimed, earning her a grin from Daniele.

"Your Italian is getting better." He knelt to help her retrieve the scattered items. "At least the cursing."

She swept her makeup and lipstick and keys—why had she bothered to bring those to Italy?—back into her macrame purse.

Daniele handed her the wallet… and lifted up a white envelope in his hand. He stared at the name and address.

Oh no. She'd meant to tell him about it. She really had. But the last few days had been so rushed, what with Sam's arrival, scattering Brad's ashes, and packing half her wardrobe for the trip to Daniele's cousin's wedding. She snatched the envelope out of his hand and stuffed it back into her purse, ignoring his raised eyebrow.

"Do you have a secret Italian lover I don't know about, *cara mia?*"

"Yes. His name's Daniele, and right now he's being a pain in the *culo.*" She regretted it as soon as she said it. It was a fair question, even if it was delivered in the form of a joke.

He crossed his arms, giving her *the look,* while he waited for her to say more.

She reached out to touch his arm. "I'm sorry. It's just… there's some guy in Italy who says he's my uncle, and wants to meet me."

That got a raised eyebrow again. "And?"

She pulled the envelope back out and handed it to him. "You might as well read it."

With a bemused expression, he took the now-crumpled envelope and flattened it on his thigh. Removing the letter, he unfolded it carefully and scanned the text. "Oooh, sounds mysterious. Is this why you agreed to come with me to Italy?" He slipped it back into its envelope and handed it to her, his eyes narrowed.

"Not at all." She stuck it back inside her purse. "I came because you asked, and because I love Rome." It was true. She'd been looking forward to the trip—and the wedding—for weeks. "But…"

"But?"

"Strangolagalli *is* nearby, right? And I've wanted to see it ever since I read those *Teresa Papavero* mysteries. If we have time…?"

He pretended to think about it. "We're going to be awfully busy, hauling around all those suitcases you brought…" He eyed the pile that teetered every time the train went around a bend, threatening to bury poor Gio, who seemed entirely unaware of his peril.

She smacked Daniele in the arm. "*Spaccapalle.*"

He relented, flashing that magnetic smile of his. "Of course we can go. I'd love to meet this… uncle of yours. Did you write him back?"

She nodded. "Email. But no response yet—" Her phone dinged. *Thank God for international phone plans.*

She pulled it out and stared at the screen. "Well, speak of the devil."

She scanned the email that had just come in. "He says he is on my mother's side. We share the same great grandmother, apparently." *I wonder why Nonna never spoke about him?* "What should I tell him?"

Daniele was staring at his own phone. "Ask if we can come see him on Sunday. We have a break in the schedule—"

"We *have* one, or you just *made* one?"

He grinned slyly. "*Uno vale l'altro.* Same difference." He hummed something she recognized as *Funiculi Funicula*—now he was just mocking her with his stereotypical Italian references—and nodded. "Looks like it's a little over two hours by car. I'll see if Elena will loan me hers. Otherwise we can take the train—that's about four-and-a-half hours."

She snorted. "I'm already tired of trains."

As if on cue, the train went around a tight curve, and the tower of luggage teetered over Gio.

Daniele's hand reached out to steady Carmelina's own personal Leaning Tower. "Monday it is, then." He kissed her cheek. "You don't need to be afraid to tell me things."

"I know. I'm sorry. I just…" Maybe, on some level, she still didn't completely trust the man who had killed her daughter, no matter that it had been nothing more than a horrible mistake two and a half decades ago.

He seemed to catch her train of thought. Sadness washed over him like a shroud. "*Lo so, cara mia. Lo so.*"

She kissed his cheek. "*Ti amo.*" Then she turned back to look out the window as the tracks wound their way into Central Rome.

"*Stazione Roma termini in cinque minuti.*" That was easy enough to decipher—Termini Station in five minutes.

And Strangolagalli in two days.

37

TRAINS & RACE CAR DRIVERS

*N*ote: *The dialogue in the Italy chapters is in Italian, but for my English readers, most of it is being presented in English.*

Evening was setting in by the time Gio reached his destination after almost twenty-four hours in transit.

He'd said goodbye to Carmelina and Daniele at Termini Station in Rome—they were off to Ostia, a seaside village just southeast of Rome. In fact, they could have gotten a cab directly there from the airport since the two were practically next door to each other. But he hadn't had the heart to tell them after they'd already gotten their train tickets. Besides, it was nice to have the company.

He'd been to Ostia Antica, the ancient city next door, once with his mother a decade and a half earlier. The ruins there were far more interesting than Pompeii, at least for a child. You could climb all over them, exploring to your little heart's content, and no one cared.

Gio's own train to Bologna was delayed—*in ritardo*, or "in a state of lateness"—by about an hour. Italians were never actually late, in his experience. They were just in that *state of lateness*, which was surely someone else's fault.

So he'd wolfed down a couple slices of awful tourist pizza from a pizzeria across from Termini Station, practicing his Italian with the employees. He was still pretty good, but he'd gotten lazy back home.

"*Americano, eh?*" the cashier had teased him.

He laughed good-naturedly. "*No, Italiano. Ma vivo adesso in America.*"

"You talks like American." The man grinned as he handed over the bag, apparently proud of his own English.

"So do you."

The man's grin widened. "*Grazie mille.*"

Once his train departed, Gio managed a couple hours of sleep on the ride to Bologna, missing Orvietto, Arezzo, Florence, and all the assorted hill towns along the way.

Another hour should have seen him in Forlimpopoli, just a few miles from Aunt Valentina's house in Bertinoro. Instead he'd gotten stuck in Bologna in the midst of a *sciopero*—a rail strike—that mysteriously lasted just seven hours.

He took a walk through the city's *centro* to stretch his legs, looking for familiar sights. He'd grown up in Bologna with his mother Luna, until Diego had come to whisk him away to America when she died when he was seventeen.

Much of it was just as he'd remembered. *Hey, if it worked in 1450, why would you tear it down now to build something new?*

And yet, there were people and pigs everywhere.

Not *actual* pigs, but depictions of them. Mortadella this and mortadella that—somehow the boring Bologna meat had gone from being a local staple to a cultural icon. And the tourists—*OMG all the tourists*—jostling through the streets like a plague of locusts, eating everything in their path.

There was even—and this made him throw up a little in his mouth—a place selling *deep-fried tortellini* in a paper cone. "A local specialty."

Gio turned away in disgust. Tourism was ruining his beloved hometown.

Now, as its brakes squealed, the train glided into the quiet, unassuming Forlimpopoli Station—a two-story rectangular building that was white on the bottom and sported bricks on top, but not in a fancy way. It wore its history in a way that was unassuming, functional, and welcome to Gio's tired eyes.

No tourists here. He grabbed his suitcase and got off the train, stepping down into the late afternoon sunlight, touching his stomach to make sure his wallet and passport were still safely strapped there, under his shirt. He pulled out his cell phone and texted his aunt.

Just arrived at Forlimpopoli. Are you here?

"Are you Gio?"

He spun around to face a teenager—no, a young man—with dark curly hair and an easy, lopsided Italian smile. "Yes… and you are?"

"Dante. Your cousin!" He wrapped his arms around Gio and lifted him a couple inches off the ground. "*Benvenuto, cugino!*"

Gio struggled to breathe after Dante finally set him down. "How did you know it was me?" he managed finally, gasping. "Where's Zia Valentina?"

"She sent me, because she had to make dinner and you are *in ritardo.* And I knew it was you because you look American."

Gio frowned. How did he *look* American? It was the second time he'd been accused of Americanness since he'd arrived. Everyone dressed pretty much the same these days. *And I am Italian, dammit.* "What's she making?"

"Your *Papà's* favorite. *Passatelli.*"

"Oooh." Gio's mouth watered.

Dante put his arm around Gio's shoulder. "Come on, *cugino.* The car's over here." They walked away from the tracks, and Gio looked around at the town that surrounded the station. This part of Forlimpopoli didn't have much Italian charm, being mostly *new* residential construction. Which in Italy usually meant it was only a couple hundred years old instead of five-hundred or a thousand.

He was a couple months too early for the *Festa Artusiana*—the famous local food festival would have been perfect for his research.

Dante guided him to a mint-green Fiat, parked half a block down the street. "Just throw your stuff in the back."

He tossed his bag into the tiny back seat. "Nice car. Yours?" Gio settled into the passenger side.

"*Magari.* It's the family car. Mamma finally upgraded a couple years back when the old one died." He grinned. "Hold on!" He peeled out onto the street and spun around the circle in front of the train station like a race car driver, sending them shooting up Via Roma.

Gio held on for dear life.

"Nice, huh? She has a lot of *vroom* for a little car."

"Yeah. Just… great." He closed his eyes, only opening them when the car slowed down as they entered Forlimpopoli's historic center. They zipped past an imposing brick edifice with wide arches and squat towers, looking more like a fortress than a— "What's that?"

"City hall." Dante gunned the engine and the car dodged through the central plaza, lined with two- and three-story brick buildings and several towers.

Bet they have amazing views.

Soon they were out of town, heading east up into the hills on Via Dante Aleghieri. Gio wondered if his cousin was named for the famous Italian writer. "Did you want to be a race car driver when you grow up?"

"What?" The little engine was doing its best to roar, but even its adorable little growls were enough to make conversation difficult.

"Never mind." They passed through a tiny village named *Ospedaletto*— little hospital?—and then veered south.

The awful pizza he'd wolfed down in Rome threatened to make a reappearance, but thankfully they soon turned off onto a smaller road called Via Badia and Dante slowed way down.

His cousin displayed those white teeth again. "Just like Foyt, huh?"

Gio frowned. "What?"

"A.J. Foyt. Famous American race car driver. What, are you American or not?" Dante frowned.

The last time he'd seen Dante, the boy had been stumbling around in the grass outside Gio's mother's funeral. Now he was this *man beast*. Gio didn't have the heart to tell him that sports were not a big thing in the Bianco-Bellei household, his own love of soccer notwithstanding. "Yeah. Just like him."

Dante laughed and nodded. "*Forza!*" He pulled the compact Fiat into a spot along the street, between a dark gray Maserati and a silver Alfa Romeo. "We're here!"

Gio stared at the semi-familiar street. He'd spent the better part of a week there, after his mother had died. *With my Dad.* Sometimes he missed his mother so much it felt like his ribs were squeezing all the breath out of him.

He'd stay with Zia Valentina couple of nights, and then set out on his grand adventure. Starting with a visit to Luna's grave outside Bologna.

He slipped out of the car, grabbed his bag, and took in a lungful of the fresh Italian countryside air. Then he followed Dante up the street to the golden glow coming from the windows of Valentina's flat, drawn by the smell of good, simple Italian cooking.

It's good to be home.

Thanks to Ilaria Maria Sala and her article on Bologna in the NY Times for the assist in descriptions of the Italian city for this chapter:

https://www.nytimes.com/2024/08/09/opinion/italy-tourists-bologna-mortadella.html

38

RULES OF THE FIRST DATE

Ben stared at his face in the mirror, his newly trimmed hair back to its usual short-cropped length. *Can anyone tell?*

He was forty-four, black, and reasonably handsome for his age. It had been more than a decade since he'd transitioned, and sometimes, when the light was just right, he could still see the contours of his old face. Softer, more feminine. Long hair, pursed lips, and green eyes staring at him from a visage he no longer recognized.

More importantly: *Would she care?*

He splashed cold water on his face and reached for a paper towel, feeling that twinge of liberal guilt at using something once and then throwing it away. One more crumpled piece of paper wasn't going to destroy the planet. Besides, the other side was already well on the way to ecological destruction, no matter what he did. He sighed.

Drying his face, he took one last look at himself in the mirror. Those moments of self-doubt came less and less often. He really had settled into being *Ben*. It was only this whole *dating again* thing that had him off his game.

Lorelei was waiting for him, her wheelchair pulled up close to one of the tables by Ragazzi's plate glass window. He'd felt a little weird keeping up the pretense, now that he knew she could walk, but she was worried her husband might spot her and make a stink if he found out she'd been lying.

She was wearing a pretty, feminine summer dress, bright green with golden flowers, that hung light on her shoulders. Her gaze was directed at the street outside, watching the passing cars.

He slipped into his own seat and picked up the menu. "Sorry about that. Should have hit the john before I left home."

She turned her radiant smile on him. "Always winning the girls over with your bathroom talk?"

His face burned. "Sorry. It's just…" He stared at her, drinking her in. It had been so long since he'd let himself just be happy. *Why not try radical honesty?* "I was in the bathroom staring at myself in the mirror, wondering what the hell I was doing here with someone as pretty as you."

Her smile broadened, and a touch of pink flashed across her own cheeks. "You're not so bad yourself." She looked down at her menu, then her gaze flicked back up to him. "You're really nervous about this?"

"What can I say? It's been a long time." He closed his eyes, seeing Ella's bright smile.

"She must have been something."

His eyes flew open and he stared at her, surprised. *What is she, psychic?* Then he laughed and shook his head. "Sorry. Not falling for it."

She tilted her head, eyes narrowing. "Falling for what?"

"First rule of the first date. *Never talk about your ex.*"

She nodded. "Fair enough. And the second?"

"*Don't start things with a lie.*"

She coughed. "I'm so sorry about that. I really didn't mean—"

"Oh, no, I wasn't talking about that." Hs face burned even hotter than before. *Ben, you're an idiot.* "You did what you had to. I don't hold that against you. Besides, technically, we weren't on a date."

She smiled shyly. "True."

His shoulders relaxed. "So forget I said anything—"

She put a finger on her lip, considering him. "What if we each tell the other something that's true? Something … I don't know. Deep. Real. I'm sick of guys who play games." She leaned forward and met his eyes, challenge and a bit of mischief sparkling there.

I like it. And I like her. A lot. He tried hard not to stare down her half-open blouse, his heart thudding in his chest. "All right. Who goes first?"

One of the waitresses passed by, carrying a tray filled with delicious-smelling Italian food—zitti and lasagna, by the look of it. "Be right with you."

Wasn't that the girl Marissa brought to the wake? He waved. "Thanks!"

"I'll go first." Lorelei took his hand, turned it over, and traced the lines on his open palm with her red lacquered nail. "When I was twenty, I worked for a year as a palm reader in a circus."

He shivered. "No shit!" He put his free hand over his mouth as Lorelei burst out laughing. "Sorry."

"It's true. I quit college and wanted to see the world. I ended up mostly visiting a bunch of crappy little hardscrabble towns stretched across the Bible Belt and the Deep South. Next time I travel, it's going to be Paris, and London, and Milan." She got a dreamy look in her eyes, and he wanted nothing more than to take her there.

He tried to ignore the stirrings her nail across his upturned hand was causing. "So what does my palm say?"

She stared at it, considering it carefully, her brow furrowed.

He waited anxiously, shifting on his wooden chair. "Well?"

"I have no fucking clue."

This time, he was the one who burst out in laughter. "I thought you said you were a palm reader?"

She flashed him a wry smile. "Not a very good one, actually. I quit when some guy with terminal cancer got pissed off because I told him he had a long, happy life ahead of him." She looked out the window again, her mouth drawn into a thin line.

"Oh crap."

"Exactly." When she turned back to him, the sparkle was gone, and she looked deadly serious. "Now it's your turn. Tell me something real."

Ben swallowed, hard. *Do I dare?* It would come out sooner or later, but he had no idea how she would react.

He was saved by the arrival of their waitress.

"Hi, my name is…" She blinked, staring at him for a second. "Ben?" She broke out in a smile.

Ben laughed. "*I'm* Ben. And it's… I wanna say Ashley?" He half closed one eye, cocking his head, hoping he was right.

She shook her head. "Ainsley. But don't worry. Folks get it wrong all the time."

Lorelei glanced at him, then at Ainsley, a puzzled look on her face. "You two know each other?"

Ben laughed. "Kind of. She came to Brad's wake with a friend of mine."

Her shoulders relaxed. "Ah."

Interesting.

"Have you two decided what you want?" The half-grin that crossed her lips told Ben she'd seen it too.

"Not yet. Give us a few more minutes?" Ben picked up the menu, though he'd been there a thousand times and knew it like the back of his hand. He wanted to give Lorelei a bit more time to decide.

"You got it." Ainsley winked at him and left them alone.

He glanced at the menu. "The *tortellini alla panna* is really good."

She nudged him with her toe under the table. "Hey, it's your turn." The mischievous look was back.

"Ah. Sure." *I was kind of hoping you'd forgotten.* "Okay. I don't like peas. Except in pea soup."

She shook her head. "Nope. Not good enough. I want something bigger."

Ben sighed. *I tried.* "All right. I'm… different from the guys you probably usually date." He looked away, not wanting to see her face when he said it. Actually said it. "I'm… trans."

Her hand found his and squeezed it. "I said something *big*."

He turned to look at her, his eyebrow arched in surprise. "Really?"

"That isn't something big. Not when I already know."

"You do?" He felt like an idiot. He'd been sure he was *passing*, though he hated that word. *Living my gender.* It had been a long time since someone had called him *ma'am*.

"Third rule of dating. *Do your research.* You're a published author. It didn't take me long to find your bio."

Ah. Beautiful and smart. How did I get so lucky? "And it doesn't bother you?"

"Why should it? My cousin is trans, and she's even girlier than I am." She grinned. "Tell me something else."

Only one other thing came to mind. "I killed my last girlfriend." It was out before he thought *not* to say it.

Her hand pulled back. "What?" Her face was ashen, her mouth open in an "o" of surprise.

"Not like that." He sighed, closing his eyes once more. Ella's face was never far away when he looked for her. "She had this thing called Fahr's Syndrome. We got her this experimental treatment, and it helped. But I brought Covid home one night and..." He choked up. It had been a horrible year—first the lockdowns and the fear, and then the reality, with Ella on a respirator in the hospital. Only able to see her via a phone screen. "It took three long weeks, but she died in the hospital, all alone." He'd thought he was past this. That the mere mention of her name would no longer bring tears. But he'd only admitted it once, to Marissa, and they'd been interrupted when Sam had texted, the night Brad died.

"Oh, Ben." She took his hands in hers. They were warm and soft. "You didn't kill her." She lifted his chin, and at last he met her eyes again, fearing he'd see disgust there, or pity.

All he saw was compassion. "If I'd just been more careful. Worn a mask. Stayed home that day." He'd been helping out a local non-profit working with restaurants to deliver food to people stuck at home. "She... I wasn't there when..." He couldn't finish. Even now, more than four years later, it still cut him to the bone. *I wasn't there.*

"She must have been something," Lorelei said again, squeezing his hands.

He pulled one away and grabbed his napkin to wipe away his tears. "First rule of dating, remember? No talk about the exes."

Her lips quirked up at the edges. "Yes, but you told me something real. And you forgot the fourth rule."

"What's that?"

"It's our damned date. We can make up the rules as we go."

He laughed, heartily this time, startling a woman at the next table. "I like you, Lorelei."

She grinned. "I like you too, Ben. Now tell me all about Ella. Then I'll tell you my own Covid story."

He stared at her for a moment, as if she might vanish into thin air. Somehow he'd told this woman his two biggest secrets, and she hadn't run away. *Maybe there's hope for us yet.*

"Okay. I first met Ella in the hospital, where she was visiting her brother, who was extorting two of my friends to get money for her experimental treatment…" It all tumbled out of him in a rush.

And by the end of the night, he was hopelessly in love.

39

BALLOON

Marcos dropped his head and pulled on his hair with one hand, stifling a groan. He was alone in his office, paying the bills, while Dave made a grocery run to Trader Joe's.

The cable bill was going up again. Maybe it was time to cut the cord, like so many of their friends had done.

But it wasn't just cable. Their adjustable-rate mortgage, which had seemed like a genius move just a couple years earlier, was biting them in the ass.

The newspaper was upwards of $1,000 a year. *Why do we still get the paper?*

He knew why. Dave loved reading it. Devoured every last page, every morning. Though with his macular degeneration... *At least that's one expense we'll be able to get rid of soon.*

Marcos sighed. That was dark, even for him.

Inflation too had taken its toll on their budget, and with less and less money coming in, things were quickly heading toward a crisis point. Now they'd need to pay for Dave's medical bills for his macular degeneration...

And then there was his biggest mistake of all.

Dave had figured out that Marcos was looking for a job. But he still didn't know what Marcos had done. The one *really bad thing*. The thing he'd done to save them both. Which would ruin everything if he didn't figure a way out. The business loan.

His financial advisor had warned him against doing it. "It'll come back to haunt you."

"I can handle it. We need the cash *now*." It had seemed like a safe bet, working with a real finance company, not some shady internet firm. It had promised twenty-thousand up front, with a credit line he could draw on as needed. When he'd taken it out in late 2019, it was the perfect solution. He'd been certain he could use the capital to turn things around.

Then Covid had hit, and they'd burned through all the money in a year. He'd applied for and gotten a couple no-interest, forgivable business assistance loans from the government, and between the loan and the Covid assistance, things had been all right for a while.

But their business had never returned to normal—the old normal, which wasn't great, but was enough. Then the coming of Generative AI had eaten even further into their margins.

He logged into the financial firm's website, hoping against hope that something had changed. That he'd been wrong about the amount.

Or maybe there was a workaround for the balloon payment that was due in just over a week.

Dammit. There it was in black and white.

$43,257.44.

He found the terms link and read through them for the hundredth time in a week, desperately looking for something—anything—that he'd missed. As he scanned through the never-ending lines of text, sweat broke out on his brow, and his knee began to bounce, his toe tapping the wooden floor like a piston.

Once again, there was nothing.

"They had those Marcona almonds you like, with the olive oil and rosemary. I got two." Dave's voice at the door shocked him.

He slammed his laptop closed, then closed his eyes. "Thank you."

"Everything okay? You're acting like you just got caught watching porn."

Marcos turned in his chair. "It's fine."

Dave had a half-smile on, his eyebrow raised. "You know you're supposed to share the good stuff."

Marcos managed a chuckle. "It's not porn. I promise."

Dave leaned over and kissed him on the cheek. "I know. Looked more like a bank statement. Banker porn?" He grinned. "Come on and help me put things away."

Marcos nodded, relieved. "I'll be right there."

"Suit yourself." Dave retreated down the hall.

Marcos reopened the laptop and closed the offending window. The time had come to admit his failure. He felt sick to his stomach.

"He'll understand."

Marcos straightened up and looked around, his eyes settling on the pesky figure who stood in the door frame where Dave had just been. The ghost who simply refused to leave. "Oh, you think so? I thought you were on your way to the pearly gates?"

Brad smirked. "Once I've finished setting things right here." His eyes grew misty. "I miss Sam. I'd give anything to be able to share our troubles again. Look, you still have Dave. Don't let him find this out on his own. He loves you, Marcos. Let him in."

Marcos nodded. "I know. I have to. I kept hoping—"

"There was a way out?"

He sighed. "We're burning through money. I should take those almonds back." He didn't need them. He didn't deserve them. Not after what he'd done.

Brad's eyes twinkled. "It's only money."

Marcos snorted. "Easy for you to say."

"Maybe." Brad's gaze met his own, his brown eyes kind. "But it's true. It can only divide you if you let it."

"Yeah. I suppose so." How often had they told each other they'd be okay even if they ended up living in a cardboard box? As long as they had each other. He might find out if it was true soon enough. "I miss you, man..."

But Brad was already gone.

With a heavy sigh, Marcos got up and headed to the kitchen.

Dave had already emptied out all the bags, and was proceeding to put things away in the pantry and the refrigerator. He flashed Marcos a welcoming smile. "I got one of those pot pies you like... the refrigerated ones, not the kind from the frozen case. Thought we could have it with a salad—"

Marcos gently took the pie from his husband and put it on the counter, screwing up his courage. "Dave, we need to talk."

His husband frowned. "Look, if you don't like it, I can take it back. But the last time we tried it, you seemed to—"

"It's not that. Come sit with me for a minute." His pulse was racing. He led Dave to the table where they'd passed so many meals together.

"What is it? Marcos, you're scaring me." Dave reached out and took his hand. "You—you're not sick, are you?"

"No, nothing like that." He closed his eyes and took a deep breath. *You can do this. It will be all right.* "I did a bad thing. Or… a thing that went bad, and I don't know how to fix it."

Dave squeezed his hands. "Tell me. Whatever it is, we can fix it. Together."

"I don't think we can." He looked up into his husband's dark brown eyes and saw only love. "I took out a loan, to save the business. Years ago."

Dave stared at him. "You never mentioned this."

"I know." He bit his lip. "We were teetering, and I thought I could save us. Save the business. Then Covid hit, and everything fell apart…" His eyes filled with tears. He felt like such a fucking useless asshole. *I did this. I ruined everything. And I can't even get a job.*

"How much do we owe?"

Another deep breath. "Forty-three thousand."

A sharp intake of breath.

I'm so sorry. He could feel Dave's confusion, his pain.

The man he loved closed his eyes. Pulled his hand away and hugged himself tightly. Took another breath. And nodded. His eyes flickered open. They were clear and bright. "It's okay. We'll figure out a way to pay it back. Get an extension. You'll find that new job you are looking for, and I'll… we'll figure something out."

Marcos shook his head. *Don't you think I've tried?*

"What?"

"It's all due next week. Every last cent of it. There's a balloon payment…" His vision blurred, and he reached out to grab Dave's hands as if they were the only thing that could keep him from drowning. "I'm so sorry. I've ruined *fucking* everything." Now he began to cry in earnest. The dam had burst, and it all came rushing out of him.

Dave pulled him close and held him tight as he sobbed. "It's all right." His warm hands rubbed Marcos's back. "We'll figure it out."

"No it's not. We're going to lose everything." Our condo. Our car. Our business. Everything they'd worked so hard to build together. *I broke it all.*

Dave held him while he sobbed, tears streaming down his face, his nose plugging up. How long they sat there like that, he'd never know, but he took solace in the warmth of Dave's chest.

At last, when his crying jag wound down, Dave released him and held him out at arm's length. "Listen to me closely. You did not screw everything up. Covid did. And all of these greedy, horrid corporations. And AI. You just tried to fix it. Sure, you failed. But we were always going to fail." He put his hand under Marcos's chin, lifting it up. "But you know what? In the end, it's just money."

Marcos stared at him. *Brad was right.* He threw his arms around Dave and hugged him tightly. "I've never loved you more than I do right now."

Dave nodded. "I love you too. We'll figure this out, *mi corazón.* Together."

For the first time in months, Marcos felt a flicker of hope. He pulled Dave close and kissed him softly. "Together."

40

NOT NERO'S TOMB

Carmelina ran her fingers through her sticky hair, trying to brush it back into some semblance of order. A fair-to-middling breeze blew in off the Mediterranean waters not thirty feet away, the constant soft lapping of the waves reminding her more of Lake Tahoe than the grand Pacific Ocean.

She was wearing a gauzy white dress that was definitely not hers—well, *technically* it was. It was two sizes too big, an Italian beachwear confection tied at the waist with a bright pink sash.

"You look beautiful, *bella ragazza*." Daniele kissed her cheek.

"I would look *more beautiful* if we were inside, without this dratted wind blowing salt and God knows what else into my hair." She said it softly under her breath, only for him, and ended it with a broad smile, just in case anyone in the crowd was listening. It was a wedding, after all, and she wasn't supposed to make herself the center of attention.

She forced herself to put her hands in her lap and let the wind do what it would with her.

It had been a hell of a day.

They'd left Fiumicino Airport bound for downtown Rome. They'd sent Gio off on his journey to his aunt's house at Termini Station, and had boarded a subway train bound for Ostia. Or so they'd thought.

Somehow they'd gotten things mixed up—their directions were for Osteria Nuova—a good 56 miles northwest of Ostia—and most definitely *not* on the Mediterranean. They'd only discovered the mistake because a nice elderly Italian man named Vito from Vitorchiano had started up a conversation with Daniele, asking him where he was headed.

Vito had given them a hearty laugh when they told him about the beachside wedding they were headed to in Ostia, and had informed them that they were heading in entirely the wrong direction.

This had led to a hasty disembarkation in some place called Tomba de Nerone on the northwestern outskirts of Rome, which the local subway agent had assured them was not *actually* the final resting place of Emperor Nero, despite the name.

They would have had enough time to make it back the way they had come if it weren't for the calling of a *sciopero,* a term Carmelina was quickly learning to detest. These strikes could occur at almost any time in Italy, and might paralyze the railways or subways for hours or days at a time.

So there they were, standing outside the subway station near the tomb that was not Nero's, when Carmelina discovered that she had left one of her pieces of luggage on the subway train. The one with most of her clothing, including her dress for the wedding.

Alas, the doors to the station were locked, and in any case, the train had already left the station. *In more ways than one.*

Daniele had called his cousin, the one getting married in just four hours. It turned out she had another cousin whose wife had a friend whose best friend's father was an undertaker who lived in La Giustiniana, the next tiny village past the tomb that was most definitely *not Nero's.*

And better yet, his mortuary was just five blocks from their subway station. And, as Daniele's cousin exclaimed excitedly in Italian, *"Nessuno è morto questa settimana." No one died this week!*

Which is how they found themselves stuffed into the back seat of an old creaky hearse that Carmelina figured must have been from the 1950's, flying down the A90, the outermost belt freeway surrounding Rome, bound at last for Ostia.

Except that someone *had actually died,* and their body needed to be transported to a mortuary in Masimilla, just west of Rome. Which is why their remaining luggage—minus Carmelina's missing bag—was stuffed in the back of the vintage hearse, tucked around the lovely pearlescent coffin. *Vintage* being a generous upgrade, in her mind.

And that's how they discovered—by driving right past the airport they had left behind hours earlier—that Ostia was just about 5.6 kilometers—or in *American*, 3.5 miles—from the place where they had started the whole land journey.

She'd thanked the man profusely—while quite possibly agreeing to use his services when her time came? She wasn't entirely sure about that part, as his Italian was too fast for her to follow, and she only caught about a third of his words.

They'd checked into the *Hotel La Scaletta* in a hurry, a charming little 4-star beachside place with green awnings a little less than a quarter mile from the beach where the wedding was to take place.

She'd managed a quick shower while Daniele contacted the subway line to try to locate her missing suitcase. No luck, at least not yet—authorities were on the lookout.

With less than thirty minutes to go before the wedding, she and Daniele had ducked into a little touristy beach shop selling mostly kaftans and blowsy beach wear, and she'd found the first thing close enough to her size that wasn't absolutely hideous.

Daniele had used the Italian *Freenow* app to call a taxi, and they'd arrived at the beach with seven minutes to spare before the purported start time of the wedding.

Which had been almost an hour earlier.

Carmelina looked over her shoulder to where the brides were supposed to be. "Is there a problem?" she whispered into Daniele's ear.

"No. Italian weddings are always like this." Still, he looked over his shoulder, his jaw muscle twitching. "They will arrive soon."

Carmelina stifled a laugh. She'd long ago discovered that *arrivo*, which literally meant *I am arriving*, was Italian shorthand for "I'll probably arrive in the next hour or so. If nothing better comes up."

As if she had summoned them, the cloth doors to the bridal tent flew open, and the two brides strode out.

Isabella was radiant, her long dark hair flowing over the white chiffon wedding dress that looked like a confection dropped from the heavens, all sparkly and white and somehow glowing, with a long train that trailed across the sand behind her. A blue floral corsage on her wrist offered a pop of color.

Something old, something new, something borrowed, something blue. Well, the bride has borrowed enough of our patience, making us wait...

Daniele's cousin Elena was next to her, striking in a pinstripe tux, complete with a turquoise bowtie and matching carnation.

The string quartet, caught flatfooted by the sudden arrival of the brides, kicked into gear rather disjointedly, but eventually settled on the traditional wedding march, and the brides proceeded across the sand to the boardwalk.

The gathered friends and family stood, and Carmelina squeezed Daniele's hand. "They are so beautiful together."

He nodded, his eyes wet. "*Certo.*"

He'd explained to her on the way back from Almost Certainly Not Nero's Tomb that queer couples were not actually allowed to marry in Italy. They had Civil Unions instead, which were in many ways equivalent to marriage, but no adoption rights.

Carmelina thought that was rather petty of the Italian government, but when in Ostia...

Elena took Isabella's hand, and their faces lit up, as radiant as Isabella's dress. The couple passed by them and proceeded to the arbor, which was wrapped in more blue carnations, just as the sun reached the water's edge behind them.

The music stopped, and everyone took their seats. The officiant raised his hands and addressed the audience.

"*Siamo qui per assistere all'unione tra queste due donne...*"

Carmelina leaned against Daniele's shoulder, not caring if she smudged her makeup or mussed her hair—it was a lost cause anyhow—and smiled.

And just like that, all of the day's trials and tribulations were washed away, as she witnessed the love of two women who had fought every step of the way to be standing together in front of friends and family to declare their love. *How can you not look at this couple and see how much they love one another?*

Suddenly it didn't matter that she felt like a reject from a college toga party who hadn't showered for a week.

It was the perfect fairytale ending to the wreck of a day.

41

IMAGES OF A MISSED LIFE

"I gotta go, *Papà*. Love you." The connection cut out, and Diego was left staring at his phone.

"Love you, *topolino*." *My little mouse.* Diego shook his head. He had to stop thinking of Giovanni that way. His son was a grown man now, a good man. An intelligent man. Someone with dreams and ideas and a life all his own. *I kept you tied to me for too long. Time for you to fly.*

Luna had raised him well. For all her flaws, she had been a good mother, and she'd left Diego a precious gift in their son.

"*Com'è il nostro topolino?*" Matteo closed the door to the downstairs and took off his shirt. Even at fifty-five, he was still a handsome man, his figure trim, bits of gray at his temples only adding to his allure.

"Not a little mouse anymore. Maybe a… how you say *proccione?*"

Matteo grinned. "A raccoon. Yeah, that sounds about right—he's an enterprising little one. So how is he?"

Diego snorted. "He's all right. With Valentina now. He goes to his mother's gravesite today. Tomorrow, our time." He shook his head. "Poor kid. We ripped him away from everything and everyone he knew—"

"You did the right thing, *tesoro*." Matteo settled in next to him and kissed him on the cheek. "You've given him a good life. He's thriving here.

I wouldn't be surprised if he went on to open a restaurant of his own one day."

Wouldn't that be something? Diego was both thrilled and scared at the prospect of Gio moving on, even if they'd been preparing for it for years. Financially, at least. "You don't think I've tied him down too much?"

Matteo laughed, but it was a kindly sound. "Oh, you absolutely have. You're a *mamma Italiana*." He squeezed Diego's hand to take the sting out of the allegation. "And he's a real *mammone*. But even a mamma's boy needs to spread his wings eventually. You did the right thing. He'll find himself there. Look what coming here did for us."

His husband was right. Moving to America—even with all of her flaws —had changed their lives. "How about you? Good night at the restaurant?"

"Good enough."

There was an undertone in his voice that Diego recognized. "What?"

"It's… nothing. I'll tell you tomorrow." He crossed his arms, and Diego knew from long experience he'd get nothing more out of Matteo on the subject. "What are you planning for class?"

Diego's spirits lifted. He loved his Sunday class, even if most of the originals had moved on. "Something new." He showed Matteo the photo for the dish he was testing.

"Oooh. So purple. Cabbage?"

Diego nodded. "*Squisito*, no?"

"Yes, it's exquisite. Just like you." Matteo got up and extended his hand. "*Andiamo a letto?*"

"Go ahead. I'll join you in bed in a little bit."

"Okay." He knelt to kiss Diego on the lips. Then vanished down the dark hall toward their bedroom, whistling Tiziano Ferro's latest hit.

Diego smiled. He leaned forward to pick up the photo album from the low glass coffee table. An image of Gio at about five years old stared back at him, mouth open in delighted laughter and eyes a twinkle, his dark hair spiked like a rock star.

Gio as Diego had never known him.

He'd rescued a bunch of old photos after Luna had passed on, memories of a life he'd missed.

He leafed through it, stopping to gaze at Gio on his ninth birthday, sitting at a wooden table with a bunch of his school friends, blowing out candles on a bright yellow limoncello cake.

A few pages later, Gio in his Bologna FC outfit at maybe eleven, holding up a grass-stained football proudly.

So many missed days. He'd long since given up on being angry at Luna for keeping Gio from him. What was the point? She was beyond regret or retribution. He just wished he could have been there. *And now I have to let him go.*

The last photo—Gio with his mother, a few months before she died. She looked sad, but resigned. Had she known the end was coming?

"Good night, bright moon." He leaned forward and kissed the last photo. Then he set the book down. Matteo was right. Gio had made a life for himself here, though he would always carry his mother—and Italy—in his heart.

Why hadn't she told him? He supposed he would never know.

Maybe she hadn't wanted to disturb his life with Matteo. He supposed he should be grateful. The revelation that they'd spent the night together might have broken up an already fragile relationship.

Or maybe she'd wanted to keep Gio all to herself.

Luna had been unstable when he'd known her, though in Gio's telling, she had straightened out her life after he had been born, and had become a model mother. Of course, no child wants to see their parents' faults. *May he never see all of mine.*

He hoped Gio found what he was looking for at his mother's final resting place.

With a heavy sigh, he got up, his middle-aged Italian bones creaking under his weight, and headed for bed. He'd find solace for his aching heart in Matteo's arms.

42

———

I'M NOT ALICE

Warning: deadnaming.

Ben hustled through the evening, making sure his staff had things well in hand, both in the front and back of house. Sunday nights at Zocalo in East Sac were usually calmer, but tonight the place was bustling, the game was on the TVs above the bar, and the margaritas were flowing like a river.

More than once during the evening, he'd had to step in between a couple of patrons before things came to blows. It was a rare thing—the place wasn't a sports bar, after all—but some nights were just like that. And it wasn't even a full moon—that was still a week-and-a-half away.

The whole time, he thought about Lorelei. He'd spilled his big, dark secret to her the night before, and she'd barely flinched. She was a remarkable woman, and they'd already made plans to see each other again the next week. His heart raced at the thought of her.

"He's still there." Maria found him checking the next week's schedule at the host stand. Her voice carried a tinge of annoyance.

Ben glanced at the man who was seated at table one, the booth all the way in the corner, next to the picture windows that looked out onto the lovely University Village parking lot. He was middle-aged, dressed in a rumpled, light blue button-down shirt that was open far enough to show his hairy chest. He had on dark sunglasses, and he'd clearly made an effort to tame his unruly black hair, with minimal success. He looked like an out-of-work secret service man who'd lost his last client. True to the stereotype, he was nursing his third margarita, as if he was working up the courage for something. "Has he been rude to you?"

The waitress shrugged. "No. He's real quiet. You know, like 'he was always such a quiet man' quiet. But he's killing my turnover."

Ben laughed. "He can't be that bad. Why don't you ask if he'd mind moving to the bar and offer him a free drink on the house?"

She smiled. "Will do, *jefe*."

He watched her approach the man, wondering why he looked so familiar. *Must have seen him around somewhere.* Probably one of those customers who comes in every now and then, not quite often enough to be remembered, but enough so that they had that strange familiarity. He turned his attention back to the schedule. Angelica was out this week—

"He said no." Maria was back, and she was pouting. "Says he wants to talk to Alice."

Ben stiffened. *Alice? It must be a coincidence.* He turned to look at the man again, and found him staring back.

Maria bit her lip. "Will you talk to him? I need that table."

"Of course." *Definitely a coincidence.* "Let me just wrap up the schedule." He turned back to the screen. Cynthia and Ruby could work Saturdays, but Marta hated weekends… "There. That should do it." But she was already gone, on one of her other customers.

The man was staring at him intently. When he caught Ben's gaze, he picked up his margarita and drained the glass, setting it back down next to the others.

Ben sighed. *Best get this over with.*

On his way over, he pulled Carlos aside. "Keep an eye on me with the customer at table one. He's had a lot to drink." *Better safe than sorry.* He didn't need another black eye.

Carlos nodded. "You got it."

He grabbed a basket of chips, some bean dip, and some salsa. Best to come offering gifts *and* get the man to get some food in his stomach.

"Hi there. I'm Ben, one of the managers here." He offered the man a broad grin and set down his peace offering. "Thought you might want some more chips and salsa. It's a bit busy in here tonight, so I wonder if you wouldn't mind moving—"

"Alice Hamil."

The words were like a thunderbolt to Ben's brain, and his world spun to a halt. "Where did you hear that name?"

The man blushed. He actually blushed. "Look, I'm sorry. I had to know, but that was a shit move."

"I don't know what you're talking about." He felt sick. Cold and clammy, but hot and sweaty too, and light-headed. Goosebumps sprang up on his arms, and his stomach flipped in his gut. The last time someone had called him that…

The man frowned. "Hey, dude, take a seat. You don't look so good."

"I'm *not* Alice." Ben sank down into the booth seat across from the stranger, staring at him.

"I know. And I hate deadnaming. My sister was trans, and if some asshole did that to her, I'd smack the words right out of his mouth, right quick."

Ben stared at him. "Who the hell are you?"

"Everything okay here?" Carlos, bless his heart, appeared with a pitcher of water. He eyed the man warily.

Ben blinked. *It most definitely is not.* But he waved Carlos away anyhow. He needed to find out why the man was there. "I can take care of it. Thank you, Carlos."

"Sure thing." Carlos nodded and backed away, his gaze flickering between the two seated men.

"Bring me a water?"

"You got it, boss." Carlos made a beeline to the kitchen, and Ben turned his attention back to the man.

The stranger leaned forward. "In answer to your question, I'm Edward Braxton the Third, PI, at your service. But my friends all call me Eddy." He handed Ben a business card. "I've been looking for you for weeks, Mr. Hammond. You're a hard man to track down."

Ben narrowed his eyes. "It's been a long time since anyone has used my deadname, Mr. Braxton, and I don't take kindly to it." He set the card down on the table and started to get up, though his shaky legs almost betrayed him. "Now if you'll excuse me—"

"She wants to see you." The pleading sound in Eddy's voice brought him back down onto his seat.

"*Who* wants to see me?" But he had a sinking feeling that he already knew.

"Your mother."

Ben's laugh was bitter. "Nice try. My mother disowned me more than a decade ago, Mr. Braxton. Please let her know I have no desire to hear from her, let alone see her—"

"She's dying."

Ben stared at the PI, his mouth gone dry. "What?"

Eddy nodded. "Emily's terminal. She sent me to find you. She wants to see you before she dies."

He slammed back down onto the booth seat. "Holy fucking crap." His mother was dying, Still, why should he care? She'd kicked him to the curb for being who he was, without a second thought.

Eddy put a big hand over his. "Look, I get it. You're hurt, and you have every right to be. When Delia told me she was trans, I went apeshit. I tried to talk her out of it. I yelled at her. And then I did the stupidest thing in my whole fucking life. I cut her off for five long years. You know what it got me? Five years of pain and sadness and loneliness. And I was lucky, Mr. Hammond. I came to my senses, and I went to her and apologized on my knees. And she forgave me." He was shaking, his eyes wet. "So look, your mother is dying, and she wants to see you. If you tell her no, you are going to regret it for the rest of your natural born life. Don't say no." He pulled his arm away and sank back against the back of the booth, seeming to shrink before Ben's eyes.

Ben shook his head. "I can't. It's too late—"

"It's never too late. Until it is. I lost Delia three years ago now, but I thank God every day that I got right with her while she was still here."

Ben took a deep breath. He was doing just fine without his mother in his life. Better than fine. He'd managed to build a life here. He had a great job, a side career as a novelist, and a circle of friends who loved him—his found family. Why let Emily Hamil ruin all of that?

She's dying.

The words reverberated through his head. What kind of man would he be if he wouldn't make his mother's dying wish come true?

"Here's the water, boss. Sorry it took so long. I got stuck on the patio—"

"It's okay, Carlos." He waved the waiter away, then took the water glass and drained it in one gulp, as if it were whiskey. Truth be told, he could have used some strong spirits right about then.

He stared at the empty glass and sighed. *She wants to see me.* Wasn't that what he'd wanted to hear for so many years? "If I agree, and that's a big if, when and where would I meet her?"

Eddy nodded. "Good man. How about tomorrow night? I can arrange a dinner for the two of you—"

"She's in town?" *Surprise after surprise.* How like his mother to go on the offensive, to bring the fight to him.

He nodded. "She flew in the moment I identified you—"

Ben's eyes narrowed. "You were in my car the other day, weren't you? That's how you figured out it was me."

Eddy laughed. "Very perceptive of you. What gave me away?"

"Things were out of order. I'm a bit of a neat freak." It should have bothered him more, but having met the man, and knowing who he was and why he was here, took some of the sting out of it. He pulled out a pen and a business card and wrote his private number on the back. "Give her this. Have her call me tomorrow morning and I'll arrange something myself."

The PI took the card and nodded. "Very well." He tucked it into his shirt pocket. "Mind if I stay and finish those chips? I had one margarita too many, I think. Need something in my stomach before I hit the road."

"Stay as long as you like. Order dinner. It's on the house." He bit his lip. "I'm sorry about your sister. She sounds like a remarkable woman."

Eddy nodded. "She was. Thank you."

He got up. "Good day, Mr. Braxton." He turned his back on the bearer of bad news.

"Good luck, Ben. You're doing the right thing." The crunching of chips accompanied him on the way back to the host stand.

"Well?" Maria was waiting for him, her eyebrow raised.

"I suspect he'll leave soon enough." *But not without stirring up a shit-storm.* "Get him something to eat first, on the house."

Her shoulders slumped. "So who's Alice?"

Ben shook his head. "No one I know." That much was true. He supposed he could say the same about Emily Hamil. "No one at all."

43

THE BELLEI BOYS

Morning sunlight streamed through *le veneziane*—Venetian blinds — to draw stark lines across the bright blue and red bedspread—Bologna Football Club's colors.

Gio sat up and rubbed his eyes, and looked around Dante's room—his cousin had slept on a couch downstairs the night before. Dante's room was so much like his own when he'd lived in Italy with Luna that it brought unexpected tears of homesickness to his eyes. Dante even had a Bologna FC poster on the wall, though the featured player was Riccardo Orsolini, not Archimede Morleo, like back in his day. *Everything changes, but everything stays the same.*

There was even a wooden desk and chair in one corner that looked astonishingly like his own. In fact, it probably was. Zia Valentina had helped take care of Luna's things after Gio's mother's death, almost a decade earlier.

Gio patted his stomach. He was still full from the impressive meal his *zia* had served up to welcome Gio back to Italy. Some *crostini* for starters sprinkled with olive oil and chopped tomatoes and garlic, the famous *passatelli*, *pizza alla bufala*, and for dessert a delicious banana chocolate *semifreddo. And they say Americans eat a lot.*

There were sounds of activity in the house outside the room—feet padding down the stairs, some clanking probably from the kitchen—and the unmistakable smell of Italian coffee slipped under the door and into the little room. *Gardelli, if I had to guess.*

He checked his iWatch—8:30 AM. With the nine-hour difference, *Babbo* would still be awake. He picked up his iPhone and called his father.

Diego answered almost immediately. "*Ciao tesoro… come sta l'Italia?*"

"Not bad. I got into Bertinoro last night. You wouldn't believe how big Dante's gotten!"

Diego chuckled. "You boys grow up so fast. How is *mia sorella?*"

"She's good. She made me *passatelli* last night. I know how you love her *passatelli.*"

Diego snorted. "I make it better than she does."

"I don't know, *Papà*. It was pretty good…" In fact Diego's *was* better, but Gio couldn't help teasing him a little over it.

There was a pointed silence on the line. Then "You are no longer my son."

Gio grinned. "Is that all it takes?"

Diego laughed.

Time to bring up the real reason for my call. "So… I'm going to see mamma today."

There was another long silence at the other end of the line.

"*Papà?*"

"Sorry." He cleared his throat, and Gio thought he heard a sniffle. "It's hard to believe it's been ten years. Almost."

"Almost." He closed his eyes, remembering that dark time clearly… the afternoon they'd buried his mother. It had been a lovely, bright day, the white towers of the crematorium rising out of the ground like some fantastical castle out of *Lord of the Rings*. Yet he'd felt only a suffocating sense of numbness. "I miss her, *Papà*. I miss her every day." He flipped over to his photos and the one of her that he had by his bedside at home. She was beautiful, ethereal, like an angel with her long dark hair mussed around her face by the wind.

"*Lo so.*" *I know.*

Diego's relationship with Luna had been distant and fractured, right up until that night one mid-October, when her beautiful soul had passed suddenly into the darkness, leaving Gio all alone with a father he didn't know.

Someone knocked on the door. "*Cugino*, you up? Mamma has breakfast ready."

Gio rolled his eyes. Dante sounded way too awake already. "I gotta go, *Papà*. Love you." He set down his phone and closed his eyes, trying to remember how his mother had smelled. *Pink. Like roses.*

"Gio, you okay in there?" Dante sounded a little annoyed.

"Yeah. Be right down."

"Good. See you in the kitchen!" The man-boy's steps echoed down the wooden stairs.

Ten minutes later, dressed and with his own dark hair combed into some semblance of order, he headed downstairs to find Dante and his sister Bianca wolfing down their meal.

"Morning, Gio." Bianca was turning into a beautiful young woman, her dark hair tucked behind elfin ears. "How was night in the *capra's* bedroom?"

Dante growled at her. "I'm not a goat."

"Well, you smell like one." She wrinkled her nose and winked at Gio.

"Bianca, be nice to your brother." Valentina glared at her daughter over her stylish Italian lenses.

Gio grinned. "Not bad. That desk looks familiar."

Zia Val nodded. "It should. It used to be yours. Have a seat. I've put out some *cornetti*, yogurt, *fragole*, corn flakes, and milk. Coffee?"

"Yes please." Gio slid into the seat next to Dante. He took a sip of the coffee—it was rich and dark, full of hidden flavors. He poured himself some corn flakes and strawberries, but when he grabbed the milk, he frowned. It was warm. Well, lukewarm. He'd forgotten that particular Italian quirk. "Zia Valentina, do you have any cold milk?"

She tsk-tsked him. "Cold liquids will make you sick." Nevertheless, she pulled a container of chilled milk from the fridge. "So you're headed out again today?"

Gio nodded. "I'm going to see mamma." She was buried in a cemetery just outside Bologna, about an hour and ten minutes north by car. Of course, they'd be going not just by car but then train and bus, so it would be twice that long, with a twenty minute walk around the cemetery at the other end to boot.

Dante stared at him. "I thought she was dead?"

"Danno!" His aunt slapped Dante upside the head. "Watch your manners."

"Ow!" His shoulders slumped. "Sorry."

Gio managed a weak smile. "It's okay. Sometimes I forget too." He poured the milk over his cereal and handed the container back to his *zia*. "*Grazie mille.*"

"*Figurati.* Then where?" She traded it for a cup of steaming coffee.

"I've made a list of places I want to visit. A few festivals, some famous restaurants, some cities known for one type of food or another. I'm looking for inspiration." He bit into one of the *cornetti*. It was delicious. "Though maybe I should just stay here and learn from you. This is fantastic."

His aunt blushed. "It's nothing special."

He finished it off in two more big bites. "No, seriously. You could sell these."

"She does." Bianca licked her own fingers clean. "Mamma makes them for the local bar."

"Can I get the recipe?" His father would love them. They were filled with just the right amount of chocolate and sprinkled with cocoa and powdered sugar.

"Not even my children have my recipes. They're locked in a safe until I die." But he could tell from the way that she said it that she was flattered. "Where will you be staying?"

"In youth hostels, mostly. I have a list." Diego had helped him fill out his itinerary.

"You're very organized." Bianca seemed to approve. "Unlike some people around here."

"Hey!" Dante scowled at her.

"Hush, *cucciolo.*" Valentina kissed Dante on the head. "Gio, I have a gift for you, and a request." She sat down at the head of the table and picked up a cornetto of her own.

"Of course. I'm indebted to you for letting me stay." He barely knew Gio's family. *It's time we rectify that.*

"*Che assurdità.* You're family. Of course you can always stay with us."

She set down the pastry. "I had Dante dig that out of storage." She pointed to a bright orange backpack in the corner of the room. The oversized kind that backpackers wore.

Gio raised an eyebrow.

"It was your father's. Far better for traveling the countryside than that heavy suitcase you brought. You can leave that here, and pick it up before you leave."

Gio nodded. He'd had a hard time dragging his suitcase—even with the wheels—across the cobblestones in Rome and Bologna. And it meant he'd have to come back to see them again. *Score one for Zia Valentina.* "*Grazie mille.* And the request?"

She leaned forward and flashed him a charming smile. "Take Dante with you."

He stared at her. *Surely she didn't just ask me to…* "*Cosa?*"

"He's just graduated from high school. Bianca is off to visit her friends in Sardinia, and my baby boy needs to see a little more of the world." She put a warm hand on his, bright red nails resting threateningly on the soft skin of his wrist. "I would really appreciate it, *tesoro.*"

It was Gio's turn to blush. How could he say no to her? She was family, after all. "I don't know…" Dante was like an oversized, overeager puppy dog who wanted to be scratched *all the time.*

"*Per favore, cugino?* I'd love to spend time with you and hear all about America. You don't think they're going to re-elect that *pallone arancione*, do you?"

Santo cielo. If he'd been a practicing Catholic, he'd have crossed himself. "Of course not." It might not be a bad thing to have someone at his side who knew Italy better than he did. He was a bit rusty after almost a decade away. And the look on Dante's face… "I guess it couldn't hurt—"

The words were cut off when his cousin threw his man-boy arms around him and squeezed the air out of him. "*Che fantastico.* I'm all packed and ready to go."

"You are? That's… great." Gio was already regretting his decision.

Zia Valentina pulled an envelope out of her pocket and slid it over to him. "Here's a little extra to help pay his way. If you need more, just text me." She leaned over the table and kissed his cheek. "*Santo cielo*, what a pleasure it will be to have a few days alone in an empty house."

I'll bet. "What do you have planned?" Gio imagined she'd get a lot of laundry done.

"A few days in bed with that handsome butcher in town. What's his name? Angelo?" She flashed him a wicked grin.

"Mamma!" Bianca looked scandalized.

"Eighteen years, taking care of you two. Mamma can take a week to herself." She got up and kissed Bianca's cheek. "Besides, you'll both be too busy to think about poor old me."

"*Assolutamente!*" Dante got up too and carried his dishes to the sink. "Hurry up, *cugino*, so we can get out of here. The world awaits the Bellei boys."

Gio rolled his eyes. *What have I gotten myself into?*

44

TO CATCH A THIEF

Sunday morning dawned bright and clear. The middle of May was turning out to be just about perfect, and the ray of sunshine that slanted in through the mostly closed bedroom drapes suggested a beautiful day.

Matteo groaned. He was not looking forward to this day, sunny or not.

First off, Gio was gone. For weeks, probably. Back to Italy, which, even if it wasn't the same country he and Diego had left a decade earlier, was still and always would be his first home. It had been strange not having Diego's son's youthful energy at Ragazzi the day before, but Matteo hoped that the time apart would do both of them good.

Diego had moped around all night in the kitchen—it was clear how much he missed his son.

But the other thing… Matteo stared up at the ceiling, willing the clock to move back an hour or so.

He was going to have to fire Ainsley Kim.

He'd carefully segregated his three top suspects in the *Mystery of the Missing Funds*. Three waiters, three separate shifts. Ainsley, Alex, and Justin.

Alex had worked the lunch hour on Thursday, and the till had come up perfect. Well, ten cents off, but nobody was gonna steal a dime.

He was rather proud of himself for the use of the very American word "gonna," even if it was only in his head.

Justin's turn had come Friday night. It had been a busy evening with over a hundred guests. And there'd actually been a $2 surplus. Which wasn't *great*—they didn't want to fleece their customers, after all, and prices were already high enough with inflation. And yet… Justin clearly wasn't the thief.

Which left Ainsley.

When he'd tallied up the totals for Saturday night, he'd hoped against hope that it wasn't her.

She'd come to him two weeks before her first semester at Sac State, desperate for a job. Her parents could barely afford her tuition, which left almost nothing to live on. And the tuition went up every year.

She'd seemed sweet and young… *so young*. Less than half of his own fifty-two years, at the time.

He'd sensed something in her. She had an innate likability, a lovely soul, and he'd rarely been wrong about such things. Everything had worked out great—she was a hard worker, and the customers all loved her.

And then the till had come up $100 short. *Again.*

He'd gone back over his notes about the last few times it had happened. Always on a Saturday night. And every time, Ainsley had been on shift.

What was she doing with that cash? It wasn't a lot in the grand scheme of things. Not enough to buy much of anything, really. Maybe she used it to go out and party after work with her friends? Though she didn't seem the type…

Maybe it was for something else. Something she didn't have a choice about.

In the end, the *why* didn't really matter. He couldn't allow someone who stole from the business to stay.

"*Ciao, bello.*" Diego stretched in bed, rubbing his eyes. "*Che ora è?*"

"It's 6:15." He could put it off a little longer—she was probably still in her dorm room, asleep. "How are you doing?"

Diego rubbed his smooth chest with one hand. Still so handsome, after all these years. "Am okay. Gio called at midnight. He is off to see Luna's grave today." A shadow crossed his face, but it was gone as swiftly as it appeared. "And you? Why you groaning this morning? Achy bones?" He leaned over to peck Matteo on the cheek.

"Ah, *una cosa difficile*. I have to let one of our servers go." Saying it out loud was painful.

Diego frowned. "*Perché?* There is enough money. We are doing well, right?"

Matteo nodded. "Yes. Though for a bit there during the pandemic…" Those had been dark times. "One of our employees has been stealing cash."

Diego sat up, alarm flashing across his handsome features. "*Cazzo. Chi?*"

"Ainsley Kim." He still couldn't believe it. There had to be an explanation. *Right? And why now, after all this time?* "Every Saturday night, there's $100 missing from the till, and she's the only one—"

Diego burst out laughing.

"*Cosa?*" *How is this funny?* He'd been agonizing over it for months.

Diego flashed him a wide grin. "Because I'm your thief."

Matteo stared at him. "*Che cosa?*"

Diego leaned forward to kiss his cheek. "*Tesoro*, every Sunday morning I must to pay one of our local produce vendors. She runs a small organic farm just outside of Placerville, and she's had the rough times lately. So I pay her *in contanti*. In cash."

Matteo frowned. "But it's not in the ledger…"

"*Sono un vecchio*. I am old man." Diego shrugged, somehow making himself even more adorable. "Sometimes I forgets?"

A wave of relief washed over him. "*Grazie al Dio!* I don't have to fire her." The day was getting better already! He narrowed his eyes. "But someone must be punished for this mistake."

Diego shrieked with feigned terror as Matteo launched himself at his lover, until his voice was muffled by a passionate kiss.

45

THE MONK'S HALF SLEEVES

"So this is the place, huh?" Oscar didn't look impressed.

Sam stared at the glass doors of the restaurant. "Yup, this is where the magic happened." He was strangely reluctant to cross the threshold into the place where he and Brad had gotten married, almost a decade before. That had been a joyful day.

How had it been that long? Today's anguish only made the memory of it burn brighter.

"You don't have to do this." Oscar put a warm hand on his shoulder.

They'd spent the last couple days crisscrossing the city, visiting places that Sam remembered from when he'd lived in Sacramento with Brad. Many of them had disappeared or been drastically changed, including the LGBT Center where Brad had worked, which had moved twice from the charming but somewhat dilapidated Victorian house on L Street next to the railroad tracks. First to a temporary home on K Street next to Faces, the mega gay bar at the heart of Lavender Heights, and then into a beautiful brick building that had once housed Electronic Arts, on the main part of 20th Street just around the corner.

"No, I want to see it. I need to see it." He had many fond memories of the place besides the wedding. Dropping Ricky off for the work-study program Brad had crafted with the Ragazzi boys. Learning to cook Italian recipes with his friends. Dinners out with Brad after a long day working.

"If you're sure…" Oscar had been his rock these past few difficult days.

"I am. Come on." He took Oscar's hand, pulled open the door, and stepped inside before he could change his mind.

The place was nearly unchanged. It still had the same comfortable, understated elegance that he remembered—none of the jarring red and white checkered tablecloths and dripping candles on wine bottles that he remembered from Italian restaurants in Tucson that he'd visited with his family as a child.

Instead, it was painted in a warm cocoa with cherrywood accents, including the long bar along one side. Immaculate white tablecloths were set with burgundy napkins wrapped around silverware, and the lights were hand-blown glass, probably from Murano in Venice. Matteo and Diego had exquisite taste.

There were a few diners, but it was still early for lunch.

The only difference he could see was the new door near the back, and the sign that announced a "cooking class *fantastico*."

Sam grinned. *Diego's work, clearly.*

A perky blond woman in a white shirt and black tie, with tattooed sleeves of bright green leaves and golden trumpet flowers on each arm, greeted them at the host's stand. "Lunch for two?"

"No…" Sam glanced at her neatly-lettered nametag. "…Aimee. We're here for the cooking class." He didn't recognize her. She must be new. At least since he and Brad had moved to Tucson.

"Ah sorry. That's in the teaching kitchen. But you can go through the door in the back." She pointed the way. "Chef Diego should be in there already." She flashed them a smile, and then went back to organizing menus.

"Thanks." He grabbed Oscar's hand again. "Come on!" He led his friend to the back of the restaurant, but before going through the door, he stopped and turned to look back toward the front windows.

"What?"

"Give me a sec." He closed his eyes.

He could still see that day as if it were yesterday. The place had been magical. *Candles everywhere, silver stars hung from the ceiling, twinkling lights on the bar… and that perfect moment when Brad kissed me after we said 'I do.'"*

"You see it too?"

Sam blinked. *That voice…*

Sure enough, Brad stood there next to him, taking in the same view.

"You… you're not really here." He looked around. The whole place was deserted. Oscar, the hostess Aimee… even the few patrons seemed to have taken their leave. "I'm losing my mind."

Brad laughed. "Maybe."

Sam snorted. "You're no help." *Here I am, talking to a ghost.*

"Sorry. It's your fault, really. I'm only here because you're not ready to let go of me yet."

"Is that so?"

Brad nodded. "I'm already in greener pastures. Or I would be, if you would let me go."

"I can't." It was too painful. He needed Brad. Needed not to be alone.

"I know." Brad exhaled sharply. "He likes you, you know."

"Who? Oscar? No he doesn't—"

"He followed you all the way here. He took time off work. He's been with you the whole time. I've seen the way he looks at you." He nodded, seeming pleased with himself.

Sam shook his head. "It's not true. And even if it was… it's too soon."

"Maybe." Brad stared at his feet. "I just want you to be happy, Sam."

"Then you shouldn't have died." It came out far more sharply than he'd intended. "I'm sorry, Brad."

But his husband was already gone.

Sam took a deep breath and then let it out, echoing Brad's gesture. "We were so happy that day."

"I know. I miss him too. Every day." Oscar squeezed his hand, and for just a second, Sam saw what Brad had told him, something in the way Oscar looked at him.

I'm not ready. He pushed the feeling away, and Oscar with it, letting go of his friend's hand.

"Sam?"

He spun around to see the chef standing in front of him. "Diego?"

"Eccomi! Ciao bello!"

He embraced his old friend. "It's good to see you again. Sorry I couldn't spend more time with you the other day at the funeral…"

Diego shook his head emphatically. "Nonsense. There was many people. You were busy. Are you here for the class?"

Sam nodded. "And my friend Oscar. But only if you have room?"

"We always have rooms for you." He ushered Sam and Oscar into the new teaching kitchen.

It was sparkling and bright, all the surfaces fresh-cleaned and smelling of bleach and Pine-sol. "This place is amazing. When did you open it?"

"A couple years ago. It was an American bar before Covid." Diego led them back to his own station at the front of the class.

"I remember." One of those old-school places, dark and moody, where you might meet a good friend for a quick drink after a long day at work. "But this… it looks great! What are we making today?"

"*Una cosa moderna.* A modern dish. I show you."

It was as if a shadow had lifted from his vision. Somehow, in crossing the threshold from the place where he and Brad had been married to this new place, full of possibility, he had crossed another threshold inside his own heart. He didn't understand it yet, but he knew it was true. "Sure. Show us."

Diego grinned. "*Avanti!* Well, you start with some onion, a little purple cabbage, and a pasta from my home region of Emilia Romagna called *mezze maniche dei frati*, or 'monks' half sleeves'…"

Sam flashed Oscar a smile, and settled into a stool next to him to listen to Diego's wayward and entertaining explanation.

Oscar's hand found his.

This time, Sam didn't let go.

46

MUFFINS ON A SUNDAY MORNING

"**A**re you fucking serious?" Marissa's smile reached her earlobes She wasn't proud of the fact that, at the end of that sentence, her voice reached one of the upper octaves usually reserved for shattering glass. But she couldn't help herself.

Ainsley had shown up on her doorstep early Sunday morning, with a mocha and a latte from the Everyday Grind in one hand and a sack of pastries in the other, grinning from ear to ear. Marissa had demanded to know what was up, but she'd insisted on laying out her purchases—two glorious apple caramel muffins, the aforementioned coffee, and a bright spray of yellow flowers.

Crocus, maybe? They were lovely little things, like golden trumpets.

Then Ainsley had dropped the news about Jun Seo.

Marissa had questions. "But wait... what about everything that happened at the gallery? Did they mention that? Will you have to work with that horrible man? Do your parents know? What about the commute—"

Ainsley stopped her with a kiss.

Marissa relaxed into it, letting go of her questions for the moment and simply enjoying the deliciously beautiful woman sitting in front of her.

How did I get so lucky? Just a few weeks before, she'd been in despair that her life would never change.

The sweet kiss lasted a couple hours, or maybe it only seemed like it, because her mocha was still hot when they finished. Still, she dialed things back a bit, taking a sip and watching Ainsley through half-lidded eyes.

"They apologized—they were really offended on my behalf. They even fired the bastard, so no, I won't have to work with him. And no. I haven't told my parents yet, but I will." Ainsley peeled off the wrapper from one of the muffins. She bit into it, and a grin spread across her face. "Oh my god. It really *is* true. The tops are the best part."

Marissa had more questions, but dammit, she was hungry too. She grabbed the other muffin and made short work of it, all but inhaling the poor thing.

Ainsley was right. It was delicious, especially the top with its apple slices and gobs of caramel. "So when do you start?" She licked the crumbs and sticky bits off her fingers.

"Tomorrow, maybe? He said this week." Ainsley was daintier with hers. Or maybe she was toying with it like a cat might do with a particularly plump and defenseless mouse. "Right now I just want to finish my breakfast and bask in the glory of it all. Working for Jun Seo!" She sank back in the gray kitchen chair and closed her eyes. "It's what I've always dreamed about."

Marissa raised an eyebrow. "Working with a non-binary Southern Korean artist, after their manager tried to sexually assault you?"

Aisley flinched.

"Sorry. I was going for funny." Marissa put a hand on Ainsley's in apology. "Too soon?"

"Yeah, maybe just a little. But no, not that *exactly*. Working with a *real artist*. Getting a leg up in the business." She finished off the muffin and took a swig of her latte.

Marissa could understand that. "What about your parents?" She hadn't met them yet, but from what Ainsley had said, they wouldn't exactly be overjoyed by her dropping out of college. Especially the part about giving up on being a doctor to pursue a more... *artistic* career.

"Let's not talk about that right now." Ainsley finished her latte and pulled Marissa in for another kiss.

It was a surprisingly effective distraction tactic, especially when Ainsley pulled away and whispered in her ear: "Wanna celebrate in a more… intimate way?" Her voice was husky, and it sent shivers up Marissa's spine.

Don't have to ask me twice. She took Ainsley's hand and pulled her toward the bedroom, her heart pounding in her chest. It was turning out to be an excellent day.

~

Ainsley lay on her side, staring out the window at the gray walls of the next building over, her breathing slowing, the sheen of sweat on her naked back and shoulder cooling under the apartment's air conditioning. Marissa's apartment was a study in white and shades of gray, almost Zen in its monochrome intensity.

Behind her, Marissa was purring like a kitten.

"Good for you, too?" A smile curved her lips.

"Oh my God. You have no idea." Marissa's voice was soft, a whisper followed by a satisfied sigh. "You were… that was incredible."

Ainsley rolled over to face her. "You were pretty good yourself." For a few moments, time had been suspended, all of her worries pushed out of her head into the ether. For a magical interval, only Marissa had existed for her—the glorious expanse of her soft skin, her warm naked lips, her heart beating rapidly under Ainsley's seeking touch like a wild thing.

But now her worries were back.

She shoved them aside, hoping for a couple more moments of peace. She traced Marissa's jawline with a finger, eliciting a ghost of a smile. "You are so beautiful. I wish I had my pencil so I could draw you."

Marissa turned to face her, the smile broadening to light up her face. "Look into my eyes."

She did as she was told. They were a beautiful, warm brown, like chocolate and honey. "I'm looking." A thrill ran through her at the intensity of Marissa's gaze.

"I want to remember you just like this. And I want you to remember me, too. No photos, no pictures, no pencils. Just the two of us here together, alone, in the gauzy Sunday morning light, the afterglow of what we just did together."

Ainsley laughed. "You have the soul of an artist."

Marissa shook her head, her eyes flashing. "I can't draw to save my life."

"Maybe not, but you see the world like one." She leaned forward and gave Marissa a soft kiss.

Marissa kissed her back, briefly, but then pulled away. "You need to call your parents."

Ainsley snorted. "Your foreplay needs work."

"Well, technically it would be *afterplay*. But I'm serious. You have two parents who love you—you don't know how lucky you are." A shadow flickered across her face but was gone in an instant. "You *need* to tell them."

Ainsley scrunched up her face. "I don't wanna."

Marissa took her hand. "You can do this. I'll help you."

"You don't have to…"

"I want to." Marissa squeezed her hand. "Look, this is what you've always dreamed of, right?"

Ainsley nodded. "Since I was a little girl. But they will be so disappointed—"

"It's your life to live, not theirs." Marissa frowned.

"What?" In that moment, they were attuned to one another, connected by a thread so fine that Ainsley could feel each little tug of Marissa's soul.

Marissa closed her eyes. "I'm an idiot. That's all."

Ainsley let go of her hand and reached up to push a lock of golden hair behind her ear. "Why?"

Marissa stared at her in mock-anger. "You're supposed to tell me I'm *not* an idiot."

Ainsley laughed. "We're *all* idiots sometimes. Why do you think you're one now?"

"Because here I am giving you advice to follow your heart. And I've let myself stop following my own." Her hand touched her chest, clutching slowly at the space above her breasts.

"Ah." Ainsley leaned forward, putting her forehead against Marissa's. "And what does your heart want you to do?"

"I want to cook." She smiled wistfully. "I was always happiest when I was working at Ragazzi—"

She could see that. "Then you should cook." It seemed simple enough to her. Suddenly Marissa's drab gray existence made sense. She was punishing herself for something.

Marissa frowned. "It's not that easy. What about my job? What will Marcos and Dave think?"

"It's your life to live, not theirs."

Marissa laughed softly. "Damn you. Using my own words against me."

"They're good words." Ainsly rolled onto her back, staring up at the ceiling. "I'll do it if you will." It sounded like a dare. *Maybe it is.*

"Change my life? I don't know…"

"Don't you *want* to be happy?" And there it was, the question that underlay everything. She wasn't happy. Marissa wasn't happy either. But maybe they could be, if they held each other's hands and stepped into the unknown together.

"I… think I do." Marissa sat up, staring down at her. "Holy crap. The idea scares the shit out of me. But I really do."

Ainsley lifted herself up and put her arms around Marissa, pulling her close again. "Then that's what we'll do. Come with me tonight to tell my parents? If you don't, I'm afraid I'll lose my nerve." She started shaking at the thought of actually going through with it. Her mother and father would be so angry.

Marissa put her warm palms on Ainsley's cheeks, looking into her eyes again. "We'll do this together. We'll choose happiness."

Ainsley looked into her eyes again. They were warm and full of love. "Happiness."

Somehow, together they'd get through all the hard parts, and reach the other side.

"I think I'm falling in love with you." Marissa's eyes searched hers, challenging her to respond.

Unable to find the words Marissa wanted from her, Ainsley kissed her again instead, hoping against hope that it was enough.

47

MOONRISE

Gio got out of the bus, shouldering his heavy, bright orange backpack. It had been a long trip. First the train ride, held in Imola for a couple hours due to some issue farther up the tracks. They finally made it into Bologna, where they stopped to grab a quick bite at the station, a place called Rosso Pomodoro, which, unlike the KFC and Burger King next door, at least seemed to be homegrown Italian.

Dante had been like a little kid, his eyes wide, his gaze darting in every direction. He must've traveled by train before, but it was his first time out on his own, without his mother. He was thrilled to see the world.

In fact, he kept wandering off like a puppy dog, chasing after one new thing after another. A tourist shop full of t-shirts. A beautiful woman who crossed his path. An African street vendor selling fashion knockoffs on a white sheet.

Gio had to keep a close eye on him so he didn't get lost. Zia Valentina would never forgive him if he lost her oldest son. It was exhausting.

Now, after a bus ride out to the northwestern corner of Bologna, they were finally within striking distance of his mother's grave.

The bus trundled off, leaving them alone on the side of the road in front of the Dolce Vita Bar. It was a quiet neighborhood, and the bus stop was actually pretty close to the cemetery.

"Is this the place?" Dante settled his own backpack on his shoulders and looked around. His eyes went wide. "Wait, this is where the Ducati Museum is?"

"I suppose." He'd never really paid attention.

"Oooh. Can we go? *Cugino*? I love the Ducati. *Vroom vroom!*"

"Maybe later." It was strange being back here, after all these years. The last time, he'd been numb, empty as the open sea—just days after his mother's death. This man from America had come to tell him that he was Gio's father, and that he was about to take him away from everything that he had ever known.

"Not much to it." Dante's gaze alighted on the pastry shop. "Hey, want to get a chocolate—"

Gio grabbed him by the ear and turned him around. "Come on. Graveside visit now. More food later."

"Ahi! What did you do that for?" Nevertheless, he followed Gio as his cousin stomped away down the sidewalk, back the way the bus had come from. "Where are we going?"

"To the cemetery."

"But the bus just came from there."

Gio sighed. He was tired of playing babysitter. "We passed the entrance a minute ago." He pulled his phone and sent a quick text to his father. *Just got to the cemetery. Will check in with you later.*

It was after midnight in California, but his father was probably still awake. He was starting to miss his real life, and his parents.

Dante caught up with him, huffing a little. "I barely remember this place. I was just a kid." He lifted his pack up and resettled it on his shoulders. "Do you think about her a lot?"

Gio nodded. "Every day." He was lucky. He knew it. He had two fathers who loved him, and a new life in America that was full of promise. But sometimes he wished he still lived here in *Italia* with his mother. It was as if something important, something as vital to him as the air he breathed, had been stolen from him.

They reached a big pink church called Santa Maria Assunta, next to a broad concrete driveway and a narrower brick path that led through an old brick wall into what looked like a park. He checked his map. "I think this is it." He felt a strange shiver of trepidation. They were here. There was no going back now. *Not that I want to.*

Dante frowned. "Wasn't there a couple of white towers? They looked like nuclear reactors?"

Or a fairytale castle… "That's on the other side. We came in that way for my mother's funeral. But unless you want a long walk…"

"No, I'm good with this one. How old do you think that wall is?" And he was off to check it out.

It was an impressively old wall, full of scars and shadows of things that had once been in front of it or attached to it.

Gio let him go. He couldn't wander far.

Across from the church was a small florist, perfectly positioned to sell flowers to anyone entering the cemetery. Temporary shelving obscured half the old wall, covered with bright blossoms of all kinds—peonies, birds of paradise, carnations, roses, hollyhocks, baby breath, and many others he didn't recognize. He poked his head into the interior. "*Salve.*"

A friendly looking woman with bright pink hair and green eyes smiled at him. "*Auguri.* What can I get you?"

"Do you have any white lilies? They were my mother's favorite."

A shadow crossed her face. "I am sorry. You look too young to have lost a mother."

"It was nine years ago. I've just come back from *gli Stati Uniti.* I wanted… I needed to visit her." *To see her again.* Though he didn't say that part out loud.

"I think I still have some." She ducked into the back, and returned a moment later, holding a dozen white lilies triumphantly. "*Eccoli!*"

"*Grazie mille.*" He pulled out his wallet. "What do I owe you?"

She squeezed his hand. "*Niente.* I was about to throw them away anyhow." She looked up into his eyes. "I have a son about your age. I hope he cares as much about me when I'm gone as you do about your mother." She pulled his head down and kissed his forehead, then patted his cheeks.

"That's very kind of you." *Some son I am. I haven't been back here in almost a decade.*

"*Di niente.*" She waved him off, and turned back to her work, but not before he noticed the moisture around her eyes.

He retreated outside to find Dante on his knees next to the wall, picking at some of the grout between the bricks. He whistled. "Here boy."

Dante looked up and blushed. "I was just trying to figure out when the wall was built. Prewar, I'd guess…" He got up and brushed off his jeans, and fell in next to Gio.

They passed through the gate together and followed the cracked pavement down a narrow road lined by Italian cypress. After a fork in the road, they passed a couple of markers with lists of names—*Died in Imprisonment. Died from Illness. Died in the Fields; Died from Wounds.*

"I think you were right about the wall." He pointed at the dates on the markers, in Roman numerals. 1925 and 1928.

Dante grinned. "I knew it." Then his expression turned somber as he read the names.

There were few other people out on the narrow road, and a car passed by only once, moving slowly as if in respect for this sacred place.

As they progressed between hundreds of markers on either side of the road, each topped with fresh flowers, Dante glanced at him repeatedly, as if he wanted to ask something but couldn't work up the courage.

"What?" It came out sharper than he intended.

"It's just… I can't remember her. She was pretty, right? What was she like?"

Gio bit his lip. "I really don't want to talk right now. Do you mind if we just walk in silence?" Flashes of her in those last few days ran through his head. Laying there on her deathbed, the spark that he remembered in her eyes slowly going out.

"Oh, sure. Sorry." Dante sounded like a wounded puppy dog.

Gio immediately felt guilty. "Look, it's not about you. I'm just… feeling a lot of things right now."

"Oh, I understand. I felt the same way after we lost *Zio Nicolo* a couple of years ago." He lapsed back into silence, casting a guilty look at Gio.

Gio sighed again. "What happened to your uncle?" He didn't remember Diego saying anything about him.

"He wasn't *really* my uncle. Just a close friend of Mamma's. He would come by at Christmas time and bring us all presents. He worked in the shipyards in Venice and there was some kind of industrial accident. It was a closed casket funeral."

"Ouch! Did they say what happened to him?" *I can imagine…*

"No, but I think something really heavy fell on top of him. Someone said he was squashed flat as a *piadina*."

Gio laughed in spite of himself. "I'm sorry. I just am picturing this piano falling on top of the poor man, like in the cartoons…"

"Seriously? It's not funny." But Dante was having a hard time suppressing a grin.

"No, it's not." He giggled, though, and soon they were both laughing so hard that tears formed at the corners of their eyes.

An old woman in a red jacket with a cane gave them a withering look. "*Peccato!*"

Shame. That just made them laugh even more.

Freed by the unexpected mirth, Gio wiped his eyes and took a deep breath, feeling lighter.

They reached another gate, this one much newer and more imposing, with concrete columns faced with travertine or marble and fancy wrought-iron grill work in between. Even Dante seemed awed into silence by the somber place.

"We're here." Gio had printed out a map of the cemetery, with his mother's gravesite marked on it. He pulled out the map and looked at it, orienting himself. Then he took a deep breath, and then stepped through the gate.

It was cooler inside, as if he'd stepped into another world.

He followed his map, turning left and proceeding with Dante along the inside wall of the cemetery. They soon came to a row of what looked like tiny houses on their left, set back from the walkway a dozen feet. *Houses of the dead.* Tombs for some of the richer permanent residents of this place. Gio shivered, wishing suddenly that Diego were here with him.

"It's like a little city," Dante whispered.

Gio nodded. "City of the dead."

The tombs thinned out, and soon another structure loomed in the distance. It was an old house, a stately two-story affair surrounded by old trees. It was in poor repair, though, all the windows broken out, and the rooftop gaping open in several places.

"That's odd." He didn't remember seeing it the last time he'd been here, but then again, he'd been numb to everything.

"The house?"

Gio nodded.

"It's probably protected. When they built this place, they had to leave it there."

"Protected? Why?" It was in ruins.

Dante shrugged. "They like to keep all the old things."

Gio snorted. It was true.

They passed the old haunted house and turned down the next lane. Gio checked his map. "Almost there."

There were a few other people visible in the cemetery—a young couple had a gravesite just off the narrow, paved road, leaving flowers for a loved one. A little farther on, a gardener was mowing part of the grass. And a little green moped zipped by, fleeing the cemetery as if being chased by zombies.

"I think her gravesite is over there." He pointed past the young couple, toward a tall oak tree. "We buried her next to the tree, but out under the sky where the moon would find her." He hurried across the grass, scanning the grave markers, and at last found what he was seeking.

Luna Mazzocco
7 Aprile 1969 - 14 Ottobre, 2015

He knelt, brushing away the dirt and bits of cut grass and leaves that had settled across her marker, and laid down the flowers. "Ciao, mamma." *I'm finally here.*

A shadow fell across the grave.

Gio looked up, expecting to see his cousin.

"Chi diavolo sei?"

Gio stared at the apparition, certain his eyes were fooling him. *"Mamma?"*

48

—————

THE ARBORETUM

The weather was unseasonably cool, with playful gusts of wind gamboling through the tree canopies above like great invisible squirrels, scampering from one branch to another and sending pollen showering down everywhere.

Dave sneezed. He was strolling through the Arboretum, virtually abandoned on a Sunday afternoon this late in the school year. In another week or so, the students would be gone for the summer, and ownership of the campus would temporarily return to folks like him who wandered in from River Park, East Sacramento, and Campus Commons for the peace and quiet the nearly abandoned campus offered.

He loved summers on campus, when it felt like someone had constructed the whole place just for him. When he'd lived in Carmelina's duplex, he had often ridden his bike there, locking it up and strolling under the great trees, imagining himself in a vast natural forest. Sometimes he'd stop by the Student Union first to grab a quick coffee, then stroll back across campus to this place of almost magical natural beauty.

Today, he'd driven across town to visit it once more, aware that he might not be able to see its verdant abundance for much longer. It was also a great balm against the financial worries he shared with Marcos. They'd find a way through them together—they always did. But for now he just wanted a little peace and quiet.

He found a quiet bench at its heart, one of his favorite places to regard the gardens, and plunked himself down on it. The old wooden planks groaned under his weight.

Not as thin as I once was. Or as young. No one was ever as young as they once were, a thought that amused him, but failed to bring much in the way of actual comfort.

He let his head fall back and stared at the bright blue patches of sky, visible here and there between all the bright green leaves of spring. He closed his eyes and listened to the myriad and wonderful sounds of the world.

Off to his right, a squirrel scampered through the grass and up the trunk of a pine tree, stopping every few feet to check for predators, or maybe to consider where to hide the acorn it had in its bulging cheeks.

Wind whipped through the trees above, partially masking the *whoosh* of the cars on J Street, maybe fifty meters away, and the rumble of a big truck as it trundled by.

A crow cawed off in the distance somewhere, and footsteps announced the passing of another visitor. Or two.

Dave opened his eyes and watched them go by. An older couple, dressed far more warmly than the weather warranted, holding hands with their heads together, sharing secrets and laughter. Maybe two professors, talking about their classes? Maybe a couple of lovers from Campus Commons, imagining themselves in San Francisco as they crossed the Guy West Bridge—a mini-version of the Golden Gate—recalling moments from their youth spent under these very same trees.

They smiled at him as they passed, and he nodded at them, giving them a fond wave.

How long until I can no longer see these things? The squirrel climbing up a hoary old oak tree. The wind blowing the branches about, making a sound like water through the birch tree leaves. Two people holding hands, remembering things only they could recall?

He closed his eyes again.

The boards of the bench creaked, as if of their own accord. "Indulging our morose thoughts again, are we?"

Dave snorted. "Took you long enough to get around to me."

"Not surprised to see me, then?" Brad sounded almost offended.

I should be the offended one. "Nothing surprises me all that much anymore. And besides, I can't *see* you. My eyes are closed."

"Touché." A long silence. "You're really not surprised? I thought you might be thrown by the whole… you know… *dead friend* thing."

Dave grinned and opened his eyes. "Marissa mentioned that she'd seen you. And Ben. Poor guy. You really went and left him in the lurch, didn't you?" He glanced over at the apparition that had once been his friend.

Brad looked away. "Not by choice."

Now I feel like an ass. Besides, Brad wasn't even *real.* He was just a manifestation of Dave's own guilt and sadness. Wasn't he? "Are you real?"

Brad looked back at him, eyes narrowing. "Define real."

"Are you really my friend Brad?" He really should be more freaked out about the whole *ghost on the bench* thing. But Brad would never do him harm. In any form.

"Ah." He leaned forward, hands on his knees, as Dave had seen Brad do a hundred times. "Honestly, I don't know. I feel like me. I mean… how do you know *you're* real?"

Dave thought about it. He held out his hands and flexed his fingers. "I don't know. I just do. I am."

Brad laughed. "Yes. Exactly."

Dave snorted again. "All right. Fair enough. Maybe it doesn't matter. Just do what you came to do. Tell me something all *afterlifey* and inspirational, and then you can go away. Mission accomplished." He was in no mood to be lectured by a phantom. Better to get it over with. He shook his shoulders and arms to loosen up his body, and then leaned back against the bench. "Hit me."

"You don't get off that easy."

Dave turned to stare at his old friend.

Brad was looking off into a stand of cypress pines.

"Seriously? You come back from the dead, and *you don't get off that easy* is all you've got?"

Brad shrugged. "What do you want me to say?"

Dave fumed. "That there's some reason for hope? That after my vision goes all dim and gray, I'll still have a reason to get up in the morning? That my life as I know it isn't coming to a dark and depressing end? I don't know. You're my spirit guide. Just pick one." He sat back hard on the old bench, and it creaked under his weight.

"Sounds like you're doing a pretty good job with that all by yourself."

Dave growled. "*Not* comforting."

"That's because it's not supposed to be." Brad got up and began to pace back and forth in front of him. "Do you want to know *why* I'm here?"

"Yes. Isn't that what I've been asking?" It was suddenly cold in the little clearing.

They were interrupted by a woman in pink Nike running shoes and matching track suit, blond ponytail streaming behind her like racing flag. She waved at him and then she was gone, swallowed up by the gardens.

When Dave turned back to Brad, he recoiled.

Brad's face was drawn and angry. "I'm here because I went into the hospital last week, and now I'm *dead*. And from here in this gray afterlife, I see the lot of you sleepwalking your way through your own lives. Marissa has a dead-end job. Diego has his apron strings wrapped so tightly around Gio's neck that it's a wonder the boy can breathe at all. Ben has taken all the blame onto himself for the loss of his girlfriend. And on and on and on… every last one of you is stuck. And you—you're the worst of all. Sure, you've been given a horrible diagnosis. No one wants to go blind. But you have something far more precious to see you through… a man who loves you, and a handful of years to spend with him. You're one of the lucky ones. Can't you see that?" He threw his translucent arms up in exasperation. "So rather than moping around this empty garden full of memories, why don't you go to him and figure out how you want to spend all that time? Figure out how to get him out of the mess he finds himself in? Because lord knows, if I still could with Sam, I would." Panting, face flushed, he collapsed back onto the bench next to Dave.

He'd never realized a ghost could seem so *alive*. "I'm so sorry, my friend." He knew how Brad felt. He'd lost his first love, John, now fourteen years past. *How can it be that long?*

Some wounds never entirely healed.

Brad crossed his arms, staring at the trees. "My chance is gone. What are you going to do with yours?"

Dave looked away. It felt… wrong to stare at his friend, ghost or not.

"I suppose I need to get my shit together and figure it out." He rubbed his shoulder absently, staring at the little tree next to the bench. *A cucumber tree.* At least according to the tag. *Do cucumbers grow on trees?* "What do you think I should say—"

He'd turned to ask Brad a question, but his friend was gone.

He sighed. Brad was right. He still had a life ahead of him, if he reached out and embraced it, and Marcos needed him too.

He chuckled. "Dave, you're an old fool." He was only useless if he let himself be.

With one final snort—it seemed to be the afternoon for it—Dave eased himself up. "Time to go. Take care of yourself, old friend." With one last look around, he turned to head back the way he'd come, toward the car. And then Marcos.

49

___

STRANGOLAGALLI

Carmelina got out of the car and stretched her arms and legs, thrilled to be done with the twisty-winding climb up through the foothills of the Apennines. It was a beautiful day, white clouds scudding through the blue sky overhead, and the rolling hills of the Frosinone region, just southeast of Rome, were bursting in verdant green—a postcard-perfect scene of an Italian countryside.

It had been a long drive, first making their way around the outskirts of southern Rome in the beltway connector, and then heading down the A1 highway toward Napoli. They got off the freeway in a small town called *Ceprano*. In typical and unsurprising Italian fashion, the road that took them the remaining fifteen kilometers changed names an astonishing *seven times*.

The town of *Strangolagalli* itself was perched on a hill overlooking the lovely region. It was a little shabby chic, full of semi-historic buildings that probably looked better from above, with a welcoming mural with an eagle's head and an aqueduct and swirls of distorted people whose depiction would have made Picasso proud. Nevertheless, it had that specific Italian charm, and apparently some very English charm, at least to go by the name of some of the local establishments. She supposed English words—to the Italians—carried a certain *je ne sais quoi*, just like Italian words did for Americans, but still, seeing the signs for *Eden Garden di De Vellis Luana* and *Hair Style Donatella* was a little jarring.

It was a warm late spring day. Out here in the countryside, things were much quieter than in Ostia Antica. It had been a wild evening after the wedding the night before. There had been bonfires and dancing on the beach, a never-ending flow of *prosecco*, and lots of spoken Italian, which had tested her language skills to the limit. But it had also been immensely enjoyable.

In the morning, they'd gotten up and borrowed Elena and Isabella's car —the couple were leaving later in the day for their honeymoon in Morocco.

Daniele and Carmelina got on the road early, but there had still been a lot of traffic around the beltway in Rome, even though it was a Sunday. Who knew the arcane rules of Italian traffic?

But none of that mattered now. *I'm here.* She was going to meet her mysterious uncle, and see what strange secret he had to tell her. *Am I adopted? Was my mother part of the Mafia? Was there a murder involved?*

She shook her head and chuckled under her breath. *Stop that. You've been reading too much Teresa Papavero.*

Chiara Moscardelli was an amazing Italian author. Carmelina had stumbled upon her books a few years earlier, while visiting a small Italian bookstore called *Libreria Pino* in San Francisco. She could readily relate to her protagonist, a middle-aged woman searching for love, whom everybody underestimated. Of course, the fact that she was kind of crazy didn't hurt either…

"So this is the place."

Daniele looked around and nodded. "Looks like it. How do you feel?"

She grimaced. "Excited. A little nervous. Have you ever been here before?" It wasn't as historic feeling as some of the Italian villages she had been in. It was a little too modern *and* a little too old at the same time. But still it had that Italian charm.

He closed the door and locked the car—it was an old Peugeot, old enough that it still had a key lock. "No, this is the first time. I grew up in Rome, but we didn't get south very much. And this is quite a ways up into the hills."

"So I'd noticed." Her stomach had gotten a little unsettled, with all those twists and turns coming up those hills. *I could use a good, stiff drink.*

"Where is this place your uncle wants to meet us at?" Daniele looked up and down the short street.

She pulled out her phone and looked up the text. "It's called *Civico 23 Bar Gelateria.*"

He indicated the building closest to them. "Is that it, across the street?"

It was a modest beige storefront, with a white roll-down vinyl shade and a newish-looking external Panasonic air conditioning unit sticking out of the wall above. A couple pots with scraggly plants tried to project a little curb appeal, and someone had painted jaunty cartoons of a gelato cone on one side and a steaming cup of coffee on the other.

"That's the one! I wonder if he's there already?" Her heart skipped in excitement.

They'd passed a group of old men seated in chairs on a little tongue of sidewalk across the street on their way into town, but otherwise the place was very quiet.

She checked the time on her watch. They were half an hour early, even after all the traffic. "Let's go grab a little something to drink."

It was probably better if she stuck to something non-alcoholic, given the state of her stomach. She wanted all her wits about her when she spoke with Uncle Angelo.

They entered the bar. It was part gelateria, part café, with a long black countertop along one side and a trio of refrigerator cases along the back. It had exactly one table.

Like the town itself it was a strange mixture of old and new, history dressed up with a fresh coat of paint and recessed lighting.

She trotted out her formal greeting. "*Auguri.*"

The server was a kid, all of sixteen years old. He had short-cropped hair, earrings in both ears, and an *AS Roma* soccer tattoo on one arm. Other than that, he could've fit in perfectly in any Starbucks in the United States. It made her wonder what Gio was up to, not that he was a teenager anymore. The boy grinned. "*Ciao. Come posso aiutarti?*"

Another sign of the new Italy. Addressing your elders in informal language, instead of the using the formal tense. Not that she really minded.

"*Vorrei un bicchieri di soda.*" Something carbonated was just what she needed.

"*Coca Cola va bene?*"

"*Certo. Con ghiacchio.*" Very few Italians took their soda with ice. Something to do with believing that it was bad for your constitution, or some such nonsense.

The kid didn't say anything, though, just a slight quirk of his lips. He turned to Daniele. "*E tu?*"

"*Dammi pure un caffee corretto.*" With alcohol.

At her raised eyebrow, he grinned. "I'm not the one who has to stay sober. Besides there's very little *actual alcohol* in it."

The barista nodded. "*Un attimo, per favore.*"

Carmelina chose the seat nearest the window, turning her chair sideways to be able to look out on the town and the hills outside.

Daniele joined her, sitting across the table from her and leaving the middle chair for their host. "Are you nervous?" He put a hand on hers.

There were butterflies in her stomach, but she wasn't about to admit it. "Not at all. It's probably nothing. But I'm enjoying being out in the Italian countryside." Worst case, she would end up having spent a day seeing someplace she likely never would've visited otherwise, a place that was near and dear to her heart because of the mystery books she'd read about it.

There were a few more people about now, going back and forth in front of the café. A little down the street she could see the group of old men chatting about their day. She wondered if people here still took a *passeggiata* in the afternoon, a walk around town just to see and be seen.

A moment later, their drinks arrived. The barista set them down on the table and flashed her a dazzling smile. "*Dimmi se hai bisogna di qualcos'altra.*"

"We will. *Lo faremo.*"

She hadn't taken but two sips of her drink before the door burst open, yielding an Italian man who was mostly balding, with a few wisps of dark gray hair combed over the top of his head and a pair of wild uncombed eyebrows to match. His teeth were crooked, but he had an engaging smile, nevertheless.

"You must be Carmelina," he said in Italian, with an accent thick enough to catch flies. He threw his arms around her and hugged her roughly, causing half the air in her lungs to erupt out of her mouth in a surprised gasp.

"A pleasure, I'm sure…" she managed between gulps of air.

He released her and held her out at arm's length. "You are the spitting image of your mother."

Her cheeks flushed. *A huge compliment.* "Thank you!" She gently wriggled out of his grasp. "And this is my partner, Daniele." The word for partner in Italian, *fidanzato*, was a little awkward, as it meant both fiancé *and* serious boyfriend, and she'd spent the last three years carefully avoiding the whole marriage question with Daniele.

He rose and shook the man's hand. "*Piacere, Signor Farelli.*"

He waved away the formality. "Call me Angelo, please. Let's sit. Are you hungry?"

Her stomach was still in knots from the twisty ride up through the hills. "Not really. I'm—"

"Fantastic. Angelo, bring us a *stesa con cioccolato*, and bring me *una birra*."

Daniele blinked twice. "His name is Angelo too?"

"It is a very common name in Strangolagalli. We have seventeen Angelos in town. None of us are related. Oh, except Angelo Morolo and Angelo Monterosi. They are married now. Nice boys."

"Ah." Nice to know he was comfortable with the gays. That said a lot about him.

He took a seat next to Carmelina, setting down an old duffel bag on the floor. "You know the *stesa, si?*"

Carmelina exchanged a glance with Daniele. "No. I don't think I do."

He grinned. "Ah, let me tell you. The *stesa* is a special kind of pizza, made only here in Strangolagalli. Well, only made *the right way* here. You make a flour and water dough with a little salt, then boil it until it's cooked, then stuff it with meat or cheese or something sweet. There's even a *festa* for it in October!"

Carmelina wasn't sure if that sounded delicious… or disgusting. It was a bit too close to the *fried everything* one found at the California State Fair. Fried jalapenos. Fried twinkies. Fried soda… "That sounds… unique."

"You try it, see if you like it, no?" He held out his hands and shrugged his shoulders.

She laughed. "Of course." He seemed like a very nice man, if a bit over-enthusiastic. And she still didn't know why he had asked her here. *Surely not just to eat a local pizza?* "*Mia mamma* never mentioned having a brother."

He stared at her for so long that she wondered if he was offended, but then he smiled and nodded vigorously. "Oh, no, sorry, that makes sense. Your mother was not my sister. She was my cousin. So I am like an uncle to you, but not exactly."

Carmelina worked it out in her head. *Grandmother's sister's son…* "Ah. You are my first cousin, once removed."

"Not the first one. I had another, but he died young—"

"No, that's what they call—never mind." She took a deep breath and pushed ahead. Her Italian had vastly improved over the last few years, but keeping up with a native Italian was proving to be a challenge. "So why did you want me to come here?"

"Ah, now we come to the reason. But first, the *stesa*."

Young Angelo appeared carrying a large white tray, decorated with hand-painted olives and olive tree branches, and set it down on the table before them. The "pizza" was a misshapen, vaguely round flatbread, golden-brown at the edges, and smothered in chocolate. The barista had cut it into pieces like a traditional pizza.

She stared at it doubtfully.

"Give it a try." Her uncle—cousin?—picked up a piece for himself. "*Delicioso. Bravo Angelo!*"

With a frown, she took a piece for herself. It was warm, and the blended aromas of pizza crust and chocolate worked their magic on her senses. She took a hesitant bite. "Oh *mio dio!*" It was like the best chocolate croissant she had ever had. "Daniele, you have to try this."

Daniele raised an eyebrow, but then took a piece of his own. "*Santo cielo!*"

Uncle Angelo flashed them a grin with his crooked teeth. "Now, you have passed the test." He finished his slice, then leaned over to open the duffel bag and fished out something heavy. Scooting the platter aside, he set it down reverently on the table and then slid it over to Carmelina.

"Oh my God. Is that Marisa?" It was a book, with an old sepia-tone photo taped to its cover. In it was a tall, handsome man in a military uniform, and next to him, a short woman with long black hair who was less than half his height. Despite her diminutive stature, she had a fierceness about her that reminded Carmelina of a tiger.

The resemblance to Teresa Papavero's governess Marisa in Chiara Moscardelli's books was uncanny.

"No, that's my *nonna*. Your *bisnonna*. Great grandmother. This book has all of her recipes."

"*Accedenti!* May I?" She felt a thrill run down her spine.

Angelo nodded, a smile playing at the corner of his lips. He held out his hand, palm up, in permission. "Please do."

She opened it carefully. The inside said *Dalla cucina di Maria Angelica Carenna. From Maria Angelica Carenna's kitchen.* Inside, it was filled with tens… no, hundreds of handwritten recipes.

Breathless, she leafed through it. There were chicken dishes, seafood dishes, dishes with beef and pork and even rabbit. Homemade pastas, sauces… and then she came to the desserts.

Her heart beat faster. *Is it here?*

When she was a child, her *nonna* had spoken of a recipe of her own mother's, by then lost to time: *una crostata di ricotta e visciole.* A kind of cheese and sour cherry pie.

She eased through the old pages, not wanting to ruin the precious book. And there it was.

She picked it up, hugged it to her chest, and closed her eyes. "What a treasure."

When she opened them, Angelo was beaming. "I am very happy to hear that you think so. Your *bisnonna* was a celebrated cook. People came from far and wide to sample her food."

Carmelina nodded, misty-eyed. "My grandmother said she had died in the war. She never mentioned your mother…"

"Angelica." He smiled again, but this time it was weaker and tinged with sadness. "They had a great fight, your mother and mine. Over my father, I think. Your grandmother went to America and never looked back."

Carmelina nodded, setting the book back on the table. They had lost one another, just like she had lost her own little girl. She put a hand on his shoulder. "So why show this to me? Why ask me to come halfway around the world to see it?"

Daniele nodded. "Surely you could have sent a photo. It would have been easier."

Uncle Angelo shook his head. "I have no children. And I have cancer. The doctors—they have given me a year."

"Oh Angelo. I'm so sorry." She leaned forward to give him a hug. She'd just met some family she'd never known she had, and now she was going to lose him.

"Thank you. I have lived a good life. I am content." He put his hand on the cookbook. "I looked for my Aunt Elena on the web. Young Angelo helped."

The barista waved. "*Non era niente.*"

"And then I found you. Imagine my surprise when I saw that you were a chef."

Carmelina blushed. "Nothing so grand as that. I make sweets and sell them in a little flower shop with… with Daniele."

Daniele's eyes narrowed, but he said nothing.

This time it was Angelo's eyes that were misty. "*Nonna Maria* worked in a flower shop too."

"Imagine that." She glanced down at the book again. "Thank you for sharing this with me. Maybe I can take photos of a couple of the recipes, if you don't mind?"

"Mind? No, you don't understand. I want you to have it." He poked her in the chest. "She would want you to have it. You are her successor." He pushed it gently back toward her.

She stared at him, only slowly becoming aware that her mouth was agape. "She… me… it?"

Daniele laughed. "Yes, I think that about sums it up." He leaned over and kissed her cheek. "She, you, it. Say 'thank you,' Carmelina."

"Thank you, Carmelina." She blinked and shook her head. "I mean, *thank you, Angelo*. It's… that's wonderful." The poor man, staring down his own mortality. And to give her such a precious gift at the same time…

"I suppose you'll be going now. It's a long trip back to Ostia." His shoulders sagged.

Carmelina glanced over at Daniele, who nodded. "We don't have to leave just yet."

His face lit up again. "*Perfetto.* Then come with me. I will show you the town. You can leave the book here. We will come back for it." He turned toward the bar. "Angelo, watch the book!"

"*Certo, Angelo!*" The boy gave them all a thumb's up and went back to wiping down the bar.

Carmelina squeezed Daniele's hand. She couldn't believe it. It was like her mother was reaching out to touch her from beyond the grave.

Daniele grinned. "Well, come on. Don't keep the poor man waiting."

She laughed and followed Older Angelo out the door. Off they went together to explore the strange, beautiful little Italian village that had come alive in the books she had read and had inspired so many of her dreams.

50

BIG NEWS

Marcos sniffed the simmering pot's contents. It smelled divine—the perfect harmony of chicken broth, tomatoes, bell peppers, onions, and zucchini.

Calabacitas. The dish that had brought him and Dave together, the one they'd been having that fateful night when Carmelina showed up all upset, when Marcos had realized how much he loved this beautiful man.

He'd made his regular Sunday morning run down to the farmer's market on X Street, the one under the freeway. *Only in Sactown.* He'd traded some of his balcony-grown basil for the fresh vegetables he'd need for the dish. Rodrigo was always happy to make the exchange.

Marcos wanted this evening to be perfect, just like that other one had been. Or had become, after he'd gotten over Carmelina's unexpected interruption.

He had *news to share,* and it was vibrating inside of him, dying to come out. He'd invited Marissa and her new person over—Ainsley seemed lovely. Maybe she would help rekindle the fire in Marissa's heart.

There was a knock at the door, and then it swung open as if of its own accord. *Speak of the devil.*

"We're here!" Marissa looked around the condo where she had come to live with him all those years ago. A smile transformed her face. "Oh my God, is that *calabacitas?*"

"*Calabawhat?*" Ainsley crossed the space between them confidently to shake Marcos's hand. "Hello, Mr. Ramirez. It's great to see you again."

"Good to see you too. And it's called *calabacitas*. It's a traditional Mexican dish made with zucchini, chicken broth, and other vegetables."

Marissa grinned, pushing a lock of blond hair behind her ear. "It's our family's version of casserole."

Comprehension dawned on Ainsley's face. "Ah, like *bibimbap*! Can I have a taste?"

Marcos laughed. "I'll take your word for it. And here you go. Blow on it first, it's hot."

She did as she was told, and then took a quick sip. "Oh my God, that's delicious."

"Just wait until he puts the cheese in it." Marissa took one of the four seats around the dining table. "Where's Dave?"

"Not sure. He turned his *find* off."

Marissa frowned. "Is that normal?"

Lately, yes. "Not all the time, but sometimes he just wants some *alone time*. I choose to think of it as healthy." He turned off the burner. He had some tortillas ready to go in a Ziploc bag, an old trick Dave had taught him—thirty seconds in the microwave and they would be as fresh and soft as when they were first made. "We've been practicing spending more time on our own, for when I get a job."

For a long time, that seemed like an unlikely event. The job market was rough, and no one wanted to hire an aging entrepreneur. And then just today… Well, he couldn't say anything about it just yet. Not until he had Dave there and everyone was seated for dinner.

As if he'd been summoned, Dave walked through the front door. "Something smells wonderful. Is that *calabacitas?*" Then he noticed Marissa and Ainsley and blinked furiously. "Were we expecting company? Is… is something wrong?"

"Well, not exactly. And no, nothing's wrong." Marcos dropped a couple potholders on the table and brought the still very hot pot over to set down on one of them while Dave leaned over and kissed his cheek. "Grab a seat. Dinner is on."

Dave sat down next to the girls and shook out his napkin.

Marissa reached over and pulled something out of his hair. "Where have you been? It looks like you've been hacking your way through the jungle." She held up a twig with a small leaf still attached.

Dave laughed, and Marcos turned to stare at him, astonished. He hadn't heard Dave laugh like that for a long time.

"I was at the Arboretum. I like to go there when I need some time to think."

Marcos pulled down now warm and pliable tortillas out of the microwave and put them into their terracotta *tortillero* to keep them warm. They joined the pot on the table, and dinner was served.

He had brought out the traditional tablecloth they used for special occasions which they'd bought on a trip to Mexico City a few years before. It was white with blue swirly designs on it and reminded him of the ceramic painted animals he'd often seen in little shops there. It was probably a super touristy thing, but he treasured it and the memory of their time there together.

He poured each of them a glass of *agua fresca*, and sat down to dinner with his family. "Dig in."

Marissa wasted no time. She sprinkled a generous handful of Mexican cheese blend into each of the bowls, and then picked up the ladle and started pouring the soup over the top of it. "The secret is all the melty cheese at the bottom."

Ainsley rubbed her hands together, a wide grin splitting her face.

Soon all of their bowls were full, and dinner began in earnest.

They each took a sip.

"Oh my God, this is delicious." Dave leaned over to kiss him on the cheek again.

Marcos grinned. "I'm glad you think so." This was it. "I'm so glad you could all make it—"

"We have some news!" Marissa squeezed Ainsley's hand, and her eyes were shining.

Marcos closed his mouth. *Guess my news can wait.* "Good news, I hope?" *We could use a bit of good news, after the last few months.*

"I'm quitting my job, and Ainsley is dropping out of school."

"What?" He was on his feet before he realized it. Dave tried pulling him back down, but he shook Dave's hand away. "You can't quit your job. How are you going to pay for your…" He was going to say mortgage, but she hadn't been able to afford a house. "Your rent? You're not moving back in here. Have you thought this through?"

Her eyes narrowed. "I'm not a kid anymore, *Marcos*. I have a fair amount saved up. I'll be fine for a few months."

He growled at the pointed use of his first name. "I'm sorry, but this sounds like a bad idea—"

Dave shushed him with a gesture. "Let her speak. She's obviously thought this through."

Marcos stared at Dave, confused. *Why aren't you backing me up here?*

Marissa flashed Dave a grateful smile. "I haven't been happy for a long time. I got my degree and then got a job, but everything has been… gray. Then I met Ainsley, and there was color again."

As if that explained it. What was this, color and black and white? Marcos glared at their guest. "She's a bad influence—"

"Marcos!" Dave stared at him, a sharp frown on his face.

"Sorry." He sank back down into his chair meekly. "Go on."

"Thank you." She took a deep breath, exhaled, and went on. "I started thinking about when I was last really happy. It was when I was in the kitchen, at Ragazzi. I *loved* cooking. I always have. I think that's what I want to do with my life."

Marcos frowned. It made no sense. She had a stable job. He didn't have to worry about her, which was such a relief, especially while he was worrying about their own finances. Why would she give that up? "That's a big step. Maybe you could take some cooking classes at night again at the restaurant… ease into it."

Dave nudged him. "Look at her, Marcos. *Really* look at her."

So he did. And then he saw it. She wasn't just happy—she was almost glowing. She had a light in her that he hadn't seen for years. She was a grown woman—holy crap, when had that happened? And she knew what she wanted. *Jesus Christ, I'm an idiot.* Still, he couldn't help himself. "Are you sure…?"

Marissa frowned. "Honestly, no. It's scary as hell." She took Ainsley's hand and squeezed it. "How much longer should I go on doing something that makes me sad? That leaves me feeling gray and lonely?"

Marcos looked from her to Dave and back again. She could make her own choices, good or bad, and she would, no matter what he said. *She's stubborn, like me.* "If it'll make you happy—" That was all he managed to get out before she squealed, threw her arms around him, and hugged him tightly.

He hugged her back. He'd find a way to get behind this, to support her, even if the whole idea scared him to death.

At last, she let go, sat down and looked at him appraisingly. "So, what's *your* big news?"

He laughed. "How do you know I have news?"

"Because this is your classic Dad move. Gather the whole family, make us our special family meal, then tell us something big. So come on. Spill it. What is it?" Her eyes sparkled. "I hope it's good news."

Touché. "Well… I got a voicemail on Friday. I didn't think much of it at the time. I've been looking for a new job for so long that sometimes it seems like nothing will ever come my way."

Dave leaned forward. "And…?"

"And I called them back this morning. They answered—on a Sunday! Remember when I interviewed to run the PRIDE Center at Sacramento State last month?"

Dave nodded. "I remember."

"They offered me the job!" His heart was racing again, just like it did when he first got the news.

Now it was Dave's turn to grin. "Oh babe, that's amazing!"

"Apparently Brad sent them a letter of recommendation that swung the whole thing in my favor. I start in two weeks!" The last thing Brad had done for him, before he'd passed away. As the former head of the LGBT Center, his words must have carried some weight. For just a second, he thought he saw Brad standing behind Dave, nodding and smiling.

"*Magnifico!*" It was Dave's turn to hug him. "I am so proud of you, *mi corazón.*"

Marcos plowed ahead. "They have great benefits for spouses—you'll be taken care of." That too had been a great relief, with Dave's macular degeneration.

Dave drew back, and picked up his napkin to dab at his eyes. "I'll be all right. I had a bit of a revelation myself, today."

Marcos raised an eyebrow.

"I'll tell you later."

There's a story there. "And best of all, I called the loan folks, and given this new income, they've agreed to restructure the balloon payment." That had been the biggest relief. *Now we're not going to be out on our asses in a week.*

Dave closed his eyes. "That's such a relief."

"Yes it is." Marcos reached over to squeeze his hand. "Well, don't let your *calabacitas* get cold! Marissa, tell me more about this crazy plan of yours." He dug into the bowl with his spoon, pulling out a steaming batch of zucchini and gooey, melted cheese.

"I'll give my notice tomorrow…" As she launched into her plan, he sat back and watched the people he loved most sharing a meal together. And he knew he'd done at least one thing right with his life.

Mi familia elegida. My chosen family.

He was the luckiest man alive.

51

THE MOON RISES ONLY FOR YOU

"*Mamma?*"

The woman stared at him, clearly debating between fight or flight.

She wasn't his mother. She couldn't be. Gio had watched her die.

She looked so much like her, but older and healthier. In the last few months before her death, Luna had become gaunt, a shell of her former herself. "Who in the hell are *you?*"

The woman took a step back, and looked from him to Dante and back again, her eyebrows creasing. "Are you Giovanni?"

He gasped, then covered his mouth with his hand. How did she know him? He clutched the bundle of lilies tightly. "Tell me who you are first."

Dante stood next to him and crossed his arms, presenting a united front. "She looks so much like your mother."

"Do you remember her?" Gio glanced over at his cousin. Some days he barely remembered what Luna looked like.

Dante nodded. "Mama has a few photos of her that she has shown me from time to time. I think she saved them from your mother's photo album."

The woman looked back and forth from one of them to the other and nodded. "Fair enough." The woman took a deep breath, and then shook her head, throwing her hair back behind her shoulders. She had long hair, blond where his mother's had been silver, but she was Luna's spitting image otherwise. She was probably approaching fifty, but she wore it well. Her gauzy top billowed around her chest like a cloud in the light breeze. "My name is Stella, and if you are Giovanni, you're my nephew. Luna Mazzocco was my sister."

Gio blinked. "My mother didn't have any family."

Stella nodded, her eyes fixed on his. She brushed a stray lock of golden hair away from her forehead with her right hand. It was a gesture so familiar to Gio that he almost choked. His mother had done exactly that when she had been playing for time, thinking about what to say next. "Your mother and I were twins. We were separated when we were four." There was a deep sadness in her voice. "You see, our own mother was an alcoholic, and she drank herself to death at a young age. Luna went to live with a local family, while I was sent away to a family in Sicily."

He shouldn't believe her, but she was here at his mother's grave, and the resemblance… *You're really my aunt.* "That must've been so difficult for you." He closed his eyes. His mother had a sister, and had never known that this woman… Stella… was still alive. He set down the flowers and stood, wiping the dirt from his hands. There was no doubt in his mind that she was telling him the truth.

His aunt took a cautious step toward him, as if afraid he might flee, and then another, and reached out to touch his cheek. "Nine years ago, I saw an obituary for someone who looked just like me. Her name was Luna. I stared at her, touching her cheek on the screen just like this, and my memory came flooding back, from when I was a little girl."

"She never said anything about you." He would've remembered if she had mentioned having a sister. Instead, she had always talked about how they were all alone in the world with no family to depend on. *We only have each other in this great wide world, tesoro.*

Stella let go of his cheek and looked away, and when her gaze returned to him, her eyes were bright and misted. "Perhaps it was for her like it was for me, like a dream. Sometimes I would lay in bed at night and picture this beautiful fairy who looked just like me, only her hair was silver, like the moon. She would smile at me and take my hand, and say 'Everything will be all right.'"

And then he remembered.

"My mother used to tell me about her imaginary friend, the one she had when she was a little girl. She was a beautiful fairy from the old country, she would tell me. A pretty girl with hair the color of the golden sun. This fairy used to look after her when she was a little girl, and mamma hoped that one day she would take care of me as well."

"It was you, wasn't it?" Dante was staring at her.

Stella smiled. "Maybe so. Maybe she remembered me the same way I remembered her."

Gio shook his head. After all this time, his mother's golden fairy had appeared to him. Still, it seemed… unlikely. "What are the odds? That you and I would be here at the same time, on the same day?"

She chuckled. "Better than you might think. When I found her again, when I found that she had passed, I was working for an old man named Agostino in an accounting office in Catania. It was a boring life, and I'd always wanted something different. I took it as a sign, and brought my daughter here as soon as I could." She put a hand on his mother's tombstone. "The day I arrived, we came here together and laid out a bouquet of white and yellow chrysanthemums on her grave. I've come to visit her every day since."

That makes sense. "White for her, and yellow for you." His mother's face, which had faded in his mind with time was suddenly bright and vivid again in his memories. Then it hit him. "Wait a minute, did you say you have a daughter?"

"Yes. She's nineteen now. Would you like to meet her?"

"Is she pretty?" Dante the puppy was back.

Gio patted Dante on the head. "Calm down, Cujo. She's your cousin too." He turned back to Stella. "I'd love to meet her. What's her name?"

"Sole. The sun of my heart."

Dante laughed, but Gio silenced him with a look. Still, it was a little funny. Luna, Stella, and Sole. Moon, Star, and Sun.

His aunt took his hand. "Kneel with me."

He did as he was told. The grass was cool on his knees, even through his jeans.

"Put your hand here, on the grass." She laid hers on the green blades.

He put his palm next to hers.

"Now close your eyes, and tell her what's on your heart."

He blinked. *What?* "It's… this feels weird."

"Only at first. Your mother is always waiting, listening for your voice. I'll tell you a secret if you promise not to laugh."

"I swear."

"Sometimes when I speak to her, I hear her voice in my head." She flashed him an embarrassed smile.

"I believe you." He thought back to his conversation with Brad. "Sometimes the spirits talk to me too."

Her smile broadened. "There you go. So talk to her. Tell her."

He looked at the headstone where his mother's name was engraved. *This is stupid.* Still, he was here. He'd come all this way to see her. And meeting Stella had to mean *something*. "Okay, I'll try. *Ciao mamma… come va?*" *How's it going?* He groaned.

He looked up at Dante, who nodded enthusiastically and gave him the okay sign. "You're doing great."

Gio shook his head. It didn't *feel* great. Still, he took another go at it. "*Ciao, mamma.* It's been nine long years. Diego… *Papà* has been great. But I miss you. Every day I miss you…" His voice caught in his throat.

Stella squeezed his shoulder in encouragement. "Go on."

He nodded. "Mamma… why did you leave me?"

And then he felt her. His chest filled with warmth, and her hands encircled his waist. "*Tesoro*, you have grown into the man I always hoped you would be. Tall and strong, *buono come il pane.* I am so sorry I had to leave you, but my time here was at an end." Her lips touched his forehead. "I am so proud of you, *il mio cucciolo.*" Then she was gone.

He laughed. *Bouno come il pane…* literally *good like bread.* "Mamma, don't go…"

"Did you hear her?" Stella's eyes fixed on his, searching.

"Yes." He lifted his hand from the grass, staring at it wonderingly. It was damp, and smelled of earth and life. He picked up the bundle of lilies and arranged the flowers on the grave, then kissed the headstone. "*Ti amo, mamma. Mi mancherai sempre.*" *I will always miss you.*

Then he got up and dusted himself off again.

Stella put her arms around him. "I'm sure she loved you very much, *tesoro.*"

She sounded so much like his mother that it made his heart ache.

Dante, however, was uncharacteristically quiet.

He tapped Dante's shoulder. "*Tutto a posto?* You okay in there?"

His cousin's gaze shifted to meet his own. "I think so. I felt her too." He was pale as a sheet.

Stella patted his cheek. "I'm sure you did. Come on, boys. I'll take you home and get you fed. Then you can meet your cousin, and ask me all the questions you want."

Gio nodded. "I'd like that." He looked up at the old, abandoned house that loomed over the neat cemetery plots, slowly collapsing to the ground. Just for a second, he thought he saw Luna waving at him from one of the empty windows.

"*Ciao mamma,*" he said one last time.

Then he turned and followed Dante and Stella out of the cemetery.

Behind him, the flowers sparkled bright green before settling down to their normal colors.

52

BETWEEN PIZZA AND PAPRIKASH

Ben stood outside the restaurant, hand resting on the door handle, unsure if he wanted to go in or flee. It was a rather strange place—plain-looking on the outside, except for the plastic green "plants" that were wrapped around the stark wrought-iron fence that surrounded the restaurant's modest outdoor seating area.

The place was called "La Trattoria Bohemia," and it occupied the end of a very plain looking, low-slung blocky building in East Sacramento on J Street, not far from Mercy Hospital. The sign on the side of the structure featured a woman dressed in puffy Renaissance gear, her head tilted to one side, and proclaimed the restaurant home to "Czech and Italian cuisine." He had passed it many times on his drive up J Street, and it always struck him as kind of strange. Was it a fusion place? Did they serve goulash pizza? Schnitzel ravioli?

He supposed he was about to find out.

He'd called Emily that morning at the number the private investigator had provided to him—the Sheraton downtown. She answered immediately, as if she'd been waiting next to the phone for his call. And maybe she had been. After all, she'd come all this way just to see him, and what else would she have to keep her busy here in Sacramento?

Even though he was *literally* standing outside the door of the restaurant with *Emily*—he refused to call her his mother—waiting for him inside, he still wasn't all that sure that he wanted to see her. After all, she had made his teenage life a living hell—always insisting that he wear frilly dresses, brightly colored blouses, and tapered skirts, and those awful fancy shoes that he hated so. They were tapered at the end, crushing his toes, and they were pink, but not just any pink—that awful shade of pink usually reserved for Pepto-Bismol, and covered in sparkly sequins. And when he finally came out to her at the age of seventeen, she had thrown him out with the trash.

Did the fact that someone was dying entitle them to forgiveness for all the horrible things they did to you earlier in your life? *Do I owe her that?*

He took a deep breath and exhaled, closing his eyes and calming his frazzled nerves.

He'd discussed it with his therapist that morning on Zoom, and she had been unequivocal about it, blue eyes fixed on him over the top of her stylish turquoise-framed glasses.

"You don't *owe* her anything. But consider this. How will you feel if you don't go to see her, and then she passes away without you ever having a chance to tell her what you think about her?"

The question had left him stunned. The whole night before, he'd been thinking about what Emily wanted or needed from him, and it had never occurred to him to think of what he might need from her. Or what she might owe him. *Now or never.*

He opened his eyes and pushed open the door.

The place was empty. There was only one person waiting, an older woman with silver white hair, pulled back and tied with a bright blue ribbon. She wore a pale blue chiffon sweater and an ankle-length gray skirt, just allowing a pair of pretty, blue sequined shoes to show under the descending cascade of fabric. She was staring up at some things on the wall —a picture of an old, white, scowling and presumably Czech man; some beer paraphernalia; a bottle of wine on a shelf; and some classic movie posters, including one for something called *Hey Mambo*, which certainly sounded Italian.

It was quite nice inside, a pleasant surprise after the unassuming exterior.

At his entrance, the woman turned, and her mouth fell open in a tiny moue of surprise.

"Hello, Emily."

It was definitely her, but she was older than he remembered, which of course was no surprise. Age had softened her, even as fine lines around her eyes and mouth robbed her of her youth.

She stood up and just stared at him for a minute.

Ben swallowed the bile that had risen up in his throat. "Go ahead and say it. You don't understand why I would choose this. You miss your *pretty little girl*. You wish I had never been born." The last one came out as a growl. It was the most painful thing she had ever said to him, and it still cut him to the core.

She grimaced, as if she too was in pain. Then she shook her head. "It's not that at all. You look so... handsome. I just didn't expect..." She stepped forward and took his hands in hers. "I'm so glad you came. I know I don't deserve it."

This time it was his mouth that fell open. This wasn't what he expected. *Not at all.* Where was the woman who had second-guessed every life choice he had made? Who had questioned his grasp on reality? He had come to the meeting expecting to see *that person*, but this woman, this stranger, unnerved him even more.

She reached up and kissed his cheek. "Come. Take a seat. Please."

He let her lead him back to the table and sat down next to her, unsure what to say next.

She carried on as if nothing strange had happened at all. "I've been looking over the menu. It's not what I expected at all. I thought they might serve goulash—"

"Pizza?"

She nodded, laughing nervously. "Jinx. But look, it's actually two separate menus. There's the Italian one, and the Czech one. Jade was telling me that the original chef and his wife were Czech and Italian. Did you know parts of Czechoslovakia used to be in Italy, and vice versa?"

Ben shook his head. "I didn't know that. Who's Jade?"

As if she had been summoned, the waitress appeared at the table. "Hello there, I'm Jade. I'm so glad you made it. Your mom has been telling me all about you." She was young, with a very friendly, open face, and the brightest green hair he had ever seen.

Ben raised an eyebrow. "She has, has she?"

Emily waved it away. "Oh nothing serious, I was just telling her how you loved to cook with me when you were a child."

He remembered it very differently, but he didn't correct her. "We haven't seen each other for a long time."

Jade smiled. "Oh good, a reunion. Can I get you something to drink?"

He considered ordering something alcoholic, but then decided he needed his wits about him. "Do you have ginger beer?"

"Of course. River City. Is that okay?"

"Perfect. In the bottle with a glass of ice?" He hated it when it got all watered down.

Jade winked at him. "You got it. I'll be back in a few minutes to take your order."

He waited until she walked away, and then turned back to Emily, impatient to get this strange meeting over. "I'm here. Your private eye said you were dying, but you look just fine to me. So tell me, *why are you here?*" He hated being *that guy,* but he had no patience for bullshit and small talk.

In response, she picked up her glass of white wine and drained it in one go. She set it down, took a deep breath, and turned all her attention on him.

Here we go. He steeled himself for the inevitable barrage.

When she spoke at last, her voice was matter-of-fact, as if she was reading the ingredients in a recipe. "I have end-stage cervical cancer. My doctors have given me three months to live, at the outside. Being told you have such a short, defined time left to live really serves to focus the mind on the things that are most important." She reached up and put her fingers under her bangs. And then in one smooth movement, she lifted her hair up and off of her head.

He gasped.

"They have these new drugs and treatments, including these cold caps that you wear, that are supposed to stop the hair loss when you go through chemotherapy. Unfortunately, none of them worked for me." She rubbed her smooth head. "I think I look a bit like Sinead O'Connor. What do you think?"

Ben was stunned that she could find humor at such a dark moment. He looked at her more closely, really *seeing* her for the first time. Her cheeks were hollow. Almost gaunt. The skin of her hands was nearly translucent. She was wearing a lot of makeup, probably to cover up the ravages of the cancer and the chemotherapy. "I am so sorry. But I'd say more Yul Brynner?"

She flashed him a feeble smile. "I'll take it. And so am I. So am I." She reached out to take his hand, running her fingers over his palm. "During my chemo sessions, I had a lot of time to reflect on the choices I've made. I found a new friend who helped me think about things in a different way."

"And what does that have to do with me?" His heart broke for her, but he still carried with him the burden of all the horrible things she had ever said to him and the awful way she had treated him. The shaming. The deadnaming. The withdrawal of her love. *What kind of mother does that?*

She nodded as if she'd been expecting the question. "Her name was Dolores. She was going through chemotherapy and radiation at the same time I was. Did you know that trans women are at an elevated risk for breast cancer, because of the estrogen they take?"

He had known that. But it was absolutely the last thing he expected to hear come out of her mouth. "Dolores is transgender?"

She squeezed his hand. "Yes. She and I talked for hours and hours. I realized she was like you right away. Well, not like you, but—"

"I get it."

Emily nodded. "She told me that she transitioned later in life. She said… I think this is how she said it… she has never been able to *pass*. Is that right? She hated that word but…"

He nodded. "Many transgender people have a love-hate relationship with the idea of passing."

"She was very clear about that, but she seemed… settled with who she was. What she was. Far more than I was. As I listened to her story, I started to think about all the ways I tried to force you to be something that you weren't. All the times that I didn't support you. I told her about you, and she didn't judge me. She just listened. She asked me questions about you, questions I should have been asking myself. She made me see what a fool I've been." She pulled her hand away and hugged her body tightly. "So many times I wished—"

"Have we decided on something for dinner?" Jade appeared at the table, unaware that she had interrupted something deep.

"Another minute?" Ben lifted up the menu. "We haven't really had a chance to look yet."

The waitress read the table and stepped back. "Of course. You two let me know when you're ready."

The doorbell chimed, and she went to greet the newcomers, leaving them alone again.

Ben returned his attention to his mother. "She sounds like an amazing person."

"She was." Emily Hamil—his mother—was shaking. "She passed away last month. The last thing she said to me was 'Go to your son. Make it right before the end.' She reminded me of something I forgot a long time ago. Love really is all that matters." Her eyes were wet. She picked up the cloth napkin and dabbed at the corners. "Look. I have no right to ask you this. You have become such a beautiful, strong, kind man. Mr. Braxton told me that—he watched you for days before he approached you. And I know that's all in spite of me, not because of me. You should throw me out of here. Tell me all the things you've been holding inside of you all these years, and then toss me out on my ear." She picked up her wig and settled it back on her head, fitting it into place and rearranging the bangs.

Ben closed his eyes. *By all rights, I should.* He'd given up on her when she disowned him.

But didn't *true regret* deserve some kind of recognition? Didn't her effort mean something? *Can I give her a second chance?*

Honestly, he didn't know. She had hurt him badly, broken his self-esteem in ways that had taken a decade to repair, and sometimes even now it was still a touch and go thing.

But she was here. She was trying. And she was dying. *If not now, when?*

He took a deep breath. Then he reached out and took her hand, pulling it back across the table gently. "I don't know how much I can give you. But I can try."

Her relief was palpable. "That's… that will do."

He nodded. *One step at a time.* "There's so much you missed in my life. But there's one thing in particular you should know about." He closed his eyes and pictured the woman he'd loved and lost. "Her name was Ella. She was the love of my life." And he told her all about the beautiful spirit who had shared a time on this green Earth with him—the joys, the tribulations, and eventually her sad passing.

One thing led to another. She shared details of her own life since he'd left. Little things. Bitter things. Beautiful things.

They laughed, they cried, and finally got around to ordering a pepperoni pizza *and* a Chicken Paprikash. Because when would they ever have the chance again?

And somewhere halfway between pizza and paprikash, between Czech and Italian, they found their way back to one another, and *Emily* became *Mother* once again.

53

A MILLION BRIGHT STARS

Daniele drove his cousin's car through the Italian foothills, winding their way back down the curvy roads toward Rome. It was well after 10 o'clock—the promised tour of Strangolagalli had turned into a community dinner where half the city had shown up meet the visitors.

Carmelina couldn't complain. It had been a marvelous evening. She'd been surrounded by the denizens of the small town who reminded her so much of their counterparts in the Papavero mysteries. There had been the famous *stesa*, as well as *lasagne*, *tortellini*, *ravioli*, *strangolapreti*, salads, fresh-baked bread, and trays and trays of *dolci*—local sweets. So many things that she couldn't remember half of them. She was stuffed to the gills, but she didn't regret a single bite.

She couldn't see the Italian countryside in the darkness, but she knew it was there. *This is a blessed land, so much different than back home.* Buildings that were historical national treasures in Sacramento might as well have been built yesterday when compared to Italy's long, storied history. The roots of the Italian culture grew deep beneath these hills.

Her palms rested over her full belly, and her great grandmother's precious book of recipes was tucked into a bag in the trunk.

After a while, the twists and turns lulled her into a light sleep, and she dreamed about cooking some of those amazing dishes.

"You look happy."

Carmelina opened her eyes. She was sitting in her favorite chair at home, a wingback rust-colored upright chair that she had bought at a yard sale and reupholstered herself twenty years earlier.

Arthur was seated across from her in his orange La-Z-Boy massage chair that went all the way back, so he could sleep there when he was too tired to get up and go to bed. She had hated that chair as much as he had loved it.

He was seated upright this time, looking at her.

"I haven't seen you for a while." He'd passed away a good ten years ago now, but she had gotten used to him showing his face every now and then, when he thought she needed his guidance.

He laughed. "You've been too busy for me. Look at the life you've made for yourself. You're a celebrated dessert chef surrounded by a circle of amazing friends. And now you're in Italy with Mr. Tall, Dark, and Handsome."

She and Arthur had gone to Italy once together, on their honeymoon, and she had never been back since, though she had always wanted to. "I wish it was *you* here with me."

He chuckled. "You're doing fine without me. But then, you do know why you're there, right?"

She blinked. "I'm not sure what you mean."

He shook his head. "You *know* why he brought you to his cousin's wedding."

Her throat went dry. She hadn't let herself think about it, but she had her suspicions. Daniele had made it clear, without ever coming out and saying it, that he wanted to spend the rest of his life with her.

She had put him off, again and again.

I'm not ready.

Her heart was still with Arthur, and there were so many other things she still wanted to do that didn't include being tied down again to a man. And maybe, just maybe, she was scared to commit to somebody, when she knew she might lose them in the end. "You don't know that."

Letting go of Arthur had been so hard—hell, he was still here. *How is this moving on?*

He laughed. "You're right. I'm just a figment of your imagination, after all. But I think *you* do."

"I'm not ready…"

"We both know that's not true."

She sat with that for a moment. *What the hell am I waiting for?* She was letting fear rule her life, which she had sworn she would never do. Daniele had been with her for nine years, and had shown himself to be nothing less than a gentleman and a true partner. She had made other commitments with him—letting him move into her house, opening the new business with him. *Why is this one so hard?*

Something jerked out of her dream.

The car had come to an abrupt halt. "Sorry about that. We're here."

Carmelina opened her eyes. "Where is here?"

He flashed her a devilish grin. "It's a surprise." He unbuckled his seatbelt, and she did the same.

She looked out through the windshield, but there wasn't much to see, only a parking rail visible in the car's headlights and some tufts of grass, and then even those vanished.

They got out of the car together. They were in a small parking lot with no other cars and only a single streetlamp to provide illumination.

She looked around doubtfully. "Are you going to kill me and dispose of the body where no one will find me?"

He rewarded her jest with an evil cackle. "Yes, you have discovered my wicked plan. Fly to Italy, show you around a bunch of people so everyone knows you're here, and then take you to an abandoned parking lot to murder you and fly home without you." He grinned, his teeth white in the moonlight. "Follow me."

She laughed. "After that confession?" Nonetheless, she did. She found she trusted him implicitly. Maybe that was the most important thing.

They walked through the parking lot, between the low fence, and onto a small trail that led up a hillside. "Seriously, where are we going?"

He winked at her. "It's a surprise." Taking her hand, he led her up the hill, along a foot path that wound through hummocks of dried grass. The sky was clear, the half-moon giving off just enough light for them to find their way, painting the pathway silver. The stars stood out like a million bright pin pricks in the velvety night sky.

They came out on top of the hill, and Carmelina gasped.

A vast city was spread out below them—it had to be Rome—its lights twinkling like reflected stars from the night sky above. "Oh my god, it's beautiful." The air was warm, and a slight breeze teased her red curls. It was a perfect night after a perfect day.

And then Daniele sank down on one knee before her, and time slowed to a halt.

"He's quite handsome."

Carmelina expected to see Arthur when she turned around. It was Brad.

He was wearing the pale yellow button-down shirt he'd had on almost every time she'd seen him, unbuttoned at the collar. His arms were crossed, and he was looking at her the way her father used to, when she'd failed a test in school.

"What?"

He inclined his head toward her frozen paramour. "He's about to ask you."

"I'm not blind." Her fear reared up again in her mind—fear of giving up her hard-won independence. Fear that it would never be as good as it had been the first time, with Arthur. Fear that he would leave her, just like Arthur had.

Brad raised an eyebrow. "He's younger than you are."

"Now you can read my mind?" Brad—the real Brad—had never been this intrusive.

He chuckled. "That's your takeaway?"

"That and the fact that I'm talking to a ghost." *It's too soon. Isn't it?*

"Look at him, down on one knee. Look how happy he is. He loves you. Even a ghost can see it."

"A ghost who's just as much of a pain in the ass in death as he was when he was alive. Maybe more." Still, she did what he said.

Daniele was looking up at her, his face almost glowing. He was a good-looking man, still as handsome as the day they'd met at Corti Brothers. The dusting of wrinkles only added a rugged gravitas to his countenance. He loved her—she could see it. It practically radiated from him.

"You have a choice. Say yes and make him the happiest man alive, or break his poor heart and tell him no. But remember, nothing lasts forever. And it can be over in the blink of an eye." And with that, Brad was gone.

She knew, somehow, that she would never see him again.

Time lurched forward, almost knocking her over, and before she could recover, Daniele was taking her hand.

"Carmelina, I know you're scared. I know I will never replace Arthur. But I love you. I have loved you since the day we met, and I can't imagine my life without you." He reached into his pocket and pulled out a small box.

Her breath caught. *This is really it.*

He opened it, and she gasped for the second time that night.

It was her mother's wedding ring—two braided bands, one silver and one gold, paired with an emerald to match her mother's fiery eyes. *Just like mine.*

Only that ring had been lost the night she'd died, misplaced in the hospital and never returned. "How…?"

"I asked a jeweler friend to recreate it from some of the old photos of your mother. I hope it's all right—"

She nodded, reaching out to touch it, not sure if it was real. "It's perfect." And suddenly she *knew.* Her fears slipped away like tendrils of fog into the night.

"Carmelina, will you do me the honor of—"

"Yes!" She took Daniele's hands and pulled him up into her embrace. Her ghosts were right. It was time to let down the last of her defenses. "Yes, Daniele Amoroso. I will marry you."

"I was just going to ask you to go steady," he murmured into his ear.

She laughed and let him go. She held out her hand for him to slip on the ring—not really her mother's, but that didn't matter.

Then she wrapped her arms around him and kissed him again, opening her heart and soul at last to the man she loved, on a hillside in Italy under a million bright stars.

54

SOLE

"Come on up! We're on the third floor." Aunt Stella's voice was encouraging, even if the ascent itself was not.

Gio stared up at the narrow stairway. He wasn't sure it was wide enough to fit even his own broad shoulders, let alone his backpack.

Stella and her daughter lived in the heart of Bologna, just off the Piazza Maggiore on a side street called Via de' Fusari, which he was pretty sure meant "really narrow old Italian street." It was almost as narrow as the stairwell before him.

"Never know until you try." Dante shrugged and muscled his way past Gio and into the stairwell. His backpack just fit. He disappeared around the corner, whistling, and Gio decided to try his own luck.

Five sweaty, struggling minutes later, he reached the third floor, hauling his bright orange backpack behind him—it was the only way it would fit through the narrow space. There was no sign of Dante, but there was an open door at the end of the hall.

He made for the light, and was drawn inside by the most enchanting smell. His nose picked out notes of tomato, basil, and oregano, but there were also some other things there that he couldn't recognize.

Stella's voice found him. "Close the door behind you, and put your things in the guest bedroom. It's just down the hall."

Gio did as he was told, finding the indicated bedroom. Dante was already busy, putting away his toiletries in the bathroom.

"Well, it's no Marriott." Gio had long ago learned that things were different in Italy. Nothing was new like it was in America, but everything had a quiet dignity about it, a storied age that spoke to you about the many lives lived there before you, if you just knew how to listen. Still, sometimes he missed *new*.

Dante nodded. "Maybe not. But it's nice. Look, there's a window."

Gio put his stuff down on the bed, and peered out through the warped glass. There was a view of the lane below, and the building right across the street, no more than ten feet away. "Yes, with a great view."

If Dante caught his sarcasm, he didn't give any indication. "I love being in the city. So many things going on all around you, all the time. Not like back home in Bertinoro, where the most interesting thing to do is pick cherries and everyone's in bed by eight."

Gio laughed. *Boy has a point.*

The room itself was nice enough, freshly painted in a bright, cheery Tuscan gold, with posters of some of the great masters—da Vinci, Caravaggio, and Michelangelo—pinned to the wall. The bed was old, but the brass headboard had been recently polished, and the duvet looked new. There was a steamer chest at the end of the bed, and a large wooden armoire next to the window where they could hang their clothes.

"Boys, dinner! Come meet your cousin!" Stella sounded eager.

"We can put these things away later. I don't know about you, but I'm hungry." Dante slipped out of the room and down the hall, and Gio followed.

His stomach rumbled.

The kitchen was just down the hall, and was the source of the wonderful aroma he'd smelled when he arrived. It was a warm, friendly room—in the place of the cabinets he was used to back in Sacramento, there were three long shelves above the counter and cooktop, filled with pots and pans, plates, ceramic bowls, and glasses. The whole room was rich with earth tones—ruddy reds, deep browns, and ivory whites, accented here and there by bright blues.

A young woman stood in front of the cooktop, her back to Gio and Dante. Stella was busy setting the table.

"Sole, say hello to your cousin Gio."

The girl turned around, and Gio noticed two things about her at once. The first was that she was stunningly beautiful. She reminded him so much of his mother when she was younger, but paler—her hair was almost white, and her skin was as light as Tahoe snow.

The second thing was that her eyes were two different colors. One was blue and the other was brown. "Hello, cousin. I'm Sole. What's your name?"

"Your eyes are different colors." Dante was staring at her.

Gio hit him up the backside of his head. "Idiot. You don't say that to someone."

Sole smiled. "It's all right. Everyone notices. How could you not? I'm used to it by now. It's called heterochromia, and it's a fancy way of saying that I was born with two different eye colors. I think it makes me quite unique."

Stella nodded, a whisp of a smile on her face, then turned back to putting out the silverware. "My daughter has a thick skin. You have to when you're born albino, as she was."

Ah, that explained the pale skin and hair. "You are unique. And beautiful. I'm Gio, by the way, and this little a-hole is my cousin—and yours—Dante. Forgive his manners. He doesn't have any."

"Hey!" Dante looked wounded. "It's true, but still…"

"Nice to meet you." She grinned at him, and then went back to stirring the pot. "Mamma texted ahead, so I made us some dinner—*tagliatelle al ragu*. I hope you like it. It's simple fare. Hand me your plates."

Dante picked up two of them from the table and handed them to her. She scooped out a handful of wide egg noodles on each one, and topped it with the sauce.

Gio took a deep breath. "What's the meat?" It smelled like a slice of heaven on Earth.

"A little minced beef and pancetta. My own variation." She filled two more plates, then turned off the oven and joined them at the table.

Stella lit a purple taper candle. "For Luna." A flash of sadness crossed her face, then was banished by a brilliant smile. "Dig in! Sole is studying to be a chef at the Culinary Institute of Bologna."

"Ah, CIBO—I get it." *Cibo* was Italian for food. "My father Diego's a chef, and I work at his restaurant. I came to Italy looking for inspiration for the restaurant."

Sole's eyes lit up. "*Certo?* What's his restaurant called?"

"Ragazzi."

Gio took a bite of the ragu, and his mouth exploded with flavor. He could *see* the farm where the tomatoes were grown, just north of Bologna, where they had ripened on the vine. He could *picture* each leaf on the basil plants as they bathed in the golden Italian sun. And he could *feel* the life force of the cow and the pig that had provided the beef and pancetta.

In an instant, he was transported by her cooking and exalted into a new realm he hadn't known existed. In that simple ragu sauce was something complex and real, something he had always lacked but had never known he was missing. "*Porco miseria.*" He dropped his fork and sat back, hands dropping to his stomach, shocked by what had just happened.

Stella nodded. "There, you see? He understands it. He sees how good your cooking is."

Good is an understatement. He felt humbled, embarrassed to realize that he had ever thought he knew how to cook. Even his father would have been dumbfounded by this.

"He's just being polite." With four words, Sole dismissed out of hand what had been one of the most transformative moments in Gio's young life.

Dante took a bite, chewed on it, and set down his fork. "Oh my God, this is good." He wolfed down all the pasta on his plate, and looked up mournfully. "Is there more?"

"You two are just being nice." Still, she seemed pleased. She took Dante's plate and heaped on another serving.

"Being nice?" He stared at his new cousin as if she'd gone mad. "This is one of the best meals I've had in my entire life, and I work for my father, who is a master chef."

Sole turned to stare at him, her multi-colored eyes narrowing. "You're not just humoring me?"

Gio shook his head vigorously. "Not at all. Sole, when I tasted your sauce, I was transported to the garden where the vegetables were grown. I could actually feel the sun on my face." He took another bite, getting some of the noodles, and he could feel her hands kneading the *impasto*—the pasta dough. "You shouldn't be taking an Italian cooking class. You should be teaching one."

Sole practically glowed, like her namesake.

Stella threw her hands wide. "I tell her this every day, and she doesn't believe me. But who am I? Just her mother." Stella leaned over to kiss Sole's cheek.

A new thought entered Gio's head, inspired by his cousin's amazing cooking. "You two need to come to America, to meet my *Papà*. Diego would love your cooking."

Sole's mouth dropped open. "I'd love to. Could we, Mamma?"

Stella frowned. "I'm not sure it's such a great idea. There's the cost, and the time away from work. And things over there are getting a little scary…"

Gio sighed. "It's different in California, I promise. And things aren't so great here, from what I've heard."

"You're not wrong about that." Stella shook her head. "This new government…"

Dante piped in. "You have to go. Gio is awesome, and I would kill for a chance to visit America."

Sole looked from her mother to Gio, and back again. "Please, Mamma? It would be nice to meet our family."

Gio grinned. *Smart, kid, playing the family card.* "My dads have a ton of frequent flier miles. I'll bet they would help out, if you wanted to come to meet them." Gio was still marveling at the fact that he had family of his own here in Italy. Since his mother had died, his only blood relative had been Diego. It was like a phantom limb that had suddenly grown back. Stella and Sole were here, for real—in flesh and bone.

Stella bit her lip. "I don't know."

Gio was struck by how much she reminded him of Luna. It was a gift, this remembering of his mother, of all her little mannerisms. "You'd love Diego, and I'm sure he'd want to meet you."

"He must be a good father, to have raised such an upstanding son." She nodded. "All right. We will come—I can probably get a few weeks off of work. But only if your father says we won't be a burden."

Gio grinned. "I'm sure it will be all right." He'd planned to spend a few weeks in Italy, but now he just wanted to go home and take these amazing people with him.

He pulled out his phone to call Diego.

Diego picked up after a couple rings. "Gio! *Come va?*"

"*Papà* and *Babbo*, you won't believe who I just met here in Bologna…"

55

LET HIM GO

Diego woke up, shivering. Which was strange, because it was the middle of May in Sacramento… well, almost the end of May… and he and Matteo had been keeping the thermostat high to save on utility costs.

Sacramento in the summertime wasn't known for its cold weather.

He sat up and looked around. Golden light from the streetlamps outside and silver light from the half-moon blended to paint the bedroom with an almost magical glow, outlining the bed posts and making them seem to hover in the inky blackness behind them.

A *clinking* noise from down the hall caught his attention. *Is someone else in the house?*

He slipped out of bed, glancing over at his still-sleeping husband, and reached underneath the bed frame to grab the baseball bat. He always kept it there—it was an old habit, born from living in a bad part of Bologna, where it wasn't uncommon to have your house broken into in the middle of the night.

Not so much here, because they were in a pretty good part of town, but there were always homeless folks down on Folsom Boulevard, and desperate people did desperate things.

If Gio were home, Diego would have figured it was just his son snagging a late-night snack in the kitchen.

He stepped as silently as he could around the bed, avoiding the squeaky floorboard next to the large armoire where they kept their clothes. Unlike apartments in Italy, this place did have actual closets, but old habits died hard.

Diego paused at the door, listening for the sound again. *Nothing.*
Maybe it was just my imagination.

He was about to go back to bed when he smelled the most amazing thing. It was one of his mother's recipes—he would know that aroma anywhere.

He followed his nose down the hall to the kitchen, wondering who would break in just to cook him a meal? *Maybe Gio came home early?*

To his surprise, the kitchen lights were on. Someone was bent over the stove, stirring something in a big, battered metal pot, one that he recognized from his childhood. They turned to smile at him.

"Tesoro." The woman reached out to pinch his cheeks. "You're looking good, if a bit more *ciccione* than before," She patted his belly and turned back to stir the pot.

"Mamma?" It couldn't be. She'd been dead for years and years. The last time he'd seen her… well, the last time he'd seen her ghost was at their surprise wedding, downstairs at the restaurant, nine years earlier.

"Don't ask questions, *cucciolo*. Just sit down at the table and get ready to eat."

He had enjoyed a full meal a few hours earlier for dinner, but suddenly he was starving. He hadn't had his mother's cooking in so long.

He did as he was told, the dutiful son, even as he stared at her impossible presence.

"Your mother has a gift for cooking. I can see that you came by it honestly."

Diego almost jumped out of his skin.

Seated across from him was another ghost, another very familiar one. "Brad?"

The man smiled. "Maybe. Or maybe just the product of your indigestion, after that huge meal you had just before bed."

"Maybe." While Diego was considering that, his mother plopped down a napkin, bowl, and spoon in front of him, and three more sets besides. Before he could figure out why there were four place settings, she had filled his bowl with a ladle of her homemade, steaming *passatelli*.

He gave into the vision and breathed in the aroma deeply. Nobody made *passatelli* like his mother. *Just as I remembered it.*

He picked up a spoon and dipped it in the rich chicken broth. Steam rose from the surface, and the breadcrumb "noodles" swirled below. He lifted the spoon to his lips, his hand shaking a little, and blew on the surface to cool it off just enough to eat it. Satisfied, he engulfed the spoon ravenously, and sighed with pleasure.

"You taught our son well. He'll be a fine chef, just like you. Just like your mamma."

Diego's eyes flew open. His mother had taken the seat to his left, and the seat to his right was now filled by his ex, Luna. Gio's mother.

He blinked, half expecting the ghost of Gina Lollobrigida to show up too. But of course there were no more available chairs, so she'd just have to stand. "Now I know I'm dreaming." But if dreaming meant he got to spend a little more time with his mamma and enjoy her home cooking, he didn't want to wake up. He took another bite, and then set the spoon down, sat back, and sighed. "So why are you all here?"

Ghosts always had a reason for visiting.

And if there was a reason, this strange dream would all make sense.

He realized he must be deep asleep for this whole affair to seem as normal as it did.

His mother reached out and took his hand in hers, wrapping her beautiful, gnarled fingers around his, each one a testament to the life she'd lived and the things she'd learned on this green Earth. "In every parent's life, there comes a time when they must let go of their children. It is never easy. We fight it for as long as we can." She rolled her eyes. "*Oddio.* For me, I'm not sure I ever did, not until I was no longer with you to guide you. Lord knows letting go is not something Italian mothers are good at."

Luna took his other hand, her soft, light skin a contrast to his calloused chef hands. "You came running when I called, and you took my baby boy home with you. You provided him with a vibrant, magical life when I no longer could. I will be forever grateful to you for that. But your mother is right. The time has come to let him go."

He looked from Luna to his mother and back again, out of sorts at being confronted by two women at once. "But I have. He's in Italy right now. How much farther do I have to let him go?" *I ache for him every day he's not here. Maybe I really am an Italian mamma.*

Ben replied with a sympathetic grin. "Things are a bit… clearer from this side. Soon, Gio will come home a changed man. It will be easy to let him fall back into his old habits. To let him live under your roof. To take care of him and treat him like a child. You have to resist. You need to let him go."

The two women nodded. "Let him go."

All three of them chanted it in unison. "Let him go. Let him go. Let him go!"

"But I can't—"

Diego's eyes flew open.

He was lying in bed, the early morning sun shining through the window. *What a strange dream.*

He glanced at the clock. 6:30 AM. Time to get up and get started with his prep for the day at Ragazzi.

He glanced over at his other half. Matteo was fast asleep.

He lay back on his pillow, savoring the remnants of the dream. He could still taste the savory broth of the *passatelli* on his tongue.

Four hours later, while he was preparing the *piadina* dough for the evening, his phone buzzed. He picked it up and glanced at the screen.

It was Gio.

You have to let him go.

The words hit him again like a thunderbolt. *I have to let him go.*

He sighed heavily, accepting the wisdom of his ghosts. He picked up the call, his heart hammering in his chest. "Gio! *Come va?*"

"*Papà* and *Babbo*, you won't believe who I just met here in Bologna…"

56

AN UNEXPECTED GIFT

Ainsley stood at the entry to her parents' mansion, staring at the double eight-foot-tall red double doors.

It truly was a mansion. Her father had made a bunch of money as a real estate agent in Folsom and El Dorado Hills, and her mother had recently retired after a career on the local news. Their 7,000 square foot home was perched on a hillside in one of the richest neighborhoods in El Dorado Hills, with a view of the Sierra Nevadas on one side and the Sacramento Valley on the other. And it was just a two-minute ride to the golf course.

Not that any of that mattered right now, though the grandness of the entry and the inescapable symbols of wealth that surrounded her served to remind her why she was there.

Marissa had planned to come with her, but in the end Ainsley had decided this was something she had to do on her own. *And if they disown me for it?*

One hard-earned piece of wisdom she had picked up during her relatively short lifetime was that when you became so sure of something, you had to make yourself do it—to move ahead, no matter the consequences.

It had happened when she had come out to her parents as a lesbian. That had begun a long, glacial period in the relationship, which they had only overcome when her auntie Eunji had intervened on her behalf. And now here she was again.

She closed her eyes and sighed. *Now or never.*

She had waited until the last minute. *Literally.* The next morning she would go to work with Jun Seo Jang. She would take up the issue of her absence from school with the university once she had talked to her parents.

She knocked three times, and dropped her hand behind her back with her other one, staring at the bright red welcome mat.

"Who is it?"

Ansley could picture her mother approaching on the other side of the door, dressed in her red silk kimono, soft slippers padding across the bamboo floor. Her mother adored red.

"*Eomma*, it's me!"

The doorbell camera blinked at her, and then the door opened and she was swept up in her mother's arms, surrounded by a cloud of Chanel N°5. "Oh, Ainsley, it is you! *Appa*, come quick. Ainsley is here!" Her mother kissed her on the cheek and beckoned her inside. "Come in, come in. It's cold out."

Ainsley slipped inside. It wasn't *that* cold out, but her mother was always freezing. The inside of the house was a good ten degrees warmer than she was comfortable with, but fortunately she didn't have to stay long.

The Kim home was decorated with an eclectic collection of beautiful Korean antiques, stylish modern furniture from Scandinavian designs, and a weird but somehow successful sampling of local artists, things bought at yard sales, and thick oriental rugs that somehow all worked together—eclecticism was her mother's signature style.

Mr. Kim came downstairs, wiping his hands on an old towel. They were covered with various colors of paint, part of his latest passion—rediscovering his artistic youth. Ainsley was convinced her own artistic talent had come from her father. While her mother had a knack for home decoration, she didn't have an artistic bone in her body.

Still, her father only viewed his artistic pursuits as a hobby, and would never have allowed himself to pursue art as a career.

"Welcome home to my beautiful daughter." He hugged her, careful to hold his splotchy hands away from her back.

"Take her into the living room. I'll make some tea. I have some cookies Mrs. Yoon at church made for us." Her mother disappeared into their palatial kitchen, while Ainsley followed her father into the living room.

Her mother often bragged that the Capital Korean Presbyterian Church was the "newest Korean Church in all of California." Whether or not that was true, the huge white building was certainly one of the most visible, right next to the freeway. *And probably also from space.*

"Oh, this is new." There was a giant red velvet couch in the middle of the room, covered with yellow cushions. Her mother also adored bright colors as a general principle.

"*Eomma* found it at an estate sale down the street. You know how she loves her estate sales." Her father gestured her to take a seat on the new acquisition, and sat down in one of the striped red and white recliners opposite it.

Her mother bustled in carrying a black lacquer tray with three steaming cups of tea and a plate of *yakgwa*—traditional honey cookies—strangely topped with powdered sugar.

How did she do that? She couldn't have been gone for more than thirty seconds.

"Here, take one." Her mother reached out with a sticky cookie.

"No thanks, *Eomma*." She wasn't hungry. In fact, her stomach was gurgling nervously. She looked down at her hands, then at her father's. His fingers were spotted with blue and green paint. Maybe he'd been painting the ocean. Or a forest and the sky. "*Appa*, you like to create art, right?"

He nodded. "I find it relaxing after a long hard day at work."

Ainsley scrunched up her nose. *Not exactly the answer I was looking for, but I can work with it.* "I like to paint too. And draw and make all kinds of art. Just like you, *Appa*."

Her mother beamed. "Your father has gotten quite good. The minister at our church put one of *Appa's* paintings on his office wall—an oak tree on a golden hillside."

Ainsley bit her lip. "That's very nice. What I'm trying to say is—"

"Our minister even took down one of the paintings by Mrs. Yoon's husband to put your *Appa's* painting up. It was that one of the horse that looked like a dog, right Jae-Seong?"

"Mamma!"

Her mother blinked and looked at her as if Ainsley had just sprung up out of the bright red couch, summoned perhaps from some heretofore unknown netherworld. "You should not be so rude to your parents."

Ainsley rolled her eyes. *If they thought that was rude…* She decided to rip the Band-Aid off. "*Eomma, Appa,* I've decided to leave school for a while. I want to be an artist, full time."

Her mother's heavy gasp overshadowed the look of disappointment on her father's face.

"Ainsley Kim, you can't do this." Her mother wrung her hands in her lap. "You have a rich future ahead of you in medicine. Your father and I have worked really hard to—"

"I hate studying medicine. I always have." Ainsley risked her mother's displeasure again by interrupting.

Her mother's mouth fell open again, but her father's features softened.

Are you so disappointed in me?

"What do you mean, you hate medicine?" Her *Eomma* shook her head vehemently. "Since you were a girl, you *always* wanted to be a doctor. You used to bandage up your little Barbie doll. Remember? You would bring her to me and tell me that she was sick and you needed me to help heal her."

"I was six years old, *Eomma*." She took a quick breath and hurried on. "I know it's what you wanted for me. I know you want me to become a doctor and become rich and famous—"

Her mother shook her head sharply. "No. That doesn't matter. Not rich. Not famous. We wanted you to be happy. To have a good life." She nodded as if to emphasize her point. "If medicine doesn't make you happy, don't do medicine."

Ainsley blinked. "Just like that?" She stared at her mother. And then glanced at her father. He seemed troubled. "*Appa?*"

He looked away, and when she followed his gaze, she realized that he was looking at a painting on the wall. It was an old black-and-white water-color, one that had been there as long as they had been in the house, the paper faded to yellow, and cracked. It was in the classic Korean style, with a couple of large hills in the background and a shorter hummock in the middle distance covered with trees. In the foreground, a house was partially hidden by more trees, showing only its roof.

"Your grandfather, Seong Hung, painted that for your mother and me for our wedding day. You never knew him. He was from the old country, and he passed away before you were born."

"It's… beautiful." She never really paid much attention to it. It had just always been there. Another piece of art in a house filled with them.

Her father nodded. "He was very talented. Just like you. He was also very poor. He gave away most of his art, and barely made a living in the small village he lived in, in South Korea." He sighed. "When I came here, I vowed to be different. To be a success. To not have to always be worried about where the money was going to come from to feed my family. To feed you."

"*Appa*, I—"

He held out his hand. "Please let me finish. I never wanted you to be unhappy the way I was unhappy when I lived with him." He held up his hands, stretching out his fingers and looking at the paint stains. "But now I see that I made the same mistake he did. I wanted you to be like me. I thought you would find happiness being like me. Working hard, working for someone else. Making lots of money."

"I… No, I never wanted that." She looked down at the coffee table and the cookies, ashamed.

He leaned forward and put a hand on her cheek, lifting her face gently to look at his. "What your *Eomma* says is right. We want you to be *happy*. Money is just money. What's in your heart?"

She felt suddenly filled with light. "There's an artist, they are from Korea. Their name is Jun Seo Jang, and they have asked me to intern with them as their assistant over the next few months. *Appa*, there's so much they could teach me."

Her father looked over at her mother. She held his gaze for a moment, and Ainsley held her breath. Then her mother nodded.

"What?" Ainsley looked from one to the other, afraid they were about to withdraw their blessing.

Instead, her father got up and crossed the room to an elaborate chest of drawers that her mother had had imported from Korea some years before. It was shaped like a vase, its red lacquer surface a good match for the couch.

He opened one of the drawers and pulled out something wrapped in burlap cloth.

Returning to the couch, he sat next to Aisley, and handed it to her. "What's this?"

He gestured with his hands. "Open it. Please."

She unwrapped the little bundle carefully, exposing three bamboo brushes. They were shiny, especially around the ends, worn smooth with time and use. "Are these…?"

Her father, nodded. "They belonged to your grandfather. And now they are yours. I am certain that you will paint many beautiful things with them."

These are precious beyond measure… She threw her arms around his neck and hugged him tight. "Thank you, *Appa*."

Her mother cleared her throat. "Nothing for your *Eomma?*"

Ainsley laughed. She let go of her father and reached out to hug her mother too. "Thank you too, *Eomma*."

"You are welcome. And when you are a rich and famous artist, you will pay us back for your college tuition."

Ainsley sat back, eyes widening. "Are you serious?"

"We will see." Her mother winked at her. "Now, tell us about this Jun Seo Jang. I want to know about this person who is stealing away my only daughter. Is there maybe something more to the story?" She sounded hopeful.

Ainsley laughed. "No, still a lesbian." She squeezed the brushes tightly in her hand, sending a quick prayer of thanks up to heaven.

She would tell them everything… even what had happened in the gallery. "It all started when this art dealer came into Ragazzi…"

57

DO YOU KNOW WHAT YOU WANT?

It was a beautiful Monday morning on the patio at Orphan, the retro-funky-chic café Carmelina had told Sam about in her last email. He'd enjoyed it so much the first time that he'd decided to come back again. It was crowded, the pleasant murmur of the gathered diners a balm for Sam's soul.

Carmelina was on her way home after a whirlwind weekend in Italy. He couldn't wait for her to return, but had rather enjoyed having her house all to himself with Oscar, complete with the pool in the back. They'd even gone skinny-dipping at midnight the night before—it had been fun to pretend he was eighteen again.

He did manage a quick glimpse of Oscar's private parts, and the man had *nothing* to be ashamed about. Still, there'd been no inappropriate behavior between them. And he wasn't convinced that there ever should be. His heart still ached for Brad. *Maybe I'd be better off alone—*

"Sam?"

He looked up to find Ricky—his hair still stubbornly pink—grinning at him like an idiot. "You made it!" He jumped up and squeezed his former foster kid tightly. "You brought Alyn too. Good!"

Ricky nodded. "I'm so glad you found time for us. I wanted to see you before you went back to Tucson. You were so busy at the scattering…"

Sam felt a twinge of pain at the memory of that day. It had been beautiful, but letting go of Brad… Truth be told, he wasn't looking forward to returning to the place he and Brad had called home, either. *Too many memories.* "Take a seat. This is my second time here. Have you guys tried it before?"

"No, we both live out in the suburbs and work in Midtown. We don't get out to East Sac very much." Ricky looked around. "It's really cute." He paged through the menu.

"Carmelina said it's one of her favorite places." It was growing on Sam too.

"Oh, is she back?" Ricky handed one of the extra menus to Alyn.

"Not yet. She flies in tonight." Sam put his own down. "I think I'm gonna have the yogurt, fruit, and granola thing. I'm trying to eat a little better these days." He patted his stomach. Brad used to tease him about letting himself go. *I wish you were still here to give me a hard time.*

Ricky gave him a once over. "Well, I think you look great." He glanced at Alan. "Wanna split the breakfast burrito?"

"Sure." He handed the menu back to Ricky. "We usually share to cut down on costs, and they serve so much food at most of these places. Prices are through the roof these days."

"That's smart. But this will be my treat." He could afford it. His books were doing well, they had built up a bit of a nest egg, and Brad had always been a planner, right down to his own life insurance.

"Thanks, Sam!" He glanced at Alyn. "Maybe the breakfast burrito and a side of rosemary potatoes?"

Alyn nodded enthusiastically. "And some fresh-squeezed orange juice?"

They both turned to look at Sam hopefully.

"Of course. You drive a hard bargain." Sam watched them both together. They looked happy. They had that sweet *boys in love* energy about them, that synergy that long term couples often had. "How long have you two been together?" He hadn't kept in touch with Ricky as well as he should have.

"About five months." Alyn took Ricky's hand. "We met just before Christmas."

Sam stared at them. "That's all? You seem like you've been a couple for much longer."

Ricky nodded. "I know, right? We both knew it was what we wanted, almost right away. It was… magic." They shared a quick, furtive glance.

Sam grinned. There was more of the story, that much was clear. Ricky would tell him in due time. He remembered the little bit of magic that had brought him and Brad together. "It thrills me to see you two so happy. Brad would've been happy too."

Ricky winced. "I'm so sorry. When I heard… I was devastated. You guys were like parents to me. It must've been so hard for you—was it quick, at least?"

Sam swallowed hard. "It was the hardest day of my life. He wasn't supposed to die. Not so soon. But yeah, it was pretty quick." *Too quick.*

He could still see them wheeling Brad's body away under a white sheet. Even then, Oscar had been at his side, holding his hand.

Ricky looked around. "Where's Oscar? I thought he was coming?"

"He stayed back at Carmelina's. Said he had some work to get done this morning. I dragged him away from everything at the last minute, and he's been really good about supporting me this whole week." As he said it, he realized how much he'd asked of his friend, and how freely Oscar had given his help, without complaining even once.

The waitress with the short blond hair he'd seen flitting around showed up at their table with a welcoming smile. "Hi there. My name is Erica. Can I get you started with something to drink?"

Sam managed a weak smile in return. "Just water for me."

"Fresh-squeezed orange juice." Ricky and Alan said it in unison.

She smiled. "Of course. Coming right up. Are you guys ready to order?"

"Another minute?" Sam hadn't fully committed to the granola yet.

"You got it." She stuck her pencil behind her ear and headed on to the next table.

"Alyn?" A cheerful brunette in a bright tie-dye shirt stopped next to their table.

"Jackie!" He got up to give her a big hug. "Sam, this is my best friend in the world—well, after Ricky. Jackie, this is Ricky's foster dad."

Sam got up and held out his hand. "Pleased to meet you."

She shook it vigorously. "Nice to meet you, Ricky's foster dad." Her eyes twinkled.

Alyn chuckled. "What are you doing down here?"

"I had a medical appointment across the street. Nothing serious." She waved it away. "I was hungry and saw this place… but it's packed. Guess I'll just head home."

"No, please. Join us." Alyn glanced at Sam. "If you don't mind?"

Sam shrugged. "Of course not. Any friend of Alyn's a friend of mine." He'd been enjoying his time with his foster son, but he didn't want to be rude.

"Oh, that'd be fabulous." She took the seat next to Sam and glanced quickly through the menu. "I know just what I want." She set it down and looked around the table. "So what were we talking about?"

"Brad." Ricky sighed. "He was my other foster father. He passed away last week."

Jackie looked stricken. She put a hand on Sam's arm. "I'm so sorry to hear that. I see a lot of that. I work with low-income families and seniors, and I've seen a lot of spouses struggling after their husbands or wives passed way."

Sam closed his eyes. "Brad was just thirty-nine." *Too soon.* "I just wish…

She squeezed his hand. "I know, I know. It's the hardest thing in the world. To lose someone like that. Then to have everyone else expect you to get back to living when the person you thought you'd grow old with is gone."

Sam nodded. "We had so many plans. Places we wanted to visit, things we wanted to learn together. How do you just let all of that go?" Puerto Vallarta. Edinburgh. Venice. They'd even talked about taking an Italian class together.

Ricky leaned forward. "When I met Alyn, I was living only for my work. I wanted to save all the kids who were living on the street, just like I was when you and Brad took me in. I forgot the most important thing— to live for myself." He leaned back and took Alyn's hand. "Then, when we met—it was magic. Like, real magic. He reminded me of all the things I wanted out of life. And I reminded him how beautiful he was."

Sam shifted uncomfortably. He and Brad had been like that together once. Young, idealistic, and ready to face the world.

Alyn grimaced. "You're not helping."

But Ricky plowed ahead. "My point is that you and Brad had a beautiful life together, a lovely dream. His dream is over, but yours is not. You have to wake up. He wouldn't want you to stay sad and alone for the rest of your life. He'd want you to find a new way to be happy. I know he would."

The earnestness in his voice tugged at Sam's heart. The kid was so young—what, all of twenty-five? He didn't know the pain the world could cause you when everything suddenly came crashing down.

Sam knew he was right. *Brad wouldn't want me to be sad.* But Brad didn't get a vote in how Sam felt anymore.

Jackie nodded. "Ricky's a smart kid—he's been so good for Alyn. You should listen to him. When my husband and I lost our last dog, Priscilla—we called her Prissy—we thought we'd never get another one. But then Petunia came into our lives." She pulled out her phone and touched the screen, and a little bulldog—it *mostly* looked like a bulldog—appeared. "There's life after loss, that's all I'm saying."

Despite the fact that she was comparing the death of her dog to the passing of his husband, she wasn't wrong, either.

Maybe he should consider his options. Brad—or the ghost of Brad—had been clear enough about his own opinions about Oscar.

He likes you, you know.

Oscar had been a good friend to them both for years, and had been there with Sam every day and every step of the way since Brad had passed.

Maybe it *was* too soon. *Of course it's too soon!* But maybe, just maybe, it was time to at least consider opening his heart to something new.

Their waitress returned. "Sorry to keep you all waiting. I see we have another guest! Welcome."

Jackie laughed. "Why thank you. I'm so happy to be here." She mimed a little curtsey.

"And we're happy to have you." She didn't roll her eyes or anything. "Can I get your order? Miss?"

"I haven't been called that in years. Thank you. I'll take the fruit and granola." She handed over her menu.

Erica took a quick note. "Of course." She turned to the boys. "And you two?"

"We'll take the breakfast burrito. We're going to split it. And a side of those rosemary potatoes." Ricky gathered up their menus.

She scribbled their order down on her pad. He loved that she still used a paper pad, and the restaurant also didn't take anything but cash. It was like stepping back into the previous century. "And you, sir? Do you know what you want?"

Sam closed his eyes. Brad was smiling at him.

I just want you to be happy.

Who knew if it would work out? If he was ready? If Oscar even wanted it?

He'd never be sure until he tried.

Sam opened his eyes and nodded. "I do now."

58

AN UNINVITED DINNER GUEST

"Mother, I want you to meet Lorelei." Ben stood back from Lorelei's front door to let the two of them assess one another.

Lorelei had graciously agreed to have the meet-and-greet at her apartment, though she'd been very nervous about meeting his mother. "What if she doesn't like me?'

"Not possible." Ben had sealed the deal with a kiss.

Now he watched with bated breath to see if things would go as well as he hoped, or if it would be more like two cats in a box.

Lorelei smiled broadly, though her hand scratching the side of her leg betrayed her nervousness. "Come on in. It's so nice to meet you, Mrs. Hamil."

"That's *Ms. Hamil* now. Mr. Hamil has been dead for a number of years." His mother stepped past Lorelei and looked around the living room. "Oh, I love the art. Where did you get it?"

"She painted them all. Lorelei is an artist." *And she's really good.* He followed them in and closed the door behind them.

His mother raised an eyebrow. "And a mother too? You didn't tell me about that little detail." She glanced at the toys strewn around the floor.

Lorelei's face flushed red. "I'm so sorry. I just got the kids off to Mr. Johnson's across the hall and didn't have time to clean up after them. He watches them sometimes when I have company." Lorelei was wringing her hands now.

Ben came to her rescue. "Yes, mama, Lorelei has two beautiful children, and she's a great mom." *Unlike some people.*

"Calm down, dear." His mother put a hand on Ben's arm. "I didn't mean any disrespect. I was just thinking I might finally become a grandmother—by marriage—if you ever make an honest woman out of this fine lady here." She put her other hand next to her mouth in a faux aside to Lorelei. "Between you and me, I don't know what you see in this lunkhead."

"Mama!" He stifled a laugh.

She raised her head in mock defiance. "Well it's true. She's far too pretty for you. Children or no."

It was Lorelei's turn to hide her laughter. "So, *Ms. Hamil,* why don't you come into the kitchen. I have dinner almost ready." Behind his mother's back, she pointed at her and mouthed *I like her.*

Ben rolled his eyes. "Come on mom, it's this way." He led her into Lorelei's small kitchen.

"It's… very cozy." She bent over to inspect the table. "But also very clean."

Ben winked at Lorelei. "That means she's impressed." He led her to one of the seats. "Mama, why don't you take a load off. I'll help Lorelei finish the meal." Dinner smelled heavenly. They had decided on something simple and difficult to criticize. Over the years feeding her kids, Lorelei had become an expert in making spaghetti, and her sauce had knocked Ben's socks off the first time he tried it. "What can I do?"

Lorelei pointed at the sink. "There's a colander there. Want to strain the pasta? I've got the sauce almost ready—just needs a bit more basil."

"You got it." He kissed her cheek, and then took the big pot off the stove and wrestled it over to the sink. Water and pasta spilled out into the colander, setting up a lovely aroma.

His mother sniffed the air. "That smells heavenly. Do I detect a bit of garlic?"

Ben refrained from staring at his mother in open surprise. She really had turned over a new leaf. When he was younger and cooked for her, there had been nothing but criticism after criticism. Apparently being faced with your own mortality really did make you reevaluate your life.

Lorelei piped in. "Yes. I have some garlic bread in the oven. Ben, can you check on that for me so it doesn't burn? There's a basket with a cloth to cover it there on the counter." She pulled down three beautiful multicolored stoneware plates from the cabinet. "I only use these on special occasions."

His mother put her hand over on chest. "I'm honored." She adjusted her wig, which had shifted slightly askew.

Ben checked on the bread, pushing down his sadness. They had agreed that this would be as normal a night as possible, under the circumstances. If his mother only had a few more months to live, he wanted to spend them with her making good memories, not fretting about what was to come. They had lost so much time. "The garlic bread looks fantastic, Lor."

He slipped it into the basket and covered it up to keep it warm, and set it down in the middle of the table.

It was soon followed by the three plates, three sets of knives and forks, some bright yellow napkins, and a trio of wine glasses.

"They say red wine usually goes best with tomato sauce, but I like a nice clean, dry white." Lorelei put a bottle down on the table—Ben's recommendation, because he knew his mother loved a good white.

His mother raised an eyebrow. "My doctor told me to avoid wine with the cancer."

Lorelei turned white as a sheet. "I'm so sorry. I didn't think—"

His mother took her by the hand and guided her gently down to the chair. "I only have a few months left to live, child, so I'm not overly concerned with what my doctor recommends. Pour me a glass."

Ben frowned. "Mama, are you sure?"

She turned to stare at Ben. "Are you really going to deny your dying mother a chilled glass of white wine?"

He laughed in spite of himself. "Are you really going to play the *dying mother card* just to get a drink?"

"Touché. But yes." She held up her glass, and Lorelei filled it and then the other two.

"*Bon apetit.*" Lorelei set the bottle down and took up her fork.

"*Bon apetit.*"

They each grabbed a piece of garlic bread, and then dug into the pasta.

A grin spread across his mother's face. "Lorelei, this is delicious. What did you put in the sauce?" She took another bite.

"It's my mother's recipe. There's a bit of sour cream in there along with some fennel and a fair amount of rosemary."

His mother put her fingers to her lips to kiss and released them in the air. "It's genius. Ben, you really need to marry this woman."

"Mama…" It was way too soon for that.

She poked him on the shoulder. "I mean it. She's perfect for you. She can cook. She's pretty. She makes beautiful things." She gestured to the art on the walls. "I'm not going to be around much longer. I want to see you happy and married before I die."

Ben and Lorelei exchanged a glance, but before he could say something there was a heavy pounding at the front door.

"Let me see who that is." Lorelei wiped the corners of her mouth, set the napkin down on the table, and vanished into the living room.

Ben followed her with his gaze. *I am so lucky.* Most people never got a second chance at true love.

His mother squeezed his shoulder. "You picked a lovely woman. I'm proud of you."

"Even if it's not the way you always hoped?" *So much water under that bridge.*

She snorted. "I gave up on that old dream a long time ago." She took the last bite of spaghetti and sighed happily. "I just want to know that you are taken care of when I'm gone."

Ben grimaced. "Mama, we still have time…"

There was a loud crash from the living room. "I knew you were lying to me. When my lawyer hears about this—"

Ben sprang up onto his feet, and was out of the kitchen in a flash.

Lorelei was cowering before a blond, bearded man a head taller than her, wearing a short-sleeve polo shirt, showing off his hairy arms, which were raised as if to strike her. One of her paintings, a watercolor of the Tower Bridge, had been smashed to pieces.

Ben inserted himself between the two of them and pushed the man away. "Back off, man."

The guy stared at him, his eyes going wide. "Lori, who's this?"

"*This* is my guest, Ben, my neighbor from downstairs. Ben, this is Garrett, my ex." The last word sounded like a curse.

"So not only are you pretending to be a cripple, you're also bringing strange men around our kids?" Garrett tried to push his way past Ben, but Ben blocked him.

"Look, I'm sorry that I lied to you." Lorelei put a hand on Ben's shoulder, staying squarely behind him. Her hand was trembling. "I really was in a wheelchair, but I didn't know how to tell you that I was better. Everything seemed to be working out—"

"Working out? I can't believe you call this working out!"

Ben crossed his arms. "I think you should leave." He said it calmly but forcefully.

Garrett growled. "Don't tell me what to do in my own home."

"This isn't your house anymore." Lorelei's hand tightened on Ben's shoulder, and now she sounded angry. "It hasn't been since you cheated on me. Thank God the kids aren't here to see you acting out like this."

"Young man, I think you should leave." Ben's mother stood in the doorway to the kitchen, her own arms crossed, a mirror image of Ben.

It was hard to keep from grinning.

"And who are you? What, Lor, are you running a boarding home for ni—"

He got no further before Ben had him pushed up against the door, a forearm against the man's windpipe. "I'd think very carefully before completing that sentence."

Garrett's eyes bulged out almost comically.

"Like my mother said, I think you should go." It had been a long time since someone had used the "n" word around him, and he wasn't about to let *this man* throw it around.

Garrett struggled under his grasp, but Ben increased the pressure on his windpipe steadily, pinning him in place.

"Am I clear?" His gaze pinned the man as much as his arm.

There was fear in Garrett's eyes now.

Not surprising. Bullies were usually timid as mice when you called their bluff. "Am. I. Clear?"

Garrett nodded rapidly. "Yes." It came out as a hoarse whisper.

Ben let him go. "Good. Now get the fuck out of here. Lorelei's lawyer will be in touch to renegotiate your custody terms." He opened the door, shoved Garret out, and slammed it behind him, locking the deadbolt.

"That was amazing." Lorelei ran to Ben and threw her arms around him.

Ben's mother nodded. "I'm very proud of you." Something about the way she said it told him she had finally, truly accepted him for who he was now, not who she wanted him to be.

He hugged Lorelei tight. "I'm sorry he scared you—"

Lorelei looked up at him, tears in her eyes. "Ask me now."

"What?" He looked from her to his mother, and back again.

His mother snorted. "He always was a little slow." She smiled at him. "Ask. Her. To. Marry. You."

Comprehension dawned. *Marry her? Am I ready for that?* Ella would want him to be happy. And Ms. Fortune herself had told him Lorelei was the one for him.

So had Brad.

You're alone. Lonely. You want to be complete again.

His old friend was right. He was so terribly lonely, ever since Ella died. Lorelei made him smile, and her bright spirit had brought him back from all the dark places.

Maybe it was time to move on. "Lorelei, would you—"

"Yes!" She reached up and kissed him.

Ben's whole world dissolved into fireworks and heart-shaped bubbles and grand orchestral music.

When he came back to down Earth, he let her go slowly. She receded from him like an ocean wave that promised to return. "Mama, I'm getting married."

"So I heard." His mother smiled, and turned around to head back into the kitchen. "Come on, you two. I want some more of that wonderful pasta."

"You're still hungry?" Ben took it as a good sign.

"Yes, for your soon-to-be-wife's wonderful pasta." Her voice came floating into the living room. "And then we can start planning your wedding."

Ben grinned. He knew just where it should take place.

59

BACK SO SOON?

Sam pulled the rental car up in front of Carmelina's house. It was dinner time already, but it would still be bright in Sacramento for another three hours. After lunch with Ricky, he'd spent the better part of the day driving around the city, sorting out his feelings.

He'd finally ended up at the State Capitol, the place where he and Brad had first met in the office of a Republican senator.

Things had been so different then. You could still talk to the other side, though sometimes those conversations were rough. The hatred that was so common these days between parties was much more on the fringe.

Brad had been so handsome, so kind, the perfect antidote to Sam's controlling ex, Grayson. And it had been Sam's first real job…

He'd gone inside that afternoon to take a look, and had ended up at his old office. Only now it belonged to a Democratic senator, a fierce Black woman in her forties—Senator Cassandra Mills. When he'd told the staff he'd worked there once upon a time, the Senator herself had come out of her office to meet him and shake his hand.

He didn't have the heart to tell her about Brad. Not that it would have mattered to her. She had never known him. Even so, he couldn't bring himself to say it. *Brad is dead.*

Now Sam was back at the place where his friend Oscar was waiting for him, and he still didn't know what he wanted. What he was supposed to want.

I'm not ready.

He almost drove off again, but he'd already made the poor guy wait all day, sending him vague texts and promising to be back in time for dinner. He'd even stopped by Café Bernardo to pick up a couple burgers and fries for dinner.

With a heavy sigh, he turned off the car.

"It's okay if you're not ready."

He almost jumped out of his seat. He looked in his rearview mirror, and Brad's warm brown eyes met his.

"Not you again." Sam didn't believe in ghosts. This was just an echo of the past, his own deep desire to go back in time conjuring up a phantom from his mind. *So why won't it leave me alone?*

He grabbed the bag and slipped out of the car, slamming the door and leaving Brad behind.

"That's what a ghost is, you know." His ex—did you call someone who was deceased an ex?—the former love of his life was blocking his path, solid as a fence.

Sam looked around, but there was no one else nearby to see what a fool he was. "What do you want from me?" He should have been over-joyed to be visited again, but instead he just found himself getting more and more angry. "You're not real."

Brad shrugged in that matter-of-fact way he had. "Maybe not. But you keep conjuring me up, for some reason. So you tell me. Why am I here?"

Sam blinked. *That's a new one.* The ghost demanding to know why it had shown up on your doorstep. "I honestly don't know."

Brad advanced on him. "Oh, I think you do."

Sam took an uncertain step back, shaking his head. "I really don't. I wanted the real Brad to come back. Not you. You're just a hallucination. Or I'm going crazy." It was possible, with all the stress he'd been under, even before Brad had died. Book deadlines, his mother's passing, his never-time-to-catch-your-breath schedule… *Maybe I am crazy.*

Brad laughed. "You know, people who think they're crazy usually aren't."

"So you can read my mind now?" *Maybe the only way out was through.*

"For God's sake, Sam, I am in your mind." Brad took a step back, holding out his hands in surrender, or placation. "Look, I know you're confused. And you have every right to be. I'm gone, but you can't seem to let go of me. You have these strange feelings about Oscar, and the guilt about that is eating you up. You don't know what to do. Is that about right?"

Sam blinked. "You're fucking kidding me, right?"

"What?" Brad's ghost blinked like a deer caught in the headlights.

"You go and die on me and leave me all alone, and you think you get to have a say in who I see once you're gone?" He threw the bag down on the concrete and it split open, spilling out the burgers and fries all over the sidewalk.

Sam didn't care. He jabbed the imaginary Brad in the chest. "You left me. You left me all alone and you broke my fucking heart. How could you do that to me?" By the end of it, he was screaming his lungs out on the sidewalk in front of God, the neighbors, and everyone.

"You okay, Sam?"

He blinked.

Oscar was standing there staring at him, an apron tied around his waist.

Sam closed his eyes and leaned back against the car. "Oh God. I must look like a fucking idiot, standing on the street and shouting at ghosts." His gaze fell on the ruined paper bag and its contents. "I brought dinner…"

Oscar looked over the ruined remains and shook his head. "They use such cheap bags these days."

Sam burst out laughing. "Such cheap fucking bags." He couldn't help himself.

Oscar laughed too, chuckling at first, but then falling into a full-blown guffaw. He leaned against the car next to Sam and held his sides, laughing so hard he started to cough.

Sam patted him on the back. "You okay there?"

Oscar sputtered a bit, then recovered. "Yeah. Man. Sorry. I needed that. It's been a bleak week." He looked over at Sam and blushed. "I mean… sorry. It must have been so much harder for you."

Sam shook his head. He'd taken Oscar and his pain at the loss of Brad for granted. "Pain is pain. Brad loved you, you know. You guys were tight. It's okay to feel like crap over losing one of your best friends."

Oscar hung his head. "Thanks. It's been hard. But seeing the places that were important to him—to you—that's helped me a lot."

"Me too." *More than you know.* Each memory had been a little *letting go.*

Oscar was staring up at the sky. "Wouldja look at that."

Sam followed his gaze. A red-tailed hawk was moving in lazy circles overhead. Warmth spread through him. Brad would always be looking out for him.

His stomach rumbled.

"You hungry?"

"Sure am. But what's this?" He pointed at Oscar's apron, which was covered in red strawberries. Definitely one of Carmelina's.

His friend blushed. "I… made you a little something for dinner. I didn't know you were going to pick something up—"

"Well, you can see how that turned out." Sam knelt and managed to scoop most of the meal back into what was left of the bag. "What did you make?"

He grinned. "Come in and see."

The sun was just dipping toward the horizon. A cool breeze kicked up, bringing the smell of honeysuckle.

Sam followed Oscar inside, dumping the spoiled meal in the trash can on the way in. The living room smelled like tomato sauce and something meaty. "Oooh, that smells lovely."

"It's my mother's secret chili recipe. I raided Carmelina's pantry and fridge to make it—I hope she doesn't mind."

Sam took another deep breath. His stomach rumbled. "I certainly don't. What's the secret?"

"Promise you won't laugh?" Oscar looked positively bashful.

Adorable. "I can't promise that."

Oscar shuffled his feet, looking down at the floor. "Promise."

"All right, I promise." He raised an eyebrow. "Is it weed?"

Oscar snorted. "Hardly. She used a couple of cans of beans and whatever she could find in the fridge and the pantry. One time we had spicy chicken rhubarb chili."

Sam covered his mouth, stifling a laugh. *A promise is a promise.* When he was sure he'd contained it, he managed to ask, "And how was it?"

"It was absolutely horrid." Oscar held his nose and made retching sounds.

Sam couldn't help but laugh with him.

Oscar looked mock-wounded. "You promised…"

"You started it. And besides, we're laughing together." He poked Oscar, and Oscar poked him back. They traded jabs, laughing and chasing each other around the kitchen, Oscar squealing as Sam chased him.

Then they were face to face with Oscar's back against the wall, and the world smelled delicious.

Sam kissed him.

Oscar's eyes opened in surprise, and then he kissed Sam back, and for a minute everything was all right—

"Hey, we're back! We caught an early flight—" Carmelina burst into the room with Daniele right behind her, holding a paper Versace bag. "Well, this is a surprise."

Sam backed away from Oscar as if he were radioactive. "Oh, hey. You're back." His face flashed seven shades of hot. He stuck his hands in his back pockets and leaned against the refrigerator.

Carmelina set her bag down. "Yes. And you and Oscar are…?"

He felt his face turning red. "It's not… we're not… it was a mistake."

Oscar stepped in to save him. "It's the secret chili's fault. Strange things are known to happen when I cook my *madre's* recipe."

Sam saw the look of hurt on his face, but Oscar turned away to stir the pot. *What am I doing?* He could almost feel Brad's eyes on him from beyond the grave. He took a deep breath, and said the words slowly and clearly. "It wasn't a mistake."

Everyone turned to look at him. "What?" they all said at once.

Sam closed his eyes and took a deep breath. When he opened them, they were all still staring at him. "It's… look, Oscar, I'm not ready for anything new yet. Brad's just left…" He still couldn't bring himself to say the word "dead" out loud yet. "Brad's… gone, and I'm hurting. And nothing makes sense. But kissing you was *not* a mistake."

Oscar crossed his arms "I'm going to need a little more than that."

Sam sank down into one of the kitchen chairs. "I'm not ready to move on yet. It's too fucking soon. But Oscar, I *like* you. You've been there for me every step of the way since Brad, since he… died." *There, I said it.* It felt cathartic. "You put your life on hold to come here with me, to bring him home to Sacramento. And it hurts. God, it hurts. I'm so not ready for anything new. Not yet. But if…"

He closed his eyes again. *This is hard.*

"If what?"

He opened them to find Oscar's eyes fixed on him.

"If you're willing to wait, then one of these days, I might be." He exhaled, and all the stress flowed out of him to evaporate like trails of steam in the air.

The happy look on Oscar's face took Sam's breath away. "Of course I'll wait. It's not like I have a bunch of other prospects knocking down the door." His expression turned more sober. "But you forgot something."

"What?" He tilted his head to the side.

Carmelina raised an eyebrow. "Do tell."

"I'm not ready yet, either. I just lost him too, you know."

"Oh." Sam sighed, deflated, his shoulders sagging. "I'm sorry. I've just made an ass of myself in front of three of my dearest friends—"

Oscar reached out to put a finger over Sam's lips. "Let me finish. If you're willing to wait for *me*, one of these days, *I* just might be ready."

Sam looked up at Oscar, and this time he was the one grinning. "Really?"

Carmelina put her hands on her hips. "All right, you two, enough is enough. You like him and he likes you, and maybe one of these days you're going to be together. But in the meantime, can we get some goddamned dinner? We've been flying for fourteen hours, and we're exhausted and starving."

Sam laughed for the third time that evening. "If Oscar doesn't mind?"

"Mind? Most of this stuff came out of Carmelina's pantry, so technically it's her dinner. Grab some chairs and I'll serve it right up."

"What's the secret?" Daniele took a seat at the little table next to Sam.

Sam shook his head. "You really don't want to know."

Carmelina laughed. "By the way, we have some big news…"

They spent a lovely evening together, one of those nights when the world opens up and suddenly things seem possible again, and Sam started, ever so slowly, to fall in love with his best friend.

60

NEW BEGINNINGS

"I want to come back." Marissa stood before Matteo, grasping the podium at Ragazzi with both hands. It felt right to be there. *You have to let me come back.*

He glanced at her. "Oh, hi there. Let's see, for tonight? I think I still got some room…"

"No, that's not what I mean." She'd spent all day Monday closing out things at her old job. She offered to stay for two weeks, but they'd surprised her. The office was apparently looking to cut staff, and her announcement had actually been taken with some relief. Which bothered her, but that was something to worry about later. "I want to come back to work here."

He looked up at her and frowned. "You want to work *here*? Don't you have a job?"

She sighed. "I haven't been happy there for a long time." She looked around at the place, still as warm and welcoming as it had been when she'd first come here as a teenager on Brad's internship program. They'd repainted, and the bar was new since the pandemic, but the heart and soul of the place was still the same.

"I see." He scratched his temple. "Well, I can't pay you very much. You'd start out as an expediter—"

She shook her head. "I don't wanna be a waiter. I want to work in the kitchen." Those times cooking at Ragazzi had been some of the happiest days of her life.

"Diego, get out here!" Matteo called out over his shoulder. He held up his index finger. "Just a second."

"Of course." She scratched her arm absentmindedly, then straightened up, wanting to put her best foot forward.

"*Eccomi.*" Diego appeared from the back, his hands and apron covered in flour. "*Ciao* Marissa!"

Matteo pointed at her with his thumb. "Marissa here wants a job."

Diego's brow furrowed and he frowned, a mirror image of Matteo's just a moment before. "But you already have a job."

"She's not happy there."

Marissa snorted. This was turning into a comedy routine.

"Ah." He scratched his head, spreading some of the flour into his hair. "We has one job for an expediter. Hank left last week."

Matteo shook his head. "She doesn't want to be a waiter. She wants to work with you, in the kitchen. She wants to cook."

Marissa stifled a laugh. It was like watching *Tweedle Dee and Tweedle Dum.*

Diego's face lit up with delight. "*Che belle notizie!* I understand now. How do they say it? You have a bug."

Marissa laughed. "I think it's 'the bug.' But yeah, I do."

Diego scratched the back of his head, spreading flour to his neck too. "I don't have anything open right now…"

Marissa swallowed hard. *You have to let me work here.* "I'll do it for free. Anything. I'll scrub pans, go to the Farmer's Market at six in the morning, take out the trash. Anything! Diego, Matteo, I really want this." She had some savings—she could weather things for a while. She and Ainsley would figure things out. *And we'll be working together when Ainsley's not with Jun Seo.*

Matteo shook his head, and for an instant, her heart fell. "Nonsense. You are family. We will find a way to make it work."

"Really?"

Matteo looked at Diego, who nodded.

"Welcome home." The chef extended his arms.

She squealed, and reached out to hug them both. "Thank you so much. I'd forgotten how much I missed it here."

They were right. She was coming home.

Ainsley got out of her father's car—the older olive-green Volvo he'd agreed to loan her until she could find transportation of her own—and stared at the wide blue bowl of sky above.

Jun Seo's rented ranch was in the heart of Amador County. She must have passed half-a-dozen wineries on the way there. The foothills shone golden, dotted with old oak trees and black outcroppings of rock, and the air smelled fresh and clean, redolent with the smell of oak trees and wildflowers.

A beaten dirt path led though the yellowed grasses to a small, trim, white farmhouse. A little farther on, there was a rustic barn, once a bright red but now faded so that it almost looked like it had sprung up from the ground in place.

She grabbed her knapsack from the back seat. She'd brought everything she could think of that she might need—her grandfather's bamboo brushes, pastels, colored pencils, watercolors, a level, and a tape measure—and had stuffed them all into the old green and beige pack she'd picked up at a surplus store. "Here we go." Taking a deep breath, she started down the new path like she was on a mission.

She'd had to put the artist off for a day to give her time to put in her paperwork at school. It was a temporary withdrawal—she could still come back the next year, if she wanted. But she really hoped she wouldn't need to. *I'm done with medicine.*

She mounted the three steps to the front door of the farmhouse and rang the bell.

It was an old building—the style, popular in the early twentieth century, and the wear on the wood paneling told her that much. But it had been refreshed with a fresh coat of paint and new hardware on the door, and a Ring camera looked at her from the doorbell.

There was no answer.

She cleared her throat. It was a bit scratchy—she'd forgotten to get something to drink to bring with her. "Hello?"

Still nothing.

She tried knocking on the door. "Anyone in there?"

"Over here!" The voice came from the barn.

That's curious. She hopped back down the stairs and strolled over to the huge structure. The barn door was ajar by a couple feet.

She slipped inside, and stood there for a few seconds to give her eyes time to adjust to the cool, dim interior. When they did, she gasped and dropped her knapsack.

"Welcome!" Jun Seo was fifteen feet up, standing on scaffolding next to the biggest canvas she had ever seen. It had to be twenty feet tall by thirty feet wide.

"Hi." Ainsley tried to take it all in. There was no paint on it yet—so far, there were only black marks—maybe from a charcoal pencil?—creating some sort of design. "What is this?"

They slid down the ladder to appear at her feet, a big grin plastered across their face. "It's my biggest work yet. A commission piece for the San Francisco Opera House. What do you think?"

She took a step closer. The seemingly random lines resolved themselves into waves, and a rocky shore. A tiny Korean village nestled there above the rocks, and in the distance, a great mountain overshadowing it all. "I think it's going to be breathtaking."

They bit their lip. "I hope you're right. Some of my critics have said I'm not thinking big enough. Maybe this will prove them wrong." Their eyes twinkled. "Come on. I hope you're not afraid of heights!"

61

AN UNCONVENTIONAL IDEA

Carmelina's news spread like wildfire among her circle of friends. Of course, part of that was the fact that she was spreading it herself—by email, Messenger, social media, phone, and even the occasional Discord or Snapchat conversation.

But there was one couple in particular she wanted to tell in person.

She opened the front door to Ragazzi and stepped inside, and was surprised to find Ben already standing there, day-off casual in jeans and a white t-shirt, looking around the empty place. It was technically open, but there was no one to be seen. The dining room was filled with the aroma of Italian cooking, a heady mix of sausage, onions, basil, oregano, tomatoes, and a dozen other flavor profiles that defied definition. She grinned. "Hey there. How are you doing?"

He grinned. "Fantastic. Such amazing news."

She nodded in agreement. "Yes, it is. It's an amazing thing, to get married again."

His grin widened, almost reaching his ears. "Never thought it would happen."

Carmelina snorted. "Hey, I'm not that old."

Ben frowned. "That's not what I meant."

They stared at each other for a long moment, eyebrows raised in a mirror image of one another.

Carmelina broke first. "What are *you* talking about?"

"I'm getting married!" His smile returned, and he hugged himself as if he was trying to reassure himself that it was true. "Lorelei proposed… or I did… it was all a bit confusing. But we're going to get married!"

She refrained from saying anything about how short their courtship had been. It didn't seem diplomatic. "That's fantastic. I'm so happy for both of you." She threw her arms around him. After Ella, he deserved to be happy.

"And what were *you* talking about?"

She let him go and held up her hand, displaying her ring. "Daniele and I are getting married too. He asked me to marry him, on a beautiful grassy hillside overlooking Rome at night, under a million stars. It was so romantic." She still felt the thrill of it all.

"Oh, that's amazing. I'm so thrilled for you too!" It was his turn to hug her.

"Thank you. I was nervous about it at first, but then I was like 'What the hell!'" She looked around. Every table was covered with a white tablecloth and set with napkins, silverware, and glasses. Still, though, there was no one to help them. "I was hoping the boys would let me hold the wedding here. Just a small affair, a few friends—"

"When?" Ben's fists clenched his shirttails.

She blinked. "This weekend. Saturday. Why?"

Ben looked crestfallen. "That's when I wanted to have *our* wedding."

Before she could reply, the kitchen door flew open and Matteo appeared. "*Buon giorno, amici! Auguri!* Did you come in for an early lunch?" He gestured around the place. "You can have any seat you want."

Ben and Carmelina looked at each other, and then at him. "We need to talk."

Matteo looked at Carmelina and then Ben, and shrugged. He called out over his shoulder, "Diego, watch the front of house. I have to take care of something." He turned back to them and gestured with a tilt of his head at the door to the training kitchen. "Come on. We'll figure this out, whatever it is. It's been an interesting day."

~

Matteo felt like he was watching one of those old-timey gun fights in the spaghetti westerns he adored so much. Carmelina and Ben sat across from each other at the main demonstration table in the teaching kitchen, glaring at each other like Billy the Kid vs. Pat Garrett. Or in this case, maybe Patricia Garrett. All that was missing was a broken down piano, a cheap glass chandelier, and a pair of those batwing doors all old western saloons seemed to have. "Okay, what's all this? What's going on between you two?"

They both spoke at once.

"Daniele asked me to marry him, and I wanted to do it here this weekend. On Saturday."

"I want to get married to Lorelei this weekend. On Saturday. Here at Ragazzi."

They returned to glaring at each other.

Matteo laughed. "Well, first of all, congratulations to both of you. I would ask if there was a reason for the rush, but..." It was extremely unlikely that either one of these "shotgun" weddings involved a pregnancy.

"I don't see why you can't wait." Carmelina sounded frustrated. "Daniele and I have been together for almost ten years, waiting for this very moment. Doesn't that count for something?"

Ben snorted. "You've had plenty of time then. What's another week's wait?" Ben jutted out his chin in defiance. "Are you saying that because Lorelei and I just met, we should have to wait? That our love is less important than yours?"

Carmelina shrugged. "Well... Yeah. Something like that. Why the rush?"

Ben sighed. He looked down at his hands, clasped in his lap, and back up at her. His eyes were wet. "Because my mother is dying."

Matteo shook his head. *Poor guy.* "I think he's got you there."

"Holy shit." She put her hand over her mouth. "I mean, I'm so sorry, Ben. I thought you and your mother weren't close?"

"Thank you." Ben unclasped his hands, absently caressing the fingers of his right hand with his left. "We weren't. But she came back into my life recently and... she has terminal cancer."

"Well, that beats whatever claim I've got." She leaned back and crossed her arms, looking flummoxed.

Matteo put a hand on Ben's shoulder. "I'm so sorry to hear that." He remembered when he'd lost his own parents. The pain of that loss still stuck with him, only a little softened by the passage of time. "But I'm afraid neither of you is getting married in the restaurant this weekend. We're fully booked. We can't afford to cancel reservations, not with the economy in such a rough place. Especially on such short notice."

It was Ben's turn to slump back into his chair. "I guess I can try to find a different venue…"

Matteo held up a finger, forestalling the rest of Ben's response. "I do have a proposal for you both. We had to cancel our usual Sunday class here in the kitchen because attendance was so low—summer vacations and all. Since you both have mostly the same friends, what if we were to do them both here… together?" He gestured around the room.

Carmelina looked around the room, then over at Ben. "That… could work." She leaned forward, hands resting on her knees. "If *you* don't mind?"

Ben's face brightened. "Mind? I would love to be at *your* wedding. But only if you want to be at mine, too."

Carmelina's eyes were alight with excitement. "That would be great. We can have it here, and we could… what if we made it a cooking class? Like old times? Get the whole gang back together." A shadow crossed her face. "Except Brad and Ella."

Ben nodded enthusiastically. "They'll be here, at least in our hearts." He put a hand on hers. "We could make a cake. A wedding cake! We've never done one of those in class."

Carmelina was clearly warming to the idea. "I like it. I didn't want a big stuffy affair, just something intimate with our friends."

"Me too. Lorelei and I have both been married before, and we decided we didn't want to make a big deal out of it."

Carmelina pounded the countertop. "Then it's settled. We'll start planning things immediately."

Matteo stared at them in bewilderment. They'd gone from Billy and Pat to Bonnie and Clyde in record time. "I don't know about the cake. I'll have to ask Diego—"

The door that led to the restaurant opened and Marissa popped her head in. "Hey Matteo, Diego needs you in the front of house. We have a few guests…." She trailed off when she saw Carmelina sitting there. "Oh, hi, Grandma."

Carmelina winced at the nickname. "Marissa, what are you doing here? Do you have the day off or something?"

"Not exactly…" She flushed bright red.

Matteo sensed the energy in the room. *Words* were about to be spoken. He stood up and gestured toward the door. "Ben, why don't you come with me? We can go over some of the details after I get our guests settled? It looks like Marissa and Carmelina have something they need to talk about."

Ben took one look at the expression on Carmelina's face and bolted. "Good idea. I don't want to get in the middle of this."

They scurried out and left the two alone together.

~

Carmelina pointed at the stool next to her. "Take a seat."

Marissa shuddered. She did as she was told. She'd known the time for this conversation would come, but she hadn't expected it to be quite this soon. Surely Carmelina would understand…

Her grandmother crossed her arms. "Now talk."

Marissa was scared of her *nonna*. Well, not scared, exactly. But Carmelina di Rosa was a formidable woman, and you didn't cross her lightly. "I'm leaving Buckman-Oldham-Rocklin-Eccles. I hate it there."

Carmelina pursed her lips, as if choosing her next words very carefully. "It's a good job. Jobs are hard to come by right now."

"I know, I know. But it kills me a little bit every day when I go into that awful, gray place. Ainsley says—"

Carmelina raised an eyebrow. "Ah, so this is Ainsley's idea?"

"No, it's not *her idea*. It was my idea." She huffed. "And you shouldn't be talking. After all, you risked everything you have to open your new dessert shop with Daniele."

Carmelina frowned. "That's different."

"Why?" She surprised herself by finding the strength to stand up to Carmelina.

They stared at one another for a good thirty seconds, neither willing to yield.

At last, Carmelina broke contact. "Because I worry about you. You're far too young and inexperienced—"

"You do?" Something inside Marissa softened at the admission.

Her *nonna* nodded. "Every day." Carmelina wiped the corners of her eyes. "You're trying to make your way in the world, and I know it's not easy for your generation. You got a raw deal, with inflation and the outrageous cost of housing and climate change and… and I won't always be around to help you."

That took the wind out of Marissa's sails, but she couldn't back down. This was too important. "You once told me that when we're young is the time to take risks. To try new things. Before we get so set in our ways that we lose out on what we might have had."

"I said that?" Carmelina blinked, but the sides of her lips twitched up in the start of a smile. "I sound like an idiot."

Marissa laughed. "You sounded like someone who loves her granddaughter very much." She reached out to take Carmelina's hands in hers. "Do I have this all figured out? Absolutely not. Is there a chance I might fail? Hell yeah. But I'd rather fail at a job I love than succeed in a job I hate. For the first time since I was seventeen, I feel excited about waking up tomorrow to see where the day might lead. Isn't that worth something?"

Carmelina squeezed her hands. "Of course it is. It's just… are you *sure?*"

This time, when their eyes met, an understanding passed between them. Marissa felt a shiver down her back and goosebumps on her arms. "Yes, *Nonna*, I am."

Carmelina was quiet for a long time, considering her granddaughter. At last she nodded, as if she had come to a decision. "In that case, I think you need to follow your heart. We'll work out the details together, if you want."

"Yeah?"

"Yeah."

She threw her arms around her *nonna*. "Thank you, Carmelina. I won't let you down."

"I know you won't. And I want you by my side when Daniele and I get married this weekend."

Marissa let go and stared at her as comprehension dawned. "What? You two are getting married?"

Carmelina held up the ring. "Right here. This Sunday."

"That's amazing!" She embraced Carmelina, this time holding on until her *nonna* gently disengaged herself.

A sly smile crossed her grandmother's face. "One more thing."

Marissa sat back, eyes widening in alarm. "What's this? What's happening? You're not changing your mind, are you? Because you just said—"

"Calm down, dear. No, I'm not changing my mind." She reached into her bag and pulled out something wrapped in paper. "I brought something back from Italy for us to share."

Marissa took the package and unwrapped it carefully. It was an old hand-written recipe book. "What… what is this?"

"It's from your great-great grandmother. It has all of our old family recipes. And I want you to help me try each and every one."

Marissa looked at it in wonder. "Really?"

"Really. Unless you have a problem spending time with your *nonna*?"

"Not at all." She set the book down on the counter and hugged Carmelina a third time. "Love you, *Nonna*."

"You too, my little *bambolina*. I love you too."

The pages of the book sparkled green for just a moment, unnoticed by either of them, and went dark.

62

COMING HOME

Gio hugged Dante tightly. "Thanks for going on this adventure with me." Getting to know Dante as a man had been worth the trip.

He'd said goodbye to his aunt Valentina and his cousin Bianca earlier in the day. Dante had driven him to the airport in Bologna—and he'd survived his cousin's race-car driver antics once again. Now Gio was ready to get on a plane with Stella and Sole and head back home. It had been a whirlwind trip, but he'd found everything he was looking for. *And more.*

"I wouldn't have missed it. But I wish we could've have gone to the Ducati Museum. We were so close."

Gio laughed. "Come visit me in Sacramento sometime and I'll take you to some real museums, in San Francisco." He let go and kissed his cousin goodbye Italian style, three times, cheek to cheek to cheek.

"I'll take you up on that." Dante flashed his white teeth and waved. "*Ci vediamo, cugino.*" Then he was gone.

See you soon. Gio turned back to his other cousin—Sole—and his other aunt Stella. *I have a wealth of new family.* "Are you two nervous about the trip?"

Sole shook her head. "I've always wanted to go to *gli Stati Uniti.*"

"I've been there once, to New York. I wasn't impressed." And yet, Stella was practically shaking with suppressed excitement. Sometimes she reminded him so much of his mother that it hurt.

"I have so many things to show you. Sacramento's such an amazing place." He hadn't thought so at first, but it had worked its magic on him. "It seems boring at first, but it grows on you… you'll see."

Stella rolled her eyes. "So you say. Come on. They're boarding now."

Gio grinned in spite of himself. Soon he'd see *Papà* and *Babbo* again.

Seventeen hours and two stops later—in Washington DC and San Francisco—they stumbled out of the terminal together, exhausted.

Gio barely had the energy to make the introductions between Diego and Matteo and Stella and Sole before they dragged him and his luggage back to the car, a bright red SUV Diego must have borrowed from someone else for the airport pick-up. They did have a lot of luggage.

He fell into a deep slumber on the way home, and had only a vague memory of climbing up the stairs to his own bedroom before crashing into a dreamless sleep.

He woke up the next morning—or maybe the next afternoon—feeling a little more human. He stared up at the ceiling where his *Papà* Diego had pasted glow in the dark stars when he'd first moved in. He'd been far too old for such things—what seventeen-year-old had plastic stars on his ceiling?—but now he treasured them.

"*Sei sveglio?*"

Gio's head snapped around to find Diego sitting at Gio's desk, the chair turned around to face the bed. "*Papà*, you scared me."

Diego chuckled. "Sorry. Did not mean to. I am so glad to have you home safe. I watched over you half the night."

That should have been creepy, but somehow it was sweet. *You were worried about me.* "I'm glad too. I've missed this place."

Diego folded his arms. "You have to move out."

Gio sat up. "What?" He realized he'd been sleeping naked, and pulled his sheets up a little higher to cover himself. "What do you mean, I have to move out?"

"You can take a month or so, until you find your own place." He held out his arms in entreaty. "Gio, you're twenty-six. You shouldn't live with your parents anymore. Also, I'm letting you go from Ragazzi."

What the hell? Gio stared at his father as if the man had gone insane. "*Papà*, what did I do? You can't just throw me out like this. I… I've never lived anywhere else but here." Was Diego mad that he'd gone in search of his mother? That he'd brought home his aunt and his cousin?

His father chuckled. He turned around to pick up a piece of paper from the desk behind him, and handed it over to Gio. "Nothing like that. I couldn't be prouder of the man you is become. But your *babbo* and I talked this over. You need to spread your wings."

Gio took the paper and looked at it. It was a lease. For a property in Folsom. "*Papà*, I don't understand."

"All this time, you been on my back to franchise Ragazzi. To open another location. Well, this week, I found a place in Folsom that's perfect. Right in downtown, needs some work, but maybe it can be as charming as the first one. With the right owner."

"Wait… what?" His *papà* had gone insane. "What are you saying?"

"And it doesn't make no sense for the owner of a Folsom restaurant to live all the way out here in East Sacramento."

Gio stared at the paper. *My own place.* "But I can't afford it. You don't pay me enough."

Diego laughed. "We pay you plenty. Besides, your *babbo* and I have been putting money away for you for this day in a… what do they call it? A DC?"

"A CD?" He couldn't believe what he was hearing.

Diego nodded happily. "A CD. So you can use it to lease this place, and buy a franchise from us."

It was a lot to take in. Did he want to run a restaurant? Let alone the same restaurant, in a different location? "But what if I don't want to run a franchise?"

Diego spread his hands. "That's up to you. We want you to be happy. What you choose to do is for you to decide."

"Did you tell him?" Matteo appeared at the doorway.

"Yes. I think he will choose the restaurant. What do you think?"

Matteo crossed his arms and leaned against the door jamb, staring at Gio. "I think he'll choose what is best for him. You raised him well, *tesoro*."

Gio's gaze jumped from one to the other and back again. "But who would take my place? You two can't run Ragazzi by yourselves."

"Don't you worry about it. I have someones in mind." Diego poked at the paper in Gio's hand. "So what do you say?"

Gio closed his eyes. This was his dream—franchising Ragazzi, and having his own place to run as he pleased? *How could I not?* "I have to see this place first."

"Of course."

"And I need to see how much money I have to work with."

Diego glanced at Matteo.

"It's about $100,000, give or take." He waved his hand side to side.

Gio's eyes bulged out. "How…"

"Your *babbo* is… how do they say? A wheeze with the investments." Diego grinned.

Gio laughed. *Close enough.* "All right. I also want Stella and Sole to come work with me on it, for as long as they are here."

"Deal."

"And I want a discount on the franchise fee. It was my idea, after all."

"We'll take that into accounts." Diego put out his hand.

I can't believe this. Gio shook it, and then pulled his father into a bear hug. "This is amazing. I love you, *Papà*."

Matteo cleared his throat.

"You too, *Babbo*." He let go of Diego and picked up the paper. "My own restaurant. What should I call it?"

"How about *Figlio*?"

"'Son'? I like it, but it's too on the nose." He thought about all the people, friends and family, who had brought him to this point in his life. "How about *Amici* instead?" *Friends.*

Diego grinned. "*Perfetto*. By the way, we have two weddings in the teaching kitchen on Sunday."

Wow. They hadn't done a wedding in years. "All right. I'll clear out—"

Diego shook his head. "No. That's not what I mean. Carmelina is marrying Daniele, at long last. And Ben is marrying that new girl. Lorelei. They want you to come."

Gio's mouth dropped open. "How did all of this happen so fast? I've only been gone less than a week!" He was thrilled for both of them. *But damn.*

"Come down for dinner. We'll fill you in!" The door closed behind his parents, but Diego's voice still came through loud and clear. "And put some clothes on first!"

63

WEDDING CAKES

Ben tapped at Lorelei's door. He was dressed in a rented tux, which, although it looked sharp as hell on him, was not ideal for working with flour. He'd wanted to look his best for Lorelei on their big day.

She opened the door and gasped. "Ben, you're so… You clean up nice."

I could say the same about you. Her blond hair was held back by a silver circlet, its tresses teased into loose curls that fell down to her shoulders. She was wearing a cute white sundress and turquoise high-heeled shoes, with a turquoise blue sash and corsage to match.

"Do I look okay?" Wrinkles creased her forehead, her only imperfection that served to make her even more beautiful.

"You look like a fairytale princess!" *How did I get so lucky?* Ella was looking down on him from somewhere.

She blushed. "And you are my Prince Charming."

He leaned forward to kiss her, but she pulled away and wagged a finger at him. "Not until after the wedding. Kids, come on! Ben is here!"

The little blond cretins—Max and Mia—scurried out of their corners, Max dressed in an adorable tiny suit and Mia in a white dress that looked like a miniature version of her mother's.

"What have you two been up to?" She brushed at the scuff marks on

Max's knees, but gave up when it became evident they weren't coming off. "At least nothing's ripped."

"Small favors. They'll be fine." He knelt on one knee. "Hello kids."

"Hello Ben," they said in unison. It sounded suspiciously rehearsed. Then Mia kicked him in the shins and ran off.

Lorelei turned three shades of red. "Mia, get your little butt back here and apologize."

Ben rubbed his shin. The kid had a surprisingly strong kick. "It's all right—"

"It's not all right. I swear, they take after their father sometimes."

"I'm sure we'll work it all out." In truth, he was terrified of becoming a father. He had absolutely no experience at it. But he'd learn. Somehow.

Lorelei peered out into the corridor. "Where's your mother?"

"Down in the car." He checked his Apple Watch. "We should go. It's almost nine-thirty."

"Come on, kids. Last one to the car gets no wedding cake!"

They whizzed past her like a couple Tasmanian devils.

Lorelei grabbed her handbag. "I'm ready. Let's go get married."

Ben had never heard sweeter words.

Marissa was having trouble getting the zipper pulled up on the black blouse she had chosen for the weddings. "Ains, could I get a hand? I can't zip this damned thing." She couldn't quite reach it.

"Sure thing, 'Riss." Ainsley made her way around a stack of boxes. She'd moved her stuff out of the dorm the day before, and they hadn't had time to get it all sorted yet. "Black's a strange color for a wedding."

Marissa laughed. "Yeah, but I look good in it. *Nonna* said this was going to be anything but a traditional affair." *Wear what you like. You'll be perfect.*

Ainsley's cool hands made short work of the zipper.

"How do I look?" Marissa did a little twirl like a fashion model. *Take that, Project Runway.*

Ainsley stared at her over her shoulder in the dresser mirror. "You're right. You look amazing." She kissed Marissa's cheek.

Marissa smirked. "Don't you want me to tell you how you look?"

"Nope. I *always* look amazing." She looked around at all the boxes still stacked in the corners of the room. "You sure you're okay with me staying here? I haven't asked my parents if they will help with the rent yet." She slipped out into the living room.

"Yup. I've got it covered for a couple months." The truth was they'd be hurting for cash soon, but that was a problem for another day. "You ready?"

"Ready if you are. Just need to pluck my eyebrows. Give me two minutes."

In twenty more, they were on their way.

Dave closed the car door, and reached down to tuck his white button-down shirt into his khakis where it had popped out on the side. "What are we supposed to wear to an event that is half bake sale and half high tea?"

Marcos snorted. "I doubt there will be any tea. With Carmelina in charge, I'd expect no fewer than five wine selections, some prosecco, a few tiny bottles of limoncello, and a whole lot of cheap Kentucky bourbon."

Dave wiggled his eyebrows. "All the better to remove the sting of disapproval from our questionable fashion choices."

"Don't be silly. You look very handsome." Marcos kissed his husband's cheek. "And if anyone says different, I'll beat the living crap out of them."

Dave grinned. "You really know the way to a man's heart." He frowned. "Oh damn. I forgot the presents. They were right there on the table by the door." *The stress must be getting to me.*

Marcos opened the hatchback and pulled out two bright blue bags, holding them up proudly.

"You brought them." Dave grinned. "Your blind-as-a-bat husband can't be trusted with anything."

Marcos shook his head. "Don't talk like that." He closed the hatch.

"Too soon?" Dave winked at him.

"Cross that bridge when we have to." He took Dave's hand and kissed his cheek. "Come on, handsome. Let's just go have a good time with our friends."

~

Gio finished wiping down the last of the prep counters in the training kitchen, making sure they were spotless for the upcoming event.

Babbo and *Papà* were helping Stella hang wedding decorations—white garland, fancy paper, bells, and bright blue sprays of flowers in alabaster white vases.

"*Ci sono troppi fiori!*" Diego spread his arms and rolled his eyes, exasperated.

Gio laughed. "It's a wedding, *Papà*. You can never have too many flowers."

"Actually, it's *two* weddings. So we need *twice as many* flowers." Matteo seemed particularly proud of himself for that math.

"You're both wrong. The number of flowers is the woman's choice." Stella was stringing more garland around the room, dangling it from wall sconce to wall sconce.

Diego and Matteo looked at each other. "Or the gay man's!" they said together.

Gio shook his head. He had a couple lovable idiots for parents.

Sole was sweeping the floor behind the main presentation counter where Diego would be working. "I think it is beautiful that your friends are getting married together. And here."

"Just like our wedding." Diego's eyes were misty. "Gio, don't forget to put out all the *ingredienti per* the cakes."

"On it, *Papà*." Diego had given him the list the night before, and he'd run over to Corti Brothers to pick up a few things that they needed that were not on hand in the kitchen. He headed into the pantry, but just before leaving the main room, he stopped and looked back over his shoulder. *This is the last time I will ever do this. At least, as part of my regular job.*

They had visited the new restaurant space on Friday, and it was perfect. It needed a lot of work— the previous tenants had trashed the place when they left, something about a rent dispute. And it had been empty for half a year. But he could already see it in his mind. Some day in the not too distant future, it would be Amici.

He glanced at the clock. *Nine AM.* They had another half hour or forty-five minutes before people started showing up.

Today they would spend with friends. Tomorrow, his real work would begin.

"Heads up! One hour to showtime!"

Carmelina climbed into the car next to Daniele, her husband to be. *Never thought I'd say that again.* Somehow, though, it didn't scare her anymore.

"*Sei belissima, cara mia.*"

She laughed. "Keep reminding me why I am marrying you." She hadn't seen her husband's ghost since that night on the hillside, but if she closed her eyes, she could feel his touch on her hand, his kiss on her cheek. *Arthur would approve.* "Besides, if you think *this* is beautiful, you've got something wrong in your head."

She was dressed in comfortable sweats and sneakers, with her favorite Italian apron wrapped around her waist, covered in puckered pink lips and the word *baci*, for kisses.

"You are always beautiful to me." Daniele was wearing a stylish Italian suit with a skinny black tie and a turquoise blue carnation on his lapel. And wrapped around the whole thing, he had on a matching apron, only *his* kisses were in red.

He started up the car and backed out of the driveway. Sam and Oscar had left an hour before, heading to a mysterious meeting. *I hope they find happiness.* "Tomorrow, I want to try out some of my *bisnonna's* recipes at the bakery, with Marissa." She'd start with her great grandmother's specialty, the *crostata di ricotta e visciole.*

"What, no honeymoon?" He sounded aggrieved, though they'd discussed it the day before. They'd take a special trip later, once things calmed down a bit.

She leaned over to kiss his cheek. "*Caro*, you *are* my honeymoon."

Diego looked around his classroom, pleased to see so many of his old friends and students there for this very special class, and for the weddings to follow. *La mia famiglia.*

"We are gathering here today to celebrate the cakes of two couples who are very much in love."

One counter was empty—Sam and his new friend Oscar hadn't yet arrived. He hoped they were okay. Sam had been through so much this year.

Matteo put an arm around Diego's waist and took over. "Because neither of these two couples getting married today is in any way traditional…"

There was a general snicker and murmur of agreement about that through the room.

"…Diego has decided to have us prepare a non-traditional wedding cake. Or rather, ten wedding cakes. It's called the *Torta Tenerina*, and it's a specialty of Ferrara, and one of the most decadent cakes Italia has to offer."

And wait until you taste it. Diego piped up again. "It's a chocolate *torta* —excuse me, cake—that we'll make with eggs, sugar, a little flour, milk, salt and butter. You should have every the things you need at your station—"

The front door opened, letting in a cool gust of morning air and a bright ray of sunshine.

"Sorry, everyone. Oscar's meeting ran a bit late." Sam brushed off his shirt, knocking a couple of leaves onto the clean floor. "Man, it's windy out there."

Carmelina chuckled. "I'm just glad you didn't burst in like that at the whole 'if anyone has a reason' part."

The whole room laughed.

"We're not doing that, right?" Daniele looked worried.

"No, *tesoro*." Carmelina kissed his cheek, and the worry lines on his face smoothed out.

He has good reason to be worried. She denied him for so long. Diego crossed his fingers for them both.

Matteo indicated the empty station. "Grab your spot. We're just getting started."

"Thanks!" Sam blushed.

When they were behind their station, Diego continued. "Let's get started. First, chop up the chocolate into little tiny pieces, like this…"

~

Carmelina dumped the chopped-up pieces of dark chocolate into the double boiler and picked up the spoon to stir the chocolate, inhaling deeply as the slivers began to melt and fuse into one another. "Nothing like the smell of melting chocolate in the morning."

Daniele looked on over her shoulder. "I love to watch you cook." He put his arms around hers as she stirred the melting chocolate.

She reached up to graze his neck with her fingertips. "I've been cooking and baking since I was a little girl at my *Nonna's* knee. I always loved the smell of chocolate." She pushed a recalcitrant piece off the edge of the pot and into the melting inferno. "Have you ever made this before?"

He shook his head. "No, my family was from farther north, near Milan. Ferrara is closer to Venice. I've had it before, though. It's delicious."

"You can't go wrong with chocolate. It's a little like brownies, right?"

He glanced over their copy of the recipe. "Yes, but it uses real chocolate instead of cocoa powder. You Americans have shortcuts for everything." He kissed her cheek.

She laughed. "It's our superpower. If you want to get something done faster—"

"Give it to a lazy man?"

"Or an American. Want to cut up the butter into little cubes?" She gestured at the wrapped-up rectangle.

"Certainly, *bella donna*. Your wish is my command." They'd been together for nine years, tested by secrets and time, and she still fell for his Italian charm *every damned time*.

Now that she had decided to marry him, she felt free, light, almost giddy inside. Like she was finally allowing herself to do something she should have done years before. To become Ms. Daniele Amoroso. Even if she hadn't yet decided if she would change her last name. *There's such a thing as too much change.*

"Here you go." He'd sliced the butter into near-perfect cubes.

She nodded approvingly. *I taught you well.* "Okay, start putting in two at a time while I stir them. Keep it up until they're all blended into the chocolate."

"Understood." A pair of butter cubes slipped off the plate into the pan and started to melt immediately. She stirred them into the chocolate, marveling at how the two blended so seamlessly into something new. *Like me and Daniele.*

And all of a sudden, she understood why Marissa wanted to come back to this. There was magic in cooking, in the kitchen, and once you'd experienced it, life out in the real world paled in comparison.

She glanced across the room and met her granddaughter's gaze. She smiled and nodded.

A grin blossomed on Marissa's face.

Then Ainsley said something to her and she broke eye contact, nodding and laughing at whatever her girlfriend had told her.

It was good to see her granddaughter smiling again. It was almost like seeing her own daughter Andrea brought back to life, watching her finding her own path. Carmelina was proud of her only grandchild.

"Do you ever think about her?" Daniele dropped two more cubes of butter into the pan.

"Who?" *Stir stir stir, watch as the butter bubbles and melts...*

"Your daughter."

Carmelina took a deep breath and sighed. It had almost killed her when she'd found out that Daniele was responsible for Andrea's death. A horrible accident, but it had come close to derailing their blossoming relationship. Now it was an old scar on her soul, smoothed out and faded by time, only felt in its tightness every now and then. "Maybe once or twice a week."

"I think of her every day."

She turned to stare at him, almost knocking the pot off the stove. "You do?"

He nodded, and she saw the old pain in his eyes, the same pain that had lived in her own heart for so many years.

She touched his cheek. "I forgave you for it long ago. You have to forgive yourself for it too."

His eyes welled up with tears. "It's hard. If only I hadn't gone out that night—"

"It happened. It wasn't your fault, and I know that. She would be happy to see Marissa here with the two of us."

He nodded. "Maybe so." His eyes went wide. "Watch the chocolate!"

Carmelina turned her attention back to the pan, stirring it before it could burn. "I got it."

He put his arms around her waist from behind and held her close. "Forever and *sempre, cara mia.*"

The warmth spread through her belly. "I love you too."

~

Marissa looked up. *Someone's watching me.*

Her *nonna* Carmelina was looking at her from across the room. When their eyes met, Carmelina smiled and nodded.

The meaning was immediately clear. *She understands.*

"And then they let me actually paint part of the canvas, these rolling hills they modeled after both the Sacramento Foothills and their home in South Korea. My brushstrokes on their canvas. It was amazing." Ainsley was almost vibrating with excitement.

Marissa laughed, delighted. "That's amazing. They're good to you?" *After what happened at the showing, they better be.* She whisked the sugar into the egg whites.

"So good. They said I was like the daughter they never had. They want me to come to the installation when the work is done." Her eyes lit up. "Hey, you could come with me. I haven't been to San Francisco since I was a child."

"I'd love to." Marissa struggled to identify what she was feeling. It was frothy and light, and it made her all warm inside. Then it hit her. *I'm happy.*

It was like emerging from gray fog into the sunlight. Her whole life was changing. She should have been scared to death, but instead she felt as if her heart was on fire. She wanted to create, to do, to become. To change lives with her culinary inventions. *To cook.*

Diego stopped by their station to check on their work. "Very good." He looked so official in his chef's whites.

Marissa beamed. "This is going to be delicious." Chocolate was one of her favorites.

Diego nodded. "You have a natural gift."

Marissa blushed. "Thank you." He had always been kind to her.

He crossed his arms. "I have a proposal for you."

"Sure." *Maybe he wants me to go full time.* So far, she'd been managing about thirty hours a week in the kitchen, mostly washing dishes, but occasionally helping with prep. *That would be amazing.*

"You may have heard that Gio is leaving to open up a new restaurant in Folsom."

"He is?" She blinked, taking that in. Somehow, she'd assumed he would always live in his little bedroom above Ragazzi. "That's great—he'll be so good at it." It felt good to see him doing so well. She'd been so guilty about how she had treated him for so long. Maybe she could let go of that now, too.

Diego nodded. "Yes, he will. But I need to replace him."

"Of course." She wasn't sure why he was asking her. She'd been there for almost a week—maybe he wanted an outsider's perspective? "Let's see. Maybe Alex? He's been here for a long time and knows the ropes—"

"Alex isn't interested." He stared at her.

She blinked. *What am I not getting?* "Then I'm not sure what you want from me."

Ainsley poked at her. "I think he means—"

"Wait, are you saying it should be me?" The idea took her aback.

"You have the gift. And you have... how do they say? A head in business?"

"A head for business." Ainsley looked back and forth between then. "Oh my God, that would be amazing. You would be so good at it."

Marissa shook her head. "I don't know."

Ainsley took her by the arms and shook her. Gently, but hard enough to get her attention. "Remember what we talked about? This is your *dream*. You were born to do this."

She shivered, whether from fear or excitement, she couldn't decide. Probably both.

Marissa bit her lip. "I guess—"

"Then say yes! Remember? Big leap together?" Ainsley's eyes met hers, and Marissa felt as if Ainsley was looking into the depths of her soul.

She'd been dreaming of something like this for so long. *I can do this.*

She turned back to Diego, trying to keep her voice from cracking. "When do I start?"

~

Gio watched Marissa's face light up with joy as Diego gave her the news.

It had been his idea—*Papà* had asked him who should replace him when he went to the new restaurant, and Gio had immediately suggested her.

She had finally confessed to him—told him what had happened between them when they'd broken up. After all these years, he was at peace with it.

Marissa was one of the smartest people he knew, and she loved cooking as much as he did. She would work well with Diego, who loved her like a daughter.

"You and she were… together?" Sole stared at him with her exotic eyes.

He had started to get used to them—the sight of them, or her very pale skin and hair no longer startled him. "A long time ago. It's good to see her happy."

"I'm sure she's happy to see you smiling again, too."

He stared at her. "Am I?" She was right. He could feel the joy coursing through him. *I'm getting my own place!*

She nodded. "Ever since we visited the restaurant the other day. You have so many ideas inside you, just bursting to get out. I am so grateful to be here with you to explore them all."

He was happy to have her too. *I don't want you to leave.* "Maybe you could stay." She already felt like a sister to him.

She shook her head. "I don't belong here. Italy is my home. But I want to learn from you, and maybe one day open a place of my own there." She reached out and took his hand, squeezing it tightly. "I am lucky to have such a smart cousin."

He laughed. "I should be saying that." How things had changed in just a week, since he'd met her and her mother Stella. "Tomorrow we'll get started on the new place. We have a ton to get accomplished."

She flashed him a shy smile. "I can't wait."

~

Marcos poured the rich, thick chocolate mixture into the round pan. It smelled absolutely delicious, the notes of melted chocolate and butter evoking memories of his mother cooking mole for them when he was a child.

From the next station over, Sam glanced at their work. "Damn, you guys are quick."

Dave grinned. "We make a great team."

Marcos nodded, pinching Dave's side playfully. "Always have. We are going to win the Great British Bakeoff."

Sam laughed. "It's not a competition." He had a long trail of melted chocolate dripping down his blue button-up shirt.

"Maybe not, but we're still going to win." He licked a little of the chocolate mixture off the spoon. "It's been good to have you guys here." It was still hard for Marcos to believe that Brad was gone. So many nights they had worked on the old LGBT Center website together in that creaky old Victorian on L street right next to the railroad tracks.

And then there was the night Brad had come with him to rescue Marissa from jail.

Sam nodded. "I didn't realize how much I missed this place." He looked at Oscar, who nodded.

"Go ahead. Tell them." He was using a rubber spatula to fill their own cake pan with batter.

Sam took a deep breath and then exhaled. "There's a chance I might be coming back to Sacramento for good."

Marcos's eyes went wide. "Seriously?"

"Marcos, watch what you're doing." Dave gently nudged his arm back over the cake pan.

"Sorry!" He looked down and realized he'd almost poured half the mix onto the counter. "How is that possible?"

"I can work from anywhere. That's one of the perks of being a writer. Though my latest book is already seriously overdue, and my editor is going to kill me. And Oscar here just interviewed for a job at the LGBT Center. With his experience and references, he's practically a shoo-in. We could be back here in a few weeks."

Dave clapped him on the back. "That's great news!"

Marcos narrowed his eyes. "Wait a minute. You said *we*. Does that mean…?"

Again, Oscar and Sam shared a glance.

"It's too soon to say." Sam closed his eyes. "I mean, I just lost Brad. Everything feels so raw. And yet… I think he'd want me to be happy." He sighed. "For now, Oscar and I are just friends, but he was looking for a change of scene, so when this opportunity came up… We've agreed to see what happens."

It was fast. As Sam said, he'd only just lost Brad. But Marcos loved Sam, and so far, he really liked Oscar too. *Everyone deserves to be happy.* "I think it's good to take it slow. If it's meant to happen, it will."

Sam wiped the corners of his eyes. "Thanks, Marcos. That means a lot, coming from you. I know how much you loved Brad."

He set down the empty pan. "Hey, Oscar and I might be working together. I just got the nod for running the LGBT Center on Sac State's campus. And it's all because of Brad. He put in a good word for me before he… passed." There it was again. Acknowledgment that Brad was truly gone.

Seeing the tears forming again in Sam's eyes, he put his arms around his longtime friend. "I know. I feel it too. Every time I think about him. But you're right. He would want us to be happy. Maybe that's the best gift we can give him."

Sam nodded, squeezing Marcos tight. "That, and always remembering him."

"That too, my friend. That too." It was a promise he was sure he could keep.

Ben peered into the oven through the thick glass window, watching their cake bake. It was about halfway done, the top just starting to crust over.

"A watched pot never boils." Lorelei put a warm hand on his shoulder, squeezing it lightly.

"Yeah, but are we sure that applies to cakes? Technically, I don't think batter can boil…"

She chuckled. "Why don't you come up here and look at me instead?"

He did as he was told. He wanted to spend the rest of his life looking at her. And baking cakes with her. And whatever else life might bring them.

She tapped his nose with her index finger. "This is certainly an untraditional wedding."

Ben's mother laughed. "My son is nothing if not *untraditional.*" She looked a bit pale but had dressed up in bright blue for the occasion.

Ben felt the blood drain out of his face. *She hates it. What was I thinking?* "I'm sorry. This was a terrible idea. You probably wanted a whole church thing, with a white dress and a minister and doves and hundreds of people and…"

She put a finger over his lips, silencing him. "I got the white dress." She spread her arms and curtseyed. "Pretty, right?"

You're just trying to make me feel better. "Yes but…"

"No buts. This wedding is perfect. We're baking a cake together, which is a beautiful metaphor for how we're going to build a life for ourselves. We're here with all of your friends, and soon I'll be able to call myself Mrs. Ben Hammond." She pulled him in for a kiss.

He didn't refuse her. Her lips were warm and soft, and she smelled like lavender.

When they separated at last, he looked deep into her eyes, searching for any trace of displeasure. "Are you sure? You're not just saying that?"

"I'm sure."

"Mom, Max won't let me use the iPad." Mia, Lorelei's youngest, tugged at her dress.

"Just a second, honey." She kissed Ben's cheek. "I gotta deal with this. Hold that thought." She followed her daughter back toward the break room, where they'd set the kids up with half a dozen entertainment options to keep them busy.

Ben's mother leaned into him, putting her arm around his waist. "I'm proud of you, my little gosling."

Ben blushed. She hadn't called him that since he was little. "Thanks, Mom."

"Lorelei's a good one. And finally I get to have some grandkids. You know I'm going to spoil them rotten for as long as I can."

For that, there was no reply.

Instead, he just held her more tightly, thanking his lucky stars for whatever time they had left.

～

Diego stood before the two engaged couples, dressed in a sharp Italian suit, though it wasn't quite as nice as Daniele's. Behind him on the main counter, a dozen chocolate cakes were cooling, dusted in powdered sugar and giving off a heavenly scent.

He clasped his hands, looking around at the expectant audience.

"We are gathered here today…" He made a show of looking at his notes. "Sorry. They wanted a non-traditional wedding. So let's forget all the usual formalness." He grinned. "Who wants to see a wedding?"

The crowd laughed and then cheered.

Matteo gave him a thumb's up from the side of the restaurant, where he was standing and ready to do his part.

"I have recently become officially ordained at SoYouWantToBeAWeddingVendor.com to perform weddings in the state of California. Carmelina, and Daniele, would you like to exchange your vows?" As an aside to the crowd, he stage-whispered, "They asked me to keep this short. There's cake and champagne waiting, after all." His stomach rumbled, as if on cue.

Their friends and family chuckled.

"If the restaurant biz ever goes south, you could do *this* for a living." Gio winked at him.

Diego gave him a thumb's up. "Daniele?"

Carmelina's fiancé flashed him his bright Italian smile, and then turned to his fiancée. "*Cara mia*, I knew, ever since that day that we bumped into each other in the grocery store line at Corti Brothers, that I would marry you someday. I just didn't think you would make me wait quite so long."

The crowd laughed.

"However, like a fine wine, you have only become better with age. I promise to make every day a new adventure… or at least to bring you your fuzzy bunny slippers every morning and rub your tired feet at night. And I will hold every dream of yours in my heart like a precious thing."

Carmelina blushed. "Not bad. And yes, I made you wait, but the longer the wait, the better the wine. I'm just glad you didn't compare me to cheese!"

This time Diego himself snorted, and covered his mouth quickly to cover his lapse. He shrugged. *Sorry.*

Carmelina ignored him. "Daniele, I promise to tell you when you are wrong, which will probably be a lot, and admit when I am, which will be considerably less. And I want to keep building our life together, one bunch of flowers and one gooey chocolate croissant at a time." She took a deep breath. "I was with my husband Arthur for decades. Letting go of him was the hardest thing I've ever had to do."

She found Sam in the crowd. Their eyes met, and he nodded solemnly. So did Ben.

"But I firmly believe the ones we loved are still here with us, and that they want more than anything to see us happy again. And I *will* be happy with you. I want to spend the rest of my life with you, however long that may be."

The audience applauded.

"The bride and groom have decided to forego an exchange of rings. Are the two of you ready to seal the deal?"

Daniele and Carmelina nodded.

"Daniele, do you promise to love and support Carmelina for as long as you walk this Earth?"

Daniele nodded, gazing into Carmelina's eyes. "I do."

"And do you, Carmelina, promise to love and support Daniele for as long as you walk this Earth, and also to supply him with tasty baked treats from time to time?"

Carmelina chuckled. "Had to get that one added, didn't you?"

"If you were marrying a woman who was as good a cook as you, wouldn't you?"

A smile of delight curved her lips. "Touché. And I do."

They really are perfect for each other. "Then I now declare you husband and wife. Carmelina, you may kiss the groom."

Carmelina wrapped her arms around Daniele and bent him over backwards, V-J Day style, for a very passionate kiss.

Their friends all cheered, and Diego fought back the urge to cry. It still amazed him, after all these years, how this group of people had found each other and become the best of friends.

"That's gonna be a hard act to follow." Ben grinned, and Lorelei pinched his arm.

"Oh come on, Ben. You're a writer." It was Sam this time, catcalling from the audience. "You're gonna knock it out of the park."

Ben did the "I'm watching you" sign with his fingers, but he grinned.

Diego cleared his throat again. "Ben and Lorelei, it's your turn. Ben, you have been a part of our little crew since the start. Lorelei, you're a new addition. But we was all talking, and we decided that if things ever—how do you say?—go south between you two, we're keeping you and dumping him."

Laughter filled the room.

Ben looked mock-offended, but then nodded. "That's fair. She's my better half, after all."

Diego winked at him. "Please share your vows."

Ben took Lorelei's hand. "I never told you this, but a drag queen led me to you. Well, technically she was a matchmaker too. But when I was lost and afraid I would never find love again, she told me that you were the one for me."

She smiled, lighting up her face. "Really?"

"Really."

She reached up and pushed a stray lock of hair back behind his ear. "Go on."

"From the moment I met you, it was magic. You brought me back from the darkness of when Ella died. You made me laugh and believe in myself again. Even unclogging your toilet was wonderful, because it meant I got to spend a little more time with you."

"This is the strangest wedding I have ever attended." Ben's mother spoke up this time. "And also one of the best."

Diego nodded in agreement. *It really is.*

Ben took Lorelei's hand. "I promise to always fix your broken things. To be there when you call. And to end each day with you, no matter how far apart we might be."

She touched his cheek. "I kind of wish my toilet had overflowed sooner."

There were chuckles of amusement from the crowd.

Lorelei pulled a card out of her pocket. "Sorry, I'm a little nervous."

Diego nodded. "That's all right. Take your time."

She took a deep breath, and began to read. "Ben, you showed up after I had stopped looking. And you became the hero I didn't know I needed. I never wanted to get married again. Once burned, twice shy, right?"

He nodded and took her free hand. The love between them was palpable.

"But you made me want to stand up here again and open my heart to trust you. You made me want to believe in love again." She looked up from the card and into his eyes. "I promise to be *your* hero, to stand up for you when no one else will, and to hold your hand like this until the day we pass from this Earth." She glanced over at Carmelina. "Oh and I'll do that tasty baked treats thing for you too, provided you keep me in the quantity of chocolate to which I have become accustomed." That was followed by a meaningful glance at the wedding cakes.

Ben grinned. "Deal." And without waiting for Diego's permission, Ben kissed his new bride.

Out of the corner of his eye, Diego caught sight of movement by the front door. He looked up, and just for a moment, he could have sworn he saw Brad standing there, giving him a smile and a nod. Then he was gone in a flash of green.

Diego rubbed his eyes. "Well…" He shrugged. "I guess they declared themselves husband and wife." *Untraditional right up to the end.* "Now it's time for the party!" He signaled Matteo, and his husband pulled the cord, dropping a velvet curtain to reveal The Three Queens, a drag queen trio and cover band who immediately broke into song with Queen's "Another One Bites the Dust."

It was the perfect ending to a ceremony.

∽

The party ran well into the evening, long after dinner had been served and all the wedding cakes consumed. All save two, which were going home with the newly married couples.

Carmelina and Daniele departed first. Ben and Lorelei excused themselves soon after, explaining that his mother had promised to watch after the kids that night, and they had a little private celebrating of their own to do at home.

When the last of the guests finally said their goodbyes, Matteo went looking for his husband. He found Diego on the back steps, sipping a cup of espresso and staring up at the trees and stars.

"Mind if I join you?" It was a gorgeous evening, the stars sparkling like little holes poked in a dark blue sheet in the clear night.

"*Certo*." His husband moved over a little to make room.

They sat in companionable silence for a few moments, listening to the wind through the branches of the big magnolia tree on 48th Street next door, and the occasional *whoosh* of a car passing by.

Diego offered him the cup.

Matteo took it and sipped some of the still warm coffee. It was early summer, but it still dropped down into the fifties later at night. It had taken him nearly a decade, but he had finally gotten used to using Fahrenheit instead of Celsius. *Mostly*.

"Tomorrow, everything changes." Diego sounded melancholy.

Matteo chuckled. "Everything is always changing." He handed back the mug.

"You know what I mean. Tomorrow my baby boy—"

Matteo snorted. "Not such a baby anymore."

"My *baby boy* moves out to start his own life." Diego took a long sip of coffee. "I'm not ready."

Matteo put an arm around Diego's shoulders and pulled him close. *I'm not ready either.* But for Diego's sake, he had to be. "He's a good young man. Luna raised him well, and you took over when she was gone. You should be proud of him."

Diego sighed. "I know. I am. I just—I don't wants to lose him."

"I know." Diego had always been the more sensitive of the two of them. Things hit him harder, and this *thing* was one of the hardest of all. "Close your eyes."

"Why?" Diego narrowed his eyes.

"Just do it." Matteo took the mug away and set it aside.

"Okay. But don't try to make me scared."

"I promise." He closed his eyes too. "Now tell me what you see when you think of Gio's future."

He was silent for a moment, his hands still in his lap. "Hmmm… I see… the new restaurant in Folsom. On opening night. It's—*affollato*?"

"Packed?"

"Yes. It's packed. And there's someone else there. A woman, with him."

"Sole? Stella?" They were both very distinctive.

"No. I don't know. It's… I think she is *with* him." There was wonder in his voice.

"He's not alone." Matteo opened his eyes.

Diego was smiling. His eyes flickered open too. "He's not alone." He frowned. "I hope I don't hate her."

Matteo shook his head and chuckled. "Me too." Gio would make his own choices now, whether they liked them or not.

"What are you guys doing out here? There's a ton of stuff to be cleaned up." Gio sounded mildly annoyed.

Matteo and Diego broke into laughter. "We'll be inside in a minute." Matteo waved Gio away. "Give your parents a little time to ourselves."

"Gross. But hurry up. I don't want to do everything myself." Gio slammed the door.

Matteo took Diego's hand in his. "We built this. You and me."

Diego kissed his cheek. "We did. You and me and our friends. And whatever happens next, we'll all deal with it. Together."

They looked up at the sky just as a bright light blazed a trail across the inky blackness.

"Make a wish?" Diego sounded playful. Under the silver light of the stars, he looked fifteen years younger than he was. *Like he did when we first met.*

"I already have everything I want." He leaned in and kissed Diego, and it was as good as that first time. Better even, because they knew so much more about life, love, and friendship than they had on that wonderful, intoxicating night.

And now, he knew for sure that things were going to be all right.

"Come on." He got up and held out his hand. "There's so much more we have to do."

Diego took his hand. Together, they went back inside.

Above the stars sparkled just a little bit brighter.

ALLA FINE

Three months later

Ben knelt next to the young oak tree where Sam had scattered Brad's ashes just a few months before. It was a warm late-summer morning, the kind that made you want to sleep in and get up after noon.

The sun's rays slanted down through the tree's branches, and it was strangely quiet. No birds sang, and Effie Yeaw Nature Center was all but abandoned. Only the American River murmured in the background, a soft counterpoint to the otherwise quiet morning.

As if the whole world stopped in her honor.

Lorelei knelt next to him, a hand on his shoulder. Even her two kids were silent, as if they too felt the solemnity of the moment. They had taken to calling his mother *grandma*, and they had cried too when she had passed away a week before.

For himself, he preferred they just call him "Ben." Garrett, for all his faults, was still their father, and Ben had no desire to come between him and his kids.

"Are you ready?" Lorelei's luminous eyes met his.

He nodded. "I think so." The funeral was over, and the memorial.

Emily had passed from this life on her own terms—in his home, surrounded by Ben, Lorelei, and his friends. "She's not hurting anymore."

He had wept for days. He hadn't known he had such feelings left in him for her, the woman who had hurt him so badly when he was a kid, trying to figure himself out. But she was his mother. She'd paid the price, and she had found her way back to him to earn her redemption in her final days.

My mama. And now she was gone.

He squeezed his eyes shut, holding back more tears, and felt Lorelei's hand on his shoulder.

Time to let her go.

He uncapped the urn, looking down at all that was left of his mother. He looked at Lorelei, who nodded. "Goodbye, mama," he whispered, and gently sprinkled her ashes around the base of the tree.

Somewhere down there, underneath the top layer of soil and fallen leaves, Brad's ashes were already becoming a part of the soil, nurturing the young oak. Now his mother's would join them. Ben liked the idea of the two of them becoming friends in the afterlife.

Lorelei reached into the bag of potting soil they'd purchased on the way over to the park, and sprinkled it lightly over her ashes, sealing them into the ground.

He closed his eyes, saying a little prayer to send her spirit on its way. He wasn't a big believer, but just then, it felt right. *Mama, I'm grateful for the time we had. And I'm thankful that we found our way back to one another before the end. Now you can be free from all the pain.*

He'd finally used up the last of Ella's old yellow bottle of shampoo, letting the ghost of her go. In a few days he and Lorelei would take her dream trip. *Paris, London, and Milan.* It was time to start living again.

Ben felt Max leaning over his shoulder. "Are you guys done yet? I'm hungry."

Mia chimed in from behind him. "Can we get In-N-Out?"

Ben laughed. Apparently their patience with ceremony had worn thin. He cherished the reminder that life still went on. "Only if I can have a chocolate milkshake!" He stood and brushed the dust off his jeans.

With one last look at the beautiful tree, he took Lorelei's hand, and stepped into their new life.

~

Five months later

"We are fortunate to have the artist of this amazing new piece here with us today. Jun Seo Jang has spent the last few months here in Northern California, working on the masterpiece we're about to reveal. Let's give them a big welcome."

The crowd applauded politely.

Ainsley squeezed Marissa's hand. "I can't believe we're here." They were at the back of the large crowd, made up of some of the finest-dressed people she'd seen in her life, that had gathered in the huge atrium at the War Memorial Opera House in the heart of San Francisco. The giant artwork that she had helped Jun Seo with was at the front, covered by a red velvet cloth.

Five months earlier, she'd been a college student studying for a life in the lab. Now she was an assistant to a world-famous artist, and had been working on some art of her own on the side with Jun's blessing.

Jun took the stage, gesturing with their hands to tamp down the sound of clapping. "I want to thank the board of the Opera House and the people of San Francisco and Northern California for your warm welcome. You have all been amazing, and I feel like this is my second home."

More applause.

"I've felt newly energized by my time spent here creating this piece. But before I reveal it to all of you extremely patient folks…"

There was a smattering of laughter.

"…I have one more person to thank. Ainsley Kim, would you please come up to the stage?" They flashed her a wicked grin across the atrium.

Ainsley felt all the blood drain out of her face. "Me?" she squeaked.

Marissa nodded. "Yes, you. Come on!" She dragged Ainsley through the crowd, toward the stage. When they reached the stairs, Marissa kissed her cheek and gave her a friendly shove. "Go show them who Ainsley Kim really is. I believe in you."

Ainsley mounted the stage, barely managing to avoid stumbling, her heart pounding at least two hundred beats a minute.

Jun smiled at her. They had been nothing but kind and supportive over the last five months, even offering helpful critiques on her own work. They turned back to the audience. "Friends and future friends, you have before you an amazing up-and-coming artist. Ainsley came to me and offered her assistance, and she has been a terrific support for someone as disorganized as me, but one day she will be the one up on a stage like this revealing her own work."

The crowd clapped appreciatively.

Jun took a step back, leaving her to say… something.

I didn't prepare anything. "I…" Her hands were shaking.

She looked over at Marissa. Their eyes met, and she nodded. *Show them.*

Ainsley cleared her throat, squared her shoulders, and spoke. "I am grateful to be here." She gazed out over the patrons of the Opera house. "Working with Jun Seo was the fulfillment of a lifetime dream. I am so proud of them, and so thankful for their support." *What else was there to say?*

Jun leaned forward and whispered in her ear.

Her eyes went wide. "Really?"

They nodded.

Well. All right then. "It is my honor to reveal Jun Seo Jang's newest piece, for installation right here in the San Francisco War Memorial Opera House. It's called *Pacific Hills*, and it blends the artistic style of their native home of South Korea with artists from the Sierra Foothills." She lifted her arm theatrically, pointing at the painting, and the cover dropped away.

It was breathtaking—somehow in the grand atrium, it looked even more impressive than it had in the barn up in the foothills. *Like it belongs here.*

Bright golden hills soared above a village that could have been somewhere in Korea or a gold-country town like Amador or Sutter, places they had both spent time in while Jun was searching for inspiration. The colors were bold and exciting, and the combination of styles spoke to a unity between nations, between people, that sent a thrill up her spine.

The room exploded into applause as the patrons leapt to their feet to express their appreciation.

Marissa bounded up on stage and hugged her. "You did it!"

"*We* did it." It had been a long and scary road, but somehow together they had found their way.

After the party, they planned to spend a couple days in the City, starting with a Tales of the City tour in the Castro. But for now, she was happy just to be where she was, when she was, with the woman who mattered to her most in all the world. "Love you, 'Riss."

For her response, Marissa kissed her in front of God, the golden hills, and the patrons of the War Memorial Opera House, sending a thrill up her back. "Love you too."

"Right here is where I want to stay, forever." *Life is sweet.*

"What's stopping us?"

Ainsley grinned. *What, indeed?*

But no matter what happened or where they went, as long as they had each other, she would be content.

~

Seven months later

Giovanni was on top of the world.

As part of his journey from his father's employee to running his own restaurant, he'd decided to go by his full Italian first name as a way to honor his mother *and* his Italian heritage. But his old friends often still called him Gio.

He stood a few steps up on the stairway that led to the building's upper floor—and the restaurant's training kitchen and his own office—and surveyed what he, Stella, Sole, and his parents had accomplished. The restaurant felt modern but warm, just like Ragazzi. Ainsley, with Jun Seo Jang's help, had created four stunning murals, each depicting an Italian city scene. His favorite was Bologna, which depicted the old house in the cemetery where his mother was buried, but refurbished and made new.

The grand opening was in full swing. A string quartet out on the boardwalk in front of Amici played Italian favorites—they were currently working through a rather inspired version of *Funiculi-Funicolà*—but later they would play some more contemporary songs rendered as classical music à la *Bridgerton.*

His friends and family were all there, having driven up from Sacramento and other parts of the valley for this special occasion. Stella had gone home months earlier, and had returned especially for the grand opening. Sole, instead, had stayed out her entire six-month traveler's visa, plus a a two-week extension. She was in the kitchen, cooking up a storm. He wasn't sure how he was going to replace her when she left, but she'd *tsk tsk'd* his worries away. "You'll be just fine."

"You should be so proud of yourself." Brianna kissed him, her hand finding his as she surveyed the scene. She'd come on as a consultant, having left a career at the library a few years before to do something *exciting* on her own. But she had quickly become more to him than just a business associate.

"I am. Believe me, I am. But I couldn't have done this without all of these people." He'd reserved the grand opening for friends and family, his way of thanking them for all that they had done for him. *Papà* and *Babbo*, his best friend Marissa and Ainsley, Sole and Stella, Marcos and Dave, Sam and Oscar—so lovely to see them together at last. Ben and Lorelei, Ricky and Alyn, and so many others.

The world was turning in strange ways. Things were happening outside these walls that were unsettling, events which made him sick with fear and rage if he thought about them for too long. Sometimes he no longer recognized his adopted country.

But for this night, here in this sacred place, everything was warm and bright and good. *Alla tavola, non si invecchia.* One of his favorite sayings— at the table, no one grows old.

Brianna frowned. "Why is that table empty? I thought we filled every seat?" The one empty table in the place really did stand out.

Giovanni nodded. "We did. Those seats are for the ones we lost. May they rest in peace, and may we never forget them."

"That's beautiful." She squeezed his hand.

He could feel them there with him too, and if he squinted, he could almost make them out.

Sam's husband Brad. Ben's wife Ella. Arthur, Carmelina's first husband. Diego's and Matteo's parents. And his own dear mother, Luna. Their approval warmed his heart.

He felt someone's eyes on him. *Papà* was looking at him.

Their eyes met. Diego's glance flicked to Brianna and back, and Giovanni's father smiled and gave him a thumb's up.

He laughed and returned the gesture.

Brianna put a hand on his shoulder. "You ready?"

He nodded. "Come with me?"

"I wouldn't be anywhere else." She kissed his cheek, and then led him down the stairs.

He picked up a glass of red wine and knife from the sideboard where he'd set them for the occasion, and clinked the side of it, capturing everyone's attention.

The room went silent, and everyone turned toward the two of them.

He held up the glass, a broad smile spreading across his face. *This is it.* "Friends and family, welcome to Amici."

On the sidewalk , a slender man in a blue suit, pressed his face against the window, looking inside.

Almost all of his friends were there. They were laughing and smiling, sharing a wonderful meal together, just the way it should be.

At the table, no one grows old.

Sam took Oscar's hand and squeezed it, and they kissed briefly, before turning back to talk with their friends.

Brad smiled. *You're going to be okay.*

Anyone watching would've heard a contented sigh and seen a brief flash of green sparks before the night faded back to black.

RECIPES

La Spianata Romagnola

Spianata Romagnola is a traditional flatbread similar to foccacia that's popular in the Emiglia Romagna region of Italy. Often made with rosemary and salt, it's perfect with salami and cheese.

Ingredients:

- 2 cups wheat flour
- 2 cups coarse whole meal flour
- 1 ½ cups water
- 1 ¼ teaspoon salt
- 1 teaspoon malt OR 1 teaspoon sugar
- 2 ¼ tablespoons olive oil
- 4/5 teaspoon of brewer's yeast

For use after preparation:

- 2 tablespoons of olive oil
- 1 sprig of rosemary
- Sea salt to taste

Sift the two flours together in a large bowl. In a small bowl, put the brewer's yeast and add the malt (or sugar) and then a little of the water. Then mix it until the yeast is entirely blended in. In the remaining water, dissolve the salt and mix in the olive oil. Add the yeast mix to the sifted flour and gently mix it in with the tips of your fingers, then add in the water, salt and oil, and mix everything together thoroughly.

Once the ingredients are combined, continue to work the dough on a pastry board for ten minutes, until it is completely blended. Sprinkle a little flour in another large bowl and set the dough inside, and cover the bowl with plastic wrap.

Put the bowl in the oven with the light on but power off, and let it rise for at least two hours. The dough should double in size.

Use a cookie sheet or baking tray with a piece of parchment paper, and sprinkle on two tablespoons of olive oil. Then put on the dough, and use your hands to flatten it and extend it to the edges of the pan. Use your fingertips to make a series of small impressions across the surface of the dough, and then sprinkle the sea salt and rosemary over the top. Put it back in the oven to rise, with the light on and power off, for 30-40 minutes more.

Bake at 400 degrees for about 30 minutes until the bread is golden brown. Place it on a wire rack, and cut and serve it as soon as it cools.

Store any leftovers for up to two days in a Ziplock bag to preserve the moisture.

Tortelli alla Lastra
(Tortelli on the Slab)
Ingredients for 6:

- 1 cup water
- 1 lb potatoes
- ½ pound of sausage
- 2 oz of grated parmigiano (or pecorino)
- Salt, Pepper, and Extra Virgin Olive Oil to taste

Boil the potatoes with their skins in lightly salted water. Once they are cooked, peel them while hot and mash them. Remove the skin from the sausages and crumble them up, and brown them in a frying pan with a little olive oil for a few minutes. Combine the potatoes, sausage, grated cheese, and a little salt and pepper in a bowl and mix well.

Put the flour and a little salt in another bowl. Add in the water slowly and knead the mixture until the dough is elastic, compact and evenly mixed. Form it into a ball and put it on a lightly floured surface. Use a rolling pin to roll it out into a thin sheet.

Spread the sausage filling evenly on one half of the rolled-out dough. Fold the other half over it and seal the edges with the flat edge of a fork. Then use a pastry wheel to cut it into four-inch squares. If you don't have a pastry wheel, use a knife, and seal the edges of each square with a fork.

Cook the tortellini on a hot griddle for three to four minutes, turning them several times, until the outsides are speckled with golden brown.

You can vary the ingredients of the filling to your own taste – like bacon, ricotta, spinach, basil, or other herbs.

Fagottini di Bresaola ai Funghi

Bresaola Parcels with Mushrooms
Makes 8 Hors d'oeuvres
Ingredients:

- 8 thin slices of bresaola
- 3 oz of fresh goat cheese
- 7 oz of sliced mushrooms
- 1 clove of garlic
- 1 teaspoon of chopped parsley
- 2 tablespoons of extra virgin olive oil
- 8 thin stalks of chives
- Salt and pepper to taste

Heat half of the olive oil in a non-stick pan. Add the garlic, then remove it as soon as it darkens. Next, add the cleaned and sliced mushrooms. Salt and pepper them to taste, and cook them over high heat for 10 minutes. Turn off the heat, add in the parsley and let the mixture cool.

Mix the goat cheese with the remaining oil until it is creamy and stir in the now-cooled mushroom mix. Line up the bresaola slices on the cutting board, place a little of the cheese-and-mushroom mixture in the center of each, the close the slices like a little sack and tie them around the neck with the chives. Keep them in a cool place until ready to serve.

Monk Sleeves With Cream of Cabbage and Crunchy Bacon

Ingredients for 2 people:

- 7 ounces of pasta (mezze maniche or similar)
- 5 1/3 ounces of purple cabbage
- 1 onion
- 2 slices of bacon
- 1/3 cup grated parmigiano
- 1/2 of a lemon
- Salt
- Oil

Chop both the onion and the red cabbage into small pieces. Use a large, flat pan and add a drizzle of oil. In a smaller pan, add the bacon. In the pan for the pasta, add water and a little salt.

Allow the water to boil while you prepare the cream of onion and purple cabbage.

Add the chopped onion and cabbage into the large pan with the oil and put it on medium heat. Stir it from time to time until the leaves of the cabbage have wilted. At the same time, chop up the bacon into small bits and fry it over low heat, turning it periodically until it is well-cooked and crunchy.

When the onion and cabbage are almost ready, add half of the parmigiano and stir it until it's blended well without sticking to the pan. Meanwhile, put the pasta in the boiling water.

Squeeze out the lemon juice and remove any seeds. Put the fresh juice into a blender, and add the rest of the parmigiano. Put the onion and cabbage cheese sauce into the blender, along with a ladle of water from the pasta pot, and blend it all until you get a purple cream sauce.

Put the purple cream back into the big pan and strain the pasta. Add it into the pan too and mix it together so the sauce coats the pasta entirely.

Put the pasta and sauce on the plates, and sprinkle the bacon bits over the top. Serve hot.

Torta Tenerina

Serves 8 people

Ingredients

- 7 oz high quality dark chocolate
- 3 medium eggs
- ¾ cup sugar
- ½ cup flour
- 3 teaspoons of warmed milk
- A pinch of salt
- ½ cup of butter

Preheat the oven to 350 degrees.

Chop up the dark chocolate bar into small pieces and melt them in a double boiler to prevent the chocolate from scorching, until it becomes creamy and smooth. Cut the butter into small cubes, and add two at a time to the chocolate over the heat, stirring the butter into the chocolate until it has been fully absorbed before adding more. Once all the butter has been blended into the chocolate, remove the pan from the heat and set it aside to cool.

In the meantime, shell the eggs and separate the yolks from the whites. Put the egg yolks in a bowl and whisk in half of the sugar until you get a light and frothy mixture. Keep whisking as you add the chocolate-butter blend into the frothy eggs and sugar.

Add the warmed milk and flour to the mixture, and stir the ingredients well to make a smoothly blended mixture with no lumps.

In another bowl, beat the egg whites, adding in the pinch of salt and the rest of the sugar until it forms a compact white cream. Then use a rubber spatula or wooden spoon to gently fold the egg white mixture into the chocolate mixture from the bottom up.

Line a 9" round pan with parchment paper and pour the cake mixture into it, spreading it smoothly around the pan with a wooden spoon or rubber spatula.

Cook the cake in the oven for 25-30 minutes, and then turn off the oven. Leave the oven door ajar, and let the cake cool for 15 minutes. Once it has cooled, carefully remove it from the pan and place it on a serving plate.

ABOUT THE AUTHOR

Scott lives with his husband Mark in a little yellow bungalow with two pink flamingoes in Sacramento. He inhabits the space between the *here and now* and the *what could be*. Indoctrinated into fantasy and sci fi by his mother at the tender age of nine, he devoured her library. But as he grew up, he wondered where the people like him were.

He decided it was time to create the kinds of stories he couldn't find at Waldenbooks. If there weren't queer characters in his favorite genres, he would remake them to his own ends.

His friends say Scott's brain works a little differently – he sees relationships between things that others miss, and gets more done in a day than most folks manage in a week. He seeks to transform traditional sci fi, fantasy, and contemporary worlds into something unexpected.

A Rainbow Award winning author, he runs Queer Sci Fi, QueeRomance Ink, Liminal Fiction, and Other Worlds Ink with Mark, sites that bring queer people together to promote and celebrate fiction reflecting their own reality. Scott was the committee chair for the Indie Authors Committee at the Science Fiction and Fantasy Writers of America (SFWA) for almost three years.

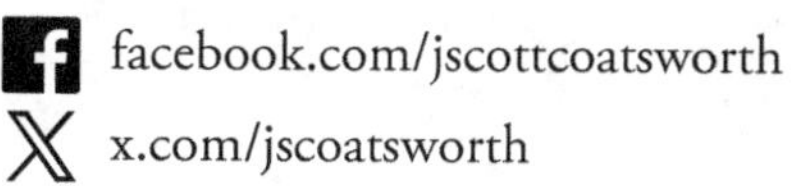

facebook.com/jscottcoatsworth

x.com/jscoatsworth

ACKNOWLEDGMENTS

There are a number of people who made *Down the River* possible, and I want to thank them all. First and foremost, my husband Mark, who has supported my writing every step of the way, and who read each chapter as I wrote it.

Next, my dear friend Kim Fielding, who was my other beta reader, and who kept me on the right path. Also thank you to Alison Behrens, who edited and proofed the book—twice. Once as I was writing it, and then she had to read the whole thing again when it was done, which I'm sure was a thrill.

And a special thanks to our dear friend Fabrizio Montanari for providing the family recipes for this book, and to his husband Marco Munda for answering my "Italian" questions, and to my author friend Jeff Baker, who encouraged me week after week.

As they say, it takes a village.

STORIES BY J. SCOTT COATSWORTH

Liminal Sky: Ariadne Cycle

The Stark Divide | The Rising Tide | The Shoreless Sea

Liminal Sky: Redemption Cycle

Dropnauts | Coredivers (Coming in 2026)

Liminal Sky: Oberon Cycle

Skythane | Lander | Ithani

Office of the Lost (with Kim Fielding)

Office of the Lost

River City

The River City Companion (Coming Soon) | The River City Chronicles | Down
the River

Tharassas Cycle

Tales From Tharassas | The Dragon Eater | The Gauntlet Runner | The Hencha
Queen | The Death Bringer

Other Sci Fi/Fantasy

The Autumn Lands | Cailleadhama | Firedrake | The Great North | Homecoming |
The Last Run | Slow Thaw | Wonderland

Short Story Collections

Spells & Stardust | Tangents & Tachyons | Androids & Aliens | Love & Limitations

Gay Own Voice Anthologies

Romance is a Drag | Romance in Autumn | Romance in Winter (November 2025)

Audiobooks

The Autumn Lands | Cailleadhama | Dropnauts | Office of the Lost (Coming Soon) | The River City Chronicles | Skythane | Lander

Writing

Suck a Little Happy Juice